PRAISE FOR AIMEE LIU'S

FACE

"Authentic in every detail, this novel should attract not only readers with Asian interests, but everyone concerned with the changing qualities of American life today."

—John Espey, author of *Minor Heresies, Major Departures: A China Mission Boyhood*

"A journey through family toward self, exquisitely layered through the lens of memory. An absorbing read."

—Paul Mantee, author of *Bruno of Hollywood*

"Impressive . . . Liu's lyrical prose is graceful and evocative."

—*Publishers Weekly*

"Structured like a mystery, around secrets and unanswered questions. . . . Liu raises compelling questions about identity, the power of memory, and the cost of forgetting."

—*Cleveland Plain Dealer*

"Reads like a kind of visual poetry. . . . Whether Aimee Liu turns to the tumult of Chinatown, the bloody chaos of Chiang's mainland China or the pain of her central character's own past, we travel there, too, in a book well worth the price of the ticket."

—Linda Phillips Ashour, author of *Speaking in Tongues* and *Joy Baby*

more . . .

"With clarity and insight, Aimee Liu has given us a glimpse into a world in which the secrets people keep are as potent as the stories they tell."

—Christina Baker Kline, author of *Sweet Water*

"A powerful examination of the Asian-American experience."

—Transpacific

"A searing story about the pain of being different and about the inescapable, often destructive hold of the past. . . . The novel creates a haunting atmosphere."

—New York Times Book Review

"Arresting and well-plotted. . . . Liu's characters are deftly delineated, and at times the descriptive lines are so beautifully written that they have the delicacy and quality of that other Oriental art form, haiku."

—Rocky Mountain News

"FACE exquisitely depicts Maibelle's slow coming to terms with the forces that made her, in a story that is part psychological drama, part rite of passage, part literary exploration of being racially divided, and part mystery."

—Milwaukee Journal

(FACE)

Also by Aimee E. Liu

Solitaire

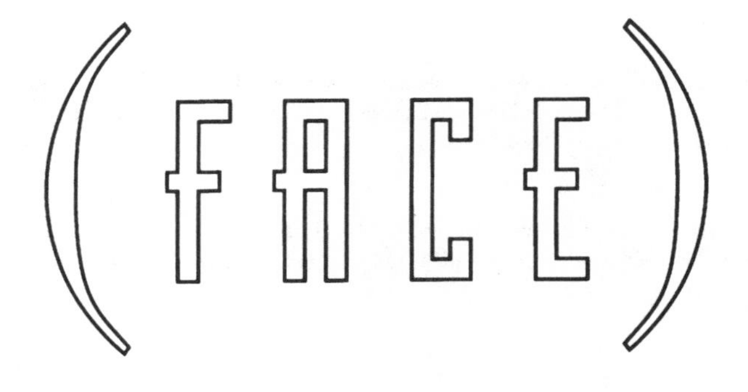

AIMEE E. LIU

A Time Warner Company

PUBLISHER'S NOTE: This novel is a work of fiction. Names, characters, places, and incidents either are the product of the author's imagination or are used fictitiously, and any resemblance to actual persons, living or dead, events, or locales is entirely coincidental.

Warner Books, Inc., 1271 Avenue of the Americas, New York, NY 10020

Printed in the United States of America

First Trade Printing: October 1995

10 9 8 7 6 5 4 2 1

Originally published in hardcover by Warner Books.

Library of Congress Cataloging-in-Publication Data

Liu, Aimee.
Face/Aimee E. Liu.
p. cm.
ISBN 0-446-67135-5
1. Chinese American women—New York (N.Y.)—Fiction. 2. Women photographers—New York (N.Y.)—Fiction. 3. Family—New York (N.Y.)—Fiction. I. Title.
PS3562.I797F33 1994
813'.54—dc20

9347143
CIP

Book design by Giorgetta Bell McRee
Photographs by Margaret Morton

For Margaret Blackstone

Acknowledgments

This novel has acquired many godparents during its long journey from impulse to publication. The first, of course, is Martin Fink, whose humor, love, and understanding sustained the author through many stretches when it seemed the story was a goner. Cai Emmons, Arnold Margolin, Hugh Gross, and Eric Edson, too, offered invaluable criticism and encouragement from early on. Willyne Bower, Nancy Fawcett, and especially Susan Bartholomew and Sarah Piel gave the finished manuscript its first of many vital blessings. Lori Andiman and Artie Pine were on hand, as always, with energetic support, while my agent, Richard Pine, provided the honest friendship, faith, and professional excellence that gave his blessing the weight of gold. Finally, Jamie Raab bestowed on this project the enthusiasm, wisdom, and generosity that are the marks of a truly gifted editor—and a true gift to this new novelist. Thank you, one and all.

I would also like to extend a special note of gratitude to my distant teachers, Joanne Hoppe, Jesse Sommer, and particularly Chic Reich, for urging me to write long before I realized I had anything to say.

Should the misted clouds survive,
They will drift to the void and let free the moon.

LIU YÜ-SHENG

Prologue

I was a child in Chinatown.

My earliest memories are filled with strangled ducks and ginseng root, parades of round, worried faces, and babies in pastel colors. Rich light slants between squeezed buildings, and winter shadows soak the streets tugging warmth from fingers and toes. I hear wailing, chattering, a multitude of tones. A language I can't understand. And the smells—I know them as well as my name—the unearthly blend of fishmongers' trash, orange peel, garlic, and sandalwood. Joss sticks lit for the dead.

I see myself in these memories as a tall, pale, redheaded girl reflected in a storefront window. A narrow face with a broad off-center nose. Too-wide eyes the color of jade and only a vague Oriental cast. Against the rest of the Mott Street crowd I stand out like a vivid flaw in a bolt of jet-black silk.

But the girls I admired most in the world—the Yellow Butterflies—stood out, too. Just one grade ahead of me and worlds apart, they had the flawless appearance of porcelain dolls. Pale skin. Flying cheekbones. Diminutive noses. Waist-length hair that hung straight, gleaming like dark cellophane, and those classic almond eyes with their smoothed-down lids, as if carved in a single stroke.

I studied the Butterflies' movements, their fashions, their games. True to their name, they dressed in yellow, light and bright, with shoes of silver or gold and hair ornaments shaped like blossoms. Their voices, alternating between Cantonese and English, made me think of the sparrows that nested in my Wisconsin grandfather's barn. Grampa said if I got too close, the sparrows would peck my eyes out, but as long as I kept my distance I could play in the barn and they'd let me be. I thought the same rule should apply to the Butterflies.

One day I followed them out of the schoolyard and heard them tittering about my height, my green eyes. They said my hair was like cock feathers. They turned and called to me in Chinese, broke into giggles when I stopped and pretended to read a nearby wall poster.

Still, I imagined them waving me forward, taking my hand. We'd stop to buy plum candies, walk to one of their homes to play. Their mothers would have a mah-jongg game going and the gentle *swish-click* of the tiles would sound in the background as I tried on the Butterflies' colors . . .

I fastened my eyes to that poster. A Ringling Brothers clown leered back. The Butterflies yelled in English.

"Who's your grandpa? Jolly Green Giant?"

"Who does your hair? Chicken Little?"

I bolted across the street, house key clenched in my fist. If I just held onto that key, the Butterflies would stay where they were, laughing and linking arms. They would leave me alone. But if I let go, they would come pull my hair out strand by strand, they would suck the color from my eyes. They would beat me with their wings until I melted into the pavement.

The key gave me safe passage.

From my father's window I watched grocer Hu scold the Butterflies over a box of lychees they had upset in the chase. They scrambled on their knees to retrieve them, and then Old Hu softened and gave each of them a nut to crack and nibble at as they moved on. I imagined the cool pink flesh between their teeth, the juice like sweet perfume. I could almost feel the brittle shell breaking and, inside, the hard, smooth pit, dark as the finest rosewood.

Much later, between years of college, I ran into one of the Yellow Butterflies selling panty hose at Bloomingdale's. She'd had her eyes done. Had the lids lifted, folded, and cut until the almond shape was gone and with it her exotic, imperious beauty. Now she looked innocent. Cute. She could pass for American.

"Donna and Bidi had their eyes done, too," she told me, "and Lily had her nose built up. None of us live in Chinatown anymore."

I didn't remember this woman's name, much less those of the other Butterflies, but I felt as though I'd come face-to-face with myself turned inside out.

Secretly, she was saying, the Butterflies used to envy me because I was real American. "If you'd stayed around, we might have been friends."

I mouthed the conventional wisdom, said those differences never should have mattered.

"No," she agreed, "but if they didn't, there would be no Chinatown."

CELEBRATE
ANCHOR SAVINGS BANK
YEAR OF THE LOAN
福來
福來傢俬
COMFORT FURNITURE
ISUZU

Part I

The Emperor State Building

....

1

Maibelle Chung
75 Sunridge Street
Playa del Rey, California

Sept. 26

Dear Maibelle—Miss Chung?

I'm not sure how to address you after all this time, especially since you may never read these words. Your mother gave me this address but said she hadn't heard from you in some years and wasn't sure if it was correct. I can only hope to reach you.

Some of your photographs appeared in a small art magazine two years ago, and I was most impressed by them. Now I am planning to write a book that would be greatly enhanced by photos. I thought of you not just because you are clearly talented but because the book will document the lives of Chinatown residents, both newcomers and some old-timers whom you might remember. Grocer Hu, whose shop was across the street from us. Friends of Uncle Li. I haven't selected all the subjects yet, as I plan to conduct the interviews over the next year or so, but my hope is that the human stories might form a bridge from Chinatown back to China. To this end I think it is important to include the faces as well as the words of those interviewed. I am not a photographer. That's why I am writing you.

I realize this comes out of the blue. But Uncle Li always said you would want to come back. I think you must return to New York sometime, as your family remains here. This might be a project for your next visit.

I look forward to hearing from you, Maibelle. We can discuss in greater detail then.

Sincerely,
T. Tommy Wah

I was two years and several addresses away from Sunridge Street when Tommy's letter arrived, not at my apartment, but in my box at work. My former landlord must have redirected the envelope, though he had never done this with any others before.

Maybe I should have recognized the note's circuitous route as a sign, but I was too unnerved by its contents: flattering, unexpected, and nothing I could even consider accepting. I hadn't touched a camera in over four years, and Tommy, Li—they were names from another lifetime. Chinatown was ancient history. I couldn't think where I'd even begin if I were to answer with any grace.

So I didn't. I tossed the letter in the trash and tried not to give it any further thought. For a while that was the end of that.

A few weeks later a near miss caused me to reconsider. I was working a charter to Pensacola. Stretch DC-8, the plane shaped like a mile-long cigar. We bounced at least six feet on impact, with all the noise of a crash. The lights flashed out. The straps of my jump seat flew off. I fell forward, slamming my head on the metal partition in front of me, and began to cry. I was shaking so hard my flying partners had to drag me into the rear closet area to get me away from the passengers, who were plenty hysterical themselves. We, as professionals, were supposed to smile and pretend this was normal. It turned out we'd missed the end of the runway, a rock jetty into the ocean, by just three and a half inches. When the copilot delivered this news, he said we were lucky sons of bitches. He called it a sign. The next week I heard he was taking early retirement.

Then I happened to pick up a *New York Times* and read that a renowned documentary photographer, a single, childless woman named Marge Gramercy, had died in lower Manhattan. That night was the first in a month I slept through without one of my nightmares.

Tommy Wah's letter. The landing in Pensacola. Marge Gramercy. Too many signs, I decided. Or warnings.

• • •

I returned to Manhattan four months ago—and four months almost to the day after Tommy's letter—on Chinese New Year. According to my calculations, it was the Year of the Rooster, but no firecrackers rattled the streets, no lion dancers came forth to welcome me. I did not go back to Chinatown, where such celebrations were surely taking place. Where Tommy, according to his return address, still lives. I did not go to the Upper West Side, where my parents now reside. I came to Greenwich Village, a territory in between, which no one in the history of my family has ever considered home.

I had an obituary in one pocket and a check for five hundred dollars from the sale of my 1973 Pinto in the other. Having grown unaccustomed to Manhattan in winter, I wore cotton, not wool, no hat, no gloves. My nose was streaming, my eyes watering. My long hair tumbled with the wind. I'd come three thousand miles to ring the bell of a weather-beaten brownstone I'd selected sight unseen.

At the front door Harriet Ratner, 140 West Eleventh Street's building manager and ground-floor tenant, looked me up and down. I stood straight and gave her my best professional smile, but Harriet had the demeanor of a career Girl Scout leader whose troops always earn the most merit badges. She warned, "We're all women here. Your boyfriend moves in, you're out."

"I don't have a boyfriend."

She held her position and continued to size me up: a redheaded stewardess out of California, single, late twenties, with no visible scars or handicaps. From the perspective of a large middle-aged woman with a double chin and orthopedic shoes I was a perfect stereotype.

"I grew up in New York."

She dug a fist into her hip and shifted her weight against the door frame.

"Yeah? Where?"

"Stuyvesant," I lied. "My parents owned a dry goods store. I joined the airlines after they died . . . I've been gone a long time."

"Stuyvesant, huh?" An invisible fault line began to shift. "Grew up in the Bronx, myself."

As I followed her inside I slid the clipping out of my pocket and tried to imagine the sweet-faced old lady in the photograph moving through this gloomy puce hallway. The single decoration was a Dutch Masters cigar box print hanging across from the door. The staircase was clean but well scuffed and creaky. The radiator moaned as we started up, and low-wattage bulbs on each landing left the corners in shadow.

Marge Gramercy had lived here for nearly thirty years, the rental agency told me, which was why they could charge only six hundred a month for her apartment. Rent stabilization. My father would be proud of me, coming up with this bargain gem long-distance, but that was only part of the story. According to her obituary, my predecessor had traveled the globe shooting mountains and native children for *National Geographic*. She'd started at the age of twenty-eight, had won awards for her work. Yet this modest brownstone was her home base. Living in her tracks, I thought, might make her achievement seem real to me. Attainable. It might bring both my life and my work back into focus.

I trailed Harriet up two flights and into a large square room with a plaster fireplace and twelve-foot ceiling. Two tall windows made the place seem lighter, airier than it really was. They looked out across a schoolyard and a couple of tight city gardens to the shops of Greenwich Avenue. A wall sliced off one edge of the main room to form a sleeping alcove barely wide enough for a double mattress. The kitchen was literally a closet that had been outfitted with a two-burner stove, vintage 1930, and a deep porcelain sink. A pull-up table was hinged to the door. The refrigerator stood in the entryway, opposite the coat closet.

It seemed a decidedly inconvenient setup for a woman of Marge Gramercy's accomplishment, not to mention her longevity here. Was the arrangement controlled by economy or indifference? Or was it simply that her real life lay elsewhere?

"Me and my mother live downstairs. These bare wood floors, we'll hear every sneeze unless you put down carpets."

I assured Harriet I was very quiet. With unemployment staring me in the face, I wasn't looking for any investments that weren't absolutely required. For the same reason, I told her not to worry about the houndstooth couch Ms. Gramercy's heirs had failed to carry away. Harriet visibly shuddered, and told me Marge's niece had found her *lying* on that sofa.

"Don't that bother you?" she asked.

"I don't know. I've never owned anything that belonged to a dead person." Which technically was true: everything I ever had from dead people was given to me before they died. Besides, I'd lost my faith in ghosts, so there didn't seem much to fear except the chance that the couch would bring bad luck. And since Ms. Gramercy had made it to eighty-six, working to the end, I figured I had some leeway in that department. It was her luck, for better or worse, that I hoped to inherit.

"She did her darkroom stuff in here, if you can imagine." Harriet swung open the door to the bathroom, a windowless cube only slightly larger than the kitchen: more maximized spatial efficiency. The sink was originally freestanding, but a sheet of plywood had been cut to fit around it as a counter extending over the tub. Crammed into the corner between the bath and toilet was a sky-blue shower with plastic walls.

"I'll take it—" I turned back to Harriet. "I'm a photographer, too."

"Oh, I see." She peered at me as if this new detail made a difference. "Hobby, huh?"

A faint odor, minty camphor or liniment, hung over the bathroom. I fingered the locket at my throat. I looked old and tired in the mirror in here, but the overhead light caught the gold heart just right and made it shine like new. Another sign?

Harriet shook her head. "Y' don't want to end up like her."

"Like how?"

"Poor Marge, broke her hip when she was seventy-eight. Slipped on the fire escape one day when she was out watchin' them kids." She jerked her head toward the closed window and the children who, despite the cold, were playing in the schoolyard. "After that, her traveling days was over. It's no fun getting old, but I guess you know, your parents and all—"

"What did she do then?"

Harriet folded her arms, tight across her chest. "Oh, Marge had chutzpah. Got some catalog company to hire her. They sent their little gadgets by UPS and she took the pictures right here."

I turned on the water. It ran rusty, but gradually cleared, dissolving my portraits of Himalayan peaks into eight-by-ten product shots.

"Gadgets."

"Yeah, like those slice 'n' dice gizmos you see on TV. She hardly had to leave the building. Real lucky stroke for old Marge."

"Real lucky."

I surveyed the main room again. Not hard to imagine how she'd done it. Some backdrop paper against the far wall, strobe, reflectors, a few stands for the little inventions. Gadgets like my father's, no doubt. All simple tripod work. And no traveling. No flying.

"Where was this company she worked for?"

"Florida, I think. Return address in Pensacola, that sound right?"

I stubbed my toe on the couch. "Pensacola?"

But she nodded. "You know Pensacola?"

I stepped on the toe to stop its throbbing and steadied myself by fixing on Harriet's opaque brown eyes. "I'll take the apartment."

Harriet squinted and pursed her lips, and I sensed her searching for my imbalance. Incredibly, she must not have found it because we shook on the deal. Her grip was firm, efficient. When she released my hand, it stayed in midair as if waiting for further instructions.

"Harriet?" I asked as she moved out into the hallway. "Was there a memorial service for Marge?"

"Not that I know. Most her relatives live in Detroit." An eerie wail lifted up the stairwell. "Never mind that," Harriet said quickly. "That's Mother. Prob'ly needs her channel changed. You move in anytime."

Anytime was the following day. I brought a bunch of lilies and daisies and spoke on Marge's behalf a made-up blessing that was a combination thank-you, memorial, and housewarming. I considered it a necessary gesture, like leaving the lights on at night, and for the first few days I actually felt safe and welcome in my new home.

• • •

I'd been here less than a week, was applying for work as a commercial photographer's assistant, and was just beginning to doubt the wisdom of quitting my job in the sky when a box arrived, addressed without name to my apartment. Postmarked in Pensacola, it contained a set of plastic coasters with interchangeable pictures of game birds, a combination sifter, grater, and dicer, five patterns of personalized embossers, and a spec sheet with the size and quantity of negatives and prints the catalogue required for each product. According to these numbers, the Hans Noble Company had paid Marge Gramercy about half the going commercial rate.

Four days later I sent the requested photographs to Pensacola along with the merchandise and an invoice informing Mr. Noble that I, Maibelle Chung, had taken over Ms. Gramercy's studio upon her death. The following week my payment arrived with a new set of merchandise and instructions on which someone had scrawled: "We pay by the job, no contracts. Fee is nonnegotiable, but you can have that photo credit you asked for. Sorry to hear about Marge."

That night was the first time my screams woke Harriet.

"It's a man, isn't it?" she demanded, wedging one foot in the doorway.

"There's no one else here."

Under her blue satin robe Harriet wore a flannel nightgown printed with elves. Her face was puffy and her hair looked as if someone had sat on it. I could hear her mother faintly whining downstairs. But Harriet was still more or less on my side back then and she didn't insist on searching my apartment.

"Men are shits, kid. They'd rather screw you than look at you. Never forget that."

I thanked her for this piece of advice and shut the door quickly before she could offer any more. There was no man that night, but there would be. I knew, inevitably there would be.

I used to think I could escape my nightmares by going away. The day I graduated from college, I was packing my car to drive across country, and my brother, Henry, said I'd never find what I was looking for that way. I told him whatever I found would be more than what I was looking for. He said no, anything would be less. Philosophy and insight not being two of my brother's strong points, I chose to laugh at him, but it turned out he was right.

Instead of driving off into oblivion that summer, I met a rich, fiftyish man in a Howard Johnson's in Nappanee, Indiana. He owned a shopping mall in Muncie where there was a consignment gallery run by an acerbic bleached blonde named Roxy who liked to talk about men who'd abused her. Though we would never claim each other as friends, I enjoyed listening to Roxy. I admired her certainty and her candor. She knew what she felt, what she thought, and why. Whatever men did to me was not something I could discuss.

The rich mall-owner lost interest when I refused to sleep with him, but Roxy said she could use more of what I had, which at that point was my student portfolio—photographs of fire hydrants lit to resemble cathedrals, and steeples that looked like knives cutting ornate cloud formations. I progressed to vintage cars, using strobes to turn their headlights to eyes, and shot landscapes in which the tops of trees became oceans and sandbars.

For half a year I traveled the Midwest, camping in Motel Sixes and photographing nature in ways that made it seem like something else. People who saw my work in the gallery called it "neat," and bought the prints as puzzles to see if their friends and neighbors could figure out what was what.

When I wasn't using tricks of light and angle to subvert the universal order, I grazed crops of men in truck stops and watched families loading and unloading cars in motel parking lots. In Menominee Falls, Wisconsin, I slept with a park ranger who fit the description of all my men—boiled gold hair, deep freckles, and eyes that seemed to have dropped from the sky. We spent twelve hours together, no hope, no expectations, and hardly more than a physical longing in common, then he went home to his wife and four children. A month later I came back to New York and my parents, but before I worked up the nerve to tell them my news, much less decide what to do about it, nature replaced my choice with an outpouring of blood, cramps, and unexpected sorrow.

Henry, the only member of the family who knew, said I probably wasn't pregnant at all.

"Wishful thinking. You know how that goes."

I told him he didn't know shit.

When I got back to my nomadic life, the fields were buried under two feet of snow. I stood on a hilltop in Illinois and stared through my circle of glass at endless miles of skeletal plants, hardened waterways, wildlife preparing to hide from the great thermal plunge into winter. Before my pregnancy I'd turned the cold into collages of lace or candy or intricately blown glass patterns. (More trick shots, most of them sold. Roxy said they'd make great postcards. She threatened to send them to art magazines and, if Tommy Wah told the truth, she eventually must have done just that because I certainly never submitted my work for publication.) But that first day back, on that bleak, frozen hill, the seasonal death defied me. I had no more tricks. I'd lost them racing toward some kind of freedom I didn't begin to understand.

I lowered the Pentax and took another look at the world unframed, let it pull itself over and around me like a vast gray paper bag. Only a fool would try to capture such immensity through a mechanical eye. Or believe the cure for terror lay in photographic alchemy. I weighed the camera briefly in one hand—metal, plastic, glass cold as ice surrounding a compartment of darkness. I let the weight of that darkness pull me to my feet, lift my arm high and wide. I felt the power, the ease of release, watched my instrument cut an arc through the frozen air and drop, clattering to the gorge below. Though I could no longer see it, I knew it was lying in shards and bent pieces all over the granite's smooth face.

That Pentax was my first camera. My mother had given it to me for my fourteenth birthday. After cracking it up I checked out of my motel room, sent what prints I had to Roxy, and traveled to Chicago. I'd heard from a coffee shop waitress that United was hiring flight attendants for openings out of Los Angeles. If I proved I could fly without falling, I thought, my nightmares would have to release me.

• • •

It's nearly the end of May now, and warm enough for kids to roller-skate in the schoolyard. From my fire escape I watch them doing backward twirls and scissor steps to boom-box rock and roll. Behind and above, the sky is the incandescent blue of a stage flat, roofs against it black. Up and down Greenwich Avenue shoppers scurry on pre-dinner errands past the dry cleaner where I take my sweaters, the grocery where I buy coffee, the record store that supplies me with the Motown greats brother Henry taught me to love. Past the photo lab where I take my color work and buy film when I don't have time to get it at discount uptown.

My upstairs neighbors, Betty and Sandra, are running a bath—probably for their new baby, Hope. Above the rush of pipes Larraine Moseley is practicing her electric guitar, and through this mesh of sounds come the smells of sautéing onions, butter, roasting meat. These sensations comfort me with their normalcy.

So does the elderly woman who lives on the ground floor of the brownstone next door. Since the weather turned warm she's come out every evening to sit in her garden with her roses and daffodils and trees shaped like lollipops. Unlike Harriet's mother, whose persistent invisibility has convinced me her daughter keeps her housebound and bedridden, my neighbor rolls herself out in her wheelchair and writes in a notebook or leafs through photo albums. I've never seen a visitor. She sits for an hour, then a large wisecracking woman in a white uniform comes to push her inside, and I tell myself the old lady is lucky, she must own the building, has the wealth to stay there and choose her own routine. She enjoyed a good enough life that she keeps poring over it, wanting to remember. Of course, for all I know, she's working out her taxes in that notebook and the albums contain shots of prospective real estate investments and she's only lived here for a few months, but I like to think she's stocking up on her past. I imagine the Village is her home, as it was Marge Gramercy's.

Product shipments now come twice a week. I've resurrected Marge's studio, leased the necessary equipment, and filled in around the couch with some folding chairs, a foam mattress in the bedroom, stacked orange crates for shelves. At the moment the crates are filled with such indispensable items as a pottery water recycler, a spring-loaded toilet seat, collapsible shoe trees, and several digital timers. Some of these products I shot back in February. I'm keeping them to show my father before I return them to Pensacola. I remember him saying once, "An inventor should always be on the lookout for concepts to improve."

One of these days I really will invite Dad to come down and visit. I'll show him the work that's paying my bills, make the necessary excuses, and admit that although it's not much to be proud of, it gives me the freedom to do my own projects. I won't lie to him. I just won't tell him what I'm making of all this freedom.

Harriet's admonishments aside, there have been men. An actor. A carpenter. A podiatrist. A hat salesman. Few lasted the whole night, none more than two weeks.

I met the last one standing in line at Ray's Pizza. He had pale Scandinavian hair and a square back, wore an embroidered denim work shirt and steel-tipped lizard boots. He ordered a single slice of the vegetarian Sicilian, then turned and, as if we'd been talking for hours, explained himself.

"Used to be fat, but I had my stomach stapled. Now I can't eat more 'n a slice."

Steady at one-sixty and five feet eleven inches tall, he had skin as smooth as a boy's and eyes the color of water in a country swimming hole.

"I'm Jed Moffitt." He claimed his pizza and offered me his free hand. Clammy.

"Maibelle Chung."

He waited, watching as I placed my order. We ate side by side at the counter looking out onto Sixth Avenue, and he told me he was a sculptor. I said I was a photographer and got up to leave.

"Two artists." He snaked his arm through mine. "Why the hell not?"

I knew perfectly well why not, but I followed Jed, anyway. By the time we reached Sheridan Square he was humming the melody from "Wichita Lineman" out the side of his mouth. He had a good, low voice and I closed my eyes to reach for the promised images of cold, clear, country nights and effortless space. But the humming stopped abruptly and we emerged from the elevator on the twelfth floor.

His sculptures were aquariums shaped like antique bottles filled with colored water, dyed oil, and floating baubles. Upgraded Lava lamps. I told him they were "neat," as if I'd never seen such creations before. He turned off the overhead lights, and the reflected greens and golds swam across our skin. I touched him first.

In short order I had my tongue in his ear, my hands pawing his back, under, on top, flattened skin-to-skin. The aggressor, I granted him neither choice nor comment. I had demanded this entry, forced my way in, and now took him by surprise.

"Wait!" He was gasping. I unrolled the condom for him, as much to preclude conversation as to protect either of us. There was no protection for what I was doing.

I nevertheless hoped for a different result.

This time, I thought as the new man straddled me, this time I will push through. I will feel him with me, beside me, in me. Somewhere. I will feel him love me.

But the closer our bodies moved together, the farther I drifted into that other familiar sensation, my own personal Doppler effect. A perversion of intimacy like a sexual narcotic, at once numbing and arousing, which heightened the sounds and smells, the darkness of moving shapes, yet erased all sensation of touch. I heard and watched as a child removed, and wondered how this could be happening.

A child wouldn't do such things. Not a child whose nakedness is a crime. A child would be plowed under by acts that make no sense. I had not been plowed under, therefore my body must belong to someone else. To prove this I went with Jed Moffitt as I had gone with so many men. I would not, would never, be plowed under.

We slept together on a mattress he'd slid into a closet in lieu of a proper bedroom. I was used to such arrangements. Nor did it surprise me the next morning when he produced a snapshot of his girl. A high school sweetheart, product of a broken home, she looked like a mouse. A twelve-year-old mouse.

"She comes up to here," he said, indicating his chest. He spoke sheepishly: she needed him; he was helping to put her through med school in Baltimore. Then he asked when he could see me again.

We slept together eight times, the last at my apartment. I never had bad dreams the nights I stayed with Jed. I wasn't fool enough to think there was anything more to it than comfort, but there was that. I admired his scar, the courage to take drastic action to salve his soul. He drank Schlitz and manufactured Lava lamps and picked up women like me, but he no longer felt ugly. If I could just identify what I needed to cut out or staple shut or transform, I might draw on Jed Moffitt's example.

Then three days ago he warned me he was going to be unavailable. The girlfriend was coming. After a few days they would leave to spend the summer in Maine with his parents.

I stared at Jed's hair, memorizing the precise color. Sand on a blazing hot day. White sand.

"I'll call you," he said.

"Why?"

"In the fall. She'll go back to school."

The fabric was pilling on Marge Gramercy's sofa. I tore at the soft nappy tufts and rolled them between my fingertips until they hardened into a ball.

Jed ran his fingers over his left eyebrow, wiping invisible perspiration. "I told you going in, Maibelle, this was the deal."

"It doesn't make any difference."

After he was gone I realized he'd left a bottle of beer in my refrigerator. I wanted to pour it down the drain, but I didn't. It's still there.

And yesterday I spotted the two of them strolling up Charles Street, laughing and bumping into each other. Hand in hand. I watched them until they turned the corner, and they never let go. Like paper dolls cut out of a chain, they stayed connected.

About two this morning I woke, thrashing and sweating, to the crack of billy clubs at my door. I pulled free of my knotted sheets, slowed my breathing to a pinched roar, and stumbled to the peephole. Outside, two overstuffed patrolmen hovered with my neighbors arrayed behind them like a geek-show audience. When I opened the door, the police backed away, but Harriet just kept coming. She wore a pink hair net and her lips curled down tight over her teeth. Her eyes squeezed against the light flooding through my doorway.

"I've had it! You either get a grip on yourself or get out. Next time you scream like that, I'm calling Bellevue. Hear me?"

Bellevue. That was a new addition. Usually it was just the threat of the street. One more chance, she'd give me. Maybe two. But now it was Bellevue: straitjacket time.

The policemen were staring past Harriet into my apartment. Sandra looked as if she was trying to decide whether I had recently ingested monstrous quantities of prescription pharmaceuticals. Larraine was sizing up the taller policeman's backside.

I apologized, assured the police that I was alone, in no danger, it wouldn't happen again. I closed the door and threw a towel across the crack underneath to make them think I'd turned out the lights. Though I sometimes dream the lamps have caught fire and my sleeping eyes open to flames just inches away, it's a risk worth taking against the alternative: darkness.

But this time I knew I couldn't return to sleep, no matter what tricks I used. I spent the remaining hours before dawn peering at the six-inch Sony at the foot of my mattress, trying to substitute whirling images of Ginger Rogers and Fred Astaire for my usual dream. The dream, of course, won. Kept playing over and over like a negative superimposed on those elegant, gleaming dance numbers. A subway chase, photographers exploding flashbulbs.

An unlit tunnel leads to stairs. I climb. And climb. When I emerge atop the statue's crown, I am up against the sky. Below, the Hudson River runs red. Bodies lie thick in the streets. I mount the howl of sirens, hard as a gale wind, and spiral over the ruined city above vacant penthouse gardens and skyscrapers shorn in half. Fifth Avenue writhes with human heads and limbs, expensive jewelry. Discarded party hats and bleeding babies. A handsome blond man frowns at the sky.

When I was little, the nightmare would abruptly change at this point and, just as the horror began to sink in, a second surge of siren sound would carry me safely home. I'd land on a red and green balcony surrounded by musical bells.

In the version of recent years there is no rescue. I spin my arms like one of those weather-vane ducks to stay aloft and only think I know where I'm going. "Home!" I scream. "Let me go!" But it's as if a cloud of white silk has eaten lower Manhattan. I cannot see beyond Canal Street, nor can I turn back. I enter the cloud and drop without warning, spin like an insect caught in a whirlpool. Down I fall, down, bracing to hit concrete, but though I feel a pain like razors being sharpened against my skin, though I open my eyes wide enough to take in all Mott Street, I see nothing. The white becomes snow as thick as ink. I plunge faster, faster. Invisible hands claw my eyes and mouth. Smoke chokes my throat but I cannot cough. Strangled voices jeer and whisper. Another minute, they tell me, another second and I will never breathe again.

• • •

The lamps have come on over the playground, and the crowd of skaters is growing. The center is given to experts who glide backward and two-step as if they were born on wheels. The shadows are filled with less ambitious couples who flirt and fight, killing time.

Nights like this in Chinatown I used to sit out on our balcony and listen to the washing of mah-jongg tiles from the terrace upstairs mix with the laughter of boys playing craps on the sidewalk directly below. I'd watch the slow procession of traffic, a pageant of shadow and mirrored light. That balcony was like a box seat at the theater with all of Mott Street the stage.

My father, who would drive an hour to save a dime on a carton of Kents, used to say our third-floor walk-up on Mott Street was the biggest bargain in Manhattan. Where else in 1960, he said, could we find a four-bedroom for under two hundred a month? Given our address and my father's Chinese birthright, you might think that apartment would have been splashed with Oriental touches, at the very least some bean curd, lotus root, or winter melon tucked into the refrigerator—but it was as though a fine dotted line traced the perimeter of my childhood home. To cross it was like stepping from Hong Kong into Geneva.

Outside, whether in the hallway or the street beyond the terrace, the air danced with fragrances of sandalwood, water chestnuts, dried shrimp, and garlic. Doors were hung with good-luck banners and appeals for protection from the gods. The reigning colors were scarlet and gold.

My mother chose to arrange our home in black and white, with an occasional accent of lemon yellow or hot pink to "punch it up." The apartment coordinated well with her wardrobe, which in the sixties was stylishly eye-popping. The kitchen was done in stainless steel, and though the native language was English, the cuisine was aggressively French. A monstrous air conditioner, which my father purchased at a factory sale in New Rochelle, was installed in the kitchen window and ran year-round to keep the smell of the neighbors' cooking from contaminating Mum's. Out on the balcony, where the locals might grow peonies or chrysanthemums, she established a garden of pots containing Alpine wildflowers.

She lived there for nearly twenty years but I never once heard my mother call Chinatown home, and after we moved away she would unfailingly correct the rest of us: "It's not our home anymore. We're uptowners now."

Perhaps that's why I so automatically rejected Tommy Wah's invitation to return. That and the fact that for years, because of my recurring nightmares, I've tried to block out all thought of the old neighborhood. But ever since Tommy's letter the memories have been creeping back, and I no longer know whether to battle or embrace them.

Now, in a corner of the schoolyard I can only dimly see, a girl has fallen, is crying. A boy stands over her shaking his fist. She twists away.

I suddenly realize I'm sweating, holding my breath. Blood flows where I've bitten my lip. The music throbs and jumps to top volume, and the boy yanks the girl to her feet. Their shadowed figures collide, then merge.

I make myself breathe in. And out. They are kissing. I have film to develop. I need to go in and work. But even in the darkroom with the door shut, the music penetrates. Pumping. Pounding. "Emotional Rescue."

* * *

My plan failed on both counts. I did not learn to fly freely or fearlessly. I clung instead to one anonymous man after another. And my nightmares clung to me.

I could say it was Tommy's letter that prompted my return. Or the incident in Pensacola. Or Marge. But the truth is, my nightmares have been driving me back for years, as relentlessly as they once pushed me away. I came to New York more determined than ever to find the source of these nightly terrors, face it down and conquer it.

But determination can be a very fickle bedfellow, and it, too, threatens to fail me now. Mystical signs and coincidences aside, unless I make some progress against my dream life soon, I will lose this apartment and even the minimal safety net I've managed to establish here.

No more men. And no more running away.

....

2

*M*y mother began teaching me practically from birth to watch the world through an imaginary viewfinder. Using the magic of the camera, she said, I could stop time cold, yet keep it alive. Through the alchemy of the darkroom, I could float the ghosts of moments I'd lived through back into shadow and light, and when I finally mastered the magic, I would feel in every photograph as though I were watching myself watch the world—and seeing the world look back. Then I would know I'd made Art.

She had such high hopes when I set off on my cross-country jaunt after college. Her plan was for me to venture, experiment, and gradually narrow my sights to a particular, salable vision. When I told her I'd settled for the view from thirty thousand feet, she made a noise at her end of the phone as if I'd spat on her.

"You can't be serious. Not you, too. You're giving up before you've begun, and to do *what*? To be a flying waitress!"

"You've always wanted to go to Europe. I can get you free airline passes."

"Not on your life. You actually think you can bribe me to approve of your squandering your talent?"

"I'll have plenty of time off. I can work then."

"Ah, yes, but will you?"

The operator interrupted. I was calling from a pay phone at Staples International. And I was out of change.

"You're quitting, Maibelle."

She didn't need to say the rest: I was quitting just like my father.

That was the last we spoke until this week.

"Darling!" she shouted when I called. "Where on earth are you? Are you all right?"

"I'm fine, Mum. I'm in New York."

"My God, Maibelle." She seemed to be catching her breath. "I thought something dreadful— Well, you know how I am about planes. I can't bear to think of you thirty thousand miles above ground all the time. Do. You. Realize. It's been three *years*."

"Feet, Mum, not miles. I realize. If you're going to be around over the weekend, I'll come uptown. We can talk then."

"I don't know if I can stand it."

"What?"

"Both daughters here at once."

"Anna's coming home?"

"Just for a few hours. Maibelle, how long are you going to be here? Why aren't you staying with us?"

"I've moved back, Mum. I have an apartment."

I pictured her gray eyes closing, the two upright worry lines plowing deeper. The impatient, manicured hand brushing a frosted wisp from her cheek.

"Excuse me?"

"Please. Let's not do this over the phone."

"There's a man. Is there a man? You haven't gone and gotten married, Maibelle!"

The receiver throbbed as if it were a direct line from her speeding heart to mine.

"There is no man, Mother. I can assure you. But I'd really prefer to discuss this in person. Is she coming Saturday or Sunday?"

My mother's voice, when she finally answered, made me think of a plate-glass window through which I was about to be thrown. "Saturday. For lunch she's coming. Around noon. If the stars are in alignment, Henry will join us, too."

Her mouth twitched when the elevator doors opened. She was standing in the hallway with two unopened bottles of champagne, and I could recount every minute of her morning just by looking at her. An hour bathing and putting on that black velveteen pantsuit and ruffled white blouse, another half hour doing her makeup and hair, then a spell in her apron making some watercress or quail salad she'd seen in *Gourmet* and shopped for at Zabar's.

"You look terrific, Mum."

"I work at it. You look beat. And you've lost weight."

I'd gone western for the day in a long riding skirt, concha belt, boots, and voluminous poet's shirt, but my mother's X-ray vision cut right through the disguise.

"Some."

"Well, we'll fix that. Come here, you."

We hugged stiffly, both holding our breath as we tried in vain to fit the points of our bodies together. Because of the bottles, it was like being embraced by someone holding barbells.

"Where's Dad?"

"It's noon. Where else would he be? Getting dressed. You're the first one here."

I trailed her into the kitchen for want of an alternative. Immaculate white with butcher-block counters and the same stainless-steel equipment she'd brought up from Chinatown, the room was either brilliantly light and breezy or sterile as a morgue. It varied with my mother's mood.

I picked up a paperweight from the counter. A solid crystal sphere filled to bursting with a real dandelion puff. I couldn't imagine how its maker had managed to keep all those feathery strands intact, encased. Each filament reached outward, pushing against the curved surface, and every one was so perfectly poised and balanced that the whole seemed about to explode.

Think light and breezy, I told myself firmly.

She put the bottles in the freezer, tied on an apron, and began emptying the cabinets. Jars, boxes, shakers, funnels, cups, and spoons soon filled the counter. Like a chemist, she proceeded to pour and measure ingredients into a huge mixing bowl. She stood with her back to me, arms popping out at odd angles as she reached and whisked. I deduced she was making salad dressing, but it looked like enough for the entire Upper West Side. She beat the concoction for three solid minutes by the Bauhaus wall clock. Dad had found that clock at a Phoenix House thrift shop and given it to her for Christmas the year before I left. He swore up and down it was brand-new, and she loved it so left it at that.

"Want some help?" I said at last.

She stopped, stock-still, then slowly turned, the whisk in her hand dripping perfect beads of oil onto her spotless floor.

"How long have you been here?"

"A few weeks."

"A few weeks."

She tossed the whisk in the sink and pulled off one large gold shell-shaped earring, rubbed the exposed lobe between her fingers. Her face seemed to list with the weight of the opposite earring.

"If you'd let me know, Scott Sazaroff had the most fabulous place in the West Seventies. He would have—"

"That's why."

"Why what?"

"I've been living on my own for years. I don't need you to find me an apartment." My voice sounded as if I were being strangled.

She let go of her ear and clenched her fist, stared at it, flattened it on the counter. The gold shell skittered among the salad dressing ingredients.

"I see. Well, in that case, I can hardly wait to see what splendid arrangement you've made for yourself."

"I didn't want to bother you and Dad."

She turned to clean up the mess she'd made and spoke slowly, deliberately, over the shoulder as she worked. "You go off God knows where—with whoever. You don't even have the courtesy of letting us know if you're dead or alive . . . but you didn't want to bother us."

She whirled around, hugging her arms to her stomach. "Are you out of your goddamn mind?"

I counted to five before answering, and my voice almost didn't shake. "I knew this would happen."

"What? What would happen?"

"You'd get defensive."

My mother replaced her earring and began pressing loose strands of hair into place. "Could we back up a little? Why, exactly, have you moved back? Have they changed your—what do you call it?"

"Base."

"Right. I'm to understand you're based out of New York now?"

I shrugged.

"I said, is that right?"

I didn't answer.

"Then you've left the airlines?"

"You'll slip on this in a minute." I took a sponge from the counter and reached down to wipe up the oil she'd spilled.

"Maibelle?"

I came up slowly so as not to get dizzy and turned the tap on over the sponge. The sun through the window caught the oil and made streaks of rainbow going down the drain. When I turned and looked her in the eye, she stamped her foot and raised her arms.

"At last you've come to your senses. I'm so glad, Maibelle. So glad!"

You'd think I'd just been freed from slavery. God almighty, free at last. Before she could hug me again, I told her to stay put, I needed some air. Having scored her first victory, she didn't object, but I could feel her jubilant eyes on me through the window as I moved across the terrace.

I stayed to the back of her garden of pots, away from the edge and her view. Here the gravity of detail gave the terrace such heft that it seemed inconceivable the real ground was twenty floors down. Detail. Like the Brown and Jordan garden furniture. Planters with evergreens and blooming peach trees. Terra-cotta pavers. Every indication that this was Mum's little slice of heaven on earth. No one would guess what a stink she put up at first.

I was thirteen the year my father finally made the killing that enabled us to leave Chinatown. Unfortunately the patent sale of his "micropore ziplock bottlecap" to a dairy distributor in New Jersey did not bring Upper East Side money, at least not the Sutton Place- or Murray Hill- or Park Avenue-type Upper East Side that my mother had in mind. But Dad, pioneering the tactic that later put me in touch with Marge Gramercy, found a lead in the obituaries. A photographer he'd known in his youth had died in a plane crash in the Andes, leaving untenanted the penthouse of a rent-controlled building at Ninetieth and Central Park West.

"Awfully close to Harlem, isn't it?" Mum asked the first day we came for a viewing.

"It belonged to a *Life* photojournalist," Dad said. "You'll love it."

The elevator was broken. The service lift stank of rotting garbage. In the kitchen a herd of cockroaches was devouring the remains of an ancient pack of pork rinds, and pea-colored paint dropped from the ceiling in chunks. Dad's friend must have been dead for some time, I thought, or else he'd been in the Andes for years without bothering to keep his cleaning lady.

"Joe," said my mother, "we're wasting our time."

"Just look at those ceilings. Ten feet at least. You can't find height like that anymore. Not for four hundred a month."

"I sure hope they'll throw in the roaches," said Anna. (Already eighteen, on her way to college and the World, my sister never did live with us uptown. Possibly my parents' combat over the apartment gave her the excuse she needed. Certainly her quest for celestial harmony became a constant in her life ever after.)

"Tommy Wah's ma says roaches are good luck," Henry said. At that time Tommy was still his best friend. "Every New Year she has me and Tommy catch one for the kitchen god."

"Maybe she'd like to move in here," Mum said. "It'd save you and Tommy all that trouble."

"How about this?" Dad led Mum outside. "Enough space for a *real* Alpine garden. Five bedrooms. Separate living and dining rooms, plus a powder room and full terrace overlooking Central Park. Diana, we'll never do better than this."

The way she looked, I could tell she was ready to explode.

But Dad tried again. "This is a real bargain—"

"And I," she shouted, "am sick of bargains! Just once in my life I'd like to forget about money. I don't want something for nothing, you see? I want to pay through the teeth—every penny, if need be—for something I absolutely love!"

Dad leaned against the balustrade and stared out over the park. "I thought you would love this."

My mother froze. "And?"

"I've already signed the lease."

Her voice, when she finally located the words, sounded like splitting wood. "You just don't see it, do you, Joe? You don't see at all."

She did not make him break the lease. She did not ask for a divorce. But she did exact retribution in decorator's and contractor's fees. Every room but Dad's workshop was transformed into Milan moderne. And, although Dad still combed the classifieds and suburban shopper gazettes, he never so much as suggested that Mum furnish the new place at discount.

"Maibee?"

He waved from the doorway as if saying goodbye instead of hello, and I was struck at once by how much older he looked. His hair was grayer, his back more stooped than I remembered. I hurried across the terrace to save him the walk.

But his appearance was deceptive. He clamped me in a bear hug with the strength of a much younger man, rumpling my hair as if I were five and surrounding me with those familiar masculine smells—tobacco, Brylcreem, the English Leather my brother ritualistically gives him for his birthday every year. I could feel the ridges of his seersucker jacket making marks in my skin. His paunch pressed against my stomach. His chest, which my arms easily encircled, felt as delicate and inviolable as the bamboo armature of a birdcage.

Finally he released me, gave my ponytail one more sweep of the hand, and stood back for a look. "Well, well." He reached into his jacket pocket and pulled out a pack of Kents, fumbled with the wrapper as he stared at me. His eyes were smiling, but his mouth worked awkwardly as if he had a candy he'd like to spit out.

"I missed you, Dad."

He slid the cigarettes back in his pocket and reached around my shoulders for another squeeze. "We missed you, too."

That was it, and about par for the course, as far as conversation with my father went. We walked back inside. I admired the rolling waves of beige in which my mother had most recently done the living room. He took his designated position behind the mahogany desk in the corner, hooked his glasses over his nose, and picked up his newspaper.

A minute or two later, he looked at me. "How have you been?"

"Fine. It's good to be home."

He nodded. "You look good."

"I quit flying."

He laid down the paper, his expression unreadable. "Mum just told me."

I checked the hallway to see if she was watching, listening, but it appeared empty and I could hear the thump of cupboard doors from the kitchen.

"I have an apartment in the Village."

"Nice down there."

"You should come visit. I'm working for a catalog company. Photographing gadgets. Some worth your taking a look at maybe."

"Ideas, eh? I'm always looking for ideas."

"Look alive, everybody!" called my mother. "Anna's here."

"I told you, it's Aneela Prem." And, with that, in strode my sister the vision in red.

Last time I saw her she wore orange, the time before mustard yellow. Now, from the scarlet ribbon in her hair right down through the garnet worship beads, ankle-length coral print skirt, and pink high-top sneakers, the only contrasting color on my sister's body was the green of her eyes, which match mine. A cosmic dress code, I was sure, but my mother managed to rationalize.

As she watched Anna fold me in her arms and carefully kiss each cheek, she said, "Aren't those colors smashing on her, Maibelle?"

"The Dhawon says they're the colors of joy and love," Anna said. "If everyone wore them, our combined auras would bring world peace."

My father made the soft, clucking noise at the back of his throat that he used to signal regret or disapproval. He came out to give Anna the usual bear hug, but retreated quickly behind his desk again.

"Well," said Mum, "the colors do wonders for your complexion."

It was true. Scrubbed clean, no makeup, my sister looked positively cherubic. I could hardly see the acne scars that had earned her the nickname Pockmark from her Chinatown classmates.

"It's the vegetarian diet. Of course, my whole life now is grounded in meditation and love, but the Dhawon says the improvement in my skin is a direct result of diet, helped by the colors. And frequency of sex, of course."

My mother clamped her jaw shut so fast I heard her teeth.

"Anna—"

"Aneela Prem. Please."

"It's so good to have both you girls home." My mother strode past us to the coffee table, laden with glasses and ice bucket, and loudly began to undo the foil on the first bottle of champagne.

Anna pressed ahead with a well-rehearsed monologue about "spiritual awareness," "articulation of joy," "knots of negativity," and "vigilance of conscience." She had just come from meditation camp in Amsterdam and wanted to tell us what she'd learned.

I wanted to ask if she still made strawberry sodas with mint chip ice cream, or woke up at three in the morning from dreams of giant toads and witches, or had the gold Chinese coin she'd unearthed long ago in Columbus Park. I wanted to ask if she still would gladly give up that coin, along with every other possession she'd ever prized, in exchange for naturally blond hair. I wanted to ask if she, by chance, knew what was wrong with me. But I didn't ask any of these questions because I knew that although the answers were probably all yes, she would tell me no—or, in the last case, that my problem was spiritual confusion intensified by unsatisfactory sex.

I helped Mum pop the champagne, but Anna said she had stopped consuming substances that altered consciousness. She would fix herself a cup of the herbal broth she'd brought with her.

"Oh, Maibelle," Mum said a little too brightly as Anna drifted into the kitchen. She took a deep gulp from her glass and blinked hard. "Someone's been calling for you. I wrote it down here somewhere. Last fall he phoned and then again last month. That boy Henry used to play with in Chinatown. Lived next door."

I knocked the tray, nearly toppling the wine, and scanned her for telltale signals, but she wasn't really paying attention. As she rummaged through a drawer in the sideboard her rings tapped like a woodpecker. "His parents ran that poultry shop. Remember?"

"Tommy Wah." The name wobbled in my mouth. He'd called again last month. That must mean he hadn't found someone else. The dare was still open, and I was sweating as if I were back aboard a diving plane.

She came at me, the white paper dangling between her fingers.

"He didn't say what he wanted." I realized too late that I'd meant to pose this as a question.

She folded the note, held it out. I wiped my dripping palm on my skirt and took the message without making eye contact.

"Four days ago I hadn't heard from you in three years and didn't know if I ever would again. I did not see any point in asking him what he wanted." If she was lying, she didn't show it. Besides, if she knew what he was asking, why would she conceal it? Not Mum. She might even approve. I wondered which would be harder to take.

I shoved the paper in my pocket, resolutely consigning Tommy and Chinatown to the nether regions of my mind, and took a glass to my father. I was about to propose a toast to Anna, who had floated back in with her tea, when my brother joined the fray.

In polo shirt and chinos, with his freshly cut hair combed neatly to one side, he was the only one of us who looked like his mother's child. He punched me in the shoulder hard enough to hurt, then kissed me between my cheek and mouth. I hugged him in return. As Anna bestowed the obligatory two-cheek kiss, he just stood blankly grinning. Then, without waiting for an invitation, he poured himself some champagne.

"Here's to my fugitive sisters who've returned however briefly to grace our family nest."

"Briefly is right," Mum said. "Can't we persuade you to at least spend the night, Anna?"

"I'm sorry. I'm scheduled to attend the Dhawon during darshan tomorrow morning."

The rest of us exchanged appropriately blank stares.

"So, Maibelle," my brother said, "how, when, where, why, and with whom, or can't you tell in present company?"

"Come again?"

"Why're you back in the Big A?"

I braced myself with a drink and told him half the truth. "Fear of flying. It's a professional liability. Besides, I was up to four years and with seniority, if I'd stayed any longer I couldn't have afforded to stop."

"Tough break. But you could have stayed out in sunny California. Why come back to the soot belt?"

"So she can get her career back on track." My mother refilled her glass.

"No. That's not why."

"Oh?" she said. "Why, then?"

I glanced at my father and felt immensely relieved when he smiled back.

"She has a job," he said. "For a catalog studio."

"Hans Noble."

"I know them," said Henry. "They're hotter than Lillian Vernon."

"Lillian Vernon!" Anna grimaced.

"Actually, I'm sort of my own studio."

"Really!" Mum sat on the arm of Henry's chair. They sipped their champagne in tandem. "How did you find this position, Maibelle?"

"Through a friend."

"What friend?"

"The woman who had my apartment before me."

"I have friends who could give you a real job."

"I know."

The vacuum cleaner had embossed colliding tracks on the rich wheat-colored carpet. Was she still doing her own cleaning on top of everything else?

"You're getting along, then, are you?" my father said.

"Just fine."

"Well, it beats waitressing, I suppose." Mum waved one hand like a baton and summoned us in to lunch.

Having inspected Mum's partridge salad with radicchio and arugula and the accompanying crisp baguette, my sister declared that she ate no animal flesh or refined-flour products. Instead she produced a bag of seeds and a slab of brown bread which she covered with a green whipped substance from a mason jar. This, with a cup of her herbal brew, was her celebration lunch.

The rest of us heaped our plates with the food Anna wouldn't touch. My father opened the second bottle of champagne, and we clinked our glasses in a toast of homecoming that was really an appeal for truce. My sister, of course, abstained.

"Henry," she said, "the Big D is holding a meditation camp down in Tennessee next month, and I really think you'd get a lot out of it . . ."

I watched my father fiddle absently with the stem of his glass. He ate his lunch and tugged at his nails (my mother outlawed smoking at the table years ago) and occasionally his gaze landed on one of us. He'd smile, and a trace of his old charm would glint through.

People used to say my father was handsome. Though handsome, to me, was Cary Grant or Gregory Peck, I knew what they meant. Dad was more like a sad Desi Arnaz. Dark with high, wide cheekbones and eyes that carefully studied the world from the shelter of heavy lids. Beneath his eyes he's always had the classic Oriental pouches, which I used to call moonpuffs. They become softer and deeper when he is tired, giving him the look of a weary wise man. I was fond of those moonpuffs until I grew up and realized I, too, had them. Then I called them bags.

Now, looking from my fanatical sister to my feckless brother, my hypercompetent mother to my muted father, I wondered for the first time if there could be more to my madness than bad dreams. Some genetic common denominator. Some shared historical virus that had twisted us all in small ways and large.

"Anna," I interrupted.

"Call me Aneela, please."

"Whatever. You remember that time down in the basement in Chinatown when we went through Dad's old boxes?"

"No."

"Oh, yes, you do. It was raining, remember? I was five and you were twelve and for possibly the only time in our entire childhood you were so bored you actually played with me."

"Maibelle." Deep in her patronizing tone I heard echoes of the girl who'd once called me a moron for not knowing the lead singer of Cream. "Maibelle, please try to understand. I have been rebirthed. I have died to the past and to the future. As the Dhawon says, I have opened myself to the timeless, eternal present. Memories are irrelevant."

With that she tossed a handful of birdseed into her mouth and began methodically to chew. Henry manfully struggled to reverse the passage of an arugula leaf that he'd snarfled into his nasal cavity during Anna's speech. My mother excused herself to make a pot of coffee, which Anna reminded her she wouldn't drink. But to my amazement my father took the bait.

"You believe that."

"Absolutely. Caffeine poisons the blood—"

"No. About memories."

"Absolutely." But then Anna swirled her tea and let her gaze amble toward the blue beyond the window. She had prepared no defense for a statement of such inherent truth.

"Sometimes I think they're all that *is* relevant," my father said. "Too bloody relevant, in fact."

"You see? They become an encumbrance, a distraction from the beauty and joy that surrounds us in the Now."

I tried to kick her under the table, but my boot fell short. "What do you mean, Dad?"

My father's face darkened. He turned away from us both. "Beauty and joy my ass."

The baize door to the kitchen swung heavily behind him. My sister started in again and Henry egged her on. Neither of them apparently considered Dad's defense of memory or the swiftness of his anger to be unusual. But then, neither of them had tripped his lock. I had, with my mention of Chinatown and the basement. The old China box. It was our memory she was talking about. Of a particular day we'd spent together which she'd just as soon forget, but those were his memories we'd dug into that day. Boxed and buried. Never mentioned. But apparently never forgotten.

When my father came back to the table, he put more sugar in his coffee than I remembered him using. As he stirred he spilled a little and cursed himself, grabbed his napkin and blotted the damage. My brother and Anna kept talking. My mother interrupted to ask Anna how the weather had been in Amsterdam, and then she went on about how she'd always wanted to go there herself, see the canals, the Van Goghs. Dad sipped his coffee and stared at the wall.

That treasure hunt had been Anna's idea. I resisted because Henry had convinced me a bogeyman lived in the second basement—a bogeyman who ate small girls. But Anna insisted Henry was full of shit and no bogeyman was going to get *her*, and once we'd left the narrow, rickety stairway and were in our own storage cubicle with the door locked from inside and all the lightbulbs burning and no bogeyman in sight, I actually started to enjoy our adventure. I liked the dank subterranean smell and the sloshing of traffic up in the street, the cut-off feet of shoppers, and the occasional drenched cat peering at us through the overhead window. The muffled squawks of birds awaiting Mr. Wah's cleaver next door made me feel as if we were in the belly of an ark nosing through an urban ocean.

Anna rummaged through Dad's discarded inventions and Mum's old clothes until at last she found the China box. It was just a pasteboard crate tied with rope, but the stamps that covered it dated back to 1937. It seemed ancient to me, and mysterious.

From the few barely legible scraps inside, my sister discovered that Dad's father, Chung Wu-tsai, was the son of a wealthy, educated official. His one remaining picture showed off a receding hairline and pudgy cheeks, but his pedigree was that of a gentleman and a scholar.

Our grandmother, Alyssa Billings, was the only child of a U.S. Navy captain. Judging from a tattered hand-tinted photograph, she'd been a pretty, blond, green-eyed child. But she had thin, tightly drawn lips that turned down at the corners and a glum stare that seemed at once resigned and dejected. I guessed I could understand that dejection when Anna told me how, after Alyssa's mother died in childbirth, her father was always leaving Alyssa with other people's families. The father—our great-grandfather—went by the name Cap Billings, and his letters chronicled my grandparents' meeting, their early years of marriage. It was like the little match girl marrying the prince, said Anna, reading between the lines. Two star-crossed lovers against the odds. No wonder it didn't work out.

My grandparents met outside a Shanghai telegraph office in 1910, on what was supposed to be my grandmother's last day in China. She'd been traveling for the summer aboard her father's ship and, the next morning, set sail as scheduled for Indochina. By the time she saw Singapore, Chung Wu-tsai had telegraphed a proposal of marriage. Alyssa never returned to America.

The captain's later letters were addressed to China. They mentioned the birth of Alyssa's three children and warned about the world war. A notice of Captain Billings's death was dated 1920. And that was the end of the written record of my father's youth. The only other document was a "We regret to inform you" letter dated 1937 from the States Steamship Company. Alyssa and her two daughters had been aboard a ship that was bombed just before it was due to set sail for America.

The trove also contained a three-tiered lacquer basket filled with calligraphy brushes, wetting stones, and ink sticks. Anna and I picked up the brushes and began to paint a scroll of air, but the play soon dissolved into dueling and she said we better put the brushes back before we ended up breaking them.

There were silk vests embroidered in peacock greens and blues, and one long coat with a golden lion brocaded on a scarlet background. Anna put on the coat and pretended to be an empress. I put on one of the vests and called her "Your Majesty," which pleased her a great deal. With her fine brown hair trailing, her upturned nose and arched eyebrows, she truly did look majestic. I knelt down, as a loyal subject should.

"Lower," she commanded. "Kowtow."

I didn't know exactly what that meant, but I bowed lower, down, down until I was practically licking the floor at her feet.

"Get up," she said at last. "You're getting the vest dirty." She took off the robe and refolded it, then turned on me. "Don't always do everything you're told."

But her mood shifted back to neutral as we repacked the box. "Maybe Dad was a *spy*," she mused, "and had to destroy his past identity to save the woman he loved."

A year or two later Anna would rather have slit her wrists than make a statement like that, but then she was still reading *Anne of Green Gables* and hadn't yet heard of Hendrix. And I still believed every word she said.

That evening when I asked my father if he really was a spy, he laughed out loud. "Who said that? Do I look like James Bond?" To which Anna screeched, "You actually thought I meant it! You retard, I bet you think Mum's Mata Hari."

"You know, you haven't changed a bit," I said now, interrupting Anna in the middle of a detailed description of "chakra enhancement seminars" (which sounded suspiciously like orgies).

She squared her shoulders, straightened her spine, looked me in the eye. "Oh, no, Maibelle, it is you who have not changed. The Dhawon says—"

"Fuck the Dhawon!"

"Oh, she does." Henry burst out laughing.

My father set down his cup and placed his hands flat on the table. He looked as if he wanted to say something, but instead bent into a cough.

"Stop it, Henry," said my mother.

"You've never really believed in anything," I said. "Not in what you say or do. Not in the people who love you. Not even Mum or Dad. Everything's always a game with you—to prove your own superiority."

Anna stiffened with a twitch I recognized from childhood as her preparation for attack. "And what is it you believe in? Oh, never mind. I know. You believe pictures of Kewpie dolls and nose-hair clippers are going to save the world. Fulfillment is just a click of the shutter away—"

"That's enough!" My father's voice erupted with an immediate, shattering clarity. His face had gone pale, eyes bulging as if he were witnessing a crime. His Adam's apple rose and fell several times, but when he opened his mouth next, all that emerged was that pinched, disapproving cluck.

• • •

Anna's wrong. Memories matter. And not just for tracking time or holding an album in your hands when everyone who ever loved you is gone. Memories contain our secrets. They answer our questions. They tell us who we are and sometimes what we need. They give Anna's "timeless, eternal present" a reason to exist by making history.

Too bloody relevant.

I can only guess what my father meant by that. Childhood in Shanghai. College in New York. Active duty as a photojournalist working the Pacific theater during World War II. Except for that one box of robes and brushes, his past lives were buried by the time I made my entrance. The dad who watched me growing up was a tinkerer, a maker of labor-saving devices. He never touched a camera, never discussed his memories. And my mother said he'd destroyed the photographs that once had made him famous.

I was a freshman in college before I saw any of those pictures. One of my teachers, eager to find out if I knew why Dad had withdrawn into obscurity, showed me some clippings she'd collected during the thirties and forties. Strange, anomalous shots. War pictures, only instead of showing the military side, they showed ordinary people in places that didn't make sense. Children running, screaming down streets strewn with shards of glass, bomb craters, and outrageous feathered and flowered hats. A white man in spats and tails cradling a bloodied black infant. A woman with a gold stud in her nose clutching a pig in the front of an army jeep. A tall blond man intently lighting a cigarette as a group of ragged Chinese rush past with a headless body in a wheelbarrow.

As I stared at the images my father had captured all those years ago I had the feeling my skin was lifting from my body, my mind was being rearranged. I recognized these pictures. I knew them. They were my dreams. My nightmares. Not exactly, of course. But so close.

My teacher fired her theories at me. Because the scenes my father had witnessed were too horrifying? Or had he gotten too close to his subjects? Maybe he felt his work was misinterpreted when it appeared in print? Or he somehow felt he'd failed to capture what he was striving for?

Her words blurred together. I must have seen these pictures before. I'd felt the exact helplessness and outrage, the same grief and love that seemed to engrave each frame. These were the terrors that, night after night, roused me screaming and weeping from sleep.

The next day I called my mother at the gallery and described the shots to her. She was very excited to hear that my teacher knew of Joe, that she had these pictures, even if they were just tear sheets. But, no, she insisted. I couldn't possibly have seen them before. Not without extensive research on my part.

"Probably just déjà vu, Maibelle. You are your father's daughter, after all. In a way, those pictures are in your blood. If you can tap into them, even intuitively, it will be to your advantage. God only knows why he quit, but in his time Joe was a master. You must never forget that. His talent—those images—are your legacy."

....

3

Tommy Wah was Henry's best friend and his partner in crime. The high point, which I believe may also have launched the slow death of their friendship, came when they were in sixth grade.

They'd worked it out with Jimmy Yang, whose father was an herbalist. He supplied a powdered aphrodisiac used in chicken breeding. Tommy and Henry sneaked into the teachers' lounge and dumped the drug into the coffee urn, and when Mrs. Dixie returned from lunch, a large rooster stood on her desk to receive the effects of the powder.

The experiment was a dud. Mrs. Dixie promptly sent for the janitor, Mr. Liberty, and told him to return the bird to Mr. Wah. Then, rather than look for the individual pranksters, Mrs. Dixie punished the whole class. The reward for mischief of this sort, she told them, was a very special medicine. And with that, she escorted Henry and Tommy down to the teachers' lounge, instructed them to carry the coffee urn back to the classroom.

"It usually tastes like the sludge of death." She motioned the boys to lift the urn straight, not to spill. "But today it's got a special flavor—tastes just like the syrup of reason."

The class grudgingly drank the brew without naming the bad boys (Henry and Tommy's popularity saved their skins) and, incredibly, not one person developed a sudden, uncontrollable urge to mate with a chicken. No one told on Mrs. Dixie, either, because to tell that this teacher made her students drink poison would beg the question "Why?" which, in turn, would lead to lost face. Since Mrs. Dixie had elected not to entangle parents or the authorities, her students accepted her justice—and the mild runs induced by the coffee elixir.

Henry was just glad he hadn't had to deal with the two-step of Mum's rage and Dad's resignation. After all, it was only a joke.

"What if old Dixie-belle had really gotten the hots for that rooster?" he said. "That would've been worth getting caught!"

He and Tommy sprawled on Henry's bed, sorting baseball cards. I was allowed to sit and watch because, as long as I kept quiet, my presence didn't count.

"Better it didn't work," said Tommy, whose father had been so astounded to see his prize bantam in the arms of the school's black janitor that that night he lectured Tommy about thieving and ordered him to spend the next week memorizing Dr. Sun Yat Sen's *First Steps in Democracy*.

"Aw, c'mon. It would've been a pisser. Gimme Roger Maris."

Tommy tossed him the card. "I mean it. Jimmy thought it was a joke, too, but if the stuff had really worked, his dad would have lost too much face."

"But if it worked, it should be great for business!"

"It's not supposed to work on people, you jerk. It's meant for chickens. And it's Jimmy's dad's job to see his medicines are used right. If his own kid fools around with the powder, it doesn't make him look too good."

"So?" Henry said.

"So people stop talking to him. The tongs tell everybody stay away from his shop. He's got to give them big money to get his face back. And Jimmy's got to pay, too."

"Yeah? How?"

"You know. Going to Chinese school. Helping in the store instead of hanging out at the arcade. Being a dutiful son."

"Sounds pretty dumb to me. There." Henry patted one last card into the box before him. "American League, 1961. A full set of Topps. Bet you can't beat that."

"Bet you don't have a single card with a Chinese ballplayer."

"There aren't any."

"So why d'you think I'd even want a full set of Topps American League 1961?"

"Because in a couple of years it'll be worth a lot of money, you dodo."

Tommy got up and crossed the room. When he reached the door, he turned and said, "Why you don't understand about face is because you have no face to lose."

• • •

I've been spotting him ever since I moved back. A wide, dark head bobbing up behind the peaches in the Bedford Street fruit stand. The chiseled face with Ray-Bans in a parked Cadillac on Broadway, or that Asian couple leaning close over engagement rings in a midtown diamond store. A man in a kung fu studio, eyes fixed with such complete concentration that I was absolutely positive. But people change between age fifteen and twenty-nine. I held my distance because I knew I wouldn't be sure of Tommy Wah if he tapped me on the shoulder.

When I called this morning, though, I knew his voice at once. Smooth and cautious, like waves against long grass.

"Maibelle. Where are you?"

"New York."

"When you didn't answer my letter, I thought—"

"You thought correctly. I guess you haven't found anyone yet."

"I've only just signed the publishing contract." The waves rippled into whitecaps. "I was hoping you'd turn up."

"I've moved back."

"Oh." He sounded confused. Possibly disappointed. "Your address sounded so perfect. Sunridge Street. Playa del Rey. It sounded rich. Happy."

"It sounded like planes taking off and landing. And used condoms washed up on the beach. I moved from there years ago."

"I see." He clearly didn't at all.

"Look, I don't know what pictures of mine you saw—"

"Landscapes. Snow."

"I thought so. No people. You want people, don't you? I don't do people."

"I have a feeling about this, Maibelle. Or I wouldn't have written you."

"Those snowflakes were an eternity ago, and I never wrote you back. Why'd you call again?"

"I saw you from a bus. You were with some blond guy in the Village."

I glanced out the window, half expecting to catch the glint of a distant telescope. I yanked the curtain.

"Then you knew I was here."

"I figured you were visiting—I wanted to catch you before you left."

I was going to be firm about this. Turn him down flat. I'd go back. I'd have to, it was all of a part, like a search-and-destroy mission. But not this way. Not with a witness. Or an escort. Certainly not someone who himself might have been part of the problem. But what he was saying now threw me. Random coincidence? I didn't believe in random coincidence.

"No," I said.

He didn't answer right away. From outside my curtain came the shouts of children, car horns, the rumble of the BMT. The return address on his letter had been Pearl Street. Chinatown. But the silence at his end of the phone was deafening. There was no silence in Chinatown. Not that I remembered.

"Meet me," he said. "Do me that favor."

I closed my eyes but failed to conjure his face.

"This afternoon," he said.

"I'm busy."

"Where you going to be?"

I had only the vaguest of plans to visit my Thirty-fourth Street discounter. "Midtown."

"Empire State Building at two?"

"I'm afraid of heights. Besides, it's for tourists."

"One of my favorite places, too. And it's a cloudy day. I'll meet you at the elevator, we can ride up together."

I could have been more creative about my afternoon agenda, or said I don't grant favors to men I don't know. I could have stood him up. Instead, I arrived early to meet this old neighbor turned stranger who'd invited me to the top of a skyscraper on a day with zero visibility.

The lobby echoed with the shuffle of feet, the gossip of idle ticket takers. Plush ropes striped the empty space in front of huge gleaming elevators. When I was six, my mother brought me here one morning on the way up to her gallery. The elevators seemed as big as monsters then, and the wind on the observation platform made me cry.

Today I waited five minutes, then turned back through the revolving doors, out to the grim June murk—and a pair of dazzling, platter blue eyes. He had a smile the width of the whole back forty. "Excuse me, ma'am." A perfect summertime drawl.

He brushed my elbow in his haste to follow a barrel-chested Japanese woman wearing flip-up sunglasses. They disappeared into the Greek deli across the street.

"I'm sorry, Maibelle."

A shadow fell and the weight lifted from my arms.

This one was about six feet tall. His eyebrows, all bunched together, looked as if they'd been painted with lacquer.

"There was a fire in the subway tunnel."

The eyes, like gleaming black glass, and the rounded slope of his forehead—a Buddha's bulge, the kids used to call it. And the liquid voice.

"It's all right." But it wasn't. He alarmed me. All the men I'd mistaken for him, and every one of them wrong. He was twice the size and stronger, sadder. Yet when he smiled, two dimples drilled holes in his cheeks. I thought, those eyebrows must fly apart like wings when he laughs.

"Still have time to go up?"

"Do I have a choice?"

He clutched my bags of photo supplies like hostages—"No"—and stepped into the revolving doors.

The observation platform was empty and gray with a cool, driving wind. The only suggestion of the city below was an occasional spire. Downtown the Twin Towers poked up like a giant's building blocks through the soft, rolling clouds. I imagined going with the wind, leaping the steel barrier that might not hold anyway, out into that endless softness. The pressure joined the magnetic sensation of the edge, drawing me forward and down, as if the floor were tipped outward.

I backed into a seat against the central wall that continued up the spire and took my packages from Tommy, held them in my lap as anchors.

He went over and leaned against the barrier, the upper half of his body floating a hundred stories high. He looked directly down.

"My parents brought me here on my fifth birthday in weather just like this," he called over his shoulder. "Pop called it the Emperor State Building."

"I really am afraid of heights," I yelled.

"He said the reason the clouds look solid when you get this far up is because of the Emperor of the Western Skies. He uses the clouds to teach us mortals about humility; if a man climbs high enough, he'll think he can just walk across and enter the gates of heaven, but when he tries he'll find out pretty quick, his path to heaven is a fast trip back to earth."

He came away from the railing. A sudden gust flattened his shirt against his narrow chest, but he walked through the wind.

I'd be a perfect victim for Tommy's Emperor. I knew the impossibility of the illusion, the end of the dream, but I felt the alternative. If not yet completely for myself, then for Johnny. I used to look out the windows of planes expecting to see him striding along with his feet in the clouds, wings spread. I never caught him, but I never stopped believing I would.

"You still bite your fingernails."

Instinctively I curled my paws.

"That's an observation, not an insult."

His hands hung open by his sides. He had long, ringless fingers, no torn edges.

"What's the 'T' for?"

"What T?"

"You signed your letter 'T. Tommy.' "

"I call myself Tai now. But you wouldn't have known me if I didn't write 'Tommy.' "

I let that digest for a moment.

"My sister calls herself Aneela. I still call her Anna."

He sat at the other end of the bench and began to talk about his work. Social history, he called it. People in places. I thought of my father's photographs. People in places, as if there were an alternative. Places without people, yes. As my own pictures proved. But not the reverse.

He crossed his legs, ankle to knee. The heel of his shoe was worn straight across the back. Mine always give along the outer edges, reminding me of a certain crookedness to my gait. Not Tommy.

Social history seemed an unlikely vocation for a poulterer's son. I wondered if it had something to do with his name change. But there was Anna chiding, no, it's not about abandonment, it's a matter of finding the truth. Truth my ass. People who shuffle their identity like a deck of cards make me suspicious. That goes for Tommy, too. Or Tai.

"Did my mother put you up to this?"

"Your mother doesn't know me from a sewer rat. Never has."

He got up and returned to the railing. I saw him flipping backward, over and down, falling silently into the great gray gauze below.

"You're giving me vertigo. Please don't stand so close to the edge."

He removed his arms from the railing and took a single step toward me. I began to shiver, but I was damned if I'd beg him.

"So. Will you help an old friend out?"

"Old friend?"

"Friend of your brother's, then." He hesitated. "And Li's."

"You haven't spoken to Henry in years. And Li's dead." Though even as I said it I could see Lao Li, his gaunt face nodding, one spidery hand lifted in amused benediction. I said, "It doesn't make sense."

"I told you, I was impressed by your work."

"My work's shit."

"All right. I can't pay. But I thought you might be interested, anyway."

My teeth chattered. Strange noises jerked and rolled up my throat. The shivering grew into something akin to a seizure. He didn't seem to notice.

"I have a publisher, but the advance is nothing. I can pay expenses, that's it. Of course, you'd share in any royalties . . ."

I turned away from him and the field of gray beyond him, and gripped the back of the bench. Still I felt myself moving backward, leaping off as I did in my dream, gliding outward, arms spread and steady, just long enough for the illusion of flight to take hold, then suddenly plunging headlong down through the gray to the white, blinding heat of the city below.

Laughter poured from my mouth like shattered glass. The wind snatched at it.

"I'm sorry." He was behind me coming closer. Leaving the edge. "I didn't mean to insult you."

"I've got to get out of here."

"Maybe—" He was turning me, both hands firm on my shoulders as if to keep me from running away, as if there were somewhere to go besides space.

"You don't want me," I warned him.

• • •

The old lady next door has a bird. She sits outside admiring the brilliant blue and green and yellow feathers. She sips her afternoon sherry with her photo album at her elbow, the bird's bill thrusting between the bars of the large domed cage. The macaw is as big as a cat.

"Pretty boy." Her voice rises an octave and quavers. "Can you talk, pretty boy?" She takes her glass with both hands and sips contemplatively. The bird pecks at the bars. I can't see its expression from where I perch, but I read it as sullen.

Suddenly my neighbor lets out a raucous, shocking wolf whistle devoid of the slightest quaver. The parrot answers with a predictable flapping of wings. One feather flies free of the cage, and she grabs it, smooths it on her lap.

"Pretty boy!" She opens her album and slides the feather into a plastic sleeve, then slams the book shut. "I know! I'll call you Euripides!"

But before the bird can reply, the old lady's nurse appears, briskly gathers up the glass and book, mutters about the mess this creature is going to make, and wheels her patient inside.

Alone, the macaw squawks ferocious, unintelligible gibberish. The noise spills over the fence to the schoolyard, where the kids pause periodically in their games to imitate the bird's sounds. That only ups the ante, and he screeches louder. Finally the old lady's nurse storms out with a black cloth in her hands.

"Hush your damn squalling!" she yells over the din.

"Awwk! Fuck you, bitch!"

"All right, bird!" the kids cheer.

The nurse yanks the cloth over the top of the cage.

"Go on, bird. You tell her," cry the children.

But the darkness has forced the bird's silence.

• • •

The phone rang eleven times. I counted, willing it to stop, let me finish this glorious, frigid shower and go to bed. Maybe a dreamless sleep. But no amount of wishing can stop my brother when he's on the prowl.

"Hey, sis. What's up?"

"Henry. It's nearly midnight. I'm dripping wet—"

"What's this? I'm trying to make a brotherly connection and you act like it's an obscene phone call."

I waited. The background roared with the street where my brother was calling from.

"I'm losing my sublet, and I figured—" A siren at close range cut him off.

"Have Mum and Dad rented out your room?"

"Maibelle. They're convinced I'm a deadbeat as it is." His next sentence dissolved in a confusion of angry male voices.

"Where are you?"

"Pay phone down the block."

"Christ, Henry. Come on up. You can crash on the couch tonight. Just tonight."

Henry is the one member of my family with whom I stayed in touch—albeit erratically—during my odyssey years. He never left New York. In fact, he lived at home most of the time, designing software on a contract basis for Atari. My mother said, after all his hands-on practice, he should be producing the crème de la crème of video games, and Henry claimed he was. Just a misunderstood artist who wasn't paid his due. Nevertheless, his last Christmas present to my parents was to move into an apartment of his own. Apparently it wasn't exactly his own.

"You weren't staying with another Miss Argentina, were you?" I asked when he'd hauled the last of his bags upstairs. For a period of time Henry had lost his heart to a call girl from Buenos Aires with an apartment the size of the Ritz and an exceedingly jealous john who killed for Baby Doc Duvalier.

"Nothing like that. This place belonged to a bond trader friend of mine. Until his SEC violations caught up with him."

I gave my brother a soda, which he downed in one long draught before looking around. He took in the tripod and lights, the compact stereo that kept me sane when setting up my shots, the rolls of backdrop paper, and display stands. The overflowing crates of ideas awaiting my father's plagiarism.

"Nice to see one of us inherited Mum's knack for interior space."

I opened the window as far as it would go and stuck my head out into the still, damp heat. "It's like being smothered in velvet."

"How poetic." My brother turned on the radio, located an oldies station playing nonstop Motown greats, and started doing the mashed potato in the middle of my set. He jumped down, bending his legs like Sammy Davis, Jr., backed into a Michael Jackson moonwalk, then segued into a complex hip-hop routine. He reached out, begging, aping an agony of desire for me to join him in the dance. I laughed and threatened to charge him for the paper he was destroying.

Then Fontella Bass began belting out "Rescue Me," and the phone rang. Harriet. The noise was giving her mother panic attacks. I did realize she was serious about Bellevue—I didn't have a man up there, did I?

"No, Harriet. There's no man up here."

Henry pantomimed horror and tiptoed across the room with his hand clapped over his mouth.

"I'll remind you once, just once. It's against the law to disturb the peace."

I silenced Ms. Franklin, and my brother collapsed on Marge's sofa.

Same old Henry. He still flung his limbs around as if they were made of rubber. Still combed his hand through his hair like a bad boy. He still watched the world through half-closed eyes, and I still wondered whether he was avoiding the view out or restricting the world's view in. Maybe that's what Tommy meant.

Why you don't understand about face is because you have no face to lose.

"I saw an old friend of yours the other day." I tossed him a sheet and blanket and pulled up a folding chair. "Tommy Wah."

"No shit! Tommy? Where?"

"Emperor State Building." I smiled.

"No shit," he said again, carefully.

"Mum didn't tell you he called?"

"No, when?"

"Last fall." I fingered my locket. "He's changed his name to Tai."

"Not him, too."

"That's what I thought."

"So? What's he want?"

"So he writes books. Calls himself a social historian. He wants me to take some pictures for his next project."

Henry snorted and got up to investigate the contents of my refrigerator—several cans of tuna fish, a basket of peaches, some moldy cheese, three cans of soda, a bottle of Schlitz.

"Mind if I have this?"

"Go ahead. I hate beer."

"Yeah? Why's it here, then?"

"Last guy who slept here left it."

He cocked an eyebrow and unscrewed the cap, resumed his position on the couch. "You going to do it?"

"No." I stretched the word for strength, let it hang in the air for emphasis. "And I'd as soon you didn't mention any of this to Mum."

Henry shrugged. "So in his old age Tommy's documenting the grand and glorious heritage of Chinatown."

I stared at him.

"Close your mouth, sis, flies'll get in. I'm not as brilliant as you think. I just knew him better 'n you did. Always thought he'd turn into Chinatown's Malcolm X, but I guess he's opted for Studs Terkel. No big deal."

In my brother's sarcasm I heard the shudder of a well-aged and deeply felt antagonism. He once loved Chinatown—and Tommy—but he'd turned on both with that cruel finality of his, and now his only way back was through jokes.

"That prophecy have anything to do with the end of your friendship?"

He tipped his head back and balanced the bottle on his forehead. "He didn't like the way I played pinball."

"Get off."

"You ask him."

"I'll do that."

He looked at me sideways. "You seeing him?"

"Hadn't planned on it till now."

He set the bottle on the floor and pushed off his shoes. "Be careful."

"What's that supposed to mean?"

"Just don't trust him too much."

"Something wrong with social history?"

"Maibelle, you and I are more Chinese than Tommy. Dad was born in Shanghai, grew up there. Tommy's family's been here three, four generations. But look who's still locked into the ethnic heritage trip. He was doing that when we were in school. It drove me crazy."

Henry's outburst confused me. This was obviously an old debate for him, and he'd firmly staked out his side, but when? And why this anger?

"When the guys in Anna's high school class got drafted, they didn't go off to fight for China, and the ones that died, died for America, not the Magic Kingdom."

"Middle Kingdom," I said, laughing in spite of Henry's uncharacteristic seriousness. "Magic Kingdom's Disneyland."

"Same difference. Disneyland and China are both based on fairy tales. It's like all these so-called Afro-Americans running around in dashikis with beads in their hair, expecting everybody to say hallelujah because they've suddenly found their roots! Give me a break. It's as bad as Anna and her fruity cult."

He finally smiled.

"As bad as Tommy changing his name to Tai," I said.

"No shit."

He closed his eyes and lavishly draped one arm over the back of the couch. In high school Henry used to sit in the kitchen while Mum was making dinner, and he'd get her steaming on something like the Cuban missile crisis or the real value of pinball arcades to the American economy. Pretty soon they'd be slamming dishes, screaming at each other, having completely flipped their original positions but remaining diametrically opposed. While they seemed to think these battles were fun, I fled whenever I heard one starting. Now, to my surprise, I felt willing and able to take Henry on.

"Aren't you ignoring one fundamental factor?"

"Hmm?"

"Looks! Skin color. Hair. Eyes. Body type. Far as most whites are concerned, Chinese are Chinese—for that matter, any Oriental is Chinese—and blacks are black. No difference where they were born or what language they speak."

"That's bull. I've heard the Movement leaders say if you've got one drop of nonwhite blood you got to consider yourself mi-nor-i-ty. That means you and I should sign on the dotted line as Chinese-Americans. Yah! Life's too short to waste on an ethnic identity crisis."

"But you're the original chameleon. With Miss Argentina, you're a Latin lover. With that girl Lina you're a Slav. In Chinatown, you were the pinball wizard, and if you'd had green hair and purple eyes it wouldn't have made a dent in your popularity. I always felt shut out because I didn't look Chinese enough to pass."

"You felt shut out because it's your nature to feel shut out. Admit it, you didn't fit in any better in high school or college than you did in Chinatown. Difference was, you could hide behind your camera, and you got a lot of stroke for your pictures."

He wasn't even looking at me. He actually had his eyes closed.

"Since when did you become my psychoanalyst?"

"Since you were born. Comes with being Big Brother. You were so busy feeling shut out, you never knew anybody noticed. No big deal. But maybe you should realize a lot of people do notice. That wounded-bird quality even turns some guys on." He opened his eyes just wide enough to leer at me.

"I'm no wounded bird!"

"I'm generalizing."

"Well, you're out of line!"

But after a few minutes sulking on my bed I realized that my reaction merely proved Henry's point. So I drew myself into a model of composure and poked my head back into the other room. He lay on the couch with the latest Noble catalog in his hands and a cryptic expression on his face.

"Good talking to you, Henry. We should do it more often."

He looked up, breaking into a grin that lifted his cheeks and narrowed his black eyes into their Chinese mode. "You always used to be too busy feeling shut out to have a serious chat. Maybe you're at some kind of turning point."

Maybe. It infuriates me when Henry's snap judgments are right. He'll trot way out to the end of a cracking limb and somehow land unscathed. Meanwhile, everyone else is a mess. I expected a full-blown panic attack as a result of our conversation. Instead I had one of my rare and cherished dreams about Johnny. My only sure antidote to nightmare.

He's a man now, big and blond, but with the sun-swept hair and blue eyes of childhood, and a kiss as soft as a whisper. We travel impossible wide, empty streets in the middle of a rainstorm, let the drops slide onto our eyelids and tongues, and roll in wet grass in Washington Square.

"Can you taste it?" His voice is a soft and rumpled blanket.

"Taste the grass?"

"No, the season. Summer. The flavor's beginning to fade, but it's still full of light and warmth."

He takes my hand and we swing arms like children. Alone in this deserted city, we cross Houston to West Broadway and a shop window filled with legless mannequins. Small objects adorn the models' bodies—carrot peelers dangling from ears, pet-food bowls on shoulders, high-tech office supplies marching across plastic breasts. A bamboo cricket cage adorns every lap.

Johnny says, "You feel the magic taking pictures of those?"

An anticrime streetlight tinges his skin an unearthly pink. I try to walk on, but he pulls me back. "Don't move." He reaches both hands beyond my shoulders. Close enough to hug, he encircles me without touching, except to briefly lick the tip of my nose.

I feel a slight stirring of air behind me, nothing more. Then he steps back and back and back, until he fades into shadow. But his hands remain, illuminated, each one offering a silver-gray mourning dove.

The birds don't struggle. They don't peck. They are soft and warm like summer, he says, stepping forward into the light. When I hold the doves, as he insists, I feel his pulse right through them, beating light and fast and sure. Their clear circle eyes shine.

I hold these two doves as long as I can, but I cannot hold them forever. I return them to the man of my dreams. He gives them back to the sky.

• • •

I couldn't admit it, but I enjoyed having Henry around, lounging on my couch like the caterpillar in *Alice in Wonderland* as I arranged my shots. I didn't need the radio; he'd sing songs from the sixties in perfect pitch, all the lyrics down cold. I can generally carry a tune, but the words of songs come back to me only in snatches. There are things about Henry that impress me.

But three days after he'd arrived Harriet caught us by the front door.

"Harriet Ratner. My brother Henry."

Henry bowed. "How d'you do?"

"You didn't tell me about any brother."

"He's just visiting."

"No men. I made that clear."

"It's against the law to discriminate, Harriet."

"Bullshit. I rented to you. Must have been out of my mind, but I did. Just you. Single occupancy is the law according to your lease, miss."

"I'll leave." Henry steered me out the door. "I'm leaving now. See me go?"

It took him twenty-four hours to find a new woman willing to take him in.

As I watched him packing all the clothes and papers and the paraphernalia that went with his laptop computer, I asked, "How many little Henry Chungs you think are marching around Manhattan?"

He plucked an undershirt from the floor where he'd dropped it the first night. "I know there aren't any."

"With your track record?" I remembered his crack about my pregnancy being wishful thinking. "Statistically it doesn't add up."

He sat on his suitcase and snapped the locks. "I had myself fixed, Maibelle. I'm not your kind of gambler."

He thanked me and hugged me and returned my key. But all I could think as he took his leave was, I'm not the only wounded bird.

Bow Luck
BOW LUCK RESTAURANT
好友

Part II

A Kingfisher's Wings

....

4

Throughout my childhood in August, when her gallery was closed, my mother would fetch the old Rambler wagon from its slot at the East End Garage, pile the three of us kids in the back, and drive to her parents' farm. The trip took three days. The address was Rural Route something. The closest neighbors were the Madisons, three miles down the road, the closest "town" a gathering of feed stores some fifteen miles away. The one landmark that distinguished this particular corner of the Midwest was the dark Gothic cathedral that rose on a hill due east of the farm like a citadel shadowing the countryside: Mount Assumption.

The farm itself was standard Wisconsin issue—a white clapboard house with plain green trim, red barn with silo and rooster weather vane, and one hundred acres of rolling fields spanned by endless sun-drenched sky. Grampa Henry grew wheat and alfalfa, kept a few chickens and sheep, and spent most of his days astride an enormous John Deere tractor. Gramma Lou grew the biggest zinnias and snapdragons in the county and would reliably have a tin of freshly baked oatmeal raisin cookies awaiting our arrival. It all made me feel like a Fresh Air Fund kid, a refugee from the city.

But the farm was also a part of me, because it was part of my mother. The living room shelves held scrapbooks crammed with everything from Diana's first baby locks to the powdered remains of her high school corsages. The stairwell was lined with photographs of her skiing and swimming and camping, looking gangly and tan, with curls tighter than mine and the same corkscrew grin as Henry.

In some of those pictures fair-haired men slung their arms possessively around her waist. When I asked about them, she'd say, "Oh, that's Bill," or Bob or George or Richard—old beaux, some of whom had begged her to marry them. Now they were real estate agents, doctors, and grain brokers. None had a last name like Chung.

"So why didn't you marry one of them?" asked Anna. "They look pretty cute to me."

"But, darling, I knew if I married any of them I'd be stuck here the rest of my life. In the Midwest, anyway."

"Too boring?"

"Suffocating."

Just how determined my mother was to escape was revealed in a steamer trunk in the attic containing hundreds of sketches for evening dresses and high-fashion women's suits. Although I was no great judge of art, I could tell these were serious drawings. The colors stayed inside the lines. The faces looked like movie stars. The detailing was minute. Each sketch was dated and signed in bold script. And some were clipped to carbons of letters addressed to the top couturiers of the day: Cristóbal Balenciaga, Coco Chanel, Christian Dior, Jacques Fath, and Lucien Lelong. "Dear Miss Chanel," read one:

> I am an aspiring young designer who *immensely* admires your work. The newspapers say that you have retired, but I do not believe it. You are too young and your ideas are too brilliant for you to quit designing. The world of haute couture needs your vision!

> Miss Chanel, you are a great artist, and I would be honored to serve as your apprentice. From the attached sketches, you can see how much your designs have influenced my own. If you would give me a chance, I will gladly pay my way to Paris, or wherever you might need me. Please consider me your humble servant. With *greatest* regard,
>
> Diana Campbell

"How'd she know who to write to?" said Henry, staring at the foreign names.

"She read the fashion pages, dummy," said Anna. "She saw what she wanted and went after it."

"Fat lot of good it did her."

Neither Chanel nor any of the other designers ever answered these letters, and my mother never saw her sketches turned into couturier clothing. The money she'd saved during high school got her as far as Chicago, where she dressed mannequins for Marshall Field until she could afford a one-way ticket on the *Twentieth Century* to New York. Saks Fifth Avenue hired her to do their windows, which was how she met my father.

Through glass.

"He was the most exotic man I'd ever seen," she told us. "And he was watching *me*. I tried to keep on working, but he motioned me outside, and just like that he asked me to a party that night. At the Rainbow Room! Do you have any idea how long I'd dreamed of going to the Rainbow Room? I can tell you, my darlings, that was the most exciting night of my life. I borrowed a green crushed-velvet dress right out of the window and had a girlfriend do up my hair. Joe danced like an angel, and I could tell from the way people treated him, he was really something special. When I found out his photographs were on the cover of *Life* magazine, I just about died. I thought, I am finally off the farm for good."

From the vantage point of Wisconsin, I could see my mother the dreamer, the frustrated sophisticate. I understood why at age sixteen she'd left the Midwest for New York. But I was also grateful that she brought her children—if not her husband—home.

I was especially grateful the summer I met Johnny Madison. The summer I was ten.

At the far end of the screened-in porch where we kids always slept sat a wooden Victrola with a crank and needle that resembled an old hearing horn. Every morning, right at dawn, Grampa Henry would crank up that Victrola, set it spinning with songs dating back to the twenties—songs like "Toot, Toot, Tootsie, Goodbye" and "Yes, Sir, That's My Baby."

"Rise and shine!" he'd bellow, clattering a wooden spoon against one of Gramma's tin pans. "Rise and shine, you slugabeds. Mornin's wastin'."

The first thing we saw when we opened our eyes was a large, deeply freckled old man dancing about in his undershirt. "Henry!" Gramma Lou would call from the kitchen. "Give the poor children some peace." But even if that had shut him up, which it never did, the aroma of her cinnamon rolls made it impossible to sleep.

Once he was satisfied that he'd roused everyone in the house, Grampa traded in the spoon for his plastic flyswatter. Thanks to the sheep and the general proximity of nature, the farm always had more than its share of winged invaders. One logical defense would have been to repair the fist-sized holes in the window and door screens, but my grandfather preferred to treat the insects as wild game. He particularly liked to hunt during meals, and breakfast was no exception.

My mother was never a morning person. She liked to lounge, contemplating the day ahead while the first few jolts of caffeine got her engine going. (Her mother's inability to make a decent cup of coffee, she said, was symptomatic of all that was wrong with the Midwest.) Wrapped in a peach silk bathrobe, her face still glossy with night moisturizers, she came to the dining room to fill her cup, then quickly headed outside to escape her father's performance.

But the morning after we arrived that summer, Mum had just begun her ritual pour when—*thwack!*—down came the swatter. Right through the stream of coffee.

"Bull's-eye!" Henry was Grampa's scorekeeper. "Number nine."

The fly that had balanced briefly on the rim of my mother's cup was now enmeshed in Gramma's lace tablecloth.

"Yah! Jew-bait!" Grampa shouted. " 'At'll teach him."

My mother put down the percolator and closed her eyes. I watched her lips move as she counted to ten.

"Anna," she said when she'd finished, "we're going into Milwaukee. Be ready in fifteen minutes."

As soon as they were gone my grandfather started Henry on the driving lessons they'd been plotting since the previous summer.

Gramma Lou put up a token protest, but it was not unusual for a country boy to learn to drive at age twelve, and she had to admit that, even if Henry never drove in the city, it wouldn't hurt him to know how to handle a gearshift on the farm. She loved her daughter dearly, Gramma said, but she'd never fought her battles for her, and this was no time to start.

Unfortunately she had stronger opinions when it came to my going along. "If you think I'm risking *two* of my grandchildren with that old coot, you've got another think coming." She handed me a wicker basket and shooed me out toward the mulberry tree to pick enough for a pie.

From the upper branches I watched Grampa's old blue sedan grinding up the lane through the middle of the farm. They weren't making much progress, and the dust they were kicking up must have made breathing uncomfortable. But I imagined them together, Grampa probably telling Henry one of his dirty jokes, making him laugh so hard he lost his concentration and ran over a boulder. Then Grampa would curse the day Henry was born, tell him he was worthless as a sheep turd, and jolly the car around the rock until they were on their way again, singing in unison Grampa's anthem:

Pooh, pooh Harvard
Pooh, pooh Yale

We do our learning through the mail.
We're no dummies,
We're no fools,
We go to correspondence school!

"Want company?"

A big boy, almost as big as Henry, was standing directly below me. He had round blue eyes and sun-bleached hair that made his skin look even redder than it really was. When Grampa Henry was a child, he might have looked like this boy.

"I'm Johnny Madison. Came to give your grandma some tomatoes from my ma. She said you might want some help."

"I guess."

He hoisted himself onto the branch below me and picked a handful of berries.

"She didn't give me anything to put 'em in."

I moved the basket within his reach.

"That your brother out there?" He nodded toward the ball of dust gathering at the crest of the hill.

"You don't have to do this, you know."

"Do what?"

"Baby-sit me."

"Baby-sitting's for girls."

"Then go someplace else to wait for Henry. I don't need any help."

"I'm not waiting for Henry." He chucked another fistful of mulberries into the basket. "I don't even like Henry."

"No? What's wrong with him?"

"Nothin'. I only met him once or twice. We just never found nothing to talk about."

My grandfather's car disappeared into the back forty. Heat waves shimmered like mirages across the space where it had been.

"Well, what *do* you like to talk about?" I asked.

"Promise you won't laugh?"

I crossed my heart.

"Flying . . . I've flown, you know. Nobody believes I have. They say I just imagine things, but honest, sometimes when I'm out in the fields by myself I start taking bigger and bigger steps, going higher and higher between each one till pretty soon I'm flying about ten feet off the ground and *staying* up there, too."

"I've dreamed I stepped off the top of the Statue of Liberty and flew all the way home."

Johnny smiled a faraway smile. "That must have been nice."

"It was only a dream."

"I did the same thing from the hayloft in your grampa's barn."

It was plain I didn't believe him.

"C'mon. I'll show you."

Before I could answer, he scooted down out of the tree and ran off. By the time I reached the barnyard fence he was standing in the opening to the hayloft, fifteen feet above me.

"Don't!"

"You don't believe I can! Just watch."

"No, I believe you, but what if it doesn't work this one time? Don't jump, please."

"I want you to see me do it." He stretched his arms.

"How about inside? Then if something goes wrong, you'll land in the hay."

Johnny rolled his eyes, and I could practically hear him thinking: Women! But he moved away from the ledge.

I did not see Johnny fly that day, but he did swoop and swerve and do loop-de-loops. We both did, for that matter.

The barn was half full of hay, with bales in the back stacked all the way to the ceiling, the rest arranged in steps down to the mounds of loose fodder that turned the floor into one great cushion. You had to be careful to avoid the trap where hay was dropped to the sheep stalls below, but otherwise it was a child's paradise, complete with floor-to-ceiling rope. When Johnny wasn't diving free, he was swinging and hollering like Tarzan.

"What religion are you?" he asked when we'd finally exhausted ourselves and lay peeking out through cracks in the siding.

"No religion."

"What d'you mean? Everybody's some religion. You're Catholic or Jewish or Protestant."

"What're you?"

"Catholic."

Through my crack I sighted Mount Assumption, a black finger raised to the sky.

"You go to church up there?" I asked.

"I been."

"What's it like?"

"Boy, you really aren't religious, are you?"

I snapped a piece of straw in two and studied the insides.

"It's boring," he said. "The priest chants all this stuff in Latin, and when you can understand what he's saying, it's usually what's going to happen after you kick."

"Kick what?"

"Kick the bucket."

"What?"

"Die, stupid!"

"Oh." I must have looked a little hurt, because Johnny apologized for calling me stupid.

"What does happen?" I asked.

"You go to heaven if you're good, and hell if you're not."

I could tell from his voice that he had nearly called me stupid again but checked himself.

"Know what I think?" I asked.

"What?"

"I think the whole world is really just a speck on the floor of a giant's throne room, and after we die we're born into that giant's kingdom, and in the next life after that we break through to the *next* giant's palace."

"I think you're a nut." But he was smiling.

I don't know why I told Johnny that. If I'd told it to Henry, he would have said something like "You have the brain of a cockroach." If I'd told Anna, she would have said I was spending too much time around Grampa. I'd never even consider telling one of the grown-ups.

But Johnny, after some thought, replied, "One day I'm going to have a plane all my own. If I fly high enough, maybe I'll meet that giant of yours."

Johnny had ten brothers and sisters. His father was a hog farmer with a fifth-grade education, his mother a harried but gentle woman who encouraged her children to dream. Johnny had never been out of Wisconsin. But he was sure he would spend his life flying.

It was the only way, he said, that you could catch a glimpse of heaven without dying.

• • •

"How cute, little Maibee's got herself a boyfriend!"

"Ask me, the kid's a demento. I mean, Jesus, he's practically my age. What's he want with a squirt like her? If he was baby-sitting, sure, but I don't *think* Gramma was paying him."

"Leave it alone!" Gramma Lou said, coming out on the porch to say good night. "Johnny's a fine boy. If you don't like him, Henry, that's all right, but Maibelle can choose her own friends."

She tucked me in and patted my hair. I pretended to be asleep.

"But I just don't get it," said Henry.

"And that's just my point," said my grandmother. "You don't need to."

• • •

Say what they would, Johnny Madison was a good friend. That summer and the next, while Henry learned to drive and my mother and Anna went off touring antique stores or into the city, Johnny showed me the sights of the country—the spring that gushed icy water deep in my grandparents' woods, the swimming holes and hidden nests you couldn't find by road.

Johnny knew the land's magic. He made soap by rubbing flowers between his palms. He pulled Indian arrowheads out of tree stumps and lured spiders from cyclone webs. He guided me into thickets where we feasted on wild raspberries and smeared our faces red. Although my mother had warned me never, ever to eat a wild mushroom, I believed that Johnny could tell the poisonous from the safe ones and, sure enough, I survived when he dared me into eating one of his "champonions"—though it tasted like dirty socks smell.

"You have to know these things if your plane crashes somewhere far away from towns or people," he said. "Trouble is, I feel like I know everything there is to know around here. It's getting too easy."

But there were a few mysteries Johnny hadn't quite mastered. Over my grandparents' back hill lay a secret hollow cut through by a creek where he claimed fairies hid their treasure. Three little bald-headed men they were, dressed in robes made of cast-off snake skins. Johnny had fallen asleep beside that creek late one afternoon and woke at midnight to see the men turning the stones to make the water run true. When they finished, they joined hands and jumped together into the deepest pool. Johnny searched for the men by moonlight, and when the sun came up, he dove to the bottom of the pool. All he found was a kingfisher's feather, bright blue-green and perfectly clean, floating on the water.

"And," he said in a hush-hush voice, "it has real gold in it."

I refused to believe this story unless he produced the feather, so one day as we spread our toes in the creek's muddy bottom he pulled it from his back pocket. And it was, as he'd said, truly beautiful, with silken colors and a shaft as hard as ivory. I couldn't tell if the dazzle of gold laced across the tip was real metal, but when I tapped it on a rock, it certainly sounded like it.

"You painted it on," I decided. But it didn't feel like paint. There was no seam and the gold wouldn't peel off.

"Jeweler in Milwaukee said he'd give me a hundred bucks for it."

"No. Why didn't you take it, then?"

"Hundred bucks won't buy a plane. Besides, if the fairies come back, I might be able to trade this for somethin' else."

"What something?"

He licked a finger and held it up to test the wind. "Something no money I know of can buy."

He looked at me hard. Serious. "Wings."

The one place Johnny refused to go was Glabber's woods. Just north of my grandparents' farm, this stretch of giant elms and beeches contained nothing more sinister than a few Swiss Jerseys and some scattered bee boxes. No one ever saw Mr. Glabber himself, except when he visited his hives, and then he was all suited up like an astronaut. But that was just it, said Johnny.

"Inside that hood of his, he's all deformed. Warts, scars. Hands are like meat hooks."

We were sitting on the old stone wall that snaked along the ridge overlooking the woods. No Trespassing signs marked every third tree. Johnny said, "My dad told me if old Glabber sees you on his land he'll shoot to kill."

"If he's as ugly as you say, maybe he's just afraid people will make fun of him."

"Dad says he was a pilot. Flew bombing missions over Japan. His plane got hit and caught fire. He parachuted out, but his whole body got burnt. That's why he looks so disgusting. Dad says when Glabber saw himself in the mirror he went nuts. Started screaming for his plane, and said he was going to get the bastards that did it to him. After they let him out of the hospital, he did go back up, but instead of going after the Japs, he started firing at the other American planes, and then he crashed. Dad says he was trying to kill himself, but they got him out of the wreck okay. Had to spend years in a insane asylum, and they never let him go up again. I bet that made him even crazier."

Johnny picked up a flat rock from the wall and skimmed it out into space. It passed over the barbed-wire fence and disappeared into the darkness between the trees. Mosquitoes swarmed in its wake. And then came a deep rumbling echo, the sound a large animal would make if trapped at the bottom of a well.

It grew louder, closer. There was a flash of white between the trees and Johnny yanked me to my feet.

"It's Glabber!"

He turned and began to run, but I kept looking over my shoulder to see what we were running from. Would this monster really rise from the forest? Was he going to eat us or burn us or steal us away?

The looking turned my feet to stone. Johnny had to practically drag me down the ridge, and because of his dragging, I never saw more than that single flash of Glabber's light.

Johnny yelled at me and his voice was strong, but all of a sudden those blue eyes were floating, and then his whole face was awash and I had this stab of worry that maybe he'd drown from the fear and effort of pulling me, and that worry set my feet to working again.

We raced across my grandfather's pasture to the skeleton of a hay shed that had been struck by lightning years before. We hid behind its widest rib and listened hard, our hearts beating as if Glabber's ghost were right on us. Finally the echo faded, and all we could hear were the sough of tall grain and the distant mutter of Grampa's tractor.

"I told you"—Johnny was still catching his breath—"he doesn't want anybody to mess with him."

"You don't know that was Glabber. It could have been anything."

"I know. It was a warning . . . God, how stupid!" He kicked the base of the upright and a chunk of its blackened shell flew off.

There was a glint in the dirt where the burned wood landed. I ran my fingers underneath and came up with a child's gold locket. A fine chain and a tiny heart-shaped case, empty.

This random find, like another mystical gift from the fairies, had a calming effect on Johnny. He polished the necklace with ash until it glistened. "Like a phoenix." He fastened it around my neck and told the story of the mythical bird that set itself on fire only to rise from the ashes reborn. He took a scrap of shiny carbon and enclosed it in the heart. I felt the metal grow warm against my skin.

"When you have your plane, where will you go?" I asked. "Where will you fly to?"

He got that dreamy look again. "Places so different I can't hardly imagine. Jungles and islands and deserts and mountains. Maybe even the moon or something. You hear about that astronaut Ed White walking out there in space? Yeah, I wouldn't mind that."

"Think you'll ever come to New York?"

He scowled at the notion. "I seen pictures. There's too many buildings, no good place to land."

"Helicopters can land on top of buildings."

"Helicopters don't have wings." As if that settled that.

"How about China, then?"

"What's in China?"

"My dad's from there. But it's communist now. Grampa calls them Pink Chinks. Says they kill white people. Mum says Grampa's prejudiced. That's why Dad never comes with us to the farm."

"Well," Johnny said, warming to the challenge. "I could be like a peace ambassador, flying in to say hello and tell them about America."

"You could find some beautiful Chinese girl and marry her."

Johnny tipped his head back and squinted at me. "Your Dad's Chinese, what's that make you?"

"Only a fourth, doesn't count."

He shrugged. "Whoever I marry, she's gotta be willing to fly."

I fingered the locket. "Well, before I get married, I'll have to go far away, maybe all around the world."

"Why's that?"

"It's just logical, silly. I mean, with all the millions of boys in the world, you think I'd meet the perfect one right in my own neighborhood?"

Johnny picked up a stick and drew a circle in the dirt.

"Here you are in New York." He made an X at one side of the circle. Then he made another X on the opposite side. "Here I am. I've flown to China. I'm living on rice and eating with chopsticks. Now you start *your* big trip and come around like this, and we run into each other along about here."

"That'd be fun."

"Well?"

"Well, what?"

"Would you marry me then?"

I was smiling. "You've got to have somebody who'll fly."

"Oh, you'll fly. You already have. From the Statue of Liberty, remember?"

"That was just a dream."

"Same difference."

I thought about that for a minute. "No. Not for me. I can do lots of things in dreams I'll never really do."

"Like what?"

"Like marry you."

• • •

Now I look back on those days with amazement, and a kind of dread. I remember the sensations, beautiful snapshots, but in the gaps between frames I sense the presence of something hideous. A demon crouching in the dark. Like Glabber.

One night soon after I started flying I awoke convinced that my internal organs had been shoved into my mouth. The next day I compared mileage logs with my flying partners, women with more seniority than I would ever have, and tallied up their crashes, near misses, and unscheduled landings until I was finally persuaded that the odds were in my favor. Still, with each takeoff I'd clutch my seat, and around my two hundredth trip, a plane went down with three new hires working their first flight. Not long after that I had my near miss in Pensacola.

The numbers would never have protected me. I was just killing time. I would not find what I was looking for in the sky, on the road, at the far end of the world. He was already long dead and gone.

....

5

When we lived in Chinatown, I would often play dolls on the window seat in my father's workshop while he puttered. That was my mother's word, and though I knew it was disrespectful, it also seemed an accurate description of how he spent his time. Puttering.

He had piles of drawings on graph paper for gizmos he never would make. Piles more of trade journals and patent bulletins which he inspected daily for new or competing ideas. The shelves that lined the room were filled with models made of everything from Erector sets and Lincoln Logs to tungsten and stainless steel.

"Toilet paper and Tupperware were ideas first," he informed me one day when I was home sick and everyone else was gone. He stood back to inspect a scramble of wire hangers on his workbench. "Clocks and crossbows, too. Chinese invented those, you know."

"And toothbrushes and spaghetti and pancakes," I said. Henry had told me that. The Chinese were geniuses, according to my brother, and that genius ran in our veins. I think Henry was the only one in the family who truly believed Dad one day would make us rich.

"Toothbrushes. Spaghetti and pancakes." My father stared at me. I nodded, smiled, but he didn't smile back.

I looked down the street toward the Six Companies building and saw Don and Julie Hsu kissing again. That was because they were ABCs—American-born Chinese. Mainlanders never kissed in public, and they thought it disgraceful if anyone did. But when it came to making families, that was something else. After Don and Julie were married, the old folks would be all over them to have babies, and if they were like most young couples—ABCs or not—they would soon comply. That would put a stop to the kissing, but the babies would keep coming. At least in that respect, my parents fit in: three kids, and I *never* saw them kiss.

"Did you used to have Chinese friends?" I asked Dad. "When you still lived in China?"

"Hmm?" He twisted a strand of wire around a corkscrew.

"Did you play with neighborhood kids when you were little? Did you think you'd marry a Chinese lady and stay in China forever?"

He stood up and began to fumble through a box of tools. No answer.

"Daddy!"

"Mm?"

"Why don't you ever tell us about China?"

He stood motionless for a second or two, his face gone flat and vacant. "Nothing worth telling about," he said, and resumed his fiddling.

Across the street, a couple of older boys were squatting on the pavement, a square box top and two tiny bamboo cages between them. They flicked open the gates to the cages and shook the contents onto the cardboard. Two dark specks let out an unnatural screech. The boys watched, motionless at first, then more animated. The specks came together, one boy shoved the other. They stared at the box top, where one of the specks no longer moved.

"Ah, shee-it!" The first boy raised his hand to his head as if to tear out his hair.

Old Mr. Wen, who some of the neighborhood kids called the Hundred Year Old Man, came shuffling from his stoop down the block. He patted the irate boy's shoulder. The boy reached into his pocket, handed his opponent a coin. Then Old Wen had the loser pick up his cage and follow him back to his building. A few minutes later they emerged from Wen's doorway. When the boy lifted his cage, its new occupant let out a triumphal chirrup, and the boy grinned straight up at me.

I tried to lift the window, but it jammed. A second later the pigeon that had caught the smile flew off the rail of the fire escape, and the boy turned back to his game.

"One good idea is all," Dad mumbled as he worked. "Good enough to stop her jabbering, anyway. Jesus! The great connoisseur—should have married goddamn Richard Avedon." He looked at the wall. "One idea. That would get us out of here . . . maybe then she'd give up the rest."

"The rest of what?" The boy had long arms and a short neck. Like a spider. His cricket won this time.

My father picked up a pencil and sharpened it. The shavings spiraled down to his wastebasket. I wanted to believe he'd confide in me, entrust me with secrets that no one else knew, but he acted as if he hadn't heard, or maybe he didn't want to confide in me, after all.

I was trying to decide whether to repeat the question when he replied, "Your mother wants her brilliant, young artist back. She doesn't realize he was the fool."

Mum, for her part, spent most days at the Foucault Gallery on East Sixty-third Street, two blocks from Central Park. It was identified only by a polished brass plaque, and customers had to make an appointment to be admitted. Inside, plush vanilla-malt carpeting absorbed noise so well that ordinary conversations were reduced to whispers. That was intentional, my mother said, so the art would speak louder than the people who came to view it.

Those people had names like Vanderbilt and Amsterdam, but they couldn't compete with the pictures, carpet or no carpet. There were paintings of dogs with the bodies of women, men with apples for heads, trees studded with babies erupting in flame, and clocks melting into the sea. Those filled the first floor. On the second were drawings and prints of those same unsettling images in pieces or variation, all personally selected by Mr. Foucault, the gallery's owner, who spent most of his time and a small portion of his enormous wealth buying art in the same capitals of Europe that filled my mother's dreams. Mum said he looked exactly like the screech owl at the Central Park Zoo. I couldn't imagine a screech owl loose in a place like this, but my mother seemed right at home.

I got to watch her in action on our Ladies' Days. That's what she called the occasional preschool days when I accompanied her to work because Dad was too busy to look after me.

She'd make me climb into one of those precious Florence Eiseman outfits that made me feel about two—like the dress with rabbits eating cherries and the matching hat with an elastic band that cut underneath my chin. She'd say I looked adorable. I'd tell her I felt stupid and beg to wear my blue jeans, but I never stood a chance. As she put it, she wasn't about to let her customers see a daughter of hers dressed like a little farm boy.

Those customers didn't stand much more of a chance with her than I did. As soon as they entered the gallery she could tell exactly how much they were worth and whether they'd part with a penny. She knew when to keep her distance and when to cozy a sale, could sense which newcomers had to be taught and which would keep her on her toes. She informed me of these talents on a regular basis, so although I was too little to know about business, I knew very well how proud Mum felt about her work.

She was especially proud of the "special collection" she'd started on the third floor. This trove of photographs was her idea, her selection, and would become her great success. Even, as she often remarked, if it was bought with Foucault money.

When I was five years old, what impressed me about the photographs was not that my mother had picked them, but how weird they were. She had work by Diane Arbus and Harry Callahan, W. Eugene

Smith, Bill Brandt and Robert Frank, but only the strangest frames, in which people looked not quite human. As strange as the artwork downstairs, only more vivid and disturbing because they were real. Who could believe a liquid clock, but that photograph of a woman with two heads really made me wonder. Those days in the gallery I'd set up my spot in the back room on the third floor, and when I wasn't coloring or playing paper dolls, I went through the drawers of prints, trying to decide if I liked them.

Once I was old enough to handle art properly—clean hands on the edges only and no close breathing or sneezing—Mum encouraged this exploration. She'd tried to interest Anna and Henry in the gallery when they were very young, but both had rebelled against the hours of imposed quiet and the boredom of nothing but visual stimulation for entertainment, so the fact that I was never bored by art relieved and delighted my mother.

Between customers and phone calls she would introduce me to her newest pieces. "You see, darling, now he's playing with light and color à la Monet?" The photograph looked to me like a picture of a Bowery bum stretched out on a park bench at dawn. "And yet it also has that social relevance. A strong Lautrec influence. Mm, really quite painterly. The shadow contrast with the warm colors and tones. Worth at least three hundred, since he's printing a limited run. He's young, but give him another ten years and I'm willing to bet he'll be one of the country's top twenty."

Then she'd heave a sigh. A meaningful look.

"Your father was at this stage when I met him. He was going to be the next Steichen."

It happened dozens of times. Just like that. And it always took me by surprise.

• • •

My mother arrived at my apartment two weeks to the day after Anna's visit. Miffed that I hadn't formally invited her, she gave me what she considered due time, then took the initiative. Naturally she was horrified.

"You can't really expect to do any decent work all cramped in like this. I wish you'd let me call Scott and see if he knows of any lofts—you could still live here if you insist, but maybe you could share work space . . ."

Her mouth opened and shut, a bright gash of lipstick. The muscles in her neck stood out. She was still holding her briefcase, a well-worn Italian calfskin tote that my father had given her before I was born. I pointed.

"You've got something to show me?"

"I thought you might like to see what all the fuss is about. Since you won't come to the gallery, I've brought it to you."

"A house call."

"You could say that."

All the fuss, as I'd read in *The New Yorker, New York,* and the *Times,* was Mum's second ground-floor photo show, by a young black artist named Delong Dupriest. "Cultural Allegories," *Artforum* dubbed his work.

Mum opened the binder to a reprint showing a fat white butcher surrounded by sides of dark, glistening beef. Laid in transparency over this image was a Ku Klux Klan Dragon presiding at the lynching of six black men. The work was in black and white. Of course.

"This piece is six feet square. I sold it on the first day, can you imagine? Twelve thousand dollars. Gerard was fit to be tied. I sold out my first one-man, too, you know. Scott's show?"

"Smashing." I closed the book without looking further.

"Smashing." She narrowed her eyes at me the way she used to when I said I felt too sick for school. "Well, then. Let's see what you've been up to!"

She did not mean my eight-by-ten product shots of the grinders, scrapers, holders, and splicers that she was conspicuously ignoring.

"I don't have anything ready."

"Oh, please. You can show me."

"I've been too busy with the job to print."

She stared at the empty mantelpiece for a moment as if she could see something hanging or leaning there that I could not. Then she put away the binder and stood up brusquely, grabbed my hair and lifted it this way and that.

"You'd be happier if you got all this stuff off your shoulders. Lighter, bouncier, less time-consuming." She pulled just this side of too tight.

For the first time I noticed the precise flecks of yellow and green that give her gray eyes their fire.

"You're twenty-eight years old, Maibelle. This is your time, your chance. If you don't pull yourself together in the next couple of years, you're going to lose it all." She yanked tighter, hurting my scalp. "Just like your father did."

"You despise Dad, don't you?"

"Maibelle!" She released my hair.

The sensation was what I imagine a dandelion might feel when its white fluff blows away. I rose from my seat. She had come uninvited. She'd insulted me and twisted the knife in my father's back as she had my whole life, over and over.

"You can't make us all blame him for disappointing you."

She sat rigid on Marge Gramercy's sofa and clenched both fists until the skin pulled white across her knuckles. She glowered at my equipment across the room, then stood up quickly, haphazardly, banging her knee on the trunk I used for a coffee table. It must have hurt, but she ignored the pain, collected her purse and hat. I was astonished to see shelves of tears in her eyes when she looked at me again.

"You don't know what's it's like to be married to a stranger for thirty years."

"I know what it's like to be his daughter. He's not a stranger to me."

The tears started to rise again. She squeezed her eyes shut and stepped into the entryway to hide them. I heard the clasp of her purse snap open. She blew her nose. Her back straightened and she spoke over her shoulder.

"The current issue of *Interiors* is devoted to small apartments. I'll send it to you."

She was gone.

The next day I asked my father down. I called and made it official because I knew he'd never drop by on his own. Beyond that, I'd been bluffing. My father was as much a stranger to me as to anyone. But when I'd said those words to my mother, something seemed to flip inside me, and I decided he couldn't stay that way.

"Mum wanted me to give you this," were his first words on arrival. The festive magazine cover illuminated the dim hallway, but it seemed to weigh on him. He was breathing hard from the climb up the stairs.

I took the *Interiors* and his umbrella. "Come on in. Sit down."

He lit a cigarette, but did not sit. He stood before my orange crate shelves and picked up one object after another, turning them between his square-tipped fingers, measured their quality with the care of an Italian matron testing plum tomatoes. I could almost hear his thoughts turning as well, methodical and focused sternly on the assortment of plastic and metal and Velcro components each item represented. Stainless-steel stovetop burner covers: *Came up with this three years ago, tossed it in the trash.* Automatic hands-free cheese grater: *Looks good, won't work.* "Instant" wine opener: *Cheap copy of the one I sold to Hammacher Schlemmer ten years ago.* He lifted a sheet of peel-and-stick safety reflectors, shook his head, and put it down. *How could I have missed this one?*

But the compact toolbox with slots for "101 household necessaries" held his interest. He's been working toward the world's most user-friendly toolbox for as long as I can remember, and though this one clearly didn't have him beat, it contained possibilities for theft. "Borrowing," he prefers to call it.

Once, when I was about eight, I went uptown with my father on one of his supply expeditions—shopping for discounted wire, metal, batteries, sheet plastic at warehouses and jobbers—and we passed a bookstore with a hardcover edition of Mary Norton's *The Borrowers* in its window. I made him stop, dragged him inside, and told him about the story's thumb-sized characters who live under floorboards and "borrow" for their own innovative uses all the odd bits of food, pen caps, matchboxes, paper clips, earrings, and handkerchiefs that humans assume they've misplaced.

"It's my *favorite,*" I pleaded. He lifted the volume, weighed it in his palm just as he was now doing with that collapsible cutting board stand. As he checked the price I held my breath, wanting that book more than any candy, any toy, any trip.

"Too expensive."

I cried as he set the book back on its shelf. I begged as he turned to the sale rack. I vowed I would never even open the paperback *Rebecca of Sunnybrook Farm* he decisively handed to the cashier. And I never did.

But I read *The Borrowers*—all five books in the series. After I reported my father's unfairness my mother bought the paperback versions, and presented them to me on unlikely holidays such as St. Patrick's Day or May Day or Halloween.

The Borrowers were scavengers. They spent their lives in hiding. And whenever anyone—even a friend—got a fix on where they were living or how, they tended to duck and run. Now, as I watched my father scavenging for ideas others wouldn't realize he'd taken, I wondered if his refusing me that book had to do with more than money. Maybe he knew the same terror as that miniature tribe of outlaws. Maybe he, too, was afraid of being found out.

I was stalling.

Dad finished his inventory. I told him he could borrow anything he thought he might use, Pensacola was in no hurry for my returns.

"What's this?" He plucked an advance copy of Noble's fall catalog off the floor. "Cover credit!"

"Mm."

"You're not pleased?"

"Sure, I guess." I sat beside him on the couch. Now that he was here I couldn't think where to begin.

He hunched forward abruptly and broke into a cough. His smoker's hack. Like exploding rocks. He'd had it for years.

I clapped him on the back. "Hey, that's a good one, Dad."

He wiped his mouth with the leathered back of his hand and shook the catalog as if it were a volume of poetry, a political manifesto, the Great American Novel.

"You should be proud of yourself," he croaked.

"It's a picture of plastic pumpkins. Cardboard witches on a picnic table with a bunch of candied apples. Big deal."

His eyes roamed the corner where I store my lights and strobe, bolts of colored backdrop paper, a stack of reflectors, and an open trunk of props—scarves, soaps, costume jewels, fake fruit, flowers, and vegetables. He took a deep, shaky breath.

"I'm proud of you, Maibelle."

I didn't say anything, so he awkwardly grabbed me around the shoulders and squeezed. I closed my eyes.

After a long minute he released me, moved to the window, and lit a cigarette. When he started to tap the ash into his palm, I handed him a glass plate to use instead. The smoke curled out over the fire escape and dissolved in liquid air.

"What happened to you in China, Dad?"

He frowned.

"I don't mean at the end," I said quickly. "But when you were little."

It was too general. I expected him to say he didn't remember and let it go. But he shook his head and ground his stub into the plate.

"Why do you think something happened?"

"Because you always say you don't remember. There's a huge hole in your life that you never talk about. Something must have happened to make you clam up like that."

He slid a thumbnail between his teeth. "I'm getting old, you know. That was a long time ago. I think Anna's right, what's the point?"

"The point is to remember and talk about it."

"And pass it on?" He made that clucking sound with his throat and turned his back to me.

"I can sort of guess. Living in Chinatown, things happened that made me feel like an outcast."

"Chinatown was nothing."

The annoyance in his voice warned me not to try that again. But it also promised answers, if I just asked the right questions.

I squatted in front of the prop trunk, rearranging the contents until I could close the lid. "Your sisters. What were their names? Annabel and Clara Mae?"

"You know they were. You and Anna were named for them."

I stared at him. "I thought Mum named me. It's French."

"It was her idea, but they were my sisters' names."

I'd never even seen a picture of my aunts, and yet I bore their names. That seemed to make them a part of me, or vice versa. A fact of my life almost since I was born, yet no one had ever bothered to tell me. It was a minor thing, but it gave me a sense of what an amnesia victim must experience on being told he has a name he doesn't recognize, that total strangers are his dear friends and family. A sense of existing on two planes at once, with no connection between them.

"What were your sisters like?"

"Maibelle, why go into all this?"

"Why not? I have a right to know about them, Dad. They were my family, too!"

His eyes changed almost imperceptibly, like a widening lens. For all his sagging flesh and gray hair, he resembled a boy who's just discovered an intruder in his favorite hiding place.

He sat on the couch and leaned forward kneading his hands. "Beautiful." He spoke to the floor. "They were fair like my mother, though of course they had dark hair and eyes."

He lit another cigarette and blew the smoke away from me.

"Was she beautiful, too?"

"Who?"

"Your mother."

"Very."

"What did the Chinese think of her?"

"Surely you can imagine."

"I can imagine all sorts of things. Tell me."

But he didn't. I put some water on for coffee. The water boiled before he spoke.

"The children. The little ones. They'd follow us in the streets whenever we left the Settlement—especially when we went to Soochow to visit my father's mother. They called Mama *bai xiangu!*"

"Which means?"

"White sorceress."

White sorceress. I juggled the words. White witch.

I poured the water slowly, wetting the sides of the filter first, moving in toward the center. The grounds bubbled up. The pot filled. White witch. I once saw the Yellow Butterflies point at our building. "The White Witch lives there!" They shaped their hands into signs to ward off the evil spirits cascading from my balcony.

My father got up from the couch and leaned on the windowsill. Colorful umbrellas scurried down Greenwich Avenue like blossoms on the backs of ants. The rain formed a soft blur around them.

"Were there people in Chinatown who knew your family back in China?"

"No one knew our family."

I brought him some coffee. "But your father was important, wasn't he? A scholar? The son of some big official?"

"My father was gone most of the time. Teaching." There was a little sneer in his voice. "You felt sorry for yourself growing up in Chinatown, Maibelle. You have no idea."

"I never said I felt sorry for myself! I loved it there." I gritted my teeth against the tears my father had prompted. He was absolutely right. I had no idea. But that's why I was asking these questions.

He started to pace the wedge of floor between the shelves of gadgets and the edge of backdrop paper where I sat. He held his cigarette impatiently, with the pads of his fingers. He was telling me something important, something I'd thought I needed. About his school in Shanghai, someone he called a head boy. Classmates—sons of wealthy industrialists with long histories of collusion with the Manchus. Brits and

Krauts, with a handful of weaker, more malleable French or Italians as support troops.

I'd asked for this. Come back from exile to demand it. I was not going to chicken out now. But I was catching only every third or fourth word, as if a subconscious censor had plugged into my hearing.

I stood up, nearly colliding with my father at the end of his pace. He kept going. I stepped into the kitchen closet, pulled up the table, and turned on the water over a pile of dishes. The bubbles of Joy puffed up to the lip of the sink.

He was talking about his exclusion—his being excluded. I tried to listen, but the water roared even after I turned off the faucet. Rain was pouring through the open window into the glass plate with all those stubs. I retrieved it and knocked the contents into a garbage bag. The metallic stench of ashes overtook the smell of detergent.

"I did quite well in my classwork. Was passably good at games, later on rode well enough to compete at polo, but . . ."

I scrubbed and rinsed.

"It was Halliday who first insulted me to my face. The others followed suit, but he was the one who coined the phrase."

"What phrase?" I stopped washing and turned toward him.

"He had his arm round my shoulder. I'd just ended first in a fifty-meter swim, and he'd led the group in a rousing chorus of 'For He's a Jolly Good Fellow.' He waited for the singing to die down. Then he had two of his buddies grab my arms. He punched me in the stomach so hard my feet lifted off the ground. There was blood in my mouth. They dropped me and held me as Halliday yanked off my swimsuit, used it to tie my wrists to my ankles. Then they dumped me back in the water and watched me nearly drown. Through it all he kept laughing. 'I say, Joseph's not half-bad for a chink bastard!' "

My father coughed. He set down his coffee and cigarette and grabbed for a handkerchief in his back pocket. He spat into it and wiped his mouth. I started to fill a glass from the tap but wasn't quick enough.

"Don't bother," he said.

I couldn't bear to hear more of the physical damage. Had they broken his ribs? How long had he been forced to thrash, injured and bound, in the water? The answers hardly mattered; his body had mended. I wanted revenge.

"You fought back, didn't you, Dad? You reported them?"

"All I could think about was my name. Joseph is not my name. It's Chou. Joe is the anglicized version. My mother enrolled me at school as Joseph. I couldn't even correct Halliday, insist that he call me by my real name, because Mama had made that impossible."

My father crushed his empty cigarette package and stepped briefly into the kitchen to put it in the trash. In that split second I imagined the door folding, pushing us together and binding us into the narrow space, like a time capsule that someone centuries ahead would open, and there would be our bones all mixed up together with the half-washed dishes and smoker's ash. But even that close, we didn't meet. There had been no revenge.

He stepped back. "They were cruel to her face, too. But she never turned. All our linen had to be bleached and starched, clothes patterned after the latest styles from home—her home. She even ordered our underwear from Sears, Roebuck." The downpour was easing. Dad picked up a sponge I'd dropped on the floor and carefully wiped off the windowsill.

"We had tea at four o'clock with white toast and marmalade. Boiled eggs and kippers for breakfast, roast beef or ham for tiffin. Chipped beef or rarebit for supper." He wrung out the sponge in the bathroom sink and handed it to me.

Our fingers pointed at each other, two nearly identical sets of torn, bitten stubs. I kept staring until he released the sponge. He tucked the user-friendly toolbox under his arm and reached for his umbrella.

"I loved congee, but the only way I could eat it was to sneak a fifth meal with the servants."

• • •

That was this afternoon.

Tonight Betty and Sandra are dancing above my head. Their footsteps pad across my darkroom ceiling to the low strains of "Moon

River." I tip my developing tank to their rhythm and time out the phases of development.

First, the evolution of shadow and light into image. Then the sudden arrest of process to freeze the moment and, finally, the careful inoculation of the "finished" picture against change. The developing tank reminds me of a martini shaker, except that it is filled not with the elixir of forgetfulness but of memory.

When I first started working in the darkroom, I imagined the metal cylinder pulsing with all those ghosts I was about to bring back to life. I really believed I had the power to pull the past forward into the present. I dared to believe time is flexible, and what's gone can be reconstructed, remolded, touched up, and fixed just by dodging in a bit of light or burning the shadows darker. I still cling to that wish, but it's getting as shriveled and tasteless as an old ginger root. In practice, I know that the snapshots in my mind are always more vibrant, more heartbreaking, more terrifyingly permanent than anything I can print in the dark.

How, for example, can you photograph a dream?

If I could capture my nightmares, stop them, get them *down,* I might destroy them. Yet in all Dad's pictures he never succeeded in stopping his schoolmates' blows, never killed the hatred in their voices.

My father accused me of feeling sorry for myself, and in the next breath shamed me because I lacked the same anguish that he'd known in China. I never before realized the strain in our family arose from a contest of sorrows.

....

6

Tommy called today. He promised not to mention his project if I'd see him again.

I asked why.

"For old times' sake."

"In old times you had no interest in me."

"New times, then. I feel bad about the other day."

I felt bad, too. I had stopped imagining him all over town, but I thought about Tommy—or Tai. What my brother had said. The Emperor State Building. His Buddha's bulge and those even, moon-shaped fingernails. It was not his fault that I was afraid of heights, or that I wasn't yet ready for Chinatown. He didn't need to know about my nightmares.

"I still think you should look for another photographer."

"Whatever you say, boss."

"No tall buildings."

"A walk, then. Solid ground."

It was warm out, clear and not too muggy. I had no pressing assignments, no excuses. Moreover, I wasn't looking for any.

"A walk would be good."

* * *

We decided to pick up where we'd left off: the corner of Thirty-fourth and Fifth. I arrived ten minutes late, and there was no sign of him. I waited five and then another five minutes and was just turning to escape the whole enterprise when I spotted him weaving hurriedly through the crowd.

Square, professorial sunglasses and a yellow short-sleeve button-down shirt. His body struck me, in a word, as spare. Not skinny or slender. Many Chinese men are so thin they look positively concave. Tommy is simply straight, up and down. No extraneous curves or bulges. No hiding places. No wonder he wears down his shoes flat across the back.

I imagined what we would look like together, the clean, straight Chinese man in his squared-off clothes and the redhead with flyaway hair. The picture made me wince.

As he reached me he started to apologize.

"I know." I turned uptown. "Fire in the tunnel."

"No, I was doing an interview that took longer than expected. I tried to call, but you'd already left."

My immediate thought was that this was a setup. Courtesy dictated a follow-up question: Oh? And what was your interview about? Right back to the forbidden subject.

I walked faster, said nothing. He kept up and didn't try to stop me, but I could feel his eyes pinching the back of my head, through that darkened glass. When we stopped for a light, I shifted from foot to foot, automatically idling as I do when jogging, grateful for the press of bodies and other people's conversation. He squeezed in beside me.

"How have you been?"

"Fine." I pulled forward before the green without looking. I wasn't really annoyed. I could let myself feel manipulated if I wanted to, but my real problem was I didn't have the faintest idea what to say. If it wasn't about work or, by extension, Chinatown, then what did we have to discuss?

His hand on my shoulder pulled without yanking. The crowd

thinned and I slowed. We walked side by side. He asked the questions he hadn't asked before. How long I'd lived in California. What I was doing there. When I'd come back. I kept my eyes on the teased hair of a woman in front of us and answered in monosyllables.

He didn't say anything for about half a block. And then the inevitable. "How could you fly if you were afraid of heights?"

His voice rose at an odd pitch. His brow was furrowed, mouth slightly pursed. The earnest concern made me smile.

"Now you don't need to ask why I quit."

His puzzled expression remained, but he stopped the questions for a few more blocks. I pretended to look at the window dressings.

Tommy stopped between the stone lions of the New York Public Library. "Come. I want to show you something."

Inside the huge, hushed reading room he called up a small pictureless volume entitled *Friends of Freedom,* published by an obscure academic press. The cover blurb described it as a history of a community of Quakers that flourished in Greenwich Village in the 1800s as a station on the underground railway. The author was T. T. Wah.

Speaking in a practiced library whisper, he said it had evolved out of class assignments for one of his graduate professors whose brother needed some gratis manuscripts to launch his new publishing company.

I flipped through the pages, more to avoid looking at Tommy than to assess his book. What a peculiar thing for him to write about. Chinatown's Malcolm X cum Studs Terkel. Like me taking pictures of Iowan snow. I stopped turning the pages and pretended to read. My eye caught on a line.

"Silence was their prison. Stories their refuge. Action their salvation."

I read the passage again. He was writing about the Quakers, but that didn't matter. I read it again and tried to sink it in. Refuge and salvation.

Tommy talked. "The professor's brother was using the nonprofit press as a tax shelter. It folded within a year. I guess I should be grateful just to be published, only this is probably the first time anyone's checked it out. You know?" But the way his fingers hovered, grasping the spine and giving the pages an almost imperceptible shake before returning the book to the desk, belied what he was saying.

"There's nothing wrong with being proud of your work," I said. "Now I want to show you something."

I scribbled some dates on a slip of paper and handed it to the librarian.

I had before me copies of *Life* magazine from 1947 and 1948. The years, my mother said, when my father enjoyed his greatest success. That's actually how she put it: enjoyment. Though she was the only one, far as I could tell, who'd taken the slightest pleasure in it. Compared to Dad's attitude about his lost career, Tommy was positively gloating over his accomplishment.

"There should be cover shots by him," I said. But the pages refused to open all the way because of the heavy binders, and it was difficult to tell the heavier cover paper from the glossy pages.

Tommy stopped my hands and closed the book to take it away. I glanced up, prepared for anger, but he was examining the compressed page edges as if conducting an experiment. He held them for me to see, and pointed to bands of white separated by almost indistinguishable stripes of cover color.

"Look how wide the white is here. And here. And here. A lot of the covers are missing. Out of a bound volume, can you imagine? Some people disgust me."

A thickness settled in the back of my throat. Without looking at Tommy's face I withdrew the volume from his hands, measured the space between the stripes, and opened to the place where a cover ought to be. Only by bending the spine nearly double could you see it, but deep in the valley between the pages a surgical slice had been made, so long ago that the edge had yellowed. I flipped to the contents page. "Cover photo of Manchurian refugees by Joe Chung." Three pages of photographs and text had also been excised from that magazine. Scores more from the rest of that and the other volume.

"Quite a methodical operation," Tommy said. His tone was cautious, and I detected a slight retreat from his earlier condemnation. "Why would anyone do this?"

"Anyone didn't."

Tommy tried to make eye contact as we left the library. I could feel the white heat of his stare boring into the side of my face. I wanted to tell him to watch where he was going. I wanted him to forget what I'd started. For the first time I felt ashamed of my father, saw his denial of the past in the context of a crime. And I—not my mother, not my professors or his former editors and audience—I was his primary victim.

I wasn't conscious of my speed, except to notice Tommy trotting to keep up. The lunchtime mob at Forty-second Street parted like water. I didn't slow down until I reached Grand Central, down past the benches of waiting room bag people, past the white travelers' clock, down to the center of the stars. There I stopped.

"You can see the whole universe from here." I pointed to the astrological map on the ceiling.

"You think I've never been in here before?"

Not only did I think it. I knew, though I was not sure how or why. Maybe because the whole time I lived in Chinatown I never came here, either. Except once. I must have been six years old.

If Tommy believed in stories, I thought, then I should tell him that story. Maybe it would make up for the magazines. Maybe, in some small way, help explain them.

So we sat at the bottom of the Vanderbilt Avenue staircase and I told him about the winter's day when my father, left in charge of Henry and me, decided for the first and last time ever to take us to the beach.

"Of course, I'd never seen a room as large as Grand Central. In those days there were no homeless to speak of. You could appreciate the distance between the floor and the stars. I remember thinking the brass on the information kiosk was gold. But Dad pulled us along so fast I seemed to be seeing in snapshots."

We'd run to catch the train—an antiquated car with ceiling fans and hard rattan seats and dull navy-green paint. I thought we would make the whole trip underground, like in a subway, but eventually we came out of the tunnel, crossed water. We kept on. Snow fell and stopped, and still we traveled, passing one commuter station after another and a world of shingled houses and trees, brown factories spurting smoke against an indifferent gray sky. From time to time I saw slices of ocean, but Dad wouldn't say where we were going or how far away from home. The fans weren't working, but the floor heaters were. Dry, dusty heat. Henry had brought along a maze book. His head nodded with the motion of the train. I fell asleep and didn't wake up until a blast of cold hit my face.

My father hadn't spoken a word the whole way, and he wasn't about to start now. We walked the length of a seaside village from the train to the beach and stood watching waves crash into huge rocks until my feet began to freeze. It was only Long Island Sound, and through the gray I could see shadowland across the water, but from the way Dad gazed out beneath his cupped hands, you'd think the whitecaps marked a trail all the way to China. Henry and I had to shout over the wind to get him moving, and even then he wasn't really reacting to us.

He picked up a stone long and thin as a shell. He worked his way down between the boulders to a place where the waves touched his toes, then lifted his arm way up over his head, and with a single flick of his fingers sent the rock gliding out over the swollen sea, so far I lost sight of it before it fell.

That was it. Just one stone. His eyes were watering. He turned, took my brother's hand and mine, and guided us back to the village, where we stopped for hot chocolate. He bought Henry a Casper the Ghost comic book and we read it together the whole way back while my father stared out the train window.

When we got home, the police were there. My mother acted as if she wanted them to arrest my father, but they wouldn't. Anna grabbed me as I walked through the door, and hugged me as if she loved me.

"It was months before Mum trusted us to my father's care again. Didn't Henry ever tell you this story?"

"No." Tommy eyed Orion. "Were you afraid?"

"Not until later that night, when I heard my mother crying. She wept like she was in pain, as if something had been cut out of her. Something she'd never get back."

He nodded. "She go on feeling that way?"

"Yes." I turned so he couldn't see my face. "But she fights it."

Lunchtime had passed, the throngs outside gradually eased. We went into a sandwich shop on Lexington that advertised itself as "The Home of the $2 Munch." In some places two dollars for a thimbleful of soup and a slice each of American cheese and Wonder bread would be considered extortion, but in Manhattan it was tantamount to a gift. Grateful that Tommy made no gesture to buy, I paid for this gift and selected a table in the corner. I sat with my back to the wall.

"Mind changing?"

I shrugged, traded places. He methodically removed everything from his tray before claiming the seat he'd requested. His meal now took up half as much space as my tray. I debated whether to follow his lead, but was worried he'd notice I was following his lead.

He looked at me, and though he seemed amused, his eyes made me think of lasers. He could turn them up so they bore down hard, or soften them until they seemed almost diffuse, but always the beam remained strong and steady. I sensed that he'd burn right through to the back of my skull if I let him hold my gaze. So we ended up playing visual tag. Looking and being seen. He was ahead, but he hadn't won yet.

I left my tray where it was, and Tommy sipped his soup. I couldn't remember if I'd ever watched him as a boy, eating.

"I don't know much about you, you know."

"Not much to know, boss."

"I wish you wouldn't call me that. Henry said your family's been here for generations."

"How is Henry?" Tommy's voice was dead calm.

"The same."

He nodded and let it go. "Not here, but in this country. My great-grandmother came from Szechuan. Her parents sold her to a trader who shipped her to California as a prostitute. My great-grandfather sold trout and salmon to the miners, he fell in love with her, paid a saloon owner one hundred dollars—fish money, my grandmother used to call it. They had three children, two died as babies."

I put down my spoon.

"When the whites in California started killing Chinese workers around the turn of the century, my great-grandparents took their son and came to New York. They opened a poultry store. My grandfather passed the business on to my father before I was born."

The baby that didn't die. I pushed the unbidden thought aside. "You chose not to carry on the tradition."

He leaned back in his chair and wove his arms into a defending brace. "My parents gave me an American name. They made me promise to stay in school, make something of my life."

I suspect he didn't mean it this way, but the last phrase came out sounding like a dare. I bit into my sandwich and waited for him to unfold his arms. Tommy's parents had been shorter than I was at ten years old. Flapping among the bodies of chickens, talking and laughing with customers as their steel blades flew faultlessly, chopping off heads and wings.

"Where are your parents now?"

"Both dead."

"Oh, God. I'm sorry."

He dropped his arms and stared at the people streaming past us on the other side of the glass. Commuters whose day had finished early, bustling for trains that would take them back to those beachfront towns.

"There are people in Chinatown who have lived in New York all their lives and never set foot north of Broome Street." He turned abruptly back to me. "Until I was fifteen years old, I was one of them."

I pushed my tray onto the empty table next to us. The only other customers now were a pair of young men in ill-fitting business suits who talked intently over monstrous hot fudge sundaes. The heel of the darker of the two jerked up and down as he talked, as disconnected and earnest as the panting of a loyal dog. The other man's feet never moved.

"Why did we change seats?"

"I don't sit with my back to the door."

I inadvertently looked around as the two men got up and left.

"Why?"

"Occupational hazard."

"Social history is dangerous?"

He picked up his sandwich, took a huge bite, and chewed slowly. Seamlessly. If he swallowed, I didn't notice.

The year Tommy Wah was fifteen years old was the same year my family left Chinatown. The last year I saw Lao Li.

• • •

It was not Li who introduced us, but in my mind Tommy and I were linked by him. Li Tsung Po. Lao Li. A mutual acquaintance? No. More.

I first met him one cold autumn day when I was eight and had strayed too far from home. I didn't recognize the street or shops and was just starting to get nervous when I came upon an enormous, brightly painted pillar rising like a god's leg in front of what was then a small curio store. Of course I stopped. Who could resist? Within the sculpted pictures lay a world of peacocks, mountains, golden leaves. A vivid green and gilt dragon wound round and round, his head rising into the clouds. Tiny white-robed women carried fruit in the palms of their hands; men held lanterns to light the way. It was magical.

The shop behind the pillar was long and narrow and dark as a wizard's den, the only source of light a lamp on a desk at the back. There sat an old, old man with a face so thin that knives of shadow stretched beneath his cheekbones.

He called out in a deep, gruff voice, "Come in, come in. Hurry up."

"I'm lost," I said from the doorway. "I need to get back to Mott Street."

"Mott Street?" He cocked his head and pulled on his chin, then slowly rose from his desk and, leaning heavily on an ivory cane, shuffled in my direction. His black robe skimmed the floor. His white hair and spindly beard made me think of cobwebs. I couldn't move.

He reached the front of the shop and pointed down the street to the right. "Mott Street is there. Not far." His front teeth glittered, solid gold. His eyes were tiny insects tucked behind old-man lids.

Before I knew what was happening, he grabbed my hand and pressed it between his own. "You call me Lao Li."

His palms were cold and I could feel the long bones just beneath his skin. It was like shaking hands with a dragon.

"You are Maibelle, *dui*?"

My hand jerked, but he had it clamped so tight that, instead of pulling away, I lost my balance and fell backward into a pile of brocaded cushions. Having failed—or refused—to let go, Mr. Li fell on top of me. We lay motionless for several seconds, and I'd just convinced myself that I'd killed him when he gave a roar.

"*Jingren de!*"

The sound erupted from deep down, the rumbling of a wizard who knew my name. Then a gurgle and shudder ran through his body, gathered into a yelp, and the old man finally rolled off of me.

"Hee, hee. Hee, hee! *Qing.*" He motioned me to rise, though he was still flat on his back.

I started for the door, but the sight of him sprawled on the floor held me. The black robe was twisted around his legs. His cane had been thrown to one side, the lion carved into its handle snarling up at me. The old man just lay there chortling at the ceiling.

I asked if he was all right, which started him up again, and though I tried to hand him his cane and help him to his feet, he was laughing so hard he could barely sit. When he took my hand this time, his palm was warm and his eyes bright.

"Okay, Mei-be." He let me pull him up.

"How do you know me?"

He shook his head. "I know lot of things. Come, Jade Maiden, I show you. My shop is very special." And then, as if I were his most valued customer, he led me on a tour.

A case near the entrance contained a trio of jade bracelets thick as doughnuts and a pair of tiny brocaded shoes inset with pearls and black jet. "If you are a girl in Old China," Li said, "you wear these when you grow up."

It was a sobering thought, since the bracelets were so heavy I could hardly lift them and already my feet were far too big to fit inside the shoes. Besides, they were all the wrong shape.

As if reading my mind, Li told me, "In China you wear tight bandages, stop bones from growing, then you have lotus feet and shoes will fit."

He smiled.

I said it sounded like torture, and people in Old China must have been very mean.

He replied that in China passion and pain could not be separated.

In one corner sat a rickshaw with worn leather seats and several wheel spokes missing. The handles were burnished and smooth as skin, and when I touched them, they were moist, as if with sweat. Mr. Li would not let me sit in the rickshaw because it was liable to break, but he insisted I try the store's centerpiece, a rosewood throne inlaid with ivory clouds and jade serpents, the legs carved into elephants. It was very uncomfortable, but that hardly mattered because as soon as I was settled, Mr. Li told me of man-eating demons and water dragons ("claws made from lightning, teeth sharp like swords") and an emperor-magician who turned his wife to stone ("that wife ask too many questions").

As he talked, his long, bony fingers moved like tentacles. I felt his black eyes watching from beneath their great sprouting brows, but I could not decide whether he viewed me with fondness, pity, or amusement.

Finally Lao Li led me to the back of the store, where the air was thick with peanut oil smells from the noodle shop next door. There, one whole wall was covered with photographs from the time when his antiques were new.

There were scared-looking children and stern old women wrapped in elaborate gowns. The women's hair was arranged in geometric shapes that stood up and out from their heads. They had the look of evil queens from some distant, alien planet. The men, always photographed separately and often in Western dress, seemed far less threatening. They had tufted eyebrows, wisps of beard, and cheeks that were either very round or hollow, like Mr. Li's.

But the pictures that intrigued me the most were not of Chinese at all. They were a series of sepia portraits of a white woman and what I assumed was her family. She had sad eyes and hair as light and curly as mine. She wore long pleated dresses with lacy trim and waists tied with broad pale ribbons. I would never have guessed she was photographed in China if it weren't for her chair, with that same inlaid wood and elephant carving, and the children standing beside her, the baby in her lap. Though dressed in starched white playsuits and gowns with ruffles and bows, these children had hair and eyes as black as those of the kids in Chinatown—the ones who really belonged there, that is, not "foreign devils" like me.

When I asked who the lady was, Lao Li wouldn't answer directly. Instead, he took me behind the counter and pulled up a couple of stools. He poured himself a bowl of tea and gave me a walnut cookie, then told about white witches who cast spells over China men.

The witches stole the enchanted men's babies for their kingdom in the sky. They raised the children as their own, teaching them wondrous magic. But when the babies were grown, the witches grew distrustful and hurled them back to earth. When the children knocked on their fathers' doors they found that the China men had new babies and did not remember the old ones. The men saw them only as witches, and begged them to go away. And so the white witches' stolen children were forced to remain forever between the earth and sky.

"Is she one of the witches?" I searched the portrait above my head for signs of mystical powers.

"Ah," said the old man fluttering his palm. "This question you ask your father."

"My father? You know my father?"

Mr. Li smiled.

"But *how* do you know my father?"

"Jade Maiden," warned Lao Li, still smiling, "you ask too many questions."

That night I asked my parents if they knew Mr. Li, and as he'd implied, they did. Li Tsung Po was his full name. He'd operated a pawnshop in Shanghai before the communist takeover, and my mother said he had the best Oriental antiques in the city. My father, bluntly and without explanation, called him a thief and forbade me to see him again, but when I asked about the pictures, Dad was silent, then started to leave the room. He reached the doorway, turned, and said, "Witches cannot be photographed."

....

7

In a used bookstore on lower Broadway I bought twenty back issues of *National Geographic* with photographs by Marge Gramercy. I have them here by my bed, in the darkroom, scattered among this next batch of gadgets awaiting the camera's eye. Not coffee-table reading or framable art, the magazines serve as a private warning system and reminder of what I hoped to accomplish by coming back.

Marge Gramercy was no one I knew before stumbling across her obituary, but she has slowly, reliably turned into a role model, confidante, and friend. The longer I live in her home, the more deeply I imagine her. Through these photographs I see where she traveled, how she saw, what she thought and loved. By extension I can see the woman herself, as she kneels before the grieving windswept child in this portrait of the Andes. I picture silver hair braided long down her back, skin the color of a sandstorm. I admire her hand-dyed vests and khaki pants, combat boots, and wild tribal earrings given by native women in exchange for Polaroids of their children.

Marge, I'm sure, had lovers at home and abroad and many invitations to marriage, but held out for the man who would not try to mold her, break her, or admire her too deeply, who would simply keep her company in love. When that man failed to materialize, she selected children in villages on all six continents and made it her life's goal to support this global family. These are her children here—a weeping Himalayan shepherd, this grinning, Nubian wrestler in Adidas shorts and body painted white, this baby crisscrossed in the netting of a hammock aboard a Vietnamese fishing boat. Others crouch under broadleaf palms or laugh invisibly in the shadows of Marge's distant peaks. Whether in grief or joy the children all have her eyes—clear, thrilled, hungry for life. But they are too trusting. She crushes this trust like a sweet, tender onion until it releases the vulnerability that makes her weep, and only when her tears are streaming does she record what she sees.

What I admire most in this mythical woman is her ability to embrace her own sorrow. Her vision is absolute and as truthful as her children are trusting. She does not travel for escape or return to this small city box with regret. She accepts the empty pockets of her life. She knows her children will probably die with their eyes clouded over by betrayal or rage, and she endures the limitations of time and love and her own brittle body that prevent her from going back to them one last time. The world is full of inescapable horror, but Marge Gramercy knows how to wrap that horror in the splendor of an infant's grin or the majesty of a snowcapped summit. She captures a whole doomed culture in a young girl's upturned hands.

I am not ashamed to talk to her photographs. I search them for guidance. And sometimes I imagine her answering me.

Stop looking for endings, she warns. The ending is only the inevitable conclusion of something that started long ago. The sources of pain and treachery and madness are also the sources of freedom.

I have called the offices of *Life* to see if I can order the back issues that contain my father's photographs. They tell me those are collector's copies, now worth up to one hundred dollars apiece. They can put me in touch with private search services, but their own archives are not for sale.

How long, I ask Marge, is long ago?

That she will not answer.

• • •

Johnny wasn't much of a writer, but he tried. Usually he sent postcards that he'd lifted from the donations box at church. On the back of glossy photographs of Mount Assumption under snow he'd scribble haphazard encouragements and news. "Went swiming in the ferry pond yestrday. Keep flying!" read one. "Hi, Chinese girl," began another. "Been to that Stachue of Librty lately?" And the really important bulletin: "My dad says Glabber's dead. Brain tumer. So it's safe to come back to the cuntry again. See ya soon, I hope."

The notes I wrote to him were more disappointing than his to me, though not for lack of thoughts or feelings. I wanted to tell him how much I missed him. I wanted to write about Chinatown and the Butterflies and Henry's goof-up with Mrs. Dixie, but as soon as I got pencil in hand my mind turned to garbage, and I'd end up writing what I always (and for years afterward) wrote when I cared too much—or not enough; I called them nothing-notes.

"School stinks, but my friend Mr. Li, the old Chinese man I told you about, he's nice to me. Wish you were here." Not exactly profound, or even informative, and to make matters worse, though I could spell better than Johnny, I still had the handwriting of a baby. The words came out looking even more stupid than they sounded.

Every time I struggled with one of these letters I thought of deaf people trying to talk. Most deaf people, I believed, would keep trying. After three or four letters, I quit.

Which meant that, when August came around again, we were six months out of touch. He was fourteen. I was twelve and sure that by now he had a girlfriend. He'd have outgrown his flying dream. He'd tell me his fairies were a joke on me and he'd lied about not liking Henry. Or maybe the Madisons had moved away and Gramma Lou hadn't told me because she thought I'd feel bad.

I mentally rehearsed the possible changes all the way to Wisconsin. Ten minutes after we arrived, Johnny found me on the back porch and called through the screen.

"Come swimming?"

He'd grown a good seven inches to my four. His hair was thicker and lighter than I recalled—near white—and his eyes, though still bright blue, had a shimmery, almost translucent quality.

"Hi," I said.

"Coming or not?"

"You're in some hurry."

"Got a new place to show you."

I grinned. "*You* found something new?"

"Hey, it's hotter 'n sheep shit out here. Come *on.*"

I dug around in my baggage for a bathing suit, but when Johnny realized what I was doing, he let out a shaming hoot.

"Swimming clothes are for city slickers. You're back in the country, Maibee. Come *on.*"

I'd never been skinny-dipping in my life, but as I contemplated Johnny's proposal, my only objection was that my brother and sister—not to mention my parents and grandparents—would be scandalized.

"Only if you're dumb enough to tell them." Johnny walked away.

We followed the main road for about a mile, then turned across a stream and onto a path through dense oak forest, emerging on a slab of rock that dropped some thirty feet to a swirl of green water below.

"Color's just like your eyes." Johnny frowned at my blushing. "Used to be a quarry about a hundred years ago."

He grabbed my hand and pulled me down the trail that zigzagged across the rock face. I tried not to look, because it made me queasy. Instead, I concentrated on the sensation of Johnny's hand around mine. It was cooler, smoother, drier than anyone's palm had a right to be on an overheated day like this.

When I went behind a shrub to get out of my shorts and T-shirt, he laughed. But he turned his back when he dropped his pants, and he dove away from me to enter the water, giving me time to jump in unseen.

Under the clear green surface, with the sun slicing long, angled swaths in the background, he looked like one of his marine fairies. He was swimming to show off, arms and legs wagging, hair a swirl of seaweed about his head. The color erased his tan and freckles, turned his body ghostly pale.

Abruptly he crunched into a ball, hung suspended for a moment, then shot off, straight for the deepest water.

I swam to the surface and waited, my sense of direction spinning. The walls of the quarry climbed in a bowl around the pool, the cloudless sky a flat lid on us. I wasn't sure where to search for Johnny. And there was no knowing how deep this went.

Finally the water burst about forty feet away. He popped straight up, waved his arm toward the opposite shore. And vanished once again.

The swimming hole, I calculated, was at least a half mile long, surrounded on all sides by rock, and beyond by impenetrable thickets and woods. No one knew where we were, and if Johnny hurt himself or went into one of the narrow inlets along the edge of the pool, I would be alone. I was not a very good swimmer. I wasn't really happy unless I could see bottom. Johnny knew this, if only he'd remember.

I was starting up the ledge toward my clothes when a horsefly chased me in again. I dunked my head and swam back to deeper water.

"Hey!"

A white tennis ball came flying toward me, trailing a long cord. Johnny's voice echoed up the quarry.

"Grab hold!" He was standing on the opposite side of the swimming hole in water up to his waist.

"*Hold!*" his voice echoed.

"I want to go," I yelled back.

"*To go!*"

He shook his head, finger to lips. The ball bobbed in front of me. He was mouthing something, but I couldn't read the words. Not that I liked that echo much, either.

I clasped the ball between my hands, pushed off, and kicked as he pulled me across. When I felt the stone below me, I let go and swam the last few feet on my own. I didn't climb past shoulder depth, though.

He was standing ahead of me. Facing me. Naked.

"We got to walk a ways."

Naked. Like the pictures in Mum's gallery she insisted on calling nudes.

"Walk?"

I'd never seen a real boy naked. Not even Henry.

"Place I want to show you."

"You mean . . ." I glanced around the quarry, anywhere else.

"Nah, I known this swimming hole all my life. *This* is something special."

And what he was showing me right now wasn't?

"I won't look." He began to turn. Anyone else would be laughing at me, but not Johnny. Not now.

"No. Wait."

I walked all the way to the top of the ledge. The water slid down me. Johnny stood, half-turned, motionless except for his eyes.

I let his gaze roam my half-formed body. I took his in, too. The long stretch of his thigh, hard and pale as marble, the flat slab of his belly. Between them, a pale, soft tangle of hair, like the down I was just beginning to grow myself. Like a nest. I felt the fullness of my breasts as I gazed at his sex, a tightening between my legs. I raised my eyes and locked into his, and in that moment understood how it feels to be savored by a man.

When I reached him, he curled his fingertips around mine and we walked through a wedge in the stone. We passed into a low stalactite-filled tunnel that raised my skin. My thigh brushed his in the darkness. We stopped as if connected by a raw, electric nerve, then started again, more slowly.

At the end of the tunnel he made me cover my eyes and promise not to peek. It wouldn't be as good, he said, if I looked too soon.

The hard floor gave way to sand beneath my feet, and my skin eased back in the warmth that now replaced the tunnel's damp chill. We walked about twenty paces. When we stopped, I was hot again. The sun turned the inside of my eyelids red, but the air was still, as if we were in a small, cramped room.

I felt Johnny moving in front of me. Standing. Almost close enough to touch. Close enough that the surface of my body felt as if it were being pulled toward him, iron to a magnet, reigniting that nerve.

"Open," he said.

I hesitated, trying to quiet the noise of my heart before taking the next step, but it was no use.

The first thing I saw when I opened my eyes was Johnny's face looking up. I followed his gaze and discovered that we were standing inside a natural dome. The rock looked as if it had been scooped out with a spoon. The sand floor was as flat and soft as a mattress with darkness licking the edges. But the darkness seemed very far away because from high up, through an opening to the sky, rained a blazing light that enclosed us in one perfect circle.

Johnny lay at my feet and crooked an arm behind his head. He smiled up at me.

"Know how this place makes me feel?" he asked.

I sat beside him and hugged my knees.

"Makes me feel like we're inside God."

Next morning, after the women were gone, Grampa embarked on this summer's project—teaching Henry to shoot. I would have been somewhere else, too, except Johnny had to finish his chores first. I was batting a croquet ball around the side lawn, waiting for him, when the gunslingers went by.

Henry and Grampa positioned themselves atop the stile that spanned the wide stone wall between the farm's lawn and pasture. Henry propped both elbows on the railing to stabilize his aim, and Grampa adjusted his fingers, made sure he had a tight grip on the butt, and cautioned him about the gun's kick. Then they scanned the middle distance for telltale shapes or movements.

"There, boy, see him?" Grampa pointed.

Henry moved the revolver slightly and cocked the trigger.

"What is it?"

"Woodchuck," said Grampa. "They got a burrow somewhere in this pasture, damn near destroyed your grandmother's vegetable garden."

I edged closer for a look. The muscles in Henry's arms were tight. Grampa's face was twitching. At the far side of the pasture sat a fat, friendly-looking creature with dark brown fur and round eyes. He had his paws up, begging.

"What the hell you waiting for—"

Kaboom!

Nothing could have prepared me for the havoc caused by that one little bullet. The explosion lifted me right off my feet. Low, deeply masculine, the throbbing bored to the bone and stayed there, drumming, for many seconds after the shot was fired.

The weapon's recoil knocked Henry backward so hard he would have dropped the gun if Grampa hadn't grabbed his hand. At first I thought Henry had been hurt, but then the two of them jumped from the stile and tore off across the field, Grampa hooting as if Henry'd scored a touchdown.

The side of the woodchuck's head was blown off, a mash now of blood and brains and jumped-up dirt. What was left of the animal lay on its back, snout and paws raised skyward, the remaining eye turned black, in the background Mount Assumption.

All the same raw material, but rearranged forever.

"See what I did, Maibee? First shot a direct hit!"

Henry's black eyes flashed. He reached with one hand and pushed his hair out of his eyes, a gesture he'd picked up from his Chinatown cronies. He had exactly the same look on his face I'd seen in the boys who won at craps in the street below our balcony.

"Now, don't go getting all high-and-mighty," said Grampa. "Beginner's luck don't count for much."

That only fueled Henry's determination to repeat his success. He galloped back to the stile. Grampa motioned for me to move away, but I needed no encouragement. I turned and ran inside the house, wishing fervently for my brother to fail.

I went up to the attic and kneeled in the gable window overlooking the main road. I thought I'd be able to see Johnny coming. Then I'd run down to meet him and we'd go back to our secret place. We'd go skinny-dipping and, afterward, he'd show me how to kiss again and insist it wasn't just practice.

Yesterday I'd tried to tell him we weren't old enough, but he said he was two years older and he was. Old enough to love me, that is. I asked how he was so sure about something as grown-up as that.

"You're the only other person I've ever met," he said, "who knows fairy stories are true."

Kaboom!

This blast shook the pane so hard I was sure the glass would shatter. I raced to the opposite window and was pleased to see my brother shaking his head. He was positioning himself for a third shot when Grampa gave a shout and the two of them were suddenly off, away from where the woodchuck had fallen, away to the other side of the pasture, the ridge by Glabber's woods.

Something about their speed, that shout, made me nervous, but I had barely cleared the stile when Henry was back, shoving me aside in his haste to get to the phone. His hand wobbled so he had to dial three times before he reached the hospital. I'd never heard his voice crack as wildly as it did saying someone had been shot.

Johnny Madison did not die that day or in the days after. The bullet caught him in the shoulder. He said it hurt like hell and made it hard to move his arm. But the doctor said it wouldn't keep him from flying, which was all Johnny really cared about.

Henry vowed to my mother that he would never touch a firearm of any kind ever again, and it seemed pretty likely that he'd keep his promise. At least it was not the kind of thing he could shrug off—or ever forget.

But Johnny told Henry he didn't hold it against him, said he'd even fired a gun once himself, though he didn't like the kick.

"Besides," he said, "I thought it was Glabber's ghost come back to get me. Heck, I was *relieved* it was you."

When he and I were alone, though, Johnny told the truth. How it felt to see his flesh torn open, the hole tunneling deep inside his body. The skin so much thicker, the bone so much farther below the surface than he'd ever imagined.

"The pain was like fire, Maibee," he said. "But it didn't seem real, almost like it was somebody else's fire, if you see. It was so sudden—when I saw the blood it didn't have nothing to do with me. There was this hunk of metal inside my arm, but I couldn't think how it got there. I didn't see Henry or your grampa. I thought it had to be Glabber. Or else it was some kinda sign."

"What do you mean, sign?"

"Like they always talk about in church. The hand of God 'n' all that." His voice quivered a little and he looked away. " 'Cause of what we were doing yesterday."

I was sitting on his bed. I'd been about to hold his hand because I thought it might make him feel better. But suddenly there was a rock in my throat, and I couldn't move.

"You told somebody?"

"Course not." He looked at me and his face crushed down a little. "But God sees. Nothing you can do about that."

"You think God thinks it's bad?"

"Naked can be bad."

"You said everybody did it."

"Well, maybe we oughtn't be like everybody."

"I thought it would be weird, but it wasn't at all."

"Yeah." He shook his head as if to convince himself. "And it wasn't God shot me, I don't think."

"Wasn't Glabber, either."

"Naw. It was just a accident." Johnny pulled his magic kingfisher's feather from the bedside table and waved it in the air. "But you can't keep a good bird down."

I leaned over and kissed him quickly, unashamedly, on the mouth and asked if he still planned to marry me.

"In China?"

"I've been thinking," I said. "Maybe we don't need to go that far, after all."

In a day or two Henry's color returned. He apologized for treating Johnny like a demento and the three of us made our peace by playing cards together. Johnny was no slouch at poker and won so much money that pretty soon Henry was acting like the victim.

My grandfather ended up taking the brunt of the blame. Gramma Lou made him write a letter explaining what happened and taking full responsibility. (Grampa considered anything to do with pen and paper to be a form of torture.) He paid for the doctoring and extra help the Madisons needed while Johnny was mending, and offered the use of his combine to finish harvesting the Madisons' rye.

Mr. Madison still might have sued, but Gramma Lou had delivered one of his children and Mrs. Madison said she would not stand for war with their closest neighbors.

The one who would not forgive Grampa was his daughter. Mum refused to even speak to him after the accident.

"I was willing to put up with his bigotry and infantile behavior for your sake," I overheard her telling Gramma Lou. "I thought it was important for the kids to know you both, to see where at least one of their parents came from. But this time he's gone too far."

I peeked into the living room, where they sat together on the faded davenport. My grandmother was nodding, holding onto Mum's hand.

"I can't bring the children back here, Mother—not as long as he's here."

My grandmother closed her eyes. She seemed suddenly very old, a cloth doll with weakening seams. Her skin was as thin and wrinkled as crêpe paper, and the flesh in certain parts of her body—around the sleeveless shoulders of her shirtdress and just above her collar—sagged as if by a gravitational pull all its own. Even her gray hair looked fatigued, sticking in fed-up wisps to her forehead and the back of her neck. When she finally opened her eyes, I realized they had gone gray, too. She turned those eyes on my mother, and they seemed to look straight through her.

"The two of you are so alike," said Gramma Lou. "You'll never forgive each other for that."

My mother drew back. Her expression hardened.

"Oh? Just exactly how am I like him?"

"Diana, ever since you were a little, tiny girl, you've done exactly what you wanted. No one could get in your way. No one could tell you right or wrong. Close the gate in your face, put a boulder in your path, and in two seconds you'd find a way around it. If this comes as news I'm very sorry, but you *are* your father's daughter."

My mother looked appalled. "Well, if I'm so goddamn determined, how come I never seem to get what I want?"

"Maybe because you pay more attention to what's holding you back than what you're aiming for."

"Maybe it's just that there's nothing to aim for here in the middle of nowhere."

"I've listened to you tell me that for thirty years, Diana. And you may be right. I assume that's why you left us. But your father and I are still your parents, and this is still where you come from. No matter how far away you go or how you change your name, you can't change that. And if any of your children want it to be, this is their home, too."

"Oh, don't go getting all sentimental, Mother."

"Everyone needs a place to come back to."

"For me and the children that place is New York."

"I don't think you really believe that."

"Well, think again. I love you, and I suppose some part of me loves Dad, but I'll be damned if I come out here anymore. The next time, the person who gets shot could be Maibelle or Anna. Or Dad."

We left the farm at dawn the next day, drove on into the night, and along about one in the morning arrived back in Chinatown.

• • •

The old lady next door is teaching her parrot to sing. She's from my grandparents' generation, give or take, so it shouldn't surprise me that she knows their songs, but the sound of her wiry, angled voice climbing through the chorus of "Toot, Toot, Tootsie, Goodbye" is hardly the way I expected to greet this morning. She wavers just like the needle on Grampa's old Victrola.

She's put a collar around the feathered neck. Now she opens the door to the cage, reaches in, and brings the macaw out on a scarlet ribbon. She lets him hop on the shoulder of her blue housedress, peck at her loose white curls. His brilliantly colored head twists as if it's screwed on.

I duck inside and come back out onto the fire escape with a telephoto lens, through which the animal's black eyes glare at me. My neighbor's skin is delicately wrinkled under a veneer of irregularly applied rouge. Her nose is sharp, narrow, her hands thin to the bone. Her head turns so I can't look into her eyes, but her profile shows the tracks of a lifetime of polite smiles, hollows where my father would have moonpuffs. I try to imagine my mother becoming this woman someday.

But you can't make substitutions for parents, and anyway, what do I know of this lady beyond my imaginings? The bird could be right. She could be a hateful old bitch, for all I know. She keeps the leash wrapped around one wrist like a noose.

And begins to warble, "La da, da da. Da, da da. Sugar's sweet, so are you."

The parrot hops off her arm to the table.

"Bye," she sings. "Bye. Blackbird."

The macaw listens intently, head cocked to one side for three or four rounds, then picks up the verse as accurately as an echo. His mistress claps her hands to her cheeks and rocks from side to side.

He lifts one leg, then the other, as if stretching from the vocal exertion. She repeats the verse and they sing in duet. "Sugar's sweet, so are you.

"Bye. Bye. Blackbird."

The old lady raises her face. Her eyes find me. She beams an indescribable smile. I lower the camera.

"Can you believe it!" she calls to me.

"You're wonderful," I holler back. "You two should go onstage."

I'm too far away to tell for sure without putting the lens back between us, but I could swear she blushed at that. She lowers her eyes, shaking her head, and strokes the ruffled feathers.

I'm off base. It's not about performing. This is not a triumph of training. The bird has replaced her photo albums and papers. He has lifted her out of her past. He has become her friend.

Part III

Chinatown Chicken

8

When I tell her I'm about to go out for my morning run, my mother tells me that New York joggers inhale two to three times more carcinogens than people who spend their free time in museums. I remind her I took up running in California, so those figures don't apply to me. Besides, the chemicals keep me going. She asks, as if she has eyes through the phone, how I can bear to be seen wearing the rags I run in. I tell her they're my only defense against muggers and besides, I'm moving too fast for anyone to get a decent look. She warns me I'll need surgery on my knees and hips before I'm thirty. I tell her I'll need a psychiatrist if I quit, and that finally shuts her up.

My mother's distaste for psychotherapy dates back to an elementary school social worker who told Mum at the age of nine that she was having difficulty with multiplication because she was in love with her father and wanted to kill her mother. Also that she'd best marry well because with her IQ the only employment she'd be fit for was waiting tables or teaching kindergarten. Mum took her revenge by clipping for her children tabloid stories about patient seductions, perfectly sane women whose lunatic therapists had locked them in asylums for years, and psychiatrists who used hypnosis to access their patients' bank accounts. "The only people who go into that line of work," she told us, "are the ones who most need it themselves." To prove it she read us chapter and verse on Freud's own sex life.

"No, Mum," I tell her now. We have come to the reason for her call. "No, I don't want to go to Delong's studio and see his latest masterpieces. I'm too busy shooting junk."

I was a junior in college and the nightmares had been stalking me for four years when I finally decided to defy my mother's conditioning. Surely the counselors at the campus psychiatric services would be different from those tabloid monsters. I was referred to a thirtyish woman who looked like Morticia Addams in leather. Dr. Elsa Gertz spoke in a breathy whisper and drank from a large mug that said "U O Me," which she refilled with black coffee twice during our hour-long session. She asked what was bothering me, and I started telling her about my nightmares, but got only as far as the Statue of Liberty before she cut me off. "People used to say that nightmares were evil spirits, like ghosts, that rose from the past to haunt or suffocate dreamers. Those evil spirits come from your childhood." My problem, said Dr. Elsa Gertz, was that my father was an alcoholic and never loved me. My mother was a doormat and—did I have brothers and sisters?—well, yes, they were as wacko as I was, of course. The only solution was to cut off ties with all of them. No phone calls, no visits, no letters. "What do you owe them?" she demanded. "You didn't choose them to be your family. You'll only get better when you choose a unit of surrogates who can retrain you to love and be loved." If I had any trouble breaking the ties, Dr. Gertz and her husband had a farm outside town where they ran a kind of "halfway family" for some of her clients. It was billable to insurance.

"I need you," Mum's saying. "His studio's in Harlem, you know, and neither Henry nor your father will go with me. Please, Maibelle. We'll take a cab up together. It'll be an adventure."

I can see her clutching the receiver, frown lines trenching her forehead. Deepest, darkest Harlem. The urban jungle. My mother, the champion of race relations.

"You've been there before, though."

"No. He's always brought his work to the gallery. Now he says if I want to show him, I have to come to him."

Her breath erupts in little gasps. I try to focus on her hypocrisy, tell myself she deserves to squirm, but the critic in me is silenced by a sudden, improbable but inescapable image of her struggling, hands trapped behind her back, face pressed against the pavement. Going down with a weapon at her throat.

I never saw Dr. Elsa Gertz again, or any other licensed psychotherapist. But for all this woman spooked me, the invitation to implicate my parents was too tempting. If I just got clear of them, I thought, we'd all be better off. My nights would become as soft and comforting as an eiderdown quilt. I would discover how to love and be loved, and they would be forced to protect each other. Which is why, on my graduation day, I drove into the sunset with them waving me off and refused to look back for five years. But all the while I was running away, I still worried about them, still hoped my flight would remove a danger I felt but couldn't name. This isn't the first time I've envisioned my mother bound and threatened.

"What do you need me to do?"

"Come with me, Maibelle. Talk to Delong."

"Why?"

"He can help you."

The image twists abruptly. Hands freed and ready, she rises, towers. Now I am the one going down. And my mother holds the weapon.

"I don't want that kind of help."

"Gerard, then. Come to the July opening." Her breath quickens. The game revealed, she's pushing for her goal. I remember how this works from all those years of listening to her sales pitch. The only danger to my mother is in my head. Always has been. "It's the first time he's been here in nearly two years. You could show him your work, at the very least talk to him, for God's sake."

"What's God got to do with it? I haven't been to one of your openings since I got sick all over that Jerry Uelsmann print."

"You were allergic to that horrible man's cigar smoke. It was only a test print, and not a very good one at that."

"What I'm allergic to is gallery openings. Especially ones where you expect me to suck up to your boss."

A long pause. "You don't mean that, Maibelle."

"I never mean what I say, do I?"

"Think about it. That's all I ask."

"I'm going out for my run now, Mother."

I'll admit it. I do get some satisfaction from my mother's taboos. The same satisfaction, I imagine, that Henry got playing pinball all those years, or still gets from his homeless status. That Anna gets from her New Age immersion. Mine seems a minor infraction by comparison, but it's a start. Dr. Gertz was right about one thing. I'd never stopped to consider whether I wanted to be the daughter my mother was assiduously grooming.

That daughter is now running ten miles a week. A drop in mileage from the West Coast, where I used to jog an hour each day along the beach, but enough to help fend off the nightmares. I've gone as long as two weeks clear of dreams when consistently running. The exercise also helps draw out some of those ghosts Dr. Gertz talked about. In a flower on a window ledge, the exhaust from a home-style bakery, a small boy flying a paper plane, I'll see or smell or hear a cue, and for the next two miles I won't notice the catcalls or feel the concrete slamming into my knees. Or think about my mother's invitation to prostrate myself before the reigning tycoon of Art.

This morning's genie is a dancing chicken in front of a Hell's Kitchen dime store. Here amid the throb of salsa and the sizzle of frying plantains, this withered fowl brings me to a full and unexpected stop. I stand gulping air and staring as the bird desultorily pecks at the wire floor of its glass cage. It cocks a leg and lifts its head and, in the space between one uncomprehending blink and the next, evokes an evening more than twenty years old that lasts the rest of my run.

It began in the Chinatown arcade, where Henry routinely took me on days when Mum left me in his charge. Not that I went willingly. The arcade was a long, dingy ell filled with smoke and swear words, the stink of beer and laughter that sounded like machine-gun fire. It was a hangout for bad boys who ditched school and carried switchblades. Henry enjoyed the hoodlum atmosphere almost as much as the games and immediately disappeared into the arcade's depths. That afternoon, like so many others, I stayed with the dancing bird up front.

At one time the chicken machine must have been a popcorn maker—the kind some old-fashioned movie theaters still have in their lobbies, with a red base and butter-colored lights inside a wide glass cage. The popcorn works had been replaced with a trough for seed and water. In the middle of the cage stood the Chinatown chicken, whose particular identity changed over the years but who always had the same mangy feathers, half a tail, and eyes glazed over with a thick white film.

When you dumped in your quarter, electric current ran through the cage's mesh floor. As long as the bird's nervous system still worked, these shocks would send it leaping and crazily flapping its wings. It looked a lot like my sister's dancing in the mid-sixties, and later, after she got into psychedelics and hooked up with her Indian guru, I wondered if she and those chickens didn't have even more in common. But I figured my sister at least had a choice in what happened to her body and mind. The chickens were trapped in the dancing machine until they simply gave out.

That day was so cold I could see my breath in the arcade's open doorway. I was trying to decide whether the chicken, too, felt cold when suddenly, without anyone even putting in a quarter, its wings started twitching, the head bobbing and smashing into the glass. Every part of the poor thing's body seemed to move in a different direction. It looked the way I thought someone would feel whose brain was sliced in half. The crazy moves lasted about a minute, then the bird keeled over. It lay on its side, those white eyes open like tiny silver dollars.

I was still staring at the dead bird when Henry grabbed my elbow, steering me toward home. Mum and Dad were taking us to Little Italy for dinner before the New Year parade, and there was a little skip in Henry's walk as he pulled me along. My brother loved Chinese New Year.

So did all of Chinatown. For days the merchants had been hanging good-luck red and gold in their doorways, displaying altars with candles and incense, fresh flowers, oranges, and fat, round New Year's cakes. Women thronged the grocer's and butcher's shops. Children compared inventories of firecrackers and imitated the lion dancers they would see that night. Ordinarily I would have been just as excited. But I couldn't forget those silver eyes, those crazy moves.

"Hey, what's eating you?" Henry asked.

"The chicken at the arcade. It died. I saw it."

"Cool."

"No! It was horrible!"

"C'mon. You know how many birds bite the dust in Chinatown every day. Just look!"

He was pointing at Wah's Imperial Poultry. That wasn't the same thing at all.

I kept seeing that dead bird's eyes all through dinner and was eager to get home, but by the time my parents had finally finished their espressos the Chinatown crowd was backed up all the way to Broome Street. Walking through it was like pushing into earth that got progressively heavier and more dense. I could hear the clamor of gongs, cymbals, and firecrackers, but for most of the way I saw only the backs of wool coats and boots stamping frozen pavement.

Then, as we crossed Canal Street, the crowd pushed back to make room for the dancing dragon. The huge red, green, and gold head bobbed and dove just inches away from me. The great mouth flapped, seemed to gobble the round heads of lettuce being lowered on strings from balconies above. The rest of the body undulated to the beat of the drums that followed, and somehow the dragon and its bearers, whose legs showed underneath, darted fluidly among the hundreds of firecrackers that were thrown skittering and clapping like pyrotechnic mousetraps, directly into its path.

As soon as the dragon passed, the mob closed in again, this time so tightly that I was lifted off my feet. My arms were sealed against my body. I had no idea who belonged to the broad tweed back into which my face was pressed, and except for the dim, sulphury glow of lanterns overhead, all I could see was black. I cried and yelled for my parents, but no one could hear me above the din. I screamed, but others were screaming, too. Finally everything within me shut down, the engine run too hard. I tried to think of the crush as safety, my grave between bodies a place where I could not get hurt.

It seemed as if I'd been suspended like that for hours when a sizzling sound drowned out the surrounding din. Like bacon frying in my ear at top volume, smelling of cannon fodder. I turned my head, caught a glimpse of pink paper—a pack of sugar candies or a party favor? I wriggled my shoulders and flailed against the surrounding backsides. The little tube rolled against my neck. I shrugged but could not get rid of the thing, and although I yelled again even louder, my voice was swallowed by the column of padding around me.

No one paid any attention until the firecracker exploded.

I was aware of the stink of burning hair before I realized it was my own. By then I'd been passed to my father's arms and the pain was shredding my skull. But the pain didn't blind me to my father's face when he realized what had happened. If anything, it magnified his reaction.

His eyebrows lifted. His cheeks twitched. His skin turned a shade as ghastly pale as that dead bird's eyes. He seemed to be looking straight through me, and as he looked he tightened his grip until I thought he might be trying to squeeze the hurt away, as if it were a bruise.

If I could have signaled past the screaming inside my head, I would have made him understand he wasn't helping. But I couldn't, and we probably would have stood there all night had my mother not snatched me from his arms. The menace in her face made people hustle out of her way, the solid wall parting just in front and reclosing immediately behind us so that I didn't realize until we'd gone several blocks that the rest of my family was with us. Henry hopped alongside to see if there was a hole in my head. Anna whined for Mum to give her the key so she could just go home. And my father, still looking dazed and disoriented, tried to catch up.

We spent the rest of the evening at Gouverneur Hospital's emergency room, where I was treated for a ruptured eardrum. After it was established, to Henry's dismay, that I had not been terminally wounded and would soon recover full hearing in the damaged ear, my mother stopped haranguing the hospital staff and began to curse the associations that organized the parade.

"Celebration, my ass. The whole thing is just a gimmick to pay off the Chinese mafia."

"Yeah?" said Henry. "How?"

She told him those red envelopes people passed to the lion dancers, those heads of lettuce coming down on strings, were all stuffed with hundreds, thousands of dollars' worth of payoffs to the tongs.

"Darling," she asked my father, "what did you say it's called?"

"*Lixi*." Although Dad's color had returned, this was the first he'd spoken in the hour we'd been at the hospital. "Lucky money."

"Extortion's what it is. Every restaurant, every store has to pony up. And they all do, too, good little sheep. So typically Chinese."

"If they don't?" asked Henry.

That stopped Mum momentarily, and she looked to my father for backup.

He took off his glasses and carefully wiped the lenses, then began fiddling with one of the hinges. Back and forth went the stem as he twisted the tiny screw deeper into the barrel.

"Look what happened to Maibelle!" said my mother at last.

Anna sighed and opened her mouth to ask if we were *ever* going home.

"What's Maibelle got to do with the tongs?" asked Henry.

Deeper and deeper went the screw in my father's glasses.

"Joe!" barked my mother. "Will you stop that!"

My father looked up, and for just an instant I saw him as a little boy caught in an act of mischief. His face became impassive. He put his glasses back on and folded his hands in his lap. When at last he spoke, he spoke to me.

"There was a story my amah used to tell at New Year's when I was about your age."

We all waited.

"About a man who was caught by spirits. The man had to entertain them, so he danced and sang . . . juggled balls. Put on costumes and acted out stories."

Henry and Anna fidgeted, annoyed by Dad's lack of timing.

"But he wasn't clever enough to outsmart the spirits, and when he ran out of ways to amuse them, they got angry. They gave him an axe and sent him to the moon."

He stopped to chew on a hangnail and watch a nurse pass by. My mother closed her handbag with a snap.

"The spirits said the man had to cut down the trees. Cinnamon trees, hundreds of them all over the moon. He hacked away. The sound of his axe cutting into the wood was like gunshot."

Mum got up and walked to the nurse's station.

"When the blade hit, sparks flew. But no matter how deep he cut, each time he pulled the axe away, the wood closed right back up."

"So what happened to him?" asked Henry.

My father leaned back, thrust his legs out in front of him.

"I used to ask that question. Every New Year, the firecrackers would remind me . . . You know, she was with us for ten years and I can't remember her name. Something Mei-lin, I think."

"But what about the man in the *story*?"

"Oh, he's still there. Yueh Lao-yeh. The Old Man in the Moon."

"Right," said Anna.

"When Mei-lin told me that, I didn't believe her, either. I always thought somehow the man would be set free . . ." Dad looked up at my mother, returning with the young Chinese doctor who had treated me. "I couldn't understand that he had been condemned."

My mother's eyes widened. Her mouth began to wobble, but before she could speak, the doctor leaned across to inspect the patch on my ear. He gave me a quick hearing test, checked my balance, told us we could leave. Then, after looking around and establishing that at least one of us belonged in the neighborhood, he exclaimed, "*Gonghe facai!*"

Happy New Year. Or, literally, Congratulations, Get Rich.

The rest of the years we lived in Chinatown we had to watch the parade from our balcony. Mum's orders, though she usually managed to have something to do uptown on those nights. Henry routinely disobeyed the edict and went out with Tommy Wah. Anna wasn't interested to begin with, so New Year came to be an occasion I shared alone with my father.

We would sit, freezing, in the dark and spy through the neighbors' windows. In each apartment the doors were covered with scarlet paper for good luck. Visitors tromped in and out with gifts of oranges, tangerines, flowers. And the food! My father could recite every dish: ants climbing trees, Buddha's delight, lion's head, jade beef, drunken chicken, and three treasures. People dropped morsels in each other's mouths like birds feeding their young. Then after feasting, their faces turned pink-orange by the round red paper lanterns strung from their balconies, they'd hurl firecrackers in groups of three to dispel the evil spirits.

For a long while after my father told me this was the firecrackers' mission I wondered if that meant I had spirits in me—perhaps the same spirits that had killed that chicken. But eventually the image of the dead bird faded and I could no longer recall the stink of burning hair.

Then what I remembered most about the night of the Chinatown chicken was the anguish on my father's face as he clutched me among all those strangers.

....

9

Located on Pell Street, around the corner from the pinball arcade, the Ming Yu Tea Parlor was a local landmark well before I was born. Its interior was a deep sea green, the ceiling painted tin, and the tiny octagonal floor tiles an unnatural but permanent gray. A New Year's dragon writhed the length of one wall, glowering at the diners who, one Sunday a month throughout my early childhood, included my family.

My father used to insist that the Ming Yu served the most authentic dim sum outside of Canton. "See, no tourists," he would say, as if this were qualitative proof. "Everybody's Chinese." With his hooded eyes and flat black hair he seemed to fit right in, and if Mum were Chinese, then our family, too, would have validated the Ming Yu's authenticity. As it was, I often felt as though we were crashing my father's party.

The only time Dad ever spoke Chinese was at the Ming Yu. "*Ni hao ma!*" he would greet the waitresses who circulated trays of dumplings around the room, and soon the table would be filled with plates of fragile shrimp balls, fried tofu, hacked duck, and meaty potstickers. Dad's grinning enthusiasm made my mother roll her eyes. "Joe, for God's sake, it's only food!" But for my father it seemed to be more. He devoured as aggressively as he ordered the dishes, and his entreaties to us to "Eat, eat!" were calls for loyalty that my mother and Anna stubbornly resisted. Henry and I tried to pick up the slack, but still, when at last we could hold no more, Dad's brow would tighten. He'd shake his head as if he'd been betrayed. Then he would forge on alone and polish every plate.

We stopped having dim sum when we moved uptown—when we went into exile, as Henry put it at the time—but when I checked the phone book this morning, I discovered the Ming Yu is still there.

This intelligence goaded me. I have to go back to Chinatown; I've known this (whether or not I'd admit it to myself) ever since Tommy's letter. There are answers there, if I can face them. If I can get past the nightmare's silken web, plant my feet on the pavement, and prove to myself that I will not fall or spin or crash. That no one will care if I come or go.

The terror in a nightmare is that it never ends. If I can bring it to a close through real life, I should be able to subvert my terror. Then I might stop focusing on what's holding me back and finally see what I'm aiming for.

The Ming Yu is a safe point of entry. And my father is free for lunch.

• • •

The first thing I notice as we enter is the wall behind the cash register, covered with paper certificates. I know what they mean. They are visible proof of the Ming Yu's many years of generous contributions to the CCBA, An Leung Association, and other tongs, fongs, and fraternities. The restaurant has paid its lucky money and thus is well protected. Nothing bad can happen here.

I can and should relax, I tell myself. My father is with me. I am wide-awake. We will sit and eat and talk as if we are anywhere. Anywhere but Chinatown.

A waitress shows us to a table. My heart gradually stops racing. I wipe my palms on my pant legs and make myself look around.

It's hardly changed. The floor and walls are still dingy, the dragon more tarnished than ever. Smells of garlic and peanut oil seem to coat every surface. The clientele remains Chinese and my father still fits in, though I am struck—and finally brought to attention—by the contrast between his presence today and my memory of him in this place.

I see him with a kind of double vision. His hair, once black, now milky gray. The sedate moonpuffs beneath his eyes, turned as full as stones. The thick black-rimmed reading glasses, on a stay-put strap of his own invention, were never there before. And the fingers, while still perpetually fiddling, knitting, picking at each other, have thickened at the joints. The same flat wedding band he's always worn has become coarse with scratches.

The most telling change today, though, is the absence of any predatory glint as he surveys the first tray of dim sum. "I can't eat so much anymore." To the waitress: "*Guo-tie, bao-zi, shao-mai. Gou. Xie xie.*"

But the next waitress hasn't heard that this small order is enough. She stops to display her tray and, for old times' sake, I point to a plate of shrimp balls and another of potstickers.

My father ruefully watches the center of the table fill with dishes. "I hope you're hungry."

"It's not a crime to leave food, Dad. Especially when it's this cheap."

He smiles. That cheers us both. He helps himself to a steamed bao. I wonder if he shares my disorientation at being back here, just the two of us, if he has any notion why I asked him. He closes his eyes and gobbles the bun, smacking his lips at the sweet pork filling.

I pick up my chopsticks and roll them between my fingers. All those dim sum lunches and I've never learned the proper way to use these things. My father tried to teach us when we were young, but only Henry got the knack. The rest of us learned to make do by balancing and skewering, but that's like hunt-and-peck versus touch typing. One more symptom that set us apart.

My father's fingers, though blunted from years of nail biting, become long and graceful, quick as talons as he swoops in on a fragile rice dumpling.

"Dad?"

"Mm?"

"Remember the night the firecracker landed on my shoulder?"

He studies the array of choices before him.

"You remember the story you told at the emergency room? About the man who chopped trees on the moon?"

"I don't remember any stories. That was an awful night."

"You talked about being condemned. What did you mean?"

"Probably having trouble with a new idea." He turns his head, does something with his mouth. A clicking noise. I realize he's adjusting his dentures. I didn't know he had dentures, and it gives me a mild shock, on top of the other changes.

But when he looks back, his eyes are piercing. "You still want to know about China?"

"I—" The dumpling at the end of my sticks falls back into its plate, splashing oil across the tablecloth. "Sure, I guess so."

He speaks as if we're arguing. "The war was a helluva mess, I tell you."

And with that he takes charge, his volume climbing, talking at me, around me. "I wanted to go back, you know, when the Japanese invaded. So I persuaded a history professor of mine at Columbia to lend me his Rollei, teach me to use it. He introduced me to a guy at the U.S. Information Agency who thought it could be useful to have someone with a foot on both sides. They didn't want to own me, so I went out freelance at first. *Life* and the news services. You know all that."

I feel as if he's pushed into high gear and my mind refuses to shift along. "I know about *Life*."

"There was a ready market, Maibelle. I needed the money. The work got me back to China, and I had a steady hand. You have a steady hand in a battle zone, you make good pictures. It takes nerve and ignorance, not talent."

Something in his delivery makes that last statement feel like a spanking. This is not what I bargained for.

"Shouldn't you be having this out with Mum?"

He blinks. His face softens. "Just listen. In '48 when USIA finally gave me a full position, I lived in a basement in Peiping. Rats the size of—" He scans the restaurant and points to the dragon's tongue, a foot-long expanse of scarlet satin. "They had me in the bloody KMT command center. I spent half my time taking family portraits at fifteen-course banquets and goddamn lawn parties. Other half shooting beggars and opium addicts they claimed were communist agitators."

"Is that why you quit?"

He lights a cigarette, takes a couple of deep drags, and speaks more quietly but no less intensely. "Photographs are like mirrors. They can always be manipulated and distorted, no two people use them the same way. In the end, I might as well have been pulling the trigger."

He stares at me, waiting as if he's asked a question. He still hasn't answered mine.

"What happened, Dad?"

"That job of yours for the catalog. That's safe. Honest. There's nothing wrong with safety."

"Nothing a lobotomy wouldn't cure."

I don't mean to be funny, it just comes out, but a smile begins somewhere in the vicinity of his chin and lifts up and up until his face beams. He throws his head back with a loud guffaw. Chinese laughter, it stops as abruptly as it started, and disintegrates into a retching cough. He catches his breath and frowns. I am crying for no reason.

"You ask what happened. I stopped caring. Not just about photographs, but what was in front of the camera. I didn't want to see it anymore. Only push it away." Dad hands me a handkerchief. "I'm not glad that happened to me, Maibelle. I would hate the same thing to happen to you. Please. Find your own way. Your eyes. Your heart. Let them guide you."

"Why? Why did you push it away?"

He shakes his head and closes his eyes. I think of the images I've seen. How many more there must have been, more that he destroyed. All with that same passionate irony?

"What do you mean, you might as well have pulled the trigger?"

"I mean what I said."

I empty the cold tea from our cups into the ashtray and pour in new. My hand wobbles.

"Mum thinks we're the same."

"Well, we're not. We all begin differently. We make different choices, and the only choices that matter are the ones we make alone. You know?"

He's made choices alone. To abandon his career. To destroy his work. To vandalize public property for the sake of his private secrets. Not only didn't he want to see that world anymore, he didn't want anyone to. Including me.

I slide the wet handkerchief across the table. A waitress counts our dishes, her bony shoulders carving narrow shelves beneath her nylon blouse. Pockmarks from some ancient sickness are written in her skin. She loses count, starts over. In the old days Dad always complimented the waitress, told how much he enjoyed the food, and she in turn laughed. "Regular customer!" Now, appearances aside, we are both strangers here and this woman seems incapable of laughter.

When she leaves, my father pulls a black leather pouch from his jacket, places it in front of me. The size of a small Bible, it is covered with years of surface scrapes and discoloration. A metal zipper runs its length.

"Open."

I am suspicious of his motives, but as I pick up the pouch, feel its compact weight, my arm jerks with the knowledge of its contents.

"Go on."

My mother would have grabbed it by now, ripped open the zipper, and raised the prize with a shout. I am too confused.

"Did Mum put you up to this?"

He doesn't answer, but I can tell from the brightness in his eyes, the stillness of his fingers just inches away, that this is between us.

I open the pouch slowly, painstakingly, not as a show of gratitude, but because my skin is jumping. The zipper slides back, a mouthful of teeth smiling wider, wider, until I hold in my palm a small, nearly weightless rectangle of aluminum and magnesium, black grain leather surrounding a circle of glass. I balance the machine on my fingertips and imagine, reflected in its lens, the scenes it has witnessed and recorded.

"Mum said you destroyed all your cameras."

Dad pretends not to have noticed the crack in my voice as he carefully chooses his next words. "No one who has ever been a photographer could destroy a Leica."

"You kept it a secret all these years."

"You could call it that if you want to. Shall we go?"

"Dad—" I put my hand out.

"I hope it helps, Maibelle. That's all I'm trying to do."

Outside the restaurant, I kiss my father as fiercely as he hugs me. But he refuses to stay and walk. He wouldn't mind taking a look around the old neighborhood, my God it's been years since he was last here, but Mum will be home from the gallery soon and he promised to do some shopping for her. Maybe another day.

Last chance, I think, as he musses my hair. We could ride together as far as the Village and I'd be back on solid ground.

He touches the leather pouch in my hand.

"I loaded it for you."

Before I can answer he gives me a light wave and steps into the current of bodies flowing north.

It's my own paranoia, I tell myself firmly, as the street starts closing in. The immediate roar of voices in Dad's wake, the laughter, car horns, the blank heat and squeeze of oncoming bodies—the mortal stares of those hanging ducks in the shop across the street—windows above, with their shades up and down, like blinking lids. These details are lifted from the way it used to be; the fact that it's the same means nothing. Nightmares may rise to suffocate dreamers, but I'm not dreaming now.

I will myself to breathe, to feel my feet planted flat on the sidewalk, to steady the buildings against that white, hot sky. I plunge my hand into my pocket, but instead of one magical house key that would make everything all right, I come up with the Leica.

Even if it doesn't seem like it, everything has changed; whatever happened to cause the instinctual terror I feel toward this place happened—or was imagined—a long time ago. My father was right, I need to do this alone. Give the past a good kick in the pants and prove to myself it's over. I remove the camera from its case and stuff it back into my pocket as I walk. I wipe the sweat from my eyes. And focus on the changes.

Modern buildings are fronted in marble now. Restaurant signs are bigger, flashier, everything else more cramped. Merchandise and produce sprawl onto the sidewalks, people throng the streets. Hong Kong music blares from digitized sound systems, and the old dancing chicken arcade is now lit up like a carnival. It roars with video-game punches and strikes. No bird. No cage.

It's all different, I tell myself. That souvenir shop sign, "Tourists welcome," means you now.

Still, I can't shake the feeling that I'm being watched. Like a child playing blindman's buff, I keep hearing my invisible observers calling, "Warmer, warmer. Cooler. Hot!" But unlike the game, I fear that if I reached my goal, stretched out my hands, and touched what ails me, I would be boiled alive.

I am only warm.

The bricks of our old building have darkened, the green and red paint on the woodwork cracked. Scarlet cloth covers the window of Dad's old workshop and an inside wall halves the window of the bedroom I used to share with Anna.

I step into an empty doorway directly across the street. It must be a typical Chinese home now. Without Mum to draw the dividing line, it must fit right in. A small stone Buddha sits on the ledge of the balcony.

The only choices that matter, he said, are the ones we make alone. My choice as a child was to live out on that balcony. I could set my watch by the appearance of old bachelor Wen, who spent warm mornings sitting in his undershirt and rolled-up pants on the stoop in front of his building, by the arrival of the two ancient Hom sisters at Mr. Hu's grocery across the street. The sisters wore dull padded jackets and pants that hung slack in the seat and walked in painful, measured steps on tiny crippled feet. They would buy their vegetables, then come across to Wah's Imperial Poultry downstairs. I'd listen to the squall of throats being slit, the slapping of Mrs. Wah's galoshes as the Homs selected their birds. I also kept watch for the babies dressed like pastel flowers, whose mothers took them to the Golden Palace Bakery across the street. They'd come out with their little mouths sunk deep into glistening sesame balls or moon cakes. Except for special banquets, the mothers and children never went into the Hop Li Association five doors down or the Chinese Six Companies on the corner. Those private clubs were reserved for the men whom I watched through the windows of smoke-filled rooms playing games or holding very serious-looking meetings. My father said the family associations were like community centers. My mother called them the Chinese mafia.

Either way, they're practically all that remains of my old vista. The bean curd factory and bakery are gone. Mr. Hu's grocery is now a seafood restaurant, and the storefront that used to be Imperial Poultry is now subdivided into a sidewalk newsstand, souvenir shop, and back room vegetable vendor. There is no space for bachelors to sit in the sun, the women with bound feet have disappeared, and this passing baby is munching a Hostess Ding-Dong.

Red lacquer lanterns now hover in the alcoves of my balcony. Mustard chrysanthemums bloom in place of Mum's Alpine hybrids. Aside from the Buddha, no one looks down on me.

I join the crowd flowing toward Chatham Square. One more stop and I can leave. I can tell Tommy—what? That I'll accept his challenge because it no longer poses a threat? Or turn him down for the same reason? I finger the Leica concealed in my pocket. He is not asking me to make salable art or disposable product shots. Not really photojournalism, either, though that's closer. History. It's about recording history. Documenting people in their places before they change. Or leave. Or die. He wants me to help him preserve time, make a bridge between past and future. Isn't that what I want, too?

As I approach the bottom of Mott Street, the crowds let up. Beyond the immediate squeeze of buildings Chatham Square opens like a vast arena, filled above with light and space, below with the thunder of buses and cars dodging potholes. On the other side of the square, streets point like spokes of a wheel to a patchwork of tall modern buildings and disintegrating tenements. It isn't likely that my destination remains or, if it does, is recognizable, but I have to look to see. Then I'll decide what to tell Tommy.

A slick air-conditioned tour bus with "National Adventures" emblazoned on its side pulls up to the curb, blocking my way. Though the windows are tinted, I know before the first of the passengers step down exactly what they will look like. Big people with puffy middles and, in spite of the air-conditioning, moist reddish faces. They'll wear travel-ready polyester and carry Instamatics, take turns snapping pictures of each other in front of the pagoda phone booth, then mosey up Mott Street in search of fortune cookies and chop suey. When they fail to find either, they'll settle for a cheongsam for the little woman to squeeze into at the next BOE costume party. I know these people from my childhood when the buses came like clockwork every Saturday and Sunday. I know them from working the cross-country flights that bring them from their homes in the West and Midwest to the buses that drive them to Chinatown. But I also know them from Wisconsin, where they seemed neither silly nor predatory but kind and honest and good-humored. They could be Johnny Madison's family. What he, in spite of himself, might have grown up to become.

Henry used to say our grandparents, too, would have seemed ridiculous if they'd ever come to Chinatown. That almost makes me glad they never did. As a child I instinctively disliked these invaders and cast myself above them. My first allegiance was to my home. If I didn't exactly belong, I thought, at least I was no outsider.

Today's passengers duck their heads as they get off the bus. The women point, wave to each other, talk nonstop. They pour onto the sidewalk and turn in circles oohing and aahing at the Chinese signs, the ornate rooflines, and of course, the phone booth. They whip off their lens caps and begin pointing, arranging wives and buddies, husbands and sisters. Eighty people, maybe more, press into the corner where I was foolish enough to get trapped.

"Helen! Yoo-hoo. Look here now, Harold."

These people are unschooled in crowd behavior. Never been on a rush-hour subway or stood in Times Square on New Year's Eve. Or been caught in a mob in Chinatown. When I push, they close in tighter. When I catch their attention, they grin. When I speak up, they say, "Howdy," and wonder how they failed to notice me in the group before.

Slowly, and with the greatest effort, I inch between their soft, damp arms and backs, have almost reached the bus when I hear chanting from beyond the phone booth. The words aren't clear at first, but they have the rhythm of protest. Ta-dum, ta-dum, ta-dum, ta-dum. Dum-ta, dum-ta, dum-ta, Da.

I ease along the side of the bus and step around the back fender. I am standing in the street, but the traffic has stopped to watch the commotion.

"Chinese people are humans too! Chinatown is not a zoo!"

Some ten men and women dressed in T-shirts and jeans bear placards with slogans such as "Tourism Promotes Racism" and "Invest in the Future, Not Fortune Cookies." About half the size of the tourists, both in height and in weight, they make up for any lack of scale by the noise they are making.

"You hate us in your neighborhoods! We hate you in ours! Tourists go home! Tourists go home!"

Their black hair gleams in the sun. Their mouths open and close over even white teeth as they string their chants on a continuous loop. Shoulder-to-shoulder they press the astonished tourists back toward the bus as car horns blare around us.

"Arnold, can't you do something?" shouts one of the passengers to her husband.

Do something. I feel as if I've forgotten a critical detail, a burner I've left on in my apartment, something I'm supposed to be doing. As if any second they'll all look my way and I'll realize I am naked. I can't move.

The tourists are clambering back into the bus when a woman steps from the center of the advancing column and screams, "You come gawk at us!"

She has thick bangs that stop just short of charcoal eyes. Her hair, coiled on top of her head, is held with an elaborate lacquered comb. She is as beautiful as I remember the Butterflies.

"You think Chinese are freaks?" She leaps forward and jabs her finger at a man with a Marine cut and red and orange Hawaiian shirt beside whom she does, in fact, look like a dwarf. "Well, how do you feel now!"

Arms rise. Metal glints in their hands. I feel the pavement slide beneath me as the tourists shriek.

"They've got guns!"

The throb of the bus's engine rises like the beating of a whale's heart, and I instinctively lean into it, warm air drawing me down and back against the wall of steel. I trip. My hands grab, close, find a dark space low to the ground. I crouch with my head pulled in, seeing nothing.

The moments stretch, immeasurable, thick with the silence of the engine's din. My eyes open. The asphalt glistens with summer heat. The tread in the bus tires travels in waves. Slowly, slowly, I remember what I'm supposed to be doing.

My fingers locate their target and begin the long return journey back through what seems a black, heavy ocean.

I am supposed to see.

But when I finally lift my eyes, I am blinded by scalding white light. Around me, the tourists not yet back on the bus tip sideways. Moans erupt. Hands fly to faces. I watch red and blue and yellow, a screen of sizzling dots.

"Again!" the beautiful woman cries, and again the world turns white.

I sense rather than see the last of the tourists escape into the bus, just as I sense the concealed faces watching from overhead windows and the deadly blur of traffic inches from my toes. I hold my circle of glass to my face as if it could protect me and dash across the path of light, directly in front of the beautiful woman, into the shade of the phone booth.

"Stop!"

A cluster of elderly merchants trotting down Mott Street waves past me. They all yell at once.

"Pay no attention! You come see. Okay tourist. Good deals for you."

The crackle of flashbulbs eases. The chant shifts.

"Uncle Tom! Uncle Tom!"

The merchants run between the protesters and the bus, laughing too loudly and hopping like wind-up toys. The doors of the bus have been pulled closed, turning the passengers to ghosts behind their protective glass.

I realize I've stopped breathing as a two-hundred-pound linebacker in a driver's cap comes around the front of the bus with a carton of take-out food in one hand and a walkie-talkie in the other.

"You kids want the cops, you got 'em."

The protesters hesitate, exchanging glances, then resume their chant.

"Marge, you there?" the driver shouts into his mouthpiece. "I got a problem down here in Chinatown."

They grudgingly form a gantlet through which the tourists may pass. The driver signs off but the merchants keep shouting, wheedling, assuring the passengers of bargains they cannot refuse, and in a few minutes the Middle Americans are back on schedule, only mildly disturbed and maybe now amused by the cluster of Chinese-American Yippies who trail them with occasional flash shots to remind them why they are here.

I follow stupidly, using only my eyes, as the parade moves back up Mott Street.

Suddenly one of the protesters, a man with a ponytail, spins around barking like a seal. The roundness of his face, like a plate, registers. I release the shutter.

"Hah! This one's got some nerve! Think we're putting on a good show, huh? Come to the Chinatown zoo, lady?" He leaps toward me.

I freeze. My hands tighten around my father's Leica, but that's the cause, not the way out this time.

The long-haired man dances close, peering at me through hands shaped like binoculars. The others form a tight circle around us, raise their cameras, taunt and jeer. The flash thunders, splinters into a thousand shards of light.

I charge my assailants, push through and run without looking across six lanes of wailing traffic. Three blocks, four. I begin to slow down. They're not coming.

At the far end of Catherine Street I finally reach the ruins of my safe haven.

The windows of Lao Li's old store have been painted blind white, their frames splintered and chipped. From the upper floors come the drone of heavy machinery, a competing hum of women's voices. The noodle shop next door is now a "Unisex Hairstylist" with a magazine stand out front. But the worst is the pillar—someone has taken a hatchet, decapitated the birds, slashed the serpentine forms, and literally gouged out the figures' faces, then smeared what was left with red, blue, and white graffiti.

As I lay my hands on the butchered forms, my fingertips turn to ice.

"*Lou fan.*"

A grunt, forced laughter. It means barbarian.

From the corner of my eye I see two boys with chiseled faces leaning into the Unisex storefront. They leer at me and shove fingers through the spikes of their hair. They spit.

I turn quickly, raising the Leica, shoot them once, twice, three times dead on, and start running. Keep running. All the way uptown.

....

10

I am watering my mother's flowers, clipping the dead leaves, wiping soot from the balcony furniture. My brother has left his *Mad* magazines on the table, and I pick one up, thumb through it without focusing. I can't see why Henry thinks Alfred E. Neuman is funny. Nothing seems funny to me in this heat. The sky pulses and glows as if the whole world has a fever.

But as I put the magazine down, the weather changes. A wind comes up, first moaning, then roaring, scalding as the sky. My feet peel upward and I grab a chair, but the wicker is too light. The twisted air pulls me onto the railing, where I perch like a high-wire artist.

I look down on a street that's vacant except for Lao Li, running but too far away and fading. Heat shoots from the pavement, pounding upward with the noise of sirens. The city falls back, scorched white, and still the sky keeps pulling, knifing me when I look up. I reach to shield my eyes.

A cool hand I can only feel, not see, presses back. Quiet.

Press, release. Press, release. It covers my eyes, strokes my face. Smooth skin scented with pine, meadow grass, and leather.

"Maibelle. You'll get heatstroke sleeping out here."

He lifts me in his arms and carries me up. Farther, away from the sky.

The television was on when I woke from this dream. The lights, too, though that was normal. I'd been watching television, fell asleep fully clothed. Normal to leave things burning. But the television is not normal.

Outside, a siren screams. I count to ten before it passes.

I was watching *The Tonight Show* on Channel 4 when I fell asleep. Now it's after three. Of course, the program would be different. A nature show about children in Tibet. But the thing is, it's on Channel 7. And the sound is off.

The listings are right here. *Tonight* 4, Tibet 7. Not a switch that can happen by itself.

Another siren breaks the night.

Marge. This is her kind of show. Something she'd want me to see. Boys no more than four years old in saffron monk's robes. Himalayan peaks shrouded in clouds.

It's for your own good.

The voice is in my head. I know that, but it doesn't belong to me. Gravelly, harsh, and loving at the same time. I want to believe it's her talking to me. That her hand turned the knob. I don't mind believing in ghosts. Quite the opposite.

But I don't believe, not enough to stop the other possibility that crouches in the next room. No creaking floorboards. No muffled breathing. I left the lights on in there, too, and no unfamiliar shadows cross the doorway.

See for yourself.

I see them, all right. They followed me home and waited for their chance. Then through the old lady's yard. Leering. Sneering. Spitting in the garden. And up the fire escape.

I grab the heavy flashlight I keep beside my bed and slide along the wall. At the threshold I stop and listen to the fading sirens. Four feet away in the shadows they run their thick practiced hands through the spikes of their hair . . .

I step around the corner quickly, brandishing my weapon.

Marge's children blink back at me. An empty sofa. Equipment and gizmos. Relentless overhead light. The explosion of my own breath exhausts me.

I touch the locket at my throat and imagine Johnny beside me, taking my hand, walking me forward. I count to twenty while opening the kitchen, the bathroom, the front closet, all empty. Check behind the backdrop paper, through the curtains. I make sure the dead bolt is turned on the door and, securely awake now, turn out the light.

Only when there is no chance of sleep can I take comfort from the dark.

I lift the window and straddle the ledge. No one. Marge is silent now, the television only a whisper beyond the wall. I must have changed it myself.

I just don't remember.

The lights of Greenwich Avenue burn through the night, but the street is as empty as in my dream. Not a sound except the renewed eruption of sirens.

• • •

"I'll do it."

The line crackled slightly. "Maibelle?"

"I can meet you this morning if you want."

"I'll be at the seniors' center on Bayard Street at ten."

"Fine."

More static. "This only works if we're partners, Maibelle."

"I don't expect you to pay me."

"Partners means this isn't just a favor you're doing me."

"Don't worry."

Two hours later he was standing on the corner of Bayard and Elizabeth with a blue loose-leaf notebook under one arm and an audio pack slung over the other. How smooth he looked. His skin, his hair, the spotless slope of his white shirt. No wrinkles, no flaws, no tortured curls or stray threads. No spike-haired companions or concealed flashbulbs. His seamlessness at once reassured me and put me on guard.

I carried two camera bags but he made no attempt to relieve me of these as he touched my arm in greeting.

"You don't have to stick with me."

I mimicked astonishment. "You're not letting me loose!"

He smiled. "Partners."

"And cover credit, of course."

"Of course." He offered his hand to shake on the deal. It felt solid, smooth as the rest of him, hairless.

I scanned for warning signals. Skidding heartbeat, ringing ears, the sweats. Nothing. The sidewalk stayed decisively beneath my feet. The sky burned blue, not white. The weekday morning traffic was light and shopkeepers nodded politely as we passed. I glanced at Tommy as he addressed them by name. Maybe I needed an escort, after all. If it worked, what was wrong with that?

If it worked, I would owe him dearly.

The senior citizen center used to be the five-and-ten where I bought my paper dolls. The outside has since been whitewashed and a red and gold sign hangs overhead. A screen painted with the stone mountains of Guilin shields the window, and fluorescent lights stripe the ceiling. As soon as we stepped into the hallway I heard the familiar shuffle of tiles, Chinese voices, hacking coughs of lifetime smokers.

"They'll see you as an outsider," he said. "They might give you white eyes at first."

"White eyes?"

"Turn up the whites to ignore you."

"Wonderful."

"Take it easy. After a while some of them might remember you. The rest will get used to you. I wouldn't try to photograph them until they do, though. Even the ones who've been here for decades, a lot still worry about deportation. They don't trust cameras."

"Or redheads."

He cupped his hand over my shoulder and squeezed. "They're suspicious of what they don't know. Human nature."

"Tai." The name was beginning to seem natural.

He took his hand away. "It's all right."

We entered a large open room filled with card tables, soft pop music, and some fifty players intent on the ivory before them. Old palms swam through the tiles, cut circles and swirls. They might have been choreographed.

A man at the closest table squinted at me. He had a wispy goatee and balloons of skin beneath his eyes. He stared for a second, then waggled his fingers low and wild to get his partners' attention, jabbed the air in my direction until everybody looked up.

I nudged Tommy. "White eyes?"

He leaned over and spoke to the man in Chinese, and a few seconds later the old face fanned wide open. The man grabbed my hand and rubbed it between his shrunken palms.

"Miss Chung! Miss Chung! You remember me, yes? Grocer Hu?" He thumped his chest. "You go 'way, all grown-up, come back a beautiful lady."

The warmth of his grip, his smile, his words worked together. My face went hot and I had to fight a sudden impulse of tears.

Tommy folded his arms across his chest. "Told you you'd meet some old friends."

I took a deep breath, squeezed Grocer Hu's hand, and leaned down to meet his mah-jongg partners. Uncle Fah-chi, a rotund figure with thick, distorting glasses and a smile like a sideways question mark, used to manage the Long Ho Restaurant on Mulberry Street, but maybe I never knew him because of his hours, two P.M. to four A.M. most nights. I wouldn't remember Auntie Mee and Auntie Soong because they had come to Chinatown only in the past ten years. "Not old-timers like you and me!" Hu cried, which set off another gale of Chinese laughter like a mad fluttering of wings.

"I do believe you're in love," Tommy whispered as we moved on.

"I didn't think he knew I existed."

"Everybody knew about you. You had the best view in Chinatown."

"I did, didn't I?" I was smiling. I was an old-timer. The notion was as exhilarating as it was absurd. All over the room heads started to wag, wizened mouths broke into grins, and black eyes snapped with curiosity. Not a single pair of white eyes.

"Maibelle, this is David Ling."

I turned and came face-to-face with the ponytailed man I'd last seen barking like a seal. His smile curled into a bemused frown. He knew me but couldn't place where. I considered not telling him, but the flush of Hu's recognition still held me in its protective bubble.

"The bus protest."

"Oh, no. You're the lunatic who ran across six lanes of traffic."

"Trying to get away from you and your welcome wagon."

"You're lucky you weren't killed."

"So are you."

"Mind filling me in?" asked Tommy.

"That bus protest last week. We confused her with the tourists—I'm afraid we came on a little too strong."

I couldn't read the dimple that appeared in Tommy's cheek, but all he said was, "Sounds like an apology is in order. And an introduction. Maibelle was living on Mott Street when you were still protesting diaper changes back in Taiwan."

We shook hands cautiously.

"Please forgive me. Sometimes political activism leads to personal stupidity."

I smiled in spite of myself. Stupidity is such a relative term; what would he think if I told him mine was caused by probable insanity?

Instead, I calmly—even sedately—answered, "No face lost."

Tommy explained that David was director of the seniors' center. It seemed that, while he objected to the tourists taking pictures of Chinatown, David fully endorsed Tommy's project. Now, as he strode across the room waving and patting backs like a politician shilling for votes, he subtly directed me toward the faces that were worth photographing.

This one, he said, was a card shark in Canton before the war, that one sold tires to the Japanese. This man with the scar across his scalp was shot by the Red Army and left for dead in a ditch. That woman with the glass eye was raped and watched her husband being beheaded by the Japanese in Nanking. Most of the men had spent their American lives working fourteen-hour shifts in laundries or restaurants. Some had been caught and sent back to China three or four times.

As David talked I had the odd, unsettling feeling that I was looking at surviving shadows of my father's photographs. These people had lived the scenes he witnessed. Some may have been his actual subjects. He claimed to know no one in Chinatown, certainly had never spoken of this common past. If it weren't for my college professor—and indirectly for Mum urging me to study photography—I would never have made this connection. Yet it was my father who, by giving me his camera and urging me to use it, had set me up for this moment and the sense of responsibility that swept over me now. A responsibility quite different from the one my mother had been hammering into me for years, this had nothing at all to do with Art, and I was utterly unprepared to fulfill it.

"These people have been through hell," said David. "But they feel safe here. This—a game of mah-jongg with friends—is their reward."

Across the room, Tommy sat next to a lady wearing a black turtleneck and glossy black wig. He laid out his tape recorder and notebook.

"Is it wise to make them relive the past?" I asked David.

"They don't forget because they want to, but because they're afraid to remember. Tai thinks recording their stories can help them get over the fear. Break Chinatown's code of silence."

"You agree?"

David smiled to a humpbacked man in a plaid beret. "Not sure. But the stories are too important to lose. For all of us."

I wandered among the players for nearly an hour before they lost interest in me. More than once I felt my body physically pulling for the exit, but Tommy or David would catch me with an encouraging glance. I finally extracted the Leica from my pocket and began to focus.

My first subject was the woman with the glass eye. I couldn't help it. If what David had said was true, she'd survived unspeakable horrors. She could conceivably have been the young wife of that headless body in my father's photograph. But would I know it to see her now? The glass eye looked at once straight ahead and out to the side—like the moon on a clear night following its watcher without ever moving. Her other eye pounced and darted from players to tiles. Lacquer birds dangled from her ears, red chopsticks pierced the knot of stark white hair at the nape of her neck. Her pink Mets sweatshirt covered her knees.

She couldn't have been taller than five feet or weighed more than eighty pounds, and though I didn't understand a word she said, I could see she ran a wicked game of mah-jongg. She played for over an hour winning virtually every hand until a mountain of chips sealed the space before her, and the others at the table were begging to switch to fan-tan. At which point she gave me exactly what I only that moment realized I'd been waiting for—a grin of exuberant, toothless triumph. Survivor as victor. Then she hoisted herself with a great deal of effort and evident pain onto two bamboo canes. Her winnings tucked inside her sweatshirt, she left her partners to their cards.

I moved on to two deaf couples who managed to simultaneously play, chain-smoke, and talk with their hands. My shot came when one of the husbands told a joke that annoyed his wife. I caught him weeping with laughter, hands shaping a swan, while she furiously sliced the air, her manicured fingers joined into a sword.

The more subjects I found, the more seemed to appear and the less I consciously thought about what I was doing. A man in a brown felt coat at least thirty years out of style hummed along with the golden canary he kept in a cage on the floor. His friend with a crewcut and skin like a walnut shell, one jet-black eye and one amber—the same colors as his teeth—broke spontaneously into a Hank Williams tune. Behind him and completely oblivious to his beat, a man and a woman in matching baby-blue sweat suits slowly, hypnotically, practiced t'ai chi. The Leica caught them all.

Finally I returned to the first table to take Lao Hu's portrait. The two aunties had joined a crew of ladies fixing tea in the kitchen, but Hu and Fah-chi were only too happy to pose for me. They each gripped the edge of the table and sat up straight, stared at the camera, and stretched their lips back until their gums showed. With that landscape screen directly behind them, their identical white shirts and pens in their pockets, with Fah-chi goggled-eyed through those Coke-bottle glasses, they looked like perfect caricatures of old Chinese power brokers. I lowered the camera, wanting a more accurate way to frame them.

Fah-chi leaned forward and stared at me so hard his eyebrows touched together. I smiled back and shot. Shot again as the old man bored through the lens. A steady hand, my father said. That's all it took. But my hand, inevitably, was shaking.

Whatever he was looking at or for, I told myself, I mustn't take it as an affront. The day had been a success. I'd passed inspection. I'd kept my head, even enjoyed myself. No villains. No demons. Now Tommy, who had spent the past half hour interviewing the Hank Williams fan, was striding across the room. In a minute or two we'd be gone.

"I know!" The tiles leapt as Fah-chi's hand slammed the table. "You are Li's girl! Mei-bi Chung, yes? His little Jade Maiden."

I glanced at Tommy, who stood just outside our circle. He folded his arms.

"You were friends?" I asked Fah-chi cautiously.

"Same fong. Same barber. I hear a lot about you for some time. I hear he taught you to write Chinese."

"No." I waved my hand to force down the blush I again felt stinging my cheeks. "No. He tried but I wasn't a very good student."

"You are like a daughter to him."

I shook my head. "I wasn't a very good daughter, either."

"Ah, you show Chinese humility. Li would be proud of you."

But I wasn't being humble at all. I was simply telling the truth.

A few minutes later I left Tommy on the corner of Canal Street with an honest hug. The morning had been a success, after all. The whole way home I couldn't stop thinking about Lao Li.

• • •

I'd ignored my father's prohibition, of course. Lao Li's tacit offer of stories and friendship had the power of a spell. In no time I was visiting once or twice a week.

Always he greeted me with a cup of tea and a cookie from the pink box under his desk. He asked after my family's health, then had me select an object in his shop. Every one of Li's artifacts, it seemed, had a mystical tale to go with it. The falling-apart rickshaw, for example, had belonged to a leper who was transformed into a monkey after helping the Emperor Yung Yen's third son escape from an evil warlord. When I asked if the leper really preferred to be a monkey, Mr. Li answered, "Monkeys very powerful. They keep away evil spirits." As if the leper could not have asked for a better fate.

A set of porcelain wine cups prompted a story of scholar-poets gathered by a country stream to drink themselves into a state of grace and compose by the light of the moon. From the ornamental dragons on an opium pipe came a tale of men enslaved by demons. And when Li took me into the river gorges of a landscape scroll, I heard the dying sighs of coolies, the cries of drowning men. The China Lao Li taught me to fear and love was a world where magic and real life mingled without warning.

One day he gave me a set of miniature masks in the form of finger puppets. Made of clay, they were smooth and cool as eggshell, the painted surface chalky.

"This story is called Pearl-sewn Shirt."

On one forefinger he placed the mask of a beautiful young woman, pink as a baby with curving red mouth and gentle, lifting eyes. On the other he placed a young merchant's face, white with darkened eyes and a serious half-smile. Lao Li danced the man and woman together, accompanying them with the high-pitched wail of Chinese opera: quick, teasing movements and song, slowing to the low swoon of courtship, then picking up to the measured beat of marriage.

"Great joy. Pure bliss. Young bride demonstrate her love by sewing for husband a shirt of pearls. Alas, husband must soon go away to sell his silks and jewels." The bride's mask plucks a white embroidered cloth. "But as reminder of fidelity, wife will keep that pearl-sewn shirt and show her face to no man until beloved returns.

"Days pour into months, months into years. Neighbors begin to whisper that young wife has been abandoned, husband killed. But one day young wife peek around compound wall. Beloved returns!" A new man's mask, all white with swooping eyes and bloodred lips, swaggers to and fro.

"No! No! This is not husband but no-name silver trader. She pull away but too late. He has seen her great beauty and cannot rest." An orange puppet quivers to a high note. "New man find town matchmaker! She bewitches our lady with stories of love and pleasure. Young wife beg her new friend stay, talk late. Deep in night, matchmaker secretly push this silver trader into our lady's bed." The white and pink masks roll together. "Such rapture! Such passion!"

(Lao Li, his delight in the story all over his face, sneaks a peek at me to see if I am following. I grin like an idiot child.)

"But young trader, too, must leave. His mistress feel such sorrow, she give him that pearl-sewn shirt!" The masks part and shift again.

"Far away, two men cross path, drink wine, and talk. The night grow late. A warm wind blows, and one man loosen his coat." Two white masks, head-to-head, the cloth suspended between them. "Husband say nothing, but he know now she has betrayed their love. He sells our lady as concubine to magistrate in faraway province." A large mask painted in blue and green twitches on the tip of Li's thumb. The wife's song arches to a sharp scream, then silence as her mask folds beneath a new lord.

"When silver trader return in one year, he learn this news of his beloved. He falls ill. Robbers steal his silver. This trader will die here, but husband send for doctor, lend this man money if he will leave town, never return. Someday die far away."

With a final grieving moan, the white masks part and lower.

I clapped for the singer and his puppets, for the compliment Li had paid me by not leaving out the sexy part. It was a sad and funny story, a lot like Lao Li. Old and young at the same time. Real and unreal.

But Li paid no attention. He sank back in his chair, eyes gone hollow. His hands, so alive just moments before, lay motionless among the painted masks.

They looked cold, those hands. I wanted to reach out and warm them with mine. I wanted to say something bright and cheery, to bring back his smile.

"Thank you for the story, Lao Li," I whispered. "I'm sorry it ended sadly."

I slid from my chair without making a sound.

"Wait." He pushed himself up, opened the cabinet beside his desk. Behind the inlaid door were stacked some twenty drawers. Li stood for a moment, surveying, reminding me of my father the one time I'd gone along to visit our safe-deposit box. Dad had disappointed me by unveiling not pirate's gold or ruby slippers, but useless, unintelligible documents.

Li opened a long middle drawer and pulled out a parcel of pale green silk tied with a black cord. His hands shook as he began to unwrap it, and I could practically see the tiny pearls glistening, bringing the story to life.

Unfortunately what emerged was even more ordinary than documents. The closest thing to pearls were the seven bone buttons that ran from the neck to the crotch. Instead of snowy silk, the fabric was a scratchy blue wool, the label Sears, Roebuck and Co.

"My pearl-sewn shirt."

As quickly as it had fallen over him, Lao Li's sadness gave way to annoyance.

"You see only underwear!" He picked up the garment and shook it for me to see that, yes, it really was a union suit. "That is no underwear. That gift of love."

But I couldn't help it. The thought of some Chinese lady giving Li Tsung Po Sears underwear as a token of love seemed so ridiculous I burst out laughing.

Lao Li looked from the suit to me and, shaking his head, packed it up again.

"Wool is great luxury in China. Everyone always cold in winter. Also, that is so—" Failing to locate the appropriate word, he crossed his arms in front of his chest.

I tried to help him. "Personal? Intimate?"

He nodded. "Intimate."

"So that's why your wife gave it to you? Because it was so intimate?"

"My wife." He grimaced. "Not my wife."

"But you said it was like the pearl-sewn shirt."

"Not my wife, my—" He paused, apparently reluctant to use the term "lover."

"Girlfriend?"

He looked at me very seriously for a moment, and then a big grin spread across his face. "My girlfriend!" He chortled, clapped his hands at the thought. He smoothed the silken wrapper.

"Do you still wear it?"

"Wear it? No." He gave me a superior smile. "I know that story of pearl-sewn shirt. I know what happen if I wear that gift."

"And it worked? Her husband didn't catch you?"

"No. Not husband."

"So what happened to her?"

His face became grave again.

"It was war. That is truth you must understand. That is lesson of pearl-sewn shirt. You know. When men fight, love die."

He turned away from me to arrange the masks in their box. When he'd finished, he said, "You know love?"

"Sure." I slid my fingers across the inlaid threads of a cloisonné vase. "I know love. I guess."

"No! You do not know love! You know *like*." He pushed the box toward me. "You. You are somebody's girlfriend?"

I could feel the heat spread across my face. "I'm only in third grade."

"In Old China third grade is old enough to marry."

The blush crept past my ears and down the back of my neck.

"Okay," he said, sparing me the need to say more. "I find boy for you. You know?"

• • •

Tommy and I met two days after the seniors' center to tour the Lower East Side. Chinatown Annex, he called it, because this territory belonged primarily to European immigrants until the seventies, when Chinese newcomers from mainland China, Vietnam, and Hong Kong quietly took it over. Not for tourists, this is where most of the sweatshops are located. Gambling dens. Slum housing stuck between brand-new high-rises built and sold at exorbitant profits by rich Taiwanese.

I tried to pay attention to Tommy's civics lesson, to behave like the rational, capable, equal partner we were both pretending that I was. But my mind kept trapping itself in scorekeeping. This was my third time back. The first was a disaster in some ways, but in all likelihood I had spooked myself, which might not have been so bad, either, since it forced my hand to try again. The second visit had gone better than I would have dared imagine. The worst I'd felt was embarrassed and inept, and though I was remembering things about Li I must have buried for years, none was unpleasant or frightening. I'd gotten through last night without dreams of any kind—preliminary evidence, surely, that my plan was working. And today, except for these mental ramblings, it really did seem like a job. An assignment.

If it was this simple, of course, then I was a perfect fool for not returning years ago. The fool part I could easily buy, but the simplicity still troubled me. If it was so simple, why the same devastating nightmare for over a decade? I couldn't shake the notion that something bad had happened to me or my family, something somehow connected to Chinatown. Maybe coming back wasn't the cure, but only a first step.

"*Ni hao ma!*" A middle-aged man with a shopping cart full of stuffed pink and blue dogs smiled at Tommy, who politely returned the greeting. When we'd moved on he said, "Just think. A million Chinese have come here since you moved away, Maibelle."

"I always knew I wasn't welcome, but I had no idea it was that bad."

He kicked a crushed paper cup out of his path. "Problem with round-eyes is they think the universe revolves around them. It would never occur to Chinese to say such a thing. Even joking."

He had the same flattened tone of voice as when he'd asked about Henry.

I looked straight ahead to a new brick apartment building on the corner. All straight angles up and down. No crisscross of fire escapes, no tangle of signs or lights, just ladders of faceless regimented windows. If you stared too long at a structure like that, it could break your heart.

"That building looks like a giant's thumb . . . What makes you think I was joking?"

He touched the fabric of my shirt. "It's not criticism but fact. Take a look."

Lower, he meant. Street level. He didn't point or single anyone out. He didn't need to. We were surrounded by people dressed in loose-fitting garments, drab prints, plain shoes, unassuming hairstyles. The women wore knee-high nylons turned down like socks. The men's collars lay flat and splayed. No ties. No jackets. Men or women, when they caught me looking, they ducked and rushed headlong into the warm dirty breeze.

"Only way they'd look you in the eye is if they thought they were invisible."

"I know just how they feel."

We walked on without speaking, but I sensed him mentally weighing my words and regretted this slip of self-pity.

"When you lived here, Maibelle, only the old people were Chinese-born. Rest of us, if we were honest, were as American as you. Now hardly any ABCs live here anymore, and nobody feels like they belong."

"You do."

"Do I?" He watched two young boys across the street crouching over bamboo cages.

"You were born here."

"So were you."

"But you—" I hunched my shoulders against the crickets' chilling screech.

"A person's geography is both outward and inward. *Zhu xin.* Bamboo heart. Traitor's heart, that's what my father called the ABCs who break tradition and cause their families to lose face."

"He didn't call you that!"

"Chinese lose face for so many reasons. I told my parents I wouldn't take over the store, I wanted a different life."

"You said they wanted you to make something of your life."

"But I wanted a *different* life."

"You rebelled. That's good. I'm still trying to figure out how to do that."

"I'm still trying to figure out how to undo it." He frowned. "Lunch?"

Noodle shops and tea rooms huddled like expectant children all along these converted streets, but instead Tommy stopped at a sidewalk vegetable vendor. He scrutinized the brightly colored flats, exchanged a few words with the grocer, and began to pluck Chinese long beans, green onions, taro root. Pretty soon, his arms were full.

"My mother had no daughters," he explained. "So I cook."

I thought of our meal together uptown, his refusal to sit with his back to the door, but banished the prickle of anxiety that followed. He nodded vigorously at something the grocer was saying. We were partners. I should trust him.

Tommy's building stood farther down toward the water, on Pearl Street. It had a small antiseptic lobby and empty white hallways. The flooring throughout, including the elevator, was a pink and tan vinyl flecked with chunks of silver and gold that looked like the crushed remnants of a little girl's birthday party. We rode up nine stories without encountering another person.

"Where is everybody?"

He grinned. "Maybe your giant ate them for lunch."

"Good. Then he won't be hungry for us."

"That's the Chinese in you, you know."

"What is?"

He turned the key and pushed open his door. "Man-eating giants."

"No. It's Li." I reconsidered. "At least partly it is."

"That's what I mean."

The apartment was one room, plain and small and filled with light from a sliding glass door that opened onto a balcony overlooking the East River. It was a magnetic view encompassing both the Manhattan and Brooklyn bridges, all the way up to Queens. Scudding clouds. Toy boats. The chop of the waves like pinpricks against the water's glossy darkness. But all that separated the concrete platform from the plunge beyond was a few metal bars and a two-inch railing.

I turned back to the room. There was no bed, just a couch that I assumed folded out and a couple of overstuffed armchairs. A kitchenette with a counter and stools. In the center of the room, covering the party leavings, was a reddish-brown Tibetan prayer rug. I began to relax. Tommy's life and passion, judging by the physical evidence, were his work.

A sawhorse table held a typewriter and stacks of books and papers, two tall file cabinets with more folders piled on top. The walls were solid with old photographs, prints, and drawings. Grinning men in bowler hats held up deer antlers. Women hid behind wedding veils. A smoke-filled opium parlor and a steaming laundry looked equally like scenes from Dante's *Inferno*. I thought of Tommy's comment about personal geography extending outward and inward. Though these people were strangers, I'd lived on their street, gone to school with their great-grandchildren, bought candy and toys at the same shops they'd built generations earlier. Somewhere back in Old China, our ancestors had been neighbors. These pictures, unlike my father's, made no demands. Instead they seemed like an offering.

I pointed. "These remind me of Li."

Tommy looked over from the kitchenette, where he was unpacking the groceries. "How so?"

"They make me feel like a kindred spirit."

"The way he did?"

I nodded.

"He once asked me, if you forget where you come from, how can you know where you're going?"

"But you wouldn't take over the store."

"My father thought that's where I came from. It wasn't what Li meant."

I came over to the kitchenette. "How did you get to be friends with Lao Li?"

"His grandparents and some of my great-grandparents came from the same village, so my father and he were in the same fong. Dad used to say he was sharing me because Li had no sons of his own. That meant I could run errands for both of them. But I liked Uncle Li, he told good stories."

He handed me a small triangular knife. "If you're going to eat, you have to work."

My relationships with men rarely venture into the kitchen, and I was so unsettled by the combination of a sharp blade and the sudden physical proximity between us that all further thought of Li fled my mind. Fortunately Tommy seemed to know without asking that I rarely ate or prepared anything more complicated than salad, and set me to work slicing vegetables while he tended the noodles and pork on the stove. After tacitly establishing our separate body zones within the limited space, we worked in companionable silence, and soon the room filled with the smells of garlic, ginger, and peanut oil.

I completed my assigned task and cleared the counter. He filled two glasses with water, placed them with chopsticks side by side in front of me.

"Do you have the life you wanted?" I asked.

"What?"

"You said your parents lost face because you wanted a different life. Did you get it?"

He sprinkled the noodles with sesame seed and poked them with long cooking sticks. "My rebellion went too far. I had to leave Chinatown for some time. A cousin of mine in Hong Kong owns this building. At first, that was the only reason I came back. Then I realized I never wanted to leave."

"Where did you go?"

"Oh, far, far away." He handed me two bowls of noodles, pale yellow with bits of meat and jewel-bright vegetables. "Hungry?"

"Where?"

"Hundred Thirty-fifth Street."

"Exile."

"You could call it that." He smiled, came around beside me, and lifted his glass. "*Gan bei!*"

"*Gan bei.* 'Bottoms up,' right?" The toast with which my father always launched lunch at the Ming Yu. "I haven't heard that in years."

"Welcome home, Mei-bi." He clinked my glass and drank.

"You're trying to distract me. Why? What do you mean, you had to leave?"

He ran a hand through his hair as if it was suddenly bothering him, then picked up his chopsticks and rolled them between his fingers. The pointed tips hovered over his bowl like a dragonfly over a pond. He leaned forward without another word and attacked his food.

Part IV

The Fairy's Rescue

....

11

Tommy and I have been meeting every three or four days, early mornings primarily, before the tourists invade. It is the time of day I remember best, when I used to feel most at home. The scratch and roll of metal grates going up. The bustle of vendors receiving their goods. Mothers and grandmothers calling, answering as early sun warmed the bricks of the buildings across the street. I had no idea as a child how little I knew of the world in which I lived.

The seniors' center was an equally benign reintroduction. I've accused Tommy of luring me with the most approachable faces in Chinatown. He doesn't deny it.

"But who said you can only photograph faces?"

So now, in back rooms and street stalls, I frame swollen hands underwater swimming with fat white noodles, chopping colorless squares of bean curd, or wielding guillotine cleavers over the heads of squawking ducks. Some of the fingers are gnarled with arthritis. Others are missing digits. Regardless, they work continuously, automatic as machines.

In sweatshops I photograph babies in baskets, their mothers zipping endless strips of denim through deafening sewing machines. In a shirt-press factory, men stripped to the waist become shadows in burning fog. In basement meat lockers pale, spindly torsos disappear beneath slabs of pork or beef twice their size, the butchers' only visible complaint the curl of their breath in the bitter cold air.

The real complaint lies in their common plan. Twelve or more hours a day at a dollar or two an hour. They save. One day they, too, will have enough to follow their ABC cousins and buy a nice house out in Queens.

Only Tommy and I are fool enough to come *back* to Chinatown by choice. For the story. The pictures. Some bastardization of memory that helps keep the nightmares at bay. My dreams have stopped cold. I am getting warmer.

It's the pictures. There are moments when I imagine my father's camera pulsing with the images it's recording, as if it's happy to be back in action. As if there really is a connection between Dad's work and mine. I try to think and not think about his photographs, let the fact of his accomplishment inform my choices without directing them, but his images and his choice to destroy them remain at the back of my thoughts. I can't decide if they're an invitation or a warning. I believe they are important.

• • •

I've always considered the gallery opening to be the art world's own exquisite form of torture. I realized as a child, when Mum used to drag me along "for the exposure," that hardly anyone at an opening bothers to look at the work on the walls. The reason people attend is to acquire, build, or flaunt social power. And social power within the rarefied world of artists and collectors is ultimately more important than talent in determining status and success. By the time I was fourteen I understood that social power was not something I was capable of developing, even if I wanted to. That was the year I threw up on Mr. Uelsmann's photograph (a purely unintentional assault on one of my mother's most revered photographic tricksters) and made Mum promise not to invite me to any more openings.

After breaking this promise last month she did not force me to think about it further. No phone calls. No invitations to lunch. No more coy requests for me to escort her through the badlands of Harlem. And, what with the trips back to Chinatown and the start of Christmas catalog work for Noble, I managed to put the whole matter out of my head, would perhaps have forgotten all about it if my brother hadn't called.

"You know anything about Foucault's new mistress?"

"Didn't know he had one."

"French. Early twenties. A brunette Deneuve."

"So Mum says, I take it."

"Well, then, you going to this opening next week?"

"Hadn't planned to."

He hummed the opening bar of the *Twilight Zone* theme. "There's intrigue afoot."

"I suppose you're the linchpin?"

"You don't need to sound so superior. She's been trying to set you up ever since you got back to New York."

"And I've been fending her off. Anyway, that's about work."

"I have a feeling this is, too. So. You coming?"

It was that fast. One second I was bantering with my brother, the next I was exposing a lie. A big one. About work.

The phrase stuck, repeated. My mother's work. My father's. A lie that spanned my entire life.

"Henry, have you ever seen any of Dad's photographs?"

"Huh?"

"His work. You know? Photojournalism. Combat photog?"

"Course not. He destroyed it all before we were born, didn't he?"

"Far as you know, Mum didn't have any of his pictures?"

"Not that she ever told me. What's this got to do with the opening?"

"Nothing," I said. "Nothing. I'll see you there."

It was a Ladies' Day over twenty-two years ago. I couldn't have been much more than four. This was before Mum encouraged me to explore, said I could only look, not touch, when I came to the gallery. But this day I was up in the third-floor storage room alone and my crayon rolled under a chest, and as I reached for it my hand tripped a hidden latch. A secret drawer popped open.

I knew I shouldn't. I should just close the drawer. Maybe if I asked about it, Mum would show me later. But it was too tempting. This was a secret drawer with hidden pictures. Something about them had to be special. And forbidden.

Ever so carefully, I lifted the layer of tissue that covered the stack and began to look through a set of black-and-white photographs my mother had never displayed. The white man with the bleeding black baby. The lady with the pig. The tall blond man looking as though he didn't even notice that headless body and all those screaming Chinese men. Children dressed in rags on a street littered with party hats. A city turned into a war zone. The makings of a nightmare.

I was staring at a pagoda like the Chinatown phone booth, only much, much bigger. I had to look close to understand and when I did I cried out loud. From those pretty, ornate roofs dangled bodies. Men's naked bodies.

My mother walked into the room.

I pulled in my hands and backed away from the pictures. But she wasn't even angry.

"What do you think?"

I expected her to punish me. I couldn't answer.

"Do you like them?"

I nodded.

"How much?"

"A lot?"

"More than that?" She pointed to a photograph on the wall, of two midgets emerging from a gorilla suit.

I nodded cautiously.

"Why?" she said.

"I just do."

And then, faster than I could move away, she grabbed me. But she still didn't shake or spank me. She hugged me. "It's no wonder you like these pictures. Your father took them. They're fabulous. And they're just some of the shots that made him famous . . . But you mustn't let him—or anyone—know I have these."

"Why? What would he do?"

"Oh . . ." She made an ugly face and shook her head so her voice quivered. "Something low-down and mean, I'm sure. You know, he's half magic, don't you?"

"He is! Really, Mum?"

She sighed and let me go. "No, not really. But I mean it about not telling him. If he gets wind of these prints, he'll destroy them, the way he did all the others."

She checked to see that the photographs were lying straight and flat, pushed in the drawer so the lock snapped. Then she twisted around and took both my hands, flipped them over as if reading my palms. Her fingers were cold and long around mine. She squatted lower to look me straight in the eye. She had her serious face on.

"You just forget you ever saw these pictures, Maibee."

"But what are you hiding them for?"

"That's for me to know and you to find out. But someday, not now. Not for a long time."

She never mentioned those hidden pictures again and the next time I tried to find them there was no secret drawer. When I asked about it, she said she didn't know what I was talking about, it must have been something I dreamed. After I started school our Ladies' Days grew less and less frequent, finally ended altogether. By then I had forgotten.

• • •

Though it was barely six o'clock when I arrived, the gallery was already full, bodies three-deep by the bar that had been set up across from the staircase. From the center of the room came frequent, social shrieks, many in elaborate foreign accents. It was a typical New York gallery opening except, instead of the usual assortment of slouching artists and trendy middle-aged collectors, tonight's crowd consisted of what Henry calls end users. Not the people who make art or broker sales, but the ones in whose homes the procured products hang.

They were, for the most part, over fifty, elaborately coiffed, perfectly manicured, and expensively (though not always tastefully) dressed in soft pastels. The women carried largish purses, the men small ones, and both favored a certain weight in both perfume and jewelry. I suspected that Elizabeth and the Queen Mum would have felt right at home.

The guest list for tonight's event was dictated by the paintings concealed behind the bodies. Over the past twenty years Mum has gradually shifted the New York gallery's main emphasis from traditional surrealism to works by newer artists, including her photographers, whom she's selected, cultivated, and persuaded Foucault to buy. For the past few years the balance sheet has left the old man no choice but to go along with Mum's picks, but he insists on one annual show of the surrealist work that he continues to buy himself. To this opening only an elite group handpicked by Foucault—the end users—are invited. My mother prefers to call them the living dead. They turn out not because they are particularly fond of surrealism themselves, but because Foucault is a little like a geriatric Gatsby, a largely invisible presence who has managed, against all the art world's conventional rules, to retain both great wealth and mystique. People come on the chance that he will make an appearance, which he does, at random and usually without notice, every few years.

Tonight as I entered I heard his name whispered, caught several women craning their heads in search of him. I hoped he'd pull one of his infamous no-shows. Then I could give my mother the satisfaction of my appearance without paying her price. Though that might make it more difficult for me to accomplish what I'd come to do.

I was standing in line by the bar when I spotted her across the room, next to a Redon portrait of a man with flowers for hair. She wore a black Dior cocktail dress that my father bought years ago at the St. Barnabas Church thrift shop. I remembered because she said it was the one bargain he'd ever found that really had never been used. He told her it made her look like Audrey Hepburn. Which was true, then and now.

She checked her watch, peered over my head, but didn't see me. A tall, elegantly dressed man spoke to her, and for an instant I thought he might be Foucault, but since no one else paid him any attention, I decided he must be a customer. She smiled at him, tossed her head, and dipped her lashes.

Something in her expression made me think of the spring she redecorated her and my father's bedroom. Draped striped chintz over the windows, laid a matching throw rug over the old black carpet, and hung two Tchelitchew lithographs of barren landscapes to "unify" the room. She pushed the twin beds together and covered them with a single king-size spread.

"I am sick to death of patterning my life after Rob and Laura Petrie," she said. "Dick Van Dyke may worry about what umpteen million viewers think when he goes to sleep in the same room as Mary Tyler Moore, but your father and I don't have that problem and it's high time we stopped conducting our married life as if we did!"

Later that week I found a two-volume *Marital Companion* wedged, spine backward, on Mum's bookshelf. Henry, who had already read it cover-to-cover, said Mum was trying to save her marriage through sex. Too embarrassed to actually read the book, I did leaf through it and was relieved it had no pictures. I preferred to think of Mum and Dad swirling around the dance floor at the Rainbow Room. What was wrong with separate beds?

Perhaps it was a credit to my mother's plan that I walked in on them for the first and only time just a few days after she'd finished redecorating. On a Sunday morning. Not that early. I'd been watching TV, had seen a machine that sliced and diced and creamed and frappéed and looked exactly like one on my father's drawing board. I thought maybe Dad had sold the idea and was about to make a million dollars (I assumed that any product advertised on TV must be worth millions of dollars to its inventor), or that someone had stolen his idea and he'd have to sue to get it back. In either case, I thought it worth waking him to see the commercial.

The door was open a crack. Silence within. The first thing I noticed was my father's side of the bed—empty. The second was the mountain of sheets loaded up on my mother's side. Nothing moved. No one made a sound. All I could see was my father's hair, black on my mother's white pillow.

I backed out and shut the door, soundless and tight, vowed never to enter that bedroom again when both of them were in there.

The advertised gizmo went clean out of my head until the next time I saw it on TV, nearly a month later, while Dad was sitting safely next to me. He said the device was neither a theft nor a bonanza but only the usual competition.

"Can I help you?" The bartender looked as if he'd been waiting awhile.

"Oh. Wine, I guess." I glanced at my mother, still chatting with the elegant man. She lifted her glass possessively and sipped. Red liquid. Red stain from her lipstick on the edge. The bartender handed me my wine and looked to the person behind me.

The liquid in my glass was the color of bleach. I left it on the corner of the bar and moved against the wall. Tanguy on one side, Ernst on the other. New old art, as Mum once called it.

She turned her head and caught my eye, immediately broke off her conversation and came over.

"Why are you just standing here?"

"I was admiring the work. No one else is."

"These people acquire art. They don't look at it."

She broke off to greet a mildly desiccated couple with a gracious-hostess smile. They reciprocated, appraised me in one querulous glance, and moved on.

"Is Henry here yet?"

She nodded through a break in the crowd. Across the room my brother was leaning over a life-sized Madame Alexander doll.

"Looks like true love."

"I hope so. Then he can move in with her."

"He's back with you again?"

She rolled her eyes.

"I've heard some small towns are buying their homeless people one-way tickets to California. He could stake his claim in Silicon Valley."

"I'm afraid he's already staked his claim on West Ninetieth Street. But if he sticks to Coralie, he might expand his territory to France."

"Henry told me Foucault has a new girl. That her?"

But more people were arriving, and she began to get the edgy, officious look that meant she was feeling compromised.

"Come," she said. "Come meet Gerard."

"That's the other half of your plan, isn't it?"

She scooped her tongue around the front of her teeth. "You didn't come just to look at the paintings, did you?"

"No," I said. "Not exactly."

Gerard Foucault was hiding in the back office. Perched on the edge of Mum's huge walnut desk (which was really, of course, his own), he did indeed look like a screech owl. The requisite hooked beak and protruding eyes, bushy white eyebrows, and colorless hair that sprouted in two wild tufts on either side of a pale scalp dome. But in spite of his ramrod posture and pin-striped suit, I was surprised to feel a stab of sympathy. The image of this old bird coupling with the little cover girl outside was as pathetic as it was grotesque.

My mother made the introductions and asked Foucault if there was anything he needed, to which he gave an ambiguous shrug. She smoothed her dress down over her hips, threw me an encouraging glance, and strode back outside.

"Please be seated." Foucault indicated an overstuffed armchair opposite the desk.

I sat.

His gaze roamed the Delvaux, Roy, and De Chirico paintings that, at his insistence, adorned the office walls. It was the gaze of a jealous child checking to see that no one had played with his toys.

"Your mother tells me you have great talent." He pronounced mother "moth-her."

"Everyone has talent. The trick is to figure out how to use it."

The great tufts lifted, and for the first time, he looked directly at me. His eyes were a queer purplish color, like eggplant.

"You are an optimist," he said.

"I wouldn't say that."

"To think that everyone has talent. That is the most sublime optimism I know."

"I didn't say genius. Talent is more like potential. We all have it, but most of us squander it. Or run from it."

"That is you?"

"Running?"

"From your own potential."

Potency-al. It was as if this conversation were a series of trapdoors, and every time I opened my mouth, another door shut behind me. I didn't answer.

"De Chirico knew about terror," he said. "All the surrealists did. They used it to focus their talent. You look at a Magritte, you enter another world full of ideas and emotions and humor. You look at some of these new paintings, what do you enter? Nothing! A white square. Drips. Dots. Pencil marks on a blank wall. Bah! They have taken art and reduced it to bullsheet."

He eased himself off the desk, walked over to a Delvaux painting of multiple dead-eyed girls who reminded me of the Stepford Wives.

"Some people would say that painting pictures of nightmares is a form of bullshit."

He spun around. "You know what is my favorite book in the world? Lewis Carroll's masterpiece, *Through the Looking-Glass.* Good art should be like a magic looking glass that pulls you inside, to a place where you will discover things you never could have guessed. A place beyond nightmares. No?"

"A place where it's easy to lie." What I remembered of my father's work took me to the heart of his nightmares as well as my own. They were not representations. They did not interpret or try to tell more than the truth. That they did not go "beyond" was a testament to their accomplishment. They did not lie.

"People who have talent can create such worlds. You think everyone has talent? If you do, my dear, I would certainly consider you to be an optimist. Or a fool."

Dad used to say he'd been a fool.

"What about you?" I asked. "Do you have that kind of talent, Gerard?"

Foucault ignored both the archness and the familiarity of my question. He casually strolled about the office picking up a paperweight here, straightening a painting there. When he arrived at the door to the gallery, he stopped and stared as if he could see through it.

"Yes," he said finally. "I believe I have talent. Not the same as a great painter, of course, but I have created something worthwhile, a kind of a world. With beauty and uncertainty, intelligence. Anxiety. Age and youth."

He turned to face me, and I noticed how his pants, impeccably tailored though they were, hung slack from his narrow waist to his shoes as if there were nothing inside.

Suddenly all sympathy, all tolerance, evaporated in the recognition of this old, pathetic man as an enemy. I remembered the one and only other time I'd seen him, on a blazing hot day in Chinatown. Around the same time that my mother redecorated her bedroom.

He'd had his driver pull up to the curb outside our apartment, and Henry and I watched from the doorway as Mum slid into the car—a silver Bentley with heavily tinted windows. She wore a white suit with a miniskirt that rode up her thigh as she sank back into the seat. She waved goodbye and, in that split second, I froze on her one naked reaching hand, her stockinged calf ending in a pale pink heel and, beyond, the dim outline of a man's pant leg. I couldn't see his face.

Now, as I caught Foucault's purple gaze, what I saw instead were those legs. His. Hers. Splitting like wishbones.

The old man turned, stroking his chin. "Do you agree, Maibelle? Do you think it takes talent to develop one of the most important galleries in New York?"

Far from arrogance, he was begging for precisely the approval and encouragement my mother had sent me to collect from him. He can make the kind of promises only the very rich are equipped to keep, she'd once told me. But she had never spelled out what he expected in return.

"Yes, Mr. Foucault." My voice sounded as if I were talking through a tin can. I'd ventured into my mother's world here, crossed a forbidden line. He was a deal she'd made for herself. A bargain with the devil maybe, but not *my* enemy. I needed to cross back.

"It does require talent," I said. "Someone with talent."

I opened the door. People turned, looked, mouthed his name, and moved toward us. A wave of disgust swept over me. I let the chosen flood in and wash me out.

When I reached the bottom of the long, curling staircase, I caught sight of Henry and Coralie in the open doorway to the street. My brother had the fingers of one hand wrapped decisively around her arm, the other spanning her narrow waist.

I shivered, unable to get the image of those parting legs out of my mind. And yet, there was my mother, working the room with the quiet efficiency of an imperial courtesan. Gracious. Confident. Seemingly untouchable. She had plans for me. Always had.

In high school, I took her promises of magic and enlightenment so to heart that I honestly believed I'd captured that feeling she described, of touching through a single image. As photographer for the yearbook I shot the basketball team doing the cancan, and the expression of astonished joy and need on Louis Havemeyer's face was such that no one who looked carefully at that photograph was surprised when Louis became the first boy in our school to bring a male date to his senior prom. I took a photograph of Mario Versacci that was divided like a diptych, one side with him curled inside his locker, the other his open locker door wallpapered with *Hustler* and *Penthouse* covers. I read in the newspaper a few years later that Mario was arrested in a single-occupancy hotel with the body of a prostitute. Then there was the close-up of Romeo and Juliet after the senior play—backstage and crotch-to-crotch in full makeup. That shot circulated and the offending couple and I were suspended from school for a week, but they got married and moved to Atlanta, had two kids, and continued to appear in community theater productions, so there was a lot of truth to that frame, too. Truth but not yet Art, Mum warned me.

Art, I learned from my college professors, combined Ideas with Intention into Images with Impact. I translated that to mean gimmickry, and steered carefully around the human form until my senior year. Then I spent months on a wall-sized mosaic of one hundred forty-four separate photographs of disconnected body parts. The bottom row consisted of lashes blown up so big they looked like wrought-iron prongs. I called the piece *Oriental I.*

The entire photography department assumed my work somehow derived from Dad, that he was grooming me to be his successor. When he appeared for the opening of my graduation show, the faculty buzz turned up so fast that he only stayed ten minutes. It was ten minutes too long for us both, especially after Mum failed to realize that *Oriental I,* the centerpiece of my show, was a self-portrait. It's never occurred to her that she doesn't know everything worth knowing about my work. For that matter, about me.

The storage cabinets in the third-floor office have multiplied since I played there as a child. It's absurd to think she'd restore the secret compartments, but I don't know how else to begin. I search two or three cabinets without luck. On the third I find a lever.

The drawer pops just as I remember. I pull it slowly, cautiously, half expecting something to jump out. The drawer is packed tight with enveloped prints. I take them one after another and search, if not for exact images, then for a sense of time and place, my father's irony or sorrow.

But the hidden pictures are not my father's. Some are famous. I recognize an Edward Weston nude and a Paul Strand photo of shadows. Most are experimental frames by Mum's protégés Dupriest and Sazaroff. I close the drawer and search another three cabinets, find another secret cache. Still no sign of Dad's work.

"What are you doing in here?"

My mother's sudden intrusion makes me jump. My thoughts scramble to get into line. I stare at the prints spread out on the floor and the images fold into the picture of her standing, one hand on the knob, just as she did the last time.

"You irritated him." Her voice trembles with an emotion I take for anger. Then I find her eyes and realize it is disappointment. What she wants me to think is disappointment.

"Where are they?"

"Maibelle?" She steps into the room and quietly shuts the door. I am aware of both of us breathing in a small closed space.

"Dad's photographs."

"What photographs, darling?"

"Dammit, Mum. I know! Stop lying to me. I know I saw them."

She clenches her arms across her chest and squints at the ceiling. If I didn't know better, I'd think she was going to cry. But I know better. I'm the one who's holding back tears.

"I've had nightmares about those pictures for years. You said I never saw them. I thought I was crazy. You've got to let me see them."

"That's ridiculous."

"I don't give a damn what you think. Let me see them!"

I sound like a child. A whining brat. That's how she looks at me. She's the mother who knows better. I am the child.

I stand up. Now I look down on her.

"All right, Maibelle." Her arms float down by her sides. Her voice is so quiet, so reserved, I feel as if I'm coated in glass. If I move, I will shatter. This, too, will be a nightmare.

But no, she flips open a wall cupboard, reaches inside, glances at me over her shoulder. There's a panel at the back, a safe behind that. She spins the knob quickly, and it makes a sound like tumbling dice. She removes a single handful of papers and closes the safe, the panel, the cupboard.

A packet of glassine envelopes. That's what she hands me. I bite the inside of my cheek to keep from speaking. She hangs on a second too long, so I feel as if I'm tugging them from her grasp, but finally she lets go.

Now, in my mother's gallery, which is not really my mother's, I look down at my father's photographs, which are not really my father's. Dead bodies float like an armada down the center of a river. Homes split like doll houses after a bombing. Grossly fat dogs feast on human corpses. I think of the glass-eyed woman in Chinatown who was raped and widowed in Nanking. The terms of her survival. My vision starts to blur. And I begin to understand.

My father saw too much.

These images could turn you to stone. That's the danger my father warned me about. Yet when I come to a one-legged baby trying to crawl to her mother's crushed body, the tears flood my face so suddenly I have to turn away to protect the photograph.

The next print is the portrait of a ghost. Just a spindly old scholar in a crowd of young men, but their arms outstretch as if to catch the elder's dying breath. Their bodies strain with that reaching, and in each of their eyes, I see the reflection of my father's dread. As he watches the world looking back at him.

"They're incredible, aren't they?"

I'd all but forgotten my mother, lurking over my shoulder. Now the muted ecstasy in her voice makes me shudder.

"What do you mean, incredible?"

"But you must see what a consummate artist he was."

I see an elderly black-jacketed Chinese woman bent from the waist before an iron fence. She is kissing a white toddler, impeccably dressed in a sailor's suit, on the other side. They are turned sideways so you can see her lips meeting his cheek between the bars. Any second now his hat, with its pompon and trailing ribbon, will fly away. He will no doubt try to run after it, but he won't run fast enough, and she won't be there to help him. He will cry. Behind them, oblivious white couples in handsome Western fashions stroll along manicured lanes of a park. In the foreground a sign reads "No dogs or Chinese."

I think of my father bent over his bits of wire and plastic, his chicken-scratch sketches and patent bulletins. The scenes that must be playing in his mind, awake, asleep. That he can't escape.

Like this next photograph, one that was in my teacher's collection. One I'd remembered. The tall blond man, hands cupped around a cigarette, his lips wound into a smirk, eyes as callused as fists not even seeming to notice that wailing band of mourners with their headless mortal cargo. It's the tall blond man, much more than the body, that sends a thrill of pain up my spine.

I turn it over. My father's name. 1947. It's the last picture in the packet.

"Where are the rest? You have more of Dad's work. I know. I remember."

She crouches beside me and the air swims with Chanel No. 9, the fragrance she adopted after my father's killing in bottle tops. She said it smelled expensive. It affects me like smelling salts.

"Somewhere safe."

"Safe." I take in the secret drawers, the concealed wall safe. My mother's war room.

"You've sold out, haven't you? You've sold Dad out."

My mother responds swiftly, with the same efficiency she applies to running the gallery. She slaps me. It is the first time she's ever done this, and it hurts, but it doesn't stop me.

"What are you and Foucault planning, anyway?"

As quickly as the anger flooded her it seems to ease away. She clasps her hands. Tight white patches appear where her knees press against her nylons.

"Gerard has no idea this portfolio exists, Maibelle."

"You really expect me to believe you've hidden this from him all these years?"

"He never checks inventory lists. He—well, he trusts me."

"That's a cute way to put it. You're using each other. You encourage me to use him. You call that trust?"

"Everyone uses each other, Maibelle. Children use parents. Parents use children. Husbands use wives, believe you me. In business you take it for granted. Trust isn't the same thing, but it's a requirement. It's hard to use people unless they trust you."

This is my mother, I remind myself. She gave birth to me. She let me slide into her bed when I was a little child. She gave me my first camera and encouraged me to strive for perfection. She lied to me. She cheated on my father.

"I need to know something."

She stands, smooths her skirt. "What?"

"How you met Foucault. How you got this job."

She doesn't answer right away. I wonder if at last I've hit some nerve that may force her to tell me the truth. When she speaks, her voice is flat.

"I didn't get the job. Joe did. We'd just married and he was about to go off to China. One of the editors he worked with at *Life* had us to a party with Foucault. Joe hated him on sight, but when Gerard said he needed someone to help him launch his New York gallery, Joe saw it as something to keep me occupied while he was gone. The two of them worked out the terms, salary, benefits."

She brushes her hands together as if to clean them off.

I focus on the eyes of the child in the sailor suit. Fine curved lines fringed with dark lashes. They are closed.

"Come on," she says. "None of this has to do with you."

"Then why am I here?"

"Because Gerard can help your career."

"Like he has yours?"

She stiffens. "I'm not an artist, Maibelle. He's been very decent to me."

She might be a poor widow talking about the town banker who doles out silver dollars at Christmas. She might still be lying through her teeth.

"Then why these? Why do this to him—to Dad?"

She smiles. "Let's just say that Gerard's idea of trust and mine are not exactly the same. The photographs settle the score. They make me happy and that makes him happy. Indirectly."

"You've had Dad's pictures stashed in here for twenty years. Nobody sees them. Nobody buys them. Who are you fooling?"

"One day—" Her voice catches sloppily. "I'll have my own gallery. The opening show—you'll see, when Joe Chung's photographs reappear they won't just be treated as art. They'll be news. And can you imagine how the press will eat it up when they find out his daughter's work is hanging alongside!"

So. After all is said and done I can ride Dad's ball and chain as he's dragged back into the limelight. Twenty years she's been plotting this. Maybe more. That little boy is never going to make it out between those iron bars.

"A lot of time has passed, Maibelle. The world is changing, and so is Joe. One of these days he'll want to be recognized for what he's accomplished. I know that, and I intend to be ready."

"Why did you lie to me all those years?"

Her breath comes in soft gasps. I realize she's trying to laugh. I grab her by the shoulders and shake. Hard. The way I want someone to shake me.

"Why!"

She looks up at me with a sharp, crooked smile. "You were too little to trust. You'd have told him."

I let her go. "I still might."

"Is that a threat?"

"I want to see the rest of Dad's pictures."

"No."

"What difference does it make now?"

Her voice drops to a whisper. "I still can't trust you."

It was a dare. She couldn't stop me. She wouldn't risk alerting everyone downstairs. Foucault. But I feel as if I've hit a dead end. I've exposed my mother's secret, not mine. The pictures might appear in my dreams, but the nightmares aren't about them.

"He'll never forgive you, you know."

She picks up the last photograph in the pile beside me. A young boy cradling a dove. His head is bent so you can't see his face, just his tiny, emaciated body deep in a bombed-out crater.

My mother sighs and looks at me. "All I'm waiting for now is you, Maibelle."

• • •

No dogs or Chinese.

A fancy lady with a thick German accent had visited Li's store. She wore a green velvet suit, diamonds in her ears, and though she must have been as old as my father, her skin had the smooth, tender look that comes with years of facials.

"It is like a miracle to find you," she said. "What will Mama say when she sees! All the way from Bubbling Well road . . ." She shook her head in amazement, staring at a brocaded love seat.

"Please." Lao Li lowered his eyes. "You say hello for me."

"Yes, yes. Of course." The lady gave him a handful of bills.

"*Xie-xie ni,*" he said. "*Xie-xie.*"

"*Xie-xie,*" she replied, delighted. "Yes. *Xie-xie ni!*"

"You knew her in China?" I asked after she was gone.

Lao Li raised his hands and dropped them. "She was a little girl. I knew her mother. Very beautiful lady. Very beautiful."

Then he winked at me in a way that said he had confided a naughty secret, and in this wink I saw that, before the cobwebs and lizard's hands, when his hair was still shiny black, he must have been a terrible ladies' man. Terrible not in the sense of evil, for, despite my first impression, I could not now imagine Lao Li as being at all bad or dangerous, but in the sense of a holy terror. My mother called such men Hairbreadth Harrys.

A Chinese Hairbreadth Harry. The thought made me burst out laughing.

"What is so funny?"

"You're funny."

"I am not funny. I am old."

"You really did like the ladies."

"Never too old to like ladies." He winked again. "And never too young to like boys, I think."

I made a face at him and changed the subject. "Tell me about China. Not ancient stories, you know. Your life. You lived in Shanghai, right? Tell me about Shanghai."

"Ai ya, your papa can tell you about that."

"But he never says *anything* about it."

"I think it is young person's duty to ask about old person's life, and it is old person's duty to tell about old times. You know. Otherwise, only ghosts know truth."

"So, tell me what Shanghai was like."

He thought for a moment. "That lady who is just here, you know? That lady live in big big house, many rooms, many servants. Her papa was officer in German navy. They had parties all night—ate whole cows, whole pigs. All around the sky light up with their dancing." He wiggled his fingers high and wide.

"Did you go to these parties?"

"I?" Li snorted. "No. Foreigners only at these parties. Foreigners only in parks. In clubs. Swimming pool. Signs say, 'No dogs or Chinese allowed.' "

"But it was *your* country!"

"You ask about Shanghai in my time. That Shanghai my time. American, English, French, Russian, Italian, German—and Japanese—own whole city. Chinese leaders take bribe money, give foreigners whatever they ask. Chinese people work for foreigners, not for China."

"But you were friendly with that lady and her mother."

"Of course. She was one of my best customers. She pawned very precious jewelry, some furniture. Paid big money to get it back." He rubbed his fingers together and smiled. "Foreigners like to gamble even more than Chinese. You know. Sometimes they gamble at their bridge and pinochle. Mostly they gamble in their stocks. In Shanghai they have big houses, cars, servants, but many times they have no money to buy gas or pay servants. Then they come to me!" He grinned and nodded his head. "The ladies come to me. Foreign men prefer to keep gambling, hope their luck will change. Until they end up with nothing. Ladies are more practical. You know."

I considered his inlaid chairs, ornate ginger jars, dragon screens, the cases of pearls and jade and ivory, hanging scrolls, and ceramic Buddhas.

"The *foreigners* pawned all this stuff?"

"Not all. Some come from Chiang's officers. They stole it from communist sympathizers, then sold quick. But most from Europeans who are not as rich as they pretend. So they get away from the Japanese."

"Didn't you run when war came?"

"*Dui*. I run. I hate Chiang. I hate Mao. Japanese take everything I own, maybe kill me, too. So right away after they begin fighting for Shanghai delta, I close my shop. I use lot of bribes, lot of *guanxi* with foreigners and friends of the Generalissimo. You know. I send everything to Hong Kong, then San Francisco."

"Then New York."

"After while. Yes, then New York."

And he had rebuilt his shop in New York. Had embraced his borrowed treasures and gone to great lengths to bring them with him across the ocean, across a foreign continent. Far from rejecting his past life, he had resurrected it here. My father had only pieces of paper, strips of celluloid to carry, but for him even that was too much.

....

12

Dad returned the toolbox this morning. I was shooting a miniature Christmas tree, the Traveling Tree, as it would be called in the catalog, on a bed of crushed Styrofoam.

He wagged his head back and forth. "Some old battle-ax gave me the third degree downstairs."

"Harriet. The building manager. What'd she want to know?"

"Who I was. Where I was going."

"You tell her?"

"Sure." He handed me the toolbox. "Any reason I shouldn't have?"

I shrugged, avoiding his eyes. "Did this help?"

"An idea or two." He watched me adjust a light, try a different filter, lower the tripod. I wondered if he had some suggestions or criticisms, but as usual it was impossible to read his expression. One thing I knew, though, he'd stay longer if I continued working. He'd think his presence made no difference.

"How close are you?"

"I put it aside."

"Working on something else?"

He sat fingering a matchbook, folded the cover diagonally, then again with attention, as if doing origami. He studied the results for a moment, then slipped it back in his shirt pocket, behind a soft pack of cigarettes. "Bad luck to talk about it."

I started shooting. "Since when are you superstitious about your work?"

What I saw through the viewfinder was a lone pine in a snowy meadow, no scale. I'd already done one set with the tree's branches covered with tiny ornaments, but I preferred this cleaner, stripped-down image. Ironically it was the more artificial; the contraption was closer to a Christmas tree than to a real pine. Noble would probably use the decorated version.

"Maibelle," my father said, "Diana's upset with you."

I tightened focus until the needles became blades of cut green plastic. "I've been busy."

"That's good."

Dad picked up the *National Geographic* lying next to him on the couch, open to Marge's photograph of an Indian boy doing a handstand on the back of a water buffalo.

"She wanted me to say something. I take it you didn't hit it off with Foucault."

I lowered the tripod. "It's not important."

My father sucked at his dentures. "The man's a horse's ass. Whatever she tells you."

"I know." I began to shoot. The hidden pictures. Mum and Foucault. The scheme to bring Dad back from the dead and screw him at the same time. The knowledge that I'd so decisively sought now felt like a bomb just waiting for me to trip it.

"That picture in your lap." I said. "It's by a woman named Marge Gramercy. She lived here before me."

"Here?" He gave the place another look around, then studied the picture. His thumb rubbed the margin of the page. He took his time. "I knew her."

Naturally I thought he was joking. But the way his thumb just kept working that paper, and he wouldn't look up, and then I began to think and it made perfect sense. She was older, but not by much. They covered some of the same territory. During some of the same years.

"She was a doctor, you know."

I pretended to take a meter reading.

"Her parents were missionaries in Singapore. They sent her back to the States to medical school. She was supposed to do God's work, but it got away from her."

He put the picture down and shook out a Kent, lit it with a steady hand. I gave him his plate, which he balanced on his knee, and pulled the curtains back just enough to open the window. A cool breeze, jagged with city sounds, blew through.

"How did you know her?"

"Burma. Rangoon during the war. There was one hotel where all the journalists stayed. She wore a Yankees cap. Backwards before her time." He smiled.

"Did you love her?"

He let out a little grunt to inform me in no uncertain terms that I was off track. "Everybody did. But I hardly knew her. Never saw her again after that."

"I feel as if I know her. From her pictures. And living here."

His eyes toured the walls, the fireplace, windows, the abbreviated kitchen. "I saw in the paper she died last winter." He closed the magazine. "You have more of these?"

I pointed to the bottom orange crate where most of the *National Geographics* were stacked.

"She never worked for *Life*, then?"

I thought I saw his head twitch, but all he said was "No." He made no move to look at the magazines or the tearsheets on the mantelpiece. I pushed the collapsible tree aside, swept the fake snow into a shoe box. I pretended Marge was guiding my hand.

"I didn't know you got Mum her job with Foucault."

The red and white checks of his shirt marched up the rise of his belly as he smoked. No answer.

"I always thought it was like her and him against you."

"And now?"

"Now I don't know."

He ground his cigarette into the plate. "Neither do I."

"But you could have stopped her. You hated the gallery. Art. When you came back from China—"

"When I came back from China, I was bloody grateful she had a paying job. She seemed to like it. That's all that mattered."

"And later?"

"Later the gallery was her career."

"But she still wants her superstar." I nearly said "back." Wants him back. I nearly told him about Mum's plan.

Not yet.

I glanced down at the old lady in the garden with her bird. It wasn't her high wheedling voice, though, or the bird's rasp.

"How are you getting along with the Leica?"

So, while arranging snowman and Santa Claus soap dispensers for the next shot, I told him about my work in Chinatown, about Tommy's book. I thanked him with the news that I'd put his gift to use. And not for art. I was looking and seeing.

Seeing shiny round men with plastic pumps growing out of their skulls.

"I could show you," I said.

"No."

The swiftness of his reply, and the decisiveness, made my hand jerk, wasting a shot. Could he see through my bluff? I had nothing developed. You can't rush free work, I'd warned Tommy. Had he called my father to complain, to urge him to push me forward? The thought was ludicrous, a diversion. That's not what Dad meant at all, and I knew it. No meant no. He wouldn't look. He didn't want to see. He wouldn't mention this to Mum, either.

"Bad luck." I straddled the stool on the edge of the set, not quite facing him.

"What?"

"You said it's bad luck to talk about your work. Is that why you hold back so much?"

"Do I?"

"When I was little, I thought you were a spy."

"I wasn't."

Two horizontal lines cut across my father's forehead. He was picking at his fingernails, his shoulders tipped forward, elbows pulled in as if he were hiding something in the center of his body. He did not straighten up.

"Did something happen to us, Dad? Something bad? When I was very little, maybe, or later. That I could have forgotten?"

"Why? Why do you ask?"

"I have nightmares."

"Oh." He patted his breast pocket, but the cigarette pack was empty. "Well. So do we all."

"Okay, then. What are yours about?"

"Awwk! Bye. Bye. Blackbird!" The parrot's song leapt over the outside sounds. It seemed to land in the center of the room and stopped as unexpectedly as it had arrived.

My father grinned, exposing large square yellowed teeth, one gold. He strode to the window, poked his head out to see the bird and its mistress. He stayed there long enough to ignore my question, but when he pulled back he gave himself a shake and said, "I don't remember my dreams. Never have. Doesn't mean I don't have them."

"Maybe if you remembered them, you might change them. For the better."

"I don't think so."

I lifted the plastic tree and folded its branches. Fully collapsed, it was the size and shape of a calligraphy brush.

"Li used to say it was important to remember, to pass those memories on. He said if we didn't, only ghosts would know the truth."

I thought that would get a rise, because of the way he used to talk about Li, because I wasn't sure if he ever knew how much time I'd spent with the old man. But Dad placed one hand on top of my head as if blessing me. Then he hitched up his pants and moved to the door. It hardly made a sound behind him.

• • •

When Li described his flight from China, he said he'd lived for a while in San Francisco before traveling to New York. Later, when I asked what he'd done there, he fluttered his hand in front of his face and closed his eyes briefly, handed me a bowl of tea.

"I wait for someone. She never did come."

"She" who gave him the pearl-sewn union suit, I thought. So it wasn't just the war. My old friend's one true love let him down, left him to live out the rest of his days as a lonely curio dealer. The admission aroused my sympathy, and then something else.

I set my bowl down with a splash. "What do you care if I have a boyfriend—if I ever get married?"

Li stared at me as if I were half-witted. "If you marry Chinese boy," he said slowly, "you have almost Chinese children."

"My children," I repeated. "If I marry a Chinese boy."

I suspect all young girls daydream about their future families, and I was no exception. I was going to have two boys and two girls, all about two years apart. But in spite of the glaring example of my own American grandmother and her Chinese husband, not to mention my American mother and her *half*-Chinese husband, in spite—or perhaps because—of living in Chinatown, I automatically assumed that white girls do not wed Chinese men.

"What about the White Witch?" I said, reaching for an argument that would not insult him. "Wasn't the moral of that story, it's bad for Chinese men to have anything to do with white ladies?"

"Aha! You think about stories I tell to you. Good. But Mei-bi, you are not white witch. You are child of witch. If you marry Chinese man, you have almost Chinese babies. If your babies grow up and marry Chinese, spell of white witch is broken. *That* is moral of story for you."

He pulled from his desk a softbound book with a cover that showed, in vivid pinks, blues, and golds, a beaming Chinese family. He'd begun this reading primer with me earlier that week.

"You're crazy, Lao Li."

"Some say so. But is very disrespectful for you to say to me."

"I'm sorry. I didn't actually mean it."

"Apology accepted." He opened the book and pointed. "This character mean 'person.' *Ren.* Like somebody walking. You know. One leg, two legs. Very simple."

But it wasn't at all simple. I didn't want to become part of Old Li's fairy package. It wasn't my fault my grandmother had married a Chinese man, so why should I have to undo the results?

"Why didn't you pick my brother or sister? They're older. They could fix the spell a lot sooner than I can."

"Not Chinese enough."

"As Chinese as I am."

"Same parents, but they are not Chinese like you."

I scowled at him and flipped my red hair. "I wish."

"Chinese spirit is strong in you. I can never mind your red hair. You hear my stories. You pay attention. You work hard. You know."

"How do *you* know I'll even have children? How do you know they'll be good Chinese? I know lots of ABC full-bloods whose parents say they're bad Chinese."

Lao Li nodded. "I know. Terrible. But not your children." He jabbed the page. "If you cross walking man, give him arms, and stretch them wide, he become 'big': *da.*"

I was staring at this character when Tommy Wah walked in.

He and Li greeted each other and talked for several minutes in a dialect I didn't recognize. When I asked about it, Tommy said, "Fuzhou dialect. He makes sure I don't forget. I see he's got you doing your lessons, too."

I looked to see if he was making fun. He grinned and shrugged, noncommittal.

Lao Li placed a wad of money in an envelope, wrapped it in red paper, and tied it with a gold string. "Take this to On Liang Association," he said to Tommy. "Tell Lao On Chou my heart on fire. I cannot come to his birthday celebration, but I wish him many years prosperity, plenty grandchildren. Make it flowery, you know."

"I'll take it if you really want me to," said Tommy. "But On Ling told me the tong hired a group of singsong girls for the party."

"No! Singsong girls in Chinatown, New York City? No good singsong girls in America."

"Maybe not good." Tommy grinned. "But you take what you can get."

"You do not want take that gift to On Chou." Li grabbed back the packet. "I will take myself!"

"What happened to the fire in your heart?" Tommy wagged his finger at the old man.

"You never mind my fire. You mind your own fire." Lao Li rolled his eyes in my direction.

Mortified by the sudden swerve of focus, I grasped for some witty, sophisticated barb, something my mother or Anna might say. When nothing came, I pretended to be engrossed in my lesson. But I'd slid too far over on my stool and now, when I leaned forward, the thing flipped right out from under me. I grabbed for a handhold and Li's tea went flying all over the desk, the primer, my shirt—

"Nice going," said Tommy. "Is that grass style or running style?"

He shouldn't have said that. Not while a full bowl of tea still remained. Because next thing I knew and faster than I could stop it, that bowl was flying after the first one, but higher, wider, and harder. It splashed directly in Tommy's face.

The bowl landed on his toe and made him jump.

"No!" Lao Li roared, and grabbed my arm. "That your future husband!"

If Tommy had been surprised by my impromptu attack, he was positively astounded by the news that we were engaged. "Future husband! Old man, you have finally gone around the bend."

"Around bend?" Lao Li released me and handed Tommy a towel.

"Too far. Wacko." Tommy skewered me with a look. "You knew about this."

I grabbed the towel from him. "Sure didn't know he had *you* in mind."

"Oh, but you were ready for him to marry you off to anybody else, huh? The ten-year-old concubine!"

"No!"

"The ten-year-old *orange-haired* concubine!" Tommy forced a laugh. "You know what 'orange' means in China? It means lots of fun, lots of babies. You get my drift?"

And suddenly I felt the sting of oncoming tears. Not daring to look or answer him, I began to mop up the desk.

"Uncle Li," said Tommy. "Let's leave each other's fire alone. *Dui?*"

"Huh!" said Li.

"*Dui?*" Tommy insisted.

"*Dui.*"

But, "He will change," Li said as soon as Tommy had gone.

"No, he won't," I replied. "I don't want him to."

The Tommy Wah of my childhood could stroke a bird with his left hand while slitting its throat with his right.

• • •

Tommy has changed. His work shows it. And his insistence on businesslike partnership. I believe he's changed and he seems intent on proving it, but the embarrassment of Li's matchmaking increasingly stands between us as the Great Unmentionable, the wall we pretend isn't there. I have not returned to his apartment and he hasn't invited me to. Nor have we met outside of working hours. Nothing that might be construed as a date. Nothing after dark.

Nothing until he called this afternoon and suggested I get some pictures of a play being staged in Columbus Park. David and some of his activist friends have a public theater company. Fairy tales for the people. Tommy would meet me there.

✲ ✲ ✲

Columbus Park is neither large nor welcoming. It has no play equipment, little grass, and because it's shadowed by the Criminal Courts Building to the west, it gets dark early. But people come, as they did when I was small. They talk, waiting for something to happen. Old men hunch over stone chess tables. Children play pavement games. Toddlers suck on long candy stems and clutch at their mothers' sleeves. Older kids taunt each other, shoot and lunge with twig weapons. As the shadows lengthen, parents pull their folding chairs beneath strings of paper lanterns.

A tent of sheets forms the backstage area. Silhouetted forms rustle the cloth. Their laughter clashes with the wary quiet of the audience outside.

He insisted he'd meet me here. Now I recognize no one. Eyes pass over me, pull away, steal hesitant glances back again. As I move, a dark circle widens around me. Without Tommy's introduction, they are afraid of me, of the bag slung over my shoulder, of my hair and eyes and skin and height. I try smiling, but my smiles glance off frozen stares.

The muttering backstage falters as a jet streaks overhead, its bright tail crossing the sky's dying band of color. The crowd grows silently. Children down in front. Parents behind. The old folks give up their game and join the spectators. But there are others now. Dim figures behind and around us. Swellings of shape and low voices. I can't see them, but I sense their breathing, their bodies adding to the midsummer's heat. There are no movie theaters in Chinatown. To sit in a close dark space here would be too dangerous and everyone knows it. Just as everyone knows why the shops must pay *lixi*. Why crimes go unreported. Why young men feel free to leer. Everyone knows. Even I know.

The women around me stoop and crouch by their children. Lights go out in windows overhead. A bird screams from the top of a tree, and my heart begins to hiccup as the surrounding space contracts. Someone is standing behind me. Eyes tight and hard, hands clenched. Long black hair. Skin glistening with sweat. The smells of salt and blood and beer.

It's in my head, I tell myself. My imagination. Because I've come alone.

I could run.

Instead I whirl and press the trigger.

The flash bursts in the eyes of a child. Mouth open, closed, wailing without a sound. A lost child.

Arms reach and snatch him up, and a woman with pink plastic elephants in her hair glowers at me, then both of them disappear. I press the camera to my face, eyes shut.

Everything I've gained in the past weeks threatens to topple back into nightmare. But I force myself to open my eyes. I won't leave. *Where* is Tommy?

A drum sounds once, twice, three times. Resolute and reassuring. Turn, it commands. Turn and listen and watch. I obey because it is something I know I can do. Gaze from a balcony into a world that never quite looks back. And find safety there.

A ripple of white silk banners makes snow. The green and blue mask of a horse canters among the folds. Other players creeping forward from the sides of the stage wear black gowns and white oval masks with the same bold details as the eggshell finger puppets Li once gave me. I look for Tommy one last time, take a reading of available light, and make the necessary camera adjustments. No flashes. The narrator addresses the audience in Chinese.

The voice I hear is Li's.

"Jade Maiden," he says. "You listen closely. This story is about you."

It was winter, snowing hard. The plows had not yet come to Catherine Street and the quiet, rare and soft as crushed silk, seemed to quilt the shop inside as well as the city without. Li said it had been a night just like this when the story began, but in Old China, in the district of Liu-ho, where a viceroy named Wu Chi lived with his wife and beautiful daughter.

"Into this night, Wu Chi's favorite steed run away. Horse name is Fortune, but in this snow and cold, Wu Chi believe horse must not be too fortunate. You know? He is wrong. Next day old man leads horse home. Oh, so old, ancient, dressed in rags, face all wrinkles, this poor gamekeeper Chu. But viceroy is so glad for his horse, he tell Chu can have any reward. Chu sees Wu Chi's daughter, jade-green eyes, skin like ivory. Chu says he is not married . . . Viceroy cry out, No! But the girl tell her father, 'Lao Chu is my fate.' And then she recite poem she spoke—a miracle!—day she was born:

Mysterious is will of Heaven!
My love in wooded darkness waits.
Ashes grown cold shall blaze anew,
Jade from gray willow sway once more.

"White turn to green to white. When green again the maiden's betrothed, Wei I-fang, ride home from duty in Emperor's army. He sees peasant woman in front of old cottage selling melons. Perfect melons, round as pearls and so fragrant! I-fang climb down from his horse to buy one, but closer he sees his beloved has become poor peasant, wife of old man. He is enraged! Draws sword against Chu. The blade shatters in his hand.

"Next day I-fang return to fight again, but finds only a peach tree with this writing:

When Jade Maiden long for earth
Immortal turns to flesh.
But fire send the fairy home,
Peach Blossom Village, Paradise.

"I-fang travels high into mountains, across deep, icy river. He sees palace of white jade near the clouds. Here gamekeeper Chu and I-fang's beloved sit in rich silks on golden throne. When I-fang comes before them, Chu tell him kowtow lower, lower, until the lady begs for mercy. Only for Jade Maiden, Chu lets I-fang go. But he tell him, 'Your fondness for violence has cost you your place in heaven. You must leave alone, never enter paradise again.'

"I-fang travels only one month home, but when he arrives, sixty years have passed. Wu Chi and his family have ascended to the skies. Only horse Fortune remains. This horse carry I-fang to an herbalist who gives him one hundred thousand strings of gold cash. I-fang use this to build new homes and roads, feed the poor. He is good and generous, soon is appointed viceroy like Wu Chi.

"One day a chariot of cranes brings Lao Chu back to earth. He tells Wei I-fang, 'You have waited long to know the truth. I am Chu the Ancient, Elder Immortal of Eternal Joy. My bride is Jade Maiden of the Upper Heaven. Her home is in Paradise, yet she longed for earth. The Celestial took pity, allowed her to go, but as she grew older He feared she would be defiled by mortal men. I was sent to rescue her and bring her back to the sky. You were wrong to oppose the will of Heaven. She could never marry you.' When finished speaking he make a sign with his hands, and fairy cranes carry him back through the clouds.

"Wei I-fang lived long and peaceful life. But he did not marry. He did not love again. And not even after death he could persuade gods to reunite him with his Jade Maiden."

A murmur runs through the audience as the players step forward, hands clasped, squinting past the lanterns. Jade Maiden, he called me. I looked it up once. It's an honest translation. Mei-bi. Little sister of Jade. He feared she'd be defiled by mortal men. But the confusion between heaven and earth, protector, beloved, mortal and god, what the maiden herself really wanted—all the rules seemed backward and suspect, and trying to figure them out made my head swim. Perhaps that's why, of all the stories Li told me, this is the one I most fully forgot. Though the outcome is true to form. For Li, true love never triumphed in the end.

Why, then, his matchmaking? To spare me from heartbreak? Or to force it on me? He reminded me of his pleasure-pain principle often enough. The thought of my old friend wishing—no, engineering—despair for me . . . But it is not impossible.

The actors blink and bow, remove their masks one by one. I recognize some of them. That's David Ling who played the viceroy and I-fang. The young woman from the bus protest. She was Jade Maiden. And Tommy.

Holding the streaked, demonic mask of Lao Chu.

I drop the camera into my bag and turn to get away before he sees me. Everywhere people are folding chairs, blankets, lifting babies over their shoulders, moving quickly and silently. I try to slip between them.

"Maibelle." The sudden closeness of his voice makes me pivot, nearly striking him. He catches my hand, holds it as if we are about to waltz.

He sees my face. "I have stage fright. If you'd known, I'd have been a mess."

"Other people knew it was you."

"Yes."

He runs his tongue across his upper lip. My right arm, clenched around the strap of my camera bag, is throbbing.

"Come to a party with me?"

I glance at the fleeing spectators. Soon the park will be empty except for the crew tearing down the stage. I concentrate on relaxing my arm.

"Party."

He grins and pulls the gown over his head. Underneath he wears a black T-shirt with "I ❤ Lubbock" printed in Day-Glo pink.

"Lubbock, Texas?"

He shrugs. "I have a friend who gets cards and gifts sent from weird places. She's never been out of New York. You'll meet her at the party."

"I didn't say I'd go."

"It's not a date, Maibelle. When we get there, I have something to give you."

"No." I catch myself. "No. I know it's not a date."

He nods, hands me his robe and mask, and picks up a backpack from the side of the stage. "Stay here a minute. I have something to take care of. Then we'll go."

He walks away from the light toward the chess tables at the far end of the park. It looks at first as though the area is filled with fireflies. Then I realize the tiny lights are cigarettes. Behind each one crouches a barely visible shadow. The pink glow of the heart and lettering on Tommy's T-shirt flashes briefly. Then, either turning or bending forward, his shadow becomes indistinguishable from the others.

Watching him disappear, I feel the same surge of panic that seized me before the play. Breathing on the back of my neck. A barely perceptible rise in temperature. Close behind me a hand spread ready to clap over my mouth. As if my brain is sweating.

"The nightmare." I say it out loud. But it's more real than that. More like déjà vu. My reaction is the dream.

I picture myself throwing the robe and mask to the ground and running from the park toward the lights of Canal Street. Uptown through Little Italy. Slowing as I reach SoHo. Walking West Broadway to Johnny and his mourning doves. Flying away with him.

My arms part. He takes something from me. He is talking. His left eyebrow has gotten tangled in itself, coarse dark hairs twisting every which way. I reach up and smooth those strands back into place.

"Lucky money," he says firmly, taking my hand. And leads me away from the shadows.

"Lin Cheng, this is Maibelle Chung."

A woman in her fifties with short salt-and-pepper hair and energetic black eyes stands in the center of a crowded loft kitchen. A best-selling cookbook author, she went to Sarah Lawrence, also works as midnight chef at Silk Road, one of the trendy new Chinese restaurants uptown.

She spots the camera bag over my shoulder.

"I need a shot for my new book. Tai says you're a professional."

I frame her against the stove with steam rising in spirals on either side. She looks like one of the witches in a Chinese production of *Macbeth*, and I'm not sure if she's serious or joking but am glad for the assignment because it gives me something to do with my hands. Tommy spent the walk up describing everyone I'd meet tonight, and I haven't retained a single detail.

"Okay, you're in!" She waves us forward. "Go join the others. We'll eat as soon as David and Lon get here."

Tommy drops his backpack in the corner, guides me past two sawhorse tables laden with food and into a dimly lit space filled with easels, painting paraphernalia, and canvases of ominous, amoebic shapes against red, white, and blue wave patterns. An assortment of old globes painted into a new world order, with whole continents shifted. I hear talking and music from the other side of the partition, but we're alone in the studio.

"Lon is a painter, too."

Lon. I grope for the connection I know I've been told. Lin Cheng's husband. He directed the play.

"Why didn't he take a bow?"

"Prefers to stay behind the scenes. Typical Chinese."

I glance down at the Leica still clutched in my hand. "What about you? Are you typical Chinese?"

"I'm joking. He's a professional actor. Doesn't want to get too attached to this amateur stuff. Especially not in Chinatown."

"No, I mean it. Which side do you prefer?"

"Of the curtain? Or my race?" When I don't reply, he says, "I prefer having a choice."

I think about that for a minute. Not what he means by it. Not even what I was really asking. Just the statement itself. A choice means multiple possibilities. Ways to go. To act. We all make different choices, and the only ones that count are those we make alone. I still don't know if I believe that.

A strong golden light slants through the doorway from the room beyond. People are dancing.

"Come here." I pull him by the shoulders until the line cuts his face in two. Half light, half dark. "Don't move. I've got fast film, but this will still take a minute."

I shoot. Again. And again with the frame wider, the exposure even longer. He plays along, looking straight through the lens. As if he can see me.

"Tai."

"What?"

"Your name. What does it mean?"

"Depends. Different intonations, different dialects, give it different meanings."

"Which do you like best?"

"Tai. Like that, with a falling tone. Means 'voice.' "

"Voice. That's a good name for a writer."

"Yes, Jade Maiden." He smiles. "Yours suits you, too."

"Tai." I push out my hand as if meeting him for the first time. He accepts, and we shake on it.

Lin Cheng's other dinner guests include Donna and LiLi, two small women who smile a lot and announce themselves as best friends, though Donna dresses like Loretta Lynn and LiLi like Laurie Anderson. Donna was the source of Tai's Texas T-shirt. LiLi is married to Ben Ying, nicknamed Dr. Shoe because he dropped out of medical school in his third year and has been selling shoes ever since. Ben entertains the ladies with yo-yo tricks. His voluptuous black hair hangs below his shoulders and he wears his pink broadcloth shirt open to reveal a gold St. Christopher medal.

Then there are Bonnie and Gene, the pair sitting cross-legged across the room arguing immigration policy. Tai whispers their story before introducing me. They were arrested three years ago for bringing recreational pharmaceuticals into the country from Hong Kong. Gene had refused to pay a tong "rent tax" on his apartment, so the associations framed him. He and Bonnie ended up being investigated by the CIA for conspiracy to dose Manhattan's water supply with Valium. They got married because their lawyer told them it would help their defense. Then the charges were dropped.

"Would you mind if I took your picture?" I ask them.

"As long as you don't publish it in Chinatown."

They pose face-to-face, like one of those figure-ground illusions; you focus on the background and see the outline of a table, the foreground a man and wife.

And suddenly everyone wants a portrait made. Kai, "the Fat Man," who runs a program for disabled children, flexes like a circus muscleman. Lee, who grew up in Staten Island and lost a brother in Vietnam, wants to be photographed doing a handstand. David Ling returns with the others from the drama troupe, and strikes the pose of Rodin's *Thinker*.

"Use a flash on me," begs Wendy, the bus protester who played the viceroy's daughter. "Go on. Right between the eyes. I'm sorry we insulted you."

What I'd feared would be viewed as a date spontaneously becomes a working session with Tai fading farther and farther from view as I spin from one set of readings to the next, establishing, however briefly and perfunctorily, a visual bridge with every person in the room. This is the first time since high school that people—friends—have asked me to take their picture.

I am dancing with Wendy, flash firing madly—friendly fire, she calls it. As she bends backward into a limbo, the Temptations break into "Ball of Confusion."

"Ball of Confucian," warbles David. Wendy falls on her back laughing.

"What! Is this disrespect for our most illustrious ancestor?" a short square man in a mauve jogging suit roars from the studio doorway. Deep furrows radiate from his eyes. His smile is like a cartoon sunrise.

"Lon," Tai explains. "Artist, director of *The Fairy's Rescue* and voice of Dynamo the Wonder Dog. You know, that collie in the dog food commercials?"

"The typical behind-the-scenes Chinese?"

"The very one."

"I spend twenty years doing small theater." Lon claps his broad hands over mine in greeting. He has a resonant, not remotely doglike voice. "I take acting lessons, go out on calls. Nothing. Then some Latino women's group pickets the advertising agency for hiring only whites, and suddenly my phone rings. If I can talk like a dog, I've got a job. Only nobody will ever see me. Nobody will know it's an Asian dog. Hah! Hah!"

He throws his head back, stretches his mouth to let out the laugh. His eyes vanish into a nest of wrinkles. "My big chance! Hah! Hah!"

It is my father's laugh. A Chinese laugh. So vast and hard it seems to crack wide open.

Instead it melts into the sound of a dinner gong. Lin Cheng calling us to feast.

It surpassed even those New Year's celebrations my father and I used to watch from our Chinatown balcony. "Ants climbing trees," Lin Cheng announced, holding a platter of crispy fried bean threads dotted with ground pork "ants." The same threadlike noodles formed the petals of "chrysanthemum flowers," which sprouted from pods of chopped prawns. Her jade rice was dotted with bright bits of spinach and pork, and in honor of the play her clear green winter melon soup was afloat with shrimp balls "pale as pearls." But the crowning glory was a whole glazed Peking duck surrounded by mounds of rice topped with cloud ears—an edible Paradise Village.

The company received this dazzling array with admiration bordering on reverence. Then, like children released from grace, they let their chopsticks fly. When plates had been filled, most of the group returned to the other end of the loft. Only Tai and I remained in the kitchen.

He poured a glass of water from the tap and watched me over the rim as he drained it. I set my plate on the counter and attempted to pick up a shrimp ball, but it slipped from my chopsticks and into the sink. He put down his glass and reached for my hand.

"You're too tense. Relax."

I tried to shake him off. "It's all right. I'm not hungry." But he moved behind me and extended my ring finger and thumb, clamping one chopstick in between, then loosened the top two fingers and slid the other stick gently between them and the tip of my thumb.

"I grew up in Chinatown." I could feel his breath on the back of my neck, the bare width of air that separated our bodies. "I've been using chopsticks all my life."

"I've watched how you use chopsticks." He pressed my middle finger to create a pincer movement and lowered his voice. "Like a crab."

His arm curled around mine, he guided my hand to the plate, then back with its pearl to my mouth. I tasted the salty smell of him and turned abruptly, dropping the shrimp ball. It rolled, leaving a warm brown trail down the front of my white shirt.

"You're not concentrating." He got down on his knees to fetch the runaway under the cabinet. An extremely disappointed cockroach scurried back into its crack. Tai retrieved his quarry but left a pinch for the kitchen guardian.

I fished among the pots in the sink and pulled out a soapy rag. The stain on my shirt grew larger instead of smaller for my efforts. The wet fabric clung to my breast. Finally, with as much finesse as I could muster, I tossed over my shoulder, "You said you had something to give me."

He cleared his throat. I heard him stand, the rustle of feet and hands, crunch of paper.

"Recognize these?" He pulled from the bag a stack of framed photographs.

Sad eyes fastened in time.

Tai placed the stack in my hands and wrapped his fingers around mine. "Li gave them to me before he died and told me to find you. He wanted you to have them."

• • •

In the weeks after Li Tsung Po named my intended husband, I watched Tommy Wah more closely. On the basketball courts he elbowed his opponents and swore as aggressively as a Brooklyn hood. In the arcade, he and Henry sang "Cool Jerk" and "Barefootin'" as duets so often and so loudly that the manager threatened to throw them out if they didn't shut up. But while Henry did his best to corrupt him, Tommy's face was still Chinese. He treated his parents with respect, worked in their store without pay. He attended Chinese school by his own choice, which was almost unheard-of for ABC boys.

"What are you doing hanging out with Li Po?" he demanded the one time he caught me watching him.

"We're friends. Do you mind?"

He stood with his hands on hips, legs apart. We were exactly equal in height, but his confidence made him seem taller.

"Friends, huh? Well, you're wasting your time."

"What are you, jealous?"

He gave a short laugh. "Don't worry, kiddo. I'm just looking out for you."

"I think you're afraid you'll end up marrying me."

"Me marry a *huaiguo ren*! No way."

"You're practically married to Henry, and he's just as Anglo as I am."

"Buddies aren't brides. Different rules apply."

"Fine by me." I pulled up tall and looked him straight in the eye. "I already have a fiancé. He has blond hair and knows how to fly."

....

13

I am standing above a moonscape, sky black with stars punched like holes over a valley of snow-swept hills and craters. I am standing on sheer, mirrored ice at the edge of a cliff with Johnny to one side, Marge Gramercy the other. Johnny squats, his thick hair lifting, white as the snow. Marge sits and dangles her legs like a child. She has been telling how she took this photograph with only moonlight by stopping all the way down, fast film, slow shutter. Her voice surrounds us in a blur of quiet, comforting detail. You can do anything you want, it insists, you are the living proof. But as she talks I feel the ice slipping beneath my feet like a treadmill to the edge. I reach for Johnny, and he catches my elbow, pulling me forward and down toward the cliff. When I look up into the sharp, weathered wrinkles where his eyes should be, I find only gaping holes.

"If you died right now," he asks, letting me fall, "how would *your* obituary read?"

• • •

Soon after Lao Li's announcement of my betrothal to Tommy Wah, my grandmother sent a photograph of Johnny taken a few months after

Henry shot him. He was pictured on the driver's seat of Grampa's tractor with Grampa standing on the platform behind, both of them grinning like maniacs. In the accompanying note, Gramma Lou said Johnny's arm was good as new, Grampa was on his best behavior, and, she added in a brave P.S., they all missed me a great deal.

"Do you think we'll go back to the farm this summer?" I asked Anna.

I was sitting at my desk, supposedly doing homework, but my attention kept getting lost in the tie-dyed swirls of fabric my sister had hung in the window. She lay on her bed, designing her nails in black and white polish. The Beatles were on the radio.

"Maybe you will, but I'm not." Anna sat up, waving toes and fingers to dry them. "I've had enough of Mum's duty trips to last me a lifetime. Let her drag you around and bitch to you what a bigoted asshole Grampa is. I know the rap already. Place bores the shit out of me, anyway."

She strolled over and picked up Johnny's picture. Her face brightened. "But then, I don't have a lover boy there."

I flushed as fast and hot as if she'd set fire beneath me. "Give me that!"

"Oo ooh." She held it above my head and lip-synched to "I Want to Hold Your Hand."

"Give it!" I lunged, grabbing and tearing the photo in two. Grampa Henry remained intact, but Johnny was beheaded.

"You bitch!" I screamed as my mother walked in.

"Maibelle! What in God's name . . ."

"Look what she did!" I was sobbing now.

"*I* did! I was just teasing. You tore the picture." Anna returned to her bed and pretended to be engrossed in a Herman's Hermits album. Anna loathed Herman's Hermits.

My mother took a deep breath and assured me that she had some tape somewhere, but I must never again call my sister a bitch.

"Are we going back to Wisconsin this summer?"

"Well," she said. "Actually, I thought we might make a tour of New England. Boston, Nantucket, see a little of Vermont. It's about time Anna started looking at colleges, and we might even get your father to come along."

"I'm not going to college," Anna said. "I'm going to work at Andy Warhol's Factory."

"Over my dead body," Mum said.

"What if I went to Wisconsin by myself?" I suggested. "You could put me on the train and Gramma Lou could pick me up in Milwaukee."

"We'll see." My mother stared at Anna's back. I could tell my summer was doomed.

The picture was still lying in pieces on the desk when my grandmother called the next day.

Anna picked up the phone. "Hi, Gramma Lou," and a moment later her face turned white. "No. Nobody's home except me and Maibelle." She listened, nodded, sat on the floor. And refused to look at me.

At last Anna said, "No, I don't think so. She's standing right here, practically on top of me. Yeah, maybe you better . . . Here." She got up to hand me the receiver, touched my shoulder. "Sit down, Maibee."

I took the phone but didn't sit down. I was too young to know that you are supposed to sit when being told bad news. So it was the touch on my shoulder, my sister's sudden gentleness, that let me know I was in trouble. In that instant I thought—what? That Grampa Henry had pneumonia? Gramma was always saying he was going to catch pneumonia because he took such lousy care of himself. That they'd lost their crop and the bank was foreclosing on the farm? There was a lot of foreclosure talk in Wisconsin. Or maybe Gramma herself was sick?

No, I was just fighting to shut out the thought that Johnny had been shot again.

But it wasn't that. It was much more obvious.

Johnny had gone flying.

Gramma was saying, "You know how he wanted to fly. But of course everybody assumed he meant later, when he was grown, maybe he'd join the service and learn how to fly a real airplane. Who knew he had this crazy idea he could fly by *himself*?"

I knew.

I pictured him standing in the hayloft window, a warm breeze lifting his silvery bangs, sunlight making him squint so that his blue eyes looked almost black. His arms were skinny, and I could trace the bones of his rib cage beneath his white T-shirt. His baggy jeans weighed him down, pinned him to the darkness inside the barn as those arms, light as feathers, reached out into space.

"Johnny was a bird in a previous life and couldn't bear to shed his wings." That would be my sister's conclusion years later, after the spiritual seed that was planted today had fully taken root. For the moment, she just stood there staring at the decapitated photograph.

"Where?" I said. "Where was he?"

"Oh, dear God." I saw my grandmother breathing deep, wiping her forehead with her white handkerchief, shutting her eyes while she chose her words. I took some deluded hope from the image, as if by feeling enough hurt ourselves, we might be able to bring him back.

"He went up the silo, honey. He went out there in the middle of the night when everybody else was asleep. His mama keeps saying he was sleepwalking, and I don't know, maybe she's right. Least, it seems to make her feel better—like he didn't know what was happening, didn't really mean it. And, I guess, if he was asleep, there wasn't much she could've done to stop it. What can you do to stop someone dreaming?"

I stopped him once. He scared me enough for that. But then he wowed me with his fairy tales, and instead of deciding he was crazy I fell under his spell. I didn't understand that I was the only one who knew. I had no idea the danger he was in.

But I should have. Flying from the hayloft was just one clue. There was his fear of Glabber, too—that crazy fear, because he was a flying man who'd crashed. And his relief at Glabber's death. Safe, he'd written. Safe for what? Safe to fly, maybe. And those imaginary men—

"Did he have anything with him when he jumped, Gramma?"

"With him?"

"You know, was he holding onto anything? Did he have anything in his pocket—"

"Oh, I see what you mean. Yes, honey, I think he did—in his pocket. Some sort of feather, they said. A real pretty feather. Blue and green."

"A kingfisher's feather?"

"I think that was it. How did you know?"

"And did anybody talk to him after . . . before he . . ."

"No. No. See, Maibelle, his neck was broken. They think it happened right away."

"Don't they *know*?" Now I saw Johnny lying in the dark, like one of those strangled ducks, like the Chinatown chicken with silver-dollar eyes. I felt sick.

Gramma was saying, "I'm just not sure, honey. No one knew it had happened till this morning . . ."

I threw the phone at Anna and raced to the bathroom, where I vomited until I lost consciousness.

It was late morning when I woke up. Dad was stroking my hair.

Anna had gone. To school, I guessed, and Henry, too. The room was quiet, except for the sound of running water. They'd washed my face and put me into a nightgown, but I still smelled the sickness on me.

"I want to take a shower."

Dad said, "Mum's run a bath."

"I don't want a bath, I want a shower." I needed to rinse off yesterday and send it down the drain. The last thing I wanted was to lie in it.

"Mei Mei."

Little Sister. He almost never called me that unless he was feeling very sentimental—and helpless.

"I *need* a shower."

How could he possibly understand? Summer after summer we went away and he stayed in Chinatown. If he'd been with us last summer, Johnny might still be alive. Dad would have stopped Henry and Grampa, for sure. And if he'd been there, I could have told him about Johnny's trying to fly. And he would have understood.

Dad reached for my hand. I punched him in the face.

My knuckles hit the bone in his jaw with a sickening crack, and the look on his face! Like a well collapsing. He grabbed me around the back and pulled me to his chest, held me there while I cried and he sat quiet as stone.

I heard the door open, my mother start to say something. Then she went away.

When I finally stopped crying, I could feel his hand smoothing my hair again. I didn't want to look at him, and he didn't push me back so I had to. He rocked me like a baby and spoke over my head, half to me, half to himself. "People will tell you you'll be all right. It will pass. It will all work out for the best. And they're right, all those things are true. But you won't ever be the same again. You don't have to worry about that, Maibelle. You won't ever be the same."

My mother came and bundled me into my bath, filled the air with words as she soaped my back and lathered my hair. Did I want to talk about what happened? She'd spoken to Gramma Lou last night, but there wasn't any more news. Everybody was holding up as well as they could. What else was there to do? A hot bath would make me feel better, and then I could have a warm cup of cocoa. Maybe we'd go out to lunch later, just the three of us.

I hardly recognized this mother hen. When President Kennedy died, she fell to pieces, and she'd never even met *him*. For Johnny she couldn't cry?

"Just leave me alone!"

She stood up without another word, put a clean towel within my reach, and left the room.

My father was right. What I feared most was that I'd be the same, that it would be as if Johnny never existed. That as I stopped grieving I'd stop remembering how special a friend he was. I didn't have enough friends to let them go like that.

Only Mr. Li now. And if Johnny could break his neck on a dream, how could I count on Lao Li?

I'd never thought about Li's age in terms of death. At first he seemed old and creepy, too strange to be my friend. Then his oldness made him more interesting. Now it was a door, threatening to shut against me.

I came out to drink my mother's cocoa but couldn't think of anything to say to her, and everything she said annoyed me. At last she decided she might as well go to work, and I retreated to Dad's workroom.

"Do you believe in ghosts?" I asked him.

"Mm." He stuck a wad of clay over the mouth of a milk bottle and began to mold it. "Not the kind you mean." He pushed the clay top flat with his thumb. "Not Halloween ghosts, or the ghosts in old Chinese stories. But people leave ghosts of themselves in other people."

"What do you mean?"

"Your friend Johnny has left his ghost in you." He swiveled in his chair to face me. "One day you'll see him walk down the street. He will be there in the mirror, you'll feel him over your shoulder, and if you tell anyone else, they'll say you're dreaming—and maybe you are, but it keeps him real. It makes him part of you. You need that to keep going."

Something in his voice made me itchy. It was too earnest, uncharacteristically direct.

"How do you know all this? Do you have a ghost in you?"

"A few."

"Are they good ones?"

"Good and bad." He picked up a file and scored the edges of the clay. "Funny thing about ghosts—when they move inside, they become much more complicated. They surprise you. Sometimes you find yourself laughing for no reason. Or you get so bloody angry you could spit."

"Angry at the ghosts?"

"At what they make you see in yourself. At the strings they pull."

I liked the idea that Johnny might weasel his way into my head from time to time, but I was crying again.

My father sat next to me. When I buried my face in his shirt, I smelled the Kents in his breast pocket, his tobacco skin and breath. Usually I hated these smells, but not today.

"I never got to say goodbye!"

"I know. That's the hardest part."

I nodded.

"If you'd been able to say goodbye," Dad said, "you might have kept him alive."

I shrugged.

"But there's another possibility."

I felt the solidity of Dad's body, the drumming of his heart. He pushed me back to look into my face. The moonpuffs seemed to intensify his concern. He cupped my cheeks in his hands.

"He might have taken you with him, Mei Mei. And that's too high a price for goodbye."

Suddenly I had to get away. My feelings ran from soothing to scalding like a temperamental shower. My father was doing his best, and his best came close—much closer than Mum's—but there were still too many hot spots where the slightest touch was agony.

I left him with his clay bottle top and went out to walk.

April in New York. On the trees around the Criminal Courts Building tiny green parcels burst from dead, gray bark. Bright sunshine threw crisp shadow branches across the pavement. Limbs reached and crossed, reached and crossed into a massive web engulfing the long skinny line of my body. A plane crossed on approach to La Guardia, and its darkness gobbled mine.

I walked over to Baxter Street, past the shabbier nontourist stores that sold plastic shoes and polyester clothing. Past Mr. Yang's medicine store, with its huge gnarled ginseng root filling the front window. Henry said the hundreds of jars and boxes inside held dried and pickled rhino's horn, eel stomach, horse's hoof, tails of lizards, dogs, and deer, tiger testicles, and sea dragon. But there were no ancient miracle cures for Johnny anymore.

"Looking for lunch?"

I jumped as if I'd been whipped. Tommy Wah laughed and took a step backward. I began to cry.

"Hey," he said. "I didn't mean to scare you."

I shook my head fiercely, but no words came and the tears refused to stop. He held out a handkerchief. A white pressed man's handkerchief of the kind old-fashioned bankers wear in their breast pockets. Too perfect to actually use. But my nose was running now, beyond anything the back of my hand could manage.

Tommy started forward. He was frowning, and as he leaned toward me the white cloth dangled at the end of his arm like a warning flag on an open tailgate.

I snatched it, spun, and ran away before he could say another word.

Without turning back I could see Tommy's startled eyes, the sudden straightening of his body, the sneakers lifting and falling, hitting the pavement faster, faster. Dodging bodies and cars, I skirted the Criminal Courts Building, headed west out of Chinatown, then south and back. I'd traveled ten blocks before I turned to make sure I'd lost him. Then I stopped and blew my nose hard, wiped my eyes.

The handkerchief was embroidered with the Wah name in Chinese characters surrounded by a circle of pale green rosettes. It was crumpled now, soggy and disgusting. Though I knew I should wash and iron it, give it back, my mind started to whirl with the complications—the possibilities for losing it in the Laundromat, the inevitable questions if my mother found it, the ridicule from Henry and Anna if they caught me pressing it. Henry would know it was Tommy's, and the cycle would start all over again. Only this time it wouldn't be worth the pain.

I balled the cloth in my fist, shoved it into an empty paper bag I found on top of a garbage can, buried the bag under a pile of orange rinds. And walked slowly to Catherine Street.

I had never mentioned Johnny to Li, so I didn't expect him to understand or sympathize. But he knew, instantly, that something was wrong. He pursed his mouth, the sides turning down, lips thrust out in a grotesque air-kiss. He didn't offer me a cookie or start winding up for a story.

He stared at me for a minute or two, then said, "You have Chinese writing set."

I had no idea what he was talking about.

"Brush. Ink. Stone. You know—Chinese writing set. Bring that here. I will teach you write Chinese."

It dawned on me that he was talking about the basket in our basement.

"How—?"

"Never mind, never mind. You go home, get that writing set. I have present for you."

I let his instructions stop my thinking, erase my fears. I followed them swiftly, but when I returned, a wall of black clouds had blocked the sun, and a cold wind churned up from the river.

"Good," Lao Li said. "Rain is bad for customers, good for lessons." He had cleared his desk as if he expected to devote the whole afternoon to instruction.

"You sit here." He arranged a plump silk pillow in his chair to boost me to working height and settled himself on a stool by my side. Then he took the basket of writing tools and slid open the top.

"Your papa has shown you how to use?" he asked.

"No."

"He never write Chinese?"

"No."

Lao Li wagged his head as he fingered the basket's contents. The movement of his hands was so full of respect that I was embarrassed by the memory of Anna and me dueling with the brushes. He took each one in turn, rolled the wooden handle between his thumb and forefinger, spit on the fingers of his other hand and used the spittle to smooth the bristles down to a perfect point. There were four brushes in all, each the length of my forearm but ranging in width from fat to skinny.

"Like people." Lao Li arranged them on the desk. He pointed to the biggest brush. "This one very rich. He eat too much, move slow, but very, very elegant." He pointed to the skinny brush. "He never have enough to eat, always work too much. He run fast, crazy. Both speak same words, make same pictures, but talk very different."

"So which do I use?"

He looked me up and down as if he'd never seen me before, then picked up a midsize brush.

"Not too fast, not too slow. Not too big, not too little." He smiled.

I picked up one of the ink sticks and rolled it between my fingers the way he'd rolled the brushes. A black chrysanthemum spread its petals beneath a black bird in flight, beneath a seal stamped gold. The carved edges resisted the pressure of my skin. But one end of the stick had been worn smooth, cutting off the top of the seal, replacing gold with air.

Lao Li placed a small lacquer cup on the desk, filled it with water from a jug by his side, then reached into the basket for the oval brass box that contained the inkstone. In one half a tiny pond of slate, in the other a dirty field of silk down. He took the brush and dabbed it in the water, painted the stone and took the ink, skated it, gold down, around the pond. His whole arm traced the circle one way, once, twice, three times, then the other, once, twice, three times. I watched the slate push into the gold, the sky below the flying bird shrink as a wash of black mud thickened across the surface of the pond.

Mr. Li's fingertips were clean. He placed the ink stick back in the basket and reached into his top drawer.

"Your present," he said. "Please. Open."

A calligraphy primer. Page after page of sheer, almost transparent paper sectioned into squares, each square filled with the dotted outline of a basic character, with arrows to direct the brush. Paint by arrow, except there were no colors and the picture was not a picture but a word.

"First number." Lao Li pointed at page one (back page), square one (right column), and in it the dotted outline of a single horizontal line. "*Yi.* One. Very easy."

He took the brush and placed it upright in my hand. Automatically I repositioned it as I would a pencil. He held the stem up and gripped my hand, forcing the fingers into position along the wood.

"Brush must always point to heaven," he said. "If not, how can gods help you?"

He guided my arm to dip the brush in water, rolled it against the silk to taper the bristles, then slid them through the ink.

"You write number one," he said. "Like this." And in the air he moved his arm in a conductor's downbeat followed by a slight lift and sideways sweep, finishing up at the level where he'd started. "Now you do."

I held the brush the way he showed me and drew a line across the square. The ink squirted over the borders, making a large blob.

"Hmm." Lao Li gave me a look, adjusted the brush in my hand again, and drew a line in the air flat above the desk. "Here is paper.

Now, like this—" and, grabbing me at the elbow, he pushed my arm through the motion he himself had just shaped.

"Like dancing," he said. "You dance in air, your feet make Chinese writing."

"You have to be a ghost to dance in air."

"Okay," he said. "Be ghost."

There were four more squares in the column with the outline of number one. I tried again.

The ink still went over the borders, but it was more of a smudge than a squirt.

"Better." Lao Li repositioned the brush and moved my arm above the next square. "Again."

Yi. Er. San. One line. Two lines. Three lines. Now I was too far inside the borders.

"No good," Li said. "Too little, too much is not just right."

"How can drawing a line be so hard!"

"You think too much, try too much. Let brush and ink think, you will do better."

"Maybe I'm just not good at this."

"Your grandfather was great scholar. Maybe these his brushes and ink. 'No good' is no excuse for you. You know? You work hard, think less, you be okay."

Once again he seemed to know more about my family than I did, but I'd given up asking how he came by these details.

"It's too much like art. I'm not good at art."

"Not art," he said. "Come."

He took my hand and led me out into the gathering thunderstorm. "Chinese writing is like wind and rain." He lifted my palm toward the east. Push push release. Push push push release. Push release.

I felt the rhythm of the weather changing in my bones.

"Like sound." He raised my hand to his lips and counted: "*Yi. Er. San. Si. Wu. Liu. Oi. Ba. Jiu. Shi.*"

I felt the rhythm of Lao Li's words moving beneath my fingertips.

"Like breath." He placed my hand on my chest. Up down. Up down. Up down.

I felt the rhythm of my own life. Strong, steady, stable.

"Everything connect." Li linked his fingers. "You breathe alone. I breathe alone. But is all same breath." He grinned and whipped up the wind with his arm.

"Old time, new time," he said. "All same time."

The rain, which had been a fine drizzle, turned to heavy drops.

"Water in clouds, in river. But is all same water." He caught a handful and pushed it through his hair. The wetness glistening on his forehead made him look vibrant, not exactly younger but as if he'd been mystically freshened. It was like some kind of blessing.

Li stuck out his tongue and drank the rain. Dirty rain, city rain, I thought—but never mind. I, too, threw back my head, let the downpour soak my face and hair.

And wept again for Johnny. For the knowledge that he would have loved this moment; for the faith I still did not quite have that my father and Li were right about Johnny always being there with me, around in his own way.

We stayed like this as the storm pressed on. Lao Li laughed as I wept and the rain washed away my tears.

The weather was clearing when my father found us. I'd stopped crying. Li and I were not talking, just standing side by side and watching the sunshine patch through the clouds. I didn't notice Dad until he called my name, but Li's whole body was turned as if he'd been tracking him for some distance. Li's lips were parted, showing just a sliver of gold teeth. His eyes were open wider than I could remember seeing them, and he didn't blink. With his hair slicked back by the rain he looked hungry. Starving.

My father slowed as he neared our end of the block. He was wearing one of those dime-store pocket raincoats that never unwrinkle, an ugly pinkish color with his checked shirt showing through. The hood had fallen back so his hair and face were drenched. I thought, this was how he would look if he cried.

Dad called my name again but he wasn't looking at me. He was squinting at Li and his arms were moving mechanically, almost like a soldier's.

It didn't occur to me to go forward to meet him. I felt as if I hadn't moved in weeks, not that I couldn't but there seemed no need to. The act of breathing seemed enough. I might have been in the audience watching my father and Li in a movie.

"I got worried with the rain." Dad was panting a little. "Are you all right?"

"She is all right," said Li quietly. "How are you?"

My father didn't answer, and now that he was with us he stopped looking at Li. He bent his legs until he reached my level. He touched my sopping hair and shirt.

"You must be freezing." His voice was a low, worried grumble. I shook my head. I felt perfectly warm. "It's time to come home, Mei Mei."

"Mei Mei?" Li nodded approvingly.

We formed a triangle the way we were standing. Li was staring at my father, my father at me. I looked back and forth. Only then did I realize that Dad might not know Li and I were friends. And then I remembered I was disobeying him by being here.

"I feel better," I said.

But he didn't sound angry. "Your mother will be back soon. She'll be frantic if you're gone."

"How is Diana?" Li asked as if he were an old friend of the family's.

My father and I both stared at him. From the beginning Li had asked me about my father, my brother and sister, but never mentioned my mother. I'd decided he either didn't know she existed or else thought of her as another white witch.

Again, Dad didn't answer. He reached for my hand, then reeled me in, first the wrist, elbow, shoulders, until he had me clasped in a hug that stopped my breathing. When he let go, his eyes were wet, and not from the rain.

"I'm okay, Dad."

"Thank you," he said.

"You are welcome, of course," said Lao Li.

My father led me away. He didn't ask what I was doing with Li, and he didn't forbid me to see him again. But just a few months later he sold his bottle cap patent. We left Chinatown within the year.

CHEN K. WONG M.D.
王景光
TEL 732-2727
CHINATOWN
VIDEO GAMES
WORLD FAMOUS
DANCING & TIC-TAC-TOE
CHICKENS
GIFTS, INC.
TEL. 732-4637
บางกอก
MUSEUM
live chicken
COST
PRECISELY
REVS

Part V

Chinaman's Whore

....

14

I received this letter this morning.

Maibelle Love,

During afternoon darshan today I saw your face so clearly, heard your complaint, felt your sadness and anger, I decided the Buddha wanted me to connect with you, and the Big D concurred. How I wish you would try a different path to the truth you are seeking. Since I surrendered to the Dhawon I have been blessed by such light and acceptance. It has cleansed me of all vile thought and confusion. Transformation is the way to enlightenment, Maibelle. You must step out of your past self as if it were a suit of ill-fitting old clothes. Leave behind what happened. The Dhawon says there are too many bodies for this planet, anyway, and too few of us fit to raise those already born. Children deserve joy and truth and harmonic bliss. If we ourselves have not yet attained enlightenment, then we have no right to create new life. This is why I have followed the Dhawon's wisdom and had myself sterilized. It is why you must not mourn or punish yourself for what is past. The new life you are creating now is your own, Maibelle. You must die to rational thought, expectation, convention. Move beyond death to the wholly compassionate welcoming grace of the Buddha, yourself, and the Universal Now.

Peace be with you.

Your loving sister,
Aneela Prem

My brother was no help at all.

"How *could* you?"

"Maibelle, calm. Breathe deeply. Transcend."

"Cut the crap. Why Anna, of all people?"

"Darling, I never told a soul. Not that I can see what the big deal is. Now, if you'd *had* the kid—"

"You're sure?"

"I told you. Not a soul."

"That includes Mum and Dad?"

"No, they've got souls, at least last time I checked."

"Asshole."

"Atta girl."

"No one?"

"No."

I listened, weighing his silence as if it were a lie detector. He had Smokey Robinson on. "Tears of a Clown."

I said, "Well. While we're on the subject, you might think about getting that operation of yours reversed."

"Do tell."

"Anna's had one, too. As it stands I'm this family's last hope of succession."

"Any prospects?"

"Not that I'd tell you. How's Coralie."

"I appreciate the confidence. Likewise, I'm sure. Don't spend it all in one place."

My brother's wit won't crack the code of my sister's message. I want to believe it's just cult babble, but there's something behind her words that unnerves me. Like a five-dollar fortune-teller who know things she can't possibly know but refuses to tell what they mean. This is my first letter from Anna since she stopped acknowledging birthdays as part of some spiritual indoctrination ten years ago.

I would call her, but there are no phones at her ashram, and the nearest town is some twenty miles away.

It's four in the morning, and I won't sleep again tonight. I've just had a new dream about Johnny. It starts all right. We're lying together beneath a huge globe. His hands are outstretched, white and transparent, full of deep blue veins. I try to touch him, but he leaps to his feet, starts running. I follow him over long green lawns toward a line of ocean. He slows to a walk, but doesn't stop at the shore. He walks on water.

"It's okay," he calls back over his shoulder. "Who needs China? Come on!"

He stops to wait for me, digs his toes into the ocean. He wears torn blue jeans and a white T-shirt, his hair a mop of light.

I run along the beach, looking for a way out to him. He continues on and I trail him. The waves lap at my feet. I sink into sand. He keeps going, farther, farther out, and I keep after him, but now I feel someone's breath against the back of my neck, pressing forward, closer.

"Stay with me," he calls. "Don't look back! You can marry me in your dreams."

I run until the breath from behind pours through me, burning my throat and crushing my chest. I let it pull me down. Johnny sinks beyond the horizon.

Then unseen hands turn my head around to a face as white as eggshell, with straw hair and blackened teeth. Eyes that glitter like jewels.

Henry's basement bogeyman.

Dear Anna,

I appreciate your letter and the concern behind it, but I am confused. What, exactly, must I leave behind? What is all this business about children? I am not angry. I really don't know what you are talking about, so I'd appreciate an explanation in clearer, more basic terms. There seems to be a lot I don't remember these days, a lot I am trying to understand.

I'm sorry we argued when you were here. I miss you, Anna.

Your sister,
Maibelle

• • •

There have been no further chopsticks lessons, no more parties, though I have seen Tai's friends in the street and they always greet me by name and stop for a casual chat. Once when I was walking alone back to my apartment, I saw Lin Cheng outside Dean and Deluca on Prince Street. I thanked her again for the sumptuous feast, apologized for taking so long with her book jacket photograph. "Oh, you are welcome," she answered. "Any friend of Tai's is friend of ours. I was just joking about the picture, anyway. I don't really need one." She meant it kindly, but the underlying statement hurt. In my own mind I still have not passed the point of needing a house key, a mission, a sponsor to gain entrance. If I tried to go back alone, I'd again feel eyes burning like switchblades into the small of my back.

But I also know I have to keep going. Marge tells me so. And the White Witch. She and her children fill the mantelpiece. Li lied, she assures me. The white witches did not cast their children out to wander forever in the ether between the living and the dead; they were good mothers, watchful mothers. The men simply misunderstood. China men. White men. Those were the two worlds between which the women were forced to wander with their children. But the children bore the blood of both worlds, and that gave them the right of safe passage.

The children are the lucky ones, their mother reassures me, if they could only see.

I must be starting to see. Harriet hasn't called the police on me in months, and my recurrent nightmares have stopped. These new dreams about Johnny and Marge are disturbing, but I wake up quickly, before the terror builds. No screaming or crying, just a quietly pounding heart. Once or twice I've actually tried sleeping with the lights out and made it through to morning.

The why is harder to figure. I'm at last allowing myself to accept—even embrace—these memories of Li and Johnny, Johnny's death; could that be the miracle cure? Or is it that I've finally disproven my falling dream and made peace with the White Witch? I have to accept the possibility that I may never know.

Anna's curious letter remains another mystery. Given my sister's fits and starts, anything is possible, but I persist in believing Henry must somehow have let my secret slip and she read into it more than was warranted.

Aside from my father's refusal to look at my work, the rest of the family front has been quiet. With Foucault—and now Coralie—back in Europe, my mother is channeling her energy into motivating Henry toward an apartment and job. She's giving me the silent treatment, for which I am truly grateful. If she knew of my work with Tai, she'd be all over me. She'd demand to view the contacts, recommend cropping, which to enlarge, which negatives to burn and which to print as Delong-sized monoliths. She'd go on about how she "sees" the exhibit. Or else she'd lay them all quietly aside and say with that restrained quaver in her voice that it's good I've finally started working again, and I'd spend the rest of the month in a funk. Because as disgusting as I consider my mother's betrayal of Dad, as willing as I am to go behind her back to seek his reviews, I still dread Mum's criticism. Especially now, when I genuinely believe my work is strong and getting better.

I can say that with some assurance, because I'm finally developing the reams of film I've collected over these weeks. Of course, I've been in the darkroom all along printing up my Noble work, but I kept putting off the Chinatown footage. Not wanting to face the potential ghosts, I suppose. Not wanting to break Tai's faith. Or my parents'.

But now I've developed it all, from those first shots of the bus protest to the footage I took this morning of *gong xi fang,* tenement rooms divided by sheets into cubbyholes where as many as fifteen men sleep like caged mice in apartments smaller than mine. The contacts hang from clothespins, still glistening from the bath, and even in this miniature format some frames—the pinch-faced men and women with downcast eyes—make me want to burn the lot. But others, in which the subjects have held on to their dignity, grant me a reprieve. The mah-jongg queen in the Mets sweatshirt flashing her mountainous winnings. Two skinny young men with their pants rolled up, feet clad in farmer's sandals, like eager novitiates at the Division Street Off-Track Betting Parlor. Lin Cheng's round, demonic laugh (it would make a *wonderful* cookbook cover) and Tai, with his handsome face halved into shadow and light. The others I've sneaked of him, squatting beside a cluster of girls playing a game with chalk and pebbles, or trading jokes with sidewalk vendors amid cymbal-clapping pandas and stuffed pink dogs.

I'm experienced enough to know that Tai's photogenic features are not the only reason his pictures are turning out right. It's been almost three months since Jed Moffitt claimed the honor of being my last affair.

I slide a negative of Tai taking his stage bow into the carrier and turn on the enlarger. I adjust knobs until his image fills the easel. A strong-featured face even in normal light, its contours leap upward in the glow of the stage lanterns. I fiddle with the focus, softening the lines of his chin and jaw. His eyes seem to widen, his mouth to move. The silk banners stretch sideways behind him in a blur. His hair slips into his eyes, disturbed by the removal of his old man's mask, which he holds like a shield in front of his chest.

I was a child when I posed Tai and Johnny Madison as adversaries and gave Johnny the winning hand. That must be why it's so hard to accept what I feel for Tai as desire, but I think of him. I linger on him.

I remember things about him that I can't account for: the smile that seems to flicker on his lips; the way he rubs the tips of his thumbs together when he's thinking, or casually tosses one leg over the other when sitting to hear a story. That he works best at five in the morning and would be a Quaker if he chose any religion, because the Quakers really do practice nonviolence. I think of the low, gentle wash of his voice as he told me these things. I've spent more time with Tai than I have with any lover, and yet the moments of intimacy have been only tentative and fleeting.

I snap off the light, place a sheet of paper on the easel. His face reappears and I make my decision.

• • •

When I invited him to my apartment to view the test prints, I half expected him to make some lewd remark: "Is that like coming up to see your etchings?" He didn't. He never would have, anyway. But that was my projection.

We had spent the last two hours at a day-care center on Henry Street listening to children's tales of harrowing border crossings and impoverished refugee camps. "Let's walk," was all Tai said.

So we walked, although the sky had the color and texture of an ocean storm. Gusts of wind sent awnings rippling in waves, and as we reached Houston Street the pent-up rain let loose a downpour. We had no rain gear, not even jackets, as it had been hot and muggy earlier. All around us people were retreating into doorways for shelter, but without giving the matter any real thought I reached over and tagged Tai's hand.

"You're on!" I shouted, running.

It was a lunatic move. We were each carrying a heavy burden of equipment. At every corner cars and buses lurched with spastic imprecision, and the downpour intermittently gave way to hailstones that rolled like marbles. But once possessed by the competitive impulse, I was its captive. I heard the horns and screeching tires from underwater. I felt the rain thick in my eyes, my clothes plastered against my body, but I felt more strongly Tai's presence behind me closing in tighter, harder, threatening to overtake and tackle me. What had started as a game acquired an edge of panic.

I ran head down, arms stroking the air like mad fish fins for block after block, never looking back. By the time I finally turned the last corner I was deafened by the roar of my own breath.

He touched my shoulder before I could get the key into the lock. I jumped as if he'd stabbed me.

"You won, Maibelle."

I was panting too hard to talk. He didn't even sound winded. I forced the key and pushed the door, but he held me from moving forward.

"Someday," he said to the back of my neck, "I'd like to know what that was all about."

There was a rushing sound above us, rhythmic thumps of feet bounding down the stairs. Larraine Moseley burst into the light. Her pink jersey catsuit showed, skintight, through a transparent slicker.

"Oh, gee. Hi!" She came to an abrupt halt at the sight of Tai and flashed me a wide-eyed grin. "God, dontcha just love this weather!" And with that, she bounced down the steps to the street and a waiting cab.

I reached up and removed Tai's hand from my shoulder. Moments later we stood laughing in front of the mirror in my apartment.

"We look like drowned muskrats."

"Not drowned. Just soggy." He stared at me in the mirror for a long moment. In the reflection we were touching. "Your teeth are chattering, Mei-bi. Better get into some dry clothes."

Instead I went searching for towels and a pair of pants and T-shirt that Henry had left behind. I expected to find Tai snooping among my things when I returned (in his place, I'd have wanted to spy), but he was staring out the window.

"Look."

I followed his gaze through the streaming glass to Greenwich Avenue. In the downpour the beams of headlights quivered like shafts of silver, and the storefronts had the watery glow of aquariums. Between these pockets of light the darkness was bleak and sinister with the trees in the old lady's garden rising like giant toadstools.

I handed Tai the towels. "Weather does strange things, doesn't it? In college I took a series of photographs of a children's jungle gym after a blizzard. First thick and soft, all padded with snow. Then draped with icicles. After it rained and froze again, it looked like glass tubing. The thing was solid steel but it was as if the weather kept trying to turn it into something else."

Tai was silent a moment rubbing his hair until it stood in soft points all over his head. The movement was so abrupt and vigorous that I regretted everything I'd just said. How pretentious I must sound! From her perch on the mantel the White Witch caught my eye and frowned.

Tai dropped the towel and combed his hair with his fingers. He spoke quietly, speculatively. "I'd like to see those pictures sometime."

"They're gone," I lied. "That's probably the only reason I think they were any good. Absence makes the heart grow fonder and all."

He accepted my brother's clothes and moved toward the bathroom, but when he reached the threshold he turned. "It's not losing something you value that causes heartbreak, Maibelle, but refusing to let anything take its place."

For the next hour Tai pored over my pictures for his book. I made tea and drank it. He turned up all the lights and spread the prints out on the floor. He made piles. He squinted and pursed his lips, compared two, three, four prints at a time, then reshuffled them like cards. He squatted and bounced on the balls of his bare feet in my brother's too-short pants. He sipped his tea without saying a word, shook his head, and moved his lips. Reached, regrouped the pictures and stared.

Looking over his shoulder, I kept seeing my father's images overshadowing mine, like Delong Dupriest transparencies. I looked up and caught the White Witch's gaze. Marge. My father pursing his mouth around the word "No."

It was crowded. Far too crowded in here.

"Well?"

Tai looked up as if he'd forgotten I was there. He braced his elbows on his knees and clasped his fingers beneath his chin. He smiled.

The phantom onlookers abruptly retreated.

"Well?" I said again.

He shook his head so the still-damp threads of hair fell forward. "I'm sorry. You just sounded so combative—so defensive and tough. Like you used to." Still smiling, he unfolded his hands and touched his fingers to his lips. His nails grew wide and strong from perfect, circular moons and ended square with his fingertips. I couldn't take my eyes off them, or think of anything else.

"Mei-bi." He unfolded himself until he was looking, just slightly, down at me. "You've caught their dignity—their face. I was afraid you wouldn't be able to get past their fear."

"That's the point of your book, isn't it? To get past that."

"Yes. But stories can be told in secret, names changed. Photographs can't be disguised."

I thought of my postgraduate wandering shots. Transmogrifications, Roxy used to call them. It was the longest word she'd ever found a use for, she told me. I said to call them disguises.

"Besides," I said, "I'm an outsider."

"Maibelle, stop it!" The touch of his hands on my arms rattled me. I couldn't look at his face. "Outsider. Insider. Those are roles. Positions you take in your own life, not in the world around you. Don't you see? The real dividing line has nothing to do with the shape of your eyes or face, what language you speak. It's inside you—are you living your life or just hiding behind that camera of yours!" He pulled away.

He had long, thin, almost bony feet with the same strong squared-off nails. They squeezed the floor as they moved across it, the bare wood sighing in return.

"That sounds dumb," he said. "But it's the way I feel about my writing—a way to establish my own position, to find where I fit. Sometimes the only way to find out where you truly belong is to try out different voices. I think photography—the kind you're doing now—is your voice."

He had his back to me, was standing in front of the shelves of gadgets where I'd left the cutout picture of Marge Gramercy's weeping shepherd. At some point while he was talking, the rain had stopped.

I'd asked Tai once how he got his subjects to reveal their stories. He said the secret to trust is to ease in slowly, the way the matchmaker in Li's story about the pearl-sewn shirt had eased himself into the young wife's life, first winning her friendship, then her confidence, and only gradually her complete trust. I pointed out that she'd then betrayed that trust by sneaking the silver trader in to rape the young wife, but Tai refused to accept that reading. He insisted the wife had been starved for sex and luckier to love two men than never to love at all. The discussion quickly escalated to a verbal brawl as I became convinced that the old woman's meddling had destroyed the young wife's life and Tai argued for Li's view of passion's dark side. No pleasure without pain, or true love without risk.

"Only fools and the very brave love with all their hearts," he'd said. "Most people prefer the safety of faking it."

"So you persuade all these people to love you and then lay bare the most painful moments of their lives."

"To trust me. Trust is only a prelude to love."

I thought of my mother's cynical analysis. "A prelude to love? Or to deception?"

I'd never trusted any of my lovers enough to let them view my work. But Tai, I reminded myself now as I felt for hard edges at the back of my closet, was not my lover.

Before I granted myself time to reconsider, we were sitting on Marge Gramercy's couch with my portfolio between us.

They were all there, like strands of hair or torn ticket stubs or dried blood on the upholstery—evidence. The fractured obsessiveness of the single, wall-sized eye. The insistence on turning objects into symbols, landscapes into some indecipherable code. Even those high school yearbook shots, like probes that somehow managed to dig beyond the surface of my subjects to expose my own anxiety.

I stopped Tai's hand. He hadn't said a word and didn't now, but looked up with a noncommittal frown.

"Mistake. I can't stand to look at this stuff. I should burn it, you know? My father was the family genius. I was always trying to prove how artistic I was so people would say I was as good as him, but that sort of thinking makes you so pretentious—" I was babbling, pulling the book from his grip, stuffing loose prints inside and zipping.

He slid one hand under the black leather binder, placed the other on top, and lifted it out of my arms.

"Please. I'd like to see the rest." He looked into me as he spoke with a quiet deliberation that was as reassuring as warm milk. He turned to the place we'd left off, an abrupt shift from the vacant freeze of midwestern nature to the shots I'd taken in the first weeks after returning to Manhattan.

For a time I'd haunted the abandoned lower West Side Drive shooting ice-encrusted litter, lunchtime joggers breathing steam at the World Trade Center, weird cloud formations hanging over the Palisades. The backs of a couple embracing in the middle of an otherwise empty six-lane highway. I was imitating a photographer, trying to get my hand back in, and each frame was technically admirable, composition correct, light exactingly balanced. But the images had a numbing oppressiveness to them, as if a great slab of granite hovered just above frame.

I shuddered. This was only seven months ago. I could still smell and taste the bitter winds that had swirled up off the river, still feel the wet sting of cold on my fingers as I fumbled for these shots. But not the desolation. I remembered it. I no longer felt it.

The last photographs—test prints and contacts—were not in sleeves but loose, stuck into the back of the binder. They'd all been shot with my father's Leica.

An old lady wept in the ground-floor window of a Greenwich Village brownstone. The same old lady laughing from a distance, arm curved upward, a blur of feathers and flapping wings. The young Chinese face of a woman screaming. A boy with the deadened stare of a killer. White-painted masks floating like moths above a field of black and green silk.

From the expression on Tai's face as he closed the book I could tell he knew this was tricky. Had he praised this work—even as he'd praised the other—I'd have hurled the portfolio out the window. If he'd dismissed it, even jokingly, I'd have thrown *him* out.

Instead, he said, "You have a beautiful voice, Mei-bi."

"Thank you." I said it without apology. Without evasion. I took the work from him but left it in plain view.

"What happened to all that stuff your family used to keep in the basement?" Tai asked after we'd spent a few minutes dodging each other's gaze.

"What stuff?"

"Things of your grandparents from China. Henry showed me once."

The question took me by surprise, the more so since I thought Anna and I were the only ones who'd ever looked into that box.

"Why?"

"Your photographs reminded me, for some reason . . . Everything handed down through my family burned in the fire."

He was looking across the room at the White Witch.

"What fire?"

"A few years after you left. It gutted the downstairs—and the basement. It's not important, I was just curious."

He picked up his wet clothes from the back of the chair where he'd laid them after changing.

"Wait," I said. "Show-and-tell night. Why not?"

I'd kept that old pasteboard box with me all through college, through my wonderings and back. Like a totem or heirloom. Yet, I'd rarely looked inside since the day I salvaged it, just before my family left Chinatown.

"I was terrified of that basement," I said as Tai removed the disintegrating twine and tape. "Those bare dangling lightbulbs, the rickety stairs, wire storage cages. Your chickens squawking. But the worst was that hole to the second basement—Henry had me convinced a bogeyman lived there."

"Good old Henry."

"I had this idea my parents would throw the box out—or leave it behind when we moved. I don't know why but that really upset me."

"So you decided to save it." The box remained closed, Tai's hands quiet on the flaps. "Even though you were scared to go alone."

"I stomped my feet, turned on every light. But there was this scuffling sound from the stairwell. Like a big rat, maybe two. Then nothing. I got the box and started to walk, but slowly, no sudden moves, you know?"

Tai nodded.

"I kept staring at the stairway to the second basement, but finally, when nothing more happened, I convinced myself I was being a fool. I laughed out loud."

And then, as if on cue, up out of that pit had risen a disembodied head, yellow hair, a dragon face with vivid blue eyes and flaming cheeks, swaying above a tattered black gown. It leaned on a long cane, like a beggar's staff, and held in one hand a rounded lamp from which smoke spiraled into the darkness. The whole thing seemed to glow in reverse, devouring light instead of releasing it, and I was sure it would devour me, too, if I came within range. I couldn't move. But then it began to screech, like chalk on blackboard. And it said my name.

" 'Maibelle'?" Tai asked.

"No, 'Mei-bi'! It said, 'Mei-bi you.' "

And suddenly I was moving, all right—fast and hard—churning the specter into an eddy of air that receded back into the hole as I charged past and up the stairs. And out.

"You tell anyone?" Tai asked.

"Only Li."

"He believed you?"

"Yes."

"I think maybe Li T'ieh-kuai," Li had said. "In life he know magic. In death his body is stolen so he take beggar's. Could be the spirits in your house are angry. Li T'ieh-kuai come warn you, you know? I think you better stay away, it will be all right."

"I'll stay away," I told Li that day. "We're moving."

He'd just nodded, which irritated me even more than his reacting to my bogeyman as if it were a ghoul on a routine house call. I hadn't told Li before that we were moving because I thought it would be hard on him. I *wanted* it to be hard on him. But he'd known all along.

Li smiled. "Go. Obey your parents. That your duty. You will come back when it is time."

"Aren't you even sorry I'm going?"

"Sorry? Why I should be sorry? It is not my fault you go."

"Sad, then."

"Sad, yes. But Mei-bi, life is full of sadness. You know. Your friend Johnny give you sadness. All pleasure, all love is pain. Like balance of good and evil. You feel most good when evil is near. Most evil when good is not far away."

He took a bite of walnut cookie. His gold teeth winked at me.

"I'll come back every weekend. I'll practice my calligraphy. Nothing will change."

"No, Mei-bi, no," Li said in that infuriating Chinese way of saying no when he meant yes. Yes, everything would change, and there was nothing I could do to stop it. "You come back. That good. You practice your calligraphy. But remember, time is long. Most important is do not forget. You know. Lao Li is your friend. This your home. You have learned here."

He took my hand between his aged palms and pressed. Squeeze, squeeze, release. Squeeze, squeeze, release. Squeeze, release, squeeze.

Then he placed in my hand a peachwood amulet. It was as smooth as glass, its lines curling so fluidly that it seemed to pour itself across my skin. An invisible hinge had been carved into the single piece of wood and, with a slight pull, the two halves opened. Pressed inside was a lock of silver-white hair.

Li's, I thought, glancing up at the familiar cobweb shag, but no.

"Keep it close," he said. "Inside is hair of child-stealing witch. It can make you safe from her."

"I believe you," I said, and I did. "I believe you."

But I did not keep my promise. Because Mum forbade me to ride the subways alone, I depended on Henry to accompany me back, and for the first month or two we visited every weekend. But after his final fight with Tai, Henry switched to an arcade uptown. I began taking photographs, and after a while the need to return didn't seem so strong.

I had not seen Li in nearly two years when my father showed me the notice in the paper about the auctioning of his shop. Dad said he might go, there were bound to be some terrific bargains. I thought of that rickshaw and dragon throne, those tiny lotus shoes. Treasures abandoned and silent. Even if Mum had not concocted a project to keep Dad home that day, I knew I could not go back.

Instead I turned our apartment upside down looking for the amulet. I found the lacquer calligraphy basket buried in my closet. I found the clay puppets, their paper backings unglued and the pink-cheeked maiden cracked in half. Old Cap Billings's letters and the silk embroidered garments for which I'd braved the basement phantom. And I found the tiny heart locket Johnny Madison had given me.

"The flying fiancé from Wisconsin." Tai touched the gold that I'd been wearing ever since.

"You remember that?"

"Of course I remember."

"He died."

"I know."

"Henry told you?"

"No, Li." He knelt beside me on the floor. "He said now you'd be free to marry me."

I stared at him, dumbfounded. I couldn't tell if he was making an apology or an inverted proposition, but that wasn't why his statement grabbed at my heart.

"I loved Johnny. Li knew that."

"Sure, but Li loved you."

"I don't know."

"Maibelle." Tai's voice caught. He moved his lips but seemed to change his mind before more sound came out. He looked down at the wads of pink tissue paper, the box's contents scattered across the floor. "There's no amulet."

"No." I began repacking. "For a while after I knew it was lost I saw the White Witch everywhere I went. In the back of the crosstown bus, in the mirrors on the Central Park carousel. Peeking around the mannequins in Bendel's windows. You know? Once I saw her under the Rockefeller Center Christmas tree. But after a few months she stopped stalking me and eventually I forgot about her."

"But?" said Tai.

"But?"

"Doesn't sound like that was the end."

"No." Lullaby music started playing upstairs. "I'm not sure. I mean, it's just occurred to me that maybe by forgetting I enabled her to catch me."

Tai's feet whispered against the bare wood. His hand folded around the back of my head, drew me toward him. I felt the brief, unfailing smoothness of his skin against my cheek.

"I think maybe you're right," he said softly, and stood to leave. "But now you've got to decide what to do about it."

• • •

The old lady is out in the garden with her parrot. A few minutes ago she looked at me drying my hair up here on the fire escape, and called hello. Over the past weeks we've established a distant familiarity. She shows off the bird. I compliment her. After I finally developed the film of the two of them, I dropped a couple of prints in her mail slot, and the next day I received a thank-you note on rose-scented paper with a coupon for a free bottle of toilet water at the drugstore on Greenwich Avenue. Her name is Emma Madson, and her writing is as delicate as a spider's web. Now whenever she sees me she waves and calls my name with a profoundly southern lilt. She tells me it's good to see me relaxing; she must envision me as some frantic workaholic. I've considered a more formal visit, but I suspect she's the sort of person who operates by invitation. She'd never make it up the stairs to come here, and since she hasn't invited me, I've let the matter slide.

"I love this old bird," she calls. "You watch this, Maibelle."

"Shut the goddamn door, Lila!" the parrot shrieks. The sun gives its green and blue feathers an iridescent gleam.

"Oh, pooh, you." Emma swivels in her wheelchair. She unlatches the door of the cage and crooks one finger over the sill. The parrot duly hop-bobbs onto her hand and up her arm. Some weeks ago they did away with the leash.

"Bubble, bubble, toil and trouble," she prompts.

"Old pisspot!"

She glances at me with an apologetic smile. "Reminds me of my husband, rest his soul."

"I think he's funny," I call.

"Funny?" She frowns and purses her lips. And says nothing more to either me or the bird.

The two of them begin to waltz. The parrot sits on the wrist of her left arm, which she holds up in dance position. With her other hand she works the wheel, forward, back, and to the side, forward and back again. She hums lightly, the sound hanging close around her like a vapor. She seems to have forgotten that anyone is watching except the bird.

But the trance falls apart when a truck backfires over on the avenue. Emma's body jerks and the startled bird immediately flaps to the corner tree. She doesn't move right away, and I'm afraid something's really wrong, but then she slowly glides the chair forward. Her voice starts up again, murmuring low and thick. I can't make out the words.

"Toot, toot, tootsie, goodbye!" yowls the bird, hopping backward up the branch. The green of its feathers blends with the leaves so I can't tell its exact location.

She lifts her crooked arm to the tree. "Come, baby, come back, darlin'." Her voice is loud and trembling.

If there were a way over the garden wall, I could climb down the fire escape and help her.

"Hold on," I call. "I'll go around front and get your housekeeper."

But she's already up and out of the wheelchair, weaving on her feet, her face lifted toward the branches and the squawking, invisible creature.

"I love you, darlin'. Please." Her voice wobbles desperately. Now I'm afraid to leave my post, as if she needs a witness.

The bird pops out at the end of a higher limb, screaming like a broken record. "Tootsie, goodbye! Tootsie, goodbye!"

"No!" Emma takes a step. Another. Grabs the trunk of the tree and stands gasping.

I feel suddenly cold in spite of the sun. It's deeply shady where the old lady now leans. The bird beats his wings and climbs even higher. She can't possibly see him, but he continues his screeching refrain. She slowly sinks to the ground.

"Jesus, Miss Madson!" The housekeeper's come at last, but too late. The bird heaves its wings outward, gives one long animal squawk, and takes off. The housekeeper feels for Emma's pulse, first the wrist, then the neck.

I scramble inside and call for an ambulance, then race downstairs.

The housekeeper answers my knock too quickly. She has alarming turquoise eyes.

"I saw what happened!"

"Excuse me?"

"Miss Madson." The name skids across my tongue. A siren erupts. St. Vincent's is just around the corner.

"Who are you?"

"I live here." I lift my hand in the general direction of next door. "Please, how is she?"

"Oh. You're the one with the pictures." She acts as if we've got all day.

"Is she all right, then?"

The housekeeper wriggles her mouth, casts an eye over my shoulder to the arriving ambulance.

"Please. I know this seems crazy, I never knew her at all, but I've watched her, I feel like I know her a little. I just want to know—"

"She's gone." She waves the paramedics through. They hurry. She places her fist on her hips and shakes her head. She's been through this process before.

I keep seeing the old lady alone, on her knees. She was dying.

"Please," I say again.

"Look, lady. I gotta go—"

"What about her family?"

"Hmph. Damned bird was her only friend in the world. Family buried down in Georgia somewhere. You want her lawyer's number?"

"No. No, I understand now. I'm sorry."

She lets out a laugh that sounds more like a grunt. "Funny thing, you're the first visitor she's had since she moved here. Five years. Too bad you waited till she's dead!"

Too bad, I think as the heavy oak door closes. The words pull together, apart. Too bad.

....

15

I went back to Wisconsin one last time, after Gramma Lou had her first stroke. It happened too suddenly for Mum to round up the whole family; Henry and Anna were off in different directions, and Dad resisted, saying he didn't want the old man blaming *him* if Lou should die; he'd wait until they both were well for his first trip to the farm. I was on summer vacation from college and felt almost as peculiar as Dad, seeing as I hadn't seen my grandparents since Johnny Madison's shooting, but I could tell my mother needed moral support. I didn't know what I could do for her. I couldn't muster the feelings of grief and profound love that I suspected one should exude in these situations. I felt sorry about Gramma Lou, of course, but she was in her eighties and I hadn't seen her in a long time, and if I got too worked up over her, I'd probably end up sidling into the question of what I'd do/how I'd feel if and when Mum died—and I wasn't prepared for that. So instead of behaving like a member of the family, I went along because it was the right thing to do. For mercy's sake.

I was afraid half Lou's face would be sliding or her arms palsied or her mouth twitching wildly up and down, but no. She'd lost some weight and gained some wrinkles. Otherwise, lying there in her hospital bed, she looked in pretty good shape.

Grampa Henry was the mess. His lower eyelids drooped open, exposing the raw blood vessels normally held inside, and he was overproducing tears, so his eyes themselves seemed to recede behind a wall of viscous liquid, which shivered each time he moved his head and then slid down his cheeks. He looked for all the world like an aged basset hound, but he had his faculties, and that was where Lou came up short.

She would sit up as perky as could be, insisting I was Diana. "Has that Miss Chanel answered your letter yet, Dydee?" she'd ask me. Or, "You go ask Minnie now, she'll set you up with some nice chiffon, and we'll fix a prom dress that'll just steal that Georgie Mark's breath away." Minnie Hamilton, my mother whispered, used to run the notions shop in Slinger and was run over by a Greyhound bus twenty years ago, and Georgie Mark had been Mum's boyfriend in sixth grade and was now a fast-food millionaire.

For the first day or so, my mother faced this displacement by bravely pushing me aside and cajoling Lou with her own memories of times they'd shared. But after a while the vacant stare my grandmother turned on her and the loving recognition with which she mistook me began to get to Mum. She stopped explaining Lou's trips to the past. She let my questions drop into the great black hole of her resentment. I had come to comfort her in her hour of need and I'd ended up stealing both her mother and her youth. Even though she knew as well as I that a short circuit in my grandmother's brain was to blame, this was not what Mum had bargained for.

Gramma Lou chattered, Grampa Henry wept, and my mother squirmed and smoldered for three days. We were having one of our, by then, silent dinners in the hospital cafeteria when we were paged. Before we could get upstairs, my grandmother was dead.

Grampa seemed to pull himself together after that. Three months later he would drop dead while shoveling sheep manure, leaving the farm and every penny he owned to a young woman of fifty to whom he'd engaged himself. But for the moment, he and Mum worked together with surprising clarity to arrange the burial and a small memorial service in the community church. I was helping my grandfather with the guest list for the service when I learned that the Madisons had moved away.

"Yup," Grampa said, "after their boy died, Lottie just kinda fell apart. You'd think with ten others she'd have some resistance, but no. Damn Catholics. They'll forgive murder with a couple of Hail Marys and a whirl of the old rosary, but suicide—now, there's a sin that'll get you eternal damnation. Poor bastard. For years she kept talking about him like he was still alive. The sinner. Newt finally decided the place was too much for her, and he up and moved 'em all out. Never heard another word about 'em. Nobody did that I know of."

My grandfather's ranting brought Johnny back for me, along with my own feelings of anger and blame at him for having abandoned me. That evening I walked back through the farm, over the stile and across the pasture, down into the hollows and up the ridge overlooking Glabber's woods, which had since been subdivided into two-acre residential parcels. But for the most part the land was still there and beautiful. And Mount Assumption still presided over the whole with its sinister, mindful warning.

As I walked, I wished Johnny's ghost did indeed reside in the spaces he'd haunted in life. I thought about his mastery of nature, his longing to cross the line between fact and fantasy. I remembered his plan to orbit the world and end up marrying me. Maybe he'd made it to heaven, maybe to the next giant's kingdom, but it seemed clear that one thing he had not yet done was rise from the ashes reborn.

When I reached the overgrown foundation where that burned-out hay shed had stood, I opened the locket we'd found there together and buried the scrap of carbon I'd kept in it all those years. Like the phoenix, I told myself, his spirit will rise again, take the body of another Johnny, a golden boy with a love of the sky, a man of nature who views the world from the awkward angle of a visionary.

That weekend I took the first of my lovers who reminded me of

Johnny, in the blue room on the plane back to New York, with my mother six rows away.

• • •

She called last week as if the gallery opening had never happened, to invite me to a party.

"I know this kind of socializing is hard for you, darling, but once you've established these contacts you really will thank me. Might even be some romantic interest. That's why I asked Henry. There's a fabulous ceramicist from Belgium who's just sold a piece to the Whitney. Reminds me of that sculptress he used to go with, remember?"

I remembered that Henry had last been seen squiring Coralie at Mum's behest.

"Will Dad be there?"

"Yes and no. You know how he is."

"Mm." I remembered the other art parties Mum had held over the years. Dad hiding alone in his workshop while Mum played Pearl Mesta outside.

"You'll come," said my mother.

"I guess." I would go, but not to pacify Mum and not to establish contacts. At least not the contacts she had in mind.

The penthouse terrace my father long ago advanced as one of the apartment's most winning attributes lends itself beautifully to parties. Purely out of spite, I'm sure, my mother never did reestablish her pots of Alpine rock plants, but created a whole new motif of trellised wisteria and beds of imported dirt from which sprout six-foot fruit trees. Tonight more than one guest would comment that Diana had created a country estate in the middle of midtown Manhattan. Lest anyone fail to draw this conclusion, my mother had hired four uniformed servants and a low-key dance band. She'd laced tiny white lights through the trees and set up a bar and a half dozen crisply clothed tables under the trellises. The guests, who ranged from the torn-jeans and bustier crowd to the leather generation, seemed uniformly out of place. Nevertheless, the backcountry aura was unmistakable and, to me, vaguely disturbing. It reminded me of another place and time, but I couldn't immediately think where.

"Maibelle!" My mother tangoed toward me in the arms of a tall bearded Neanderthal. She grasped my hand.

"This is Scott Sazaroff."

A true photo-stallion. He bowed gracefully and excused himself before she could further detain him.

"We'll talk later," she called after him. "Don't pay any attention, Maibelle. You're only as good as your work in Scott's eyes. Once he sees your portfolio he'll do anything to help you. I'm really pleased you came, darling." And for the first time she took a good look at me.

I was wearing a plain white button-down blouse, a seersucker skirt, black flats. Decidedly ordinary. Inconspicuous. Mediocre. Clothes I'd intended to hide in. But in this crowd the ordinariness stood out like a dead bloom in a fresh bouquet. She pursed her lips and straightened my collar.

My brother, across the terrace, had adopted a much more appropriate camouflage of hip olive drabs. He appeared to be having no difficulty impressing Deniece Williams, the rock-star portraitist often featured in *Interview,* whom my mother had long been courting.

"Why don't you get Henry into photography?"

"God help me. Henry wouldn't know a picture if it sliced him between the eyes."

"But he's so much better at networking than I'll ever be."

"Henry's a hustler," my mother said with a wistful quiver of pride. "But you're my artist. Don't ever forget it."

"I am not your artist and never have been."

"You could do with less sarcasm and more confidence, Maibelle."

"I'm going to tell Dad about your plan."

"No, you're not." It was a statement, not a command, not an invitation for follow-up. She put an arm out to stop a middle-aged man with a blue stripe through his hair.

"Lester! This is my daughter Maibelle. Maybe you remember her as a child—she used to just live at the gallery with me. Now she's an artist herself."

I wanted to bore a hole through the terrace. Whatever the people downstairs were into—S&M, war games, international terrorism—it had to be easier than this.

Lester thrust one pink-fleshed hand in my direction. He flicked his tongue like a snake and engaged my mother in a discussion about profit margins in performance art.

As I turned to make my escape a young woman with a high, southern twang butchered my father's name. "I hear he's still alive. Sumpin' musta gone wrong, though. Like maybe he's brain-dead, you think?"

"Maibee." Henry blocked my path with a tumbler of wine.

I pulled his hand over and drank the whole glass, but the alcohol only squeezed my head tighter. "How can you stand this!"

"I live here, remember?"

"Like I said, how can you stand it?"

"Won't be long now. I'm just about ready to put my program on the market. But since you brought it up, I was sort of wondering if you'd mind my crashing with you again."

"It is getting to you."

"Mum calls Dad and me the Two Putterers and leaves IBM executive trainee ads on my bed all the time. Dad waits up for me until three, four in the morning. He calls me Skipper. It gets old."

"Poor you." I pressed circles into my forehead to stop the throbbing. Henry put down his wine and massaged my shoulders.

"Any reason I *shouldn't* come visit for a while?"

"Harriet."

"I'll cross-dress. Anything else?"

"What's that supposed to mean?"

"You seeing anybody?"

"All right. Come tonight if you want. After this."

"Tommy? Ah, see that? I can feel you tensing up."

I shook him off me. "It's 'Tai.' And not like that."

"Then how?"

With my mother hovering like a hungry vulture, it seemed an inopportune moment for confidences.

"Work," I said.

"He paying you?"

"Yes. Henry, why *did* you turn against him?"

"You ask him?"

"Yes." A helicopter circled overhead. Red lights. Green lights. I pictured it landing in the middle of the party, everyone running for cover. "He said he couldn't remember."

My brother folded his arms across his chest.

"I told you. Pinball. I was playing this FOB guy who couldn't even speak English. Maybe it wasn't fair, but I was creaming him. Tommy got on my case. Hell, I would've quit, but the guy was like in a trance. He dug his own hole."

"You were playing for money?"

My brother shot me a look of profound disbelief. "We're talking Chinatown, Maibelle. What'd you think?"

"I—I just never thought about it."

He shrugged. "Stakes got up to three hundred, and he pulled a gun on me."

"The FOB?"

"No. Lover boy." Henry let his arms flop to his sides and spat the next word as if it were a wad of old chewing tobacco. "Face!"

And it dawned on me that he was talking about Tai.

"A gun?"

"Bang-bang, best friends. Asshole."

I couldn't process what my brother was saying for the sudden pain behind my left eye. The glittering lights, the throb of music, my brother's voice all darkened.

"I need some aspirin."

"Hall bathroom. Hey, Maibelle—"

My mother blocked my way.

"Delong just told me he's looking for an assistant." She pulled my hand from my head and steered me into the crowd. "I'm not going to let you creep away this time."

"Gotta trade on your skin, man." The voice was husky and polished as sea glass. "Like a package, gotta be a come-odd-ity." A long, skinny trombone of a man with a long, skinny cigarette in one hand and a long, skinny glass full of dark liquor in the other. Delong towered over a man twice his age who gazed up at him as if he were Moses. "Gotta be out there."

"See," Mum whispered from the corner of her mouth as she prepared to cut in. "Networking."

And then there were hands pumping, fingers to palm, the clasp of bone beneath flesh. The throbbing climbed up my head.

"Hey, honey. Your beautiful mama says you're lookin' for a studio job."

My mother has pale gray eyes, Delong feather black ones. I imagined a band between them—elastic—snapping the two faces together like a Marx Brothers or Three Stooges routine.

My partner carried a gun. He pulled it on his best friend. On my brother. The words ran circles inside my skull as my mother stood petting me like an imbecile.

"Excuse me." I lurched away. "I'm not looking for anything."

I found some aspirin in the powder room—Excedrin, extra strength, with a triple dose of caffeine. The effect was like a dry eraser on chalkboard, quick relief but with a cloudy residue. The image staring back at me from the mirror looked normal, no deep creases between the eyes, no blotches discoloring cheeks or throat, no wild bloodshot stripes on the eyeballs. But I felt all those physical strains even if I couldn't see them. I felt as if any moment a much larger eraser would sweep the mirror and take me out of the picture. I leaned forward until I was touching my reflection. If only I could see whose hand held that eraser, I would know how to force it back.

"Dad, it's me. You in there?" I hugged the wood and whispered through the keyhole. A woman had just gone into the bathroom down the hall, and the kitchen was bustling with Mum's caterers and a group of people playing cards at the counter. I imagined they'd give their nose rings for a glimpse of Joe Chung, the phantom *Life* photog.

The door opened a crack and I slipped through. My father shut it and spun the lock, without a word sat back down on his stool, and returned his attention to the sheet of cardboard before him. His wide, stubby fingers bent and pushed, scored and folded the cardboard into a box. He took an X-acto knife and sliced off wedges of paper from the sides, tucked and glued. It was several minutes before he held up the finished product.

"A cigarette pack?"

He nodded. "But look." He flipped the lid down. It clicked. He pulled it up. A slender flap along the front lip popped out. "Freshness seal. And a stay-closed lock. Been working on this for weeks. What do you think?"

Music and party voices from outside jiggled the window glass, but my father was oblivious. His eyes were bright with the success of his invention. "No one's come up with a new cigarette packaging idea in decades. They could use this for candy, too."

He was sweet, my father. Sweet and innocent. I put my arms around him and buried my face in the soft, frayed collar of his shirt.

"Good for you, Dad."

He worked on, plying his origami masterpieces. Smoke curled from the ashtray beside him. Only when working hard would he let his cigarettes lie. He drummed his fingers, but didn't bite them. His eyes were focused, not glassy. It came to me suddenly. When he was working, he seemed whole and alive. Otherwise, when he was around my mother or the family, without the focus of his "puttering," he twitched with some buried impulse for escape. Puttering was safe for him, as he thought catalog work was for me. He had said we weren't alike, yet his advice presumed we were.

I thought of the furtive way Tai had bent over his plate when I asked why he had to leave Chinatown. He wouldn't look at me. He wouldn't answer. Through his work wasn't he, too, looking for escape? Now I understood that guilt lay at the core of Tai's secrecy. Was it the same for my father? Might as well have been pulling a trigger, he'd said. Had his subjects really been shot, killed? And if Dad and I were really so alike, where did that leave me?

I felt exhausted. The layers of shame and deceit seemed to run to the bone.

"Dad?"

"Mm?"

"There's a question—well, there are lots of questions, but one I've wondered since I was little. About us in Chinatown. I mean, you and Mum had no friends there. So what were we doing living there?"

He rubbed his hands together as if they hurt. He took his time. "Someone must have told you."

"No. Except you said it was the cheapest place in New York."

His throat growled for a moment, but the growl quickly turned to that terrible clucking sound. "It was."

Then gradually, while his cigarette burned itself out and the room filled with an acrid, deathly stink to which he seemed entirely oblivious, he told me the larger story.

At first after he came back from China, he said, they stayed in the one-room apartment on East Thirty-third Street that my mother had leased since she came to New York. Although he'd quit photography, my father was supposed to be completing his graduate degree in history. He had a handful of professional and college acquaintances who were friendly without being friends. Diana had the gallery.

"And Foucault, God knows, eating out of her hand," my father said.

They were living on Diana's salary and what was left of Dad's. He spent his days sketching space-saving ideas for undersized apartments. Trundle beds, hideaway ironing boards, convertible stovetops, and pull-down cabinets.

"Graduate school didn't work out. I stayed home. It wasn't that I was afraid. But I'd been all over the world, seen what was worth seeing and plenty more that wasn't. I'd seen enough."

"And Mum wouldn't understand that?"

He sucked on his cigarette. "She went to work, to her parties, museums, shopping. Pressured me to come with her. I said I had to work. She reminded me that she had married a very different man."

"She's never stopped reminding you, or any of the rest of us."

He shook his head without looking at me. "She kept it up until finally I relented."

"How?"

It was a summer Saturday, hot and airless. Not many people in town. They had no particular destination. Just out browsing, as my mother put it. Joe followed Diana through several East Side galleries, bookstores, and boutiques. There was no air-conditioning in those days. What my father was looking for was a working fan. They found one in a store that sold expensive bed linens and imported ceramics, the same useless accessories that had festooned Dad's home in Shanghai.

"But Mama could never have afforded this store. Even Diana was stunned by the prices, and we steered away from the clerks. Still, it was cool. We passed a water fountain and I took a drink. Diana looked through a pile of satin pillowcases and, as casually as if she were telling me she planned to go to the park, she announced that she was pregnant."

She wasn't looking at him but at a small embroidered rectangle—a baby's pillowcase.

"She had it all planned: now I was to shower her with delighted kisses, lift her off her feet, and fork over the ten dollars for that bloody pillowcase."

Suddenly my father couldn't breathe. He had to get out of that store, out from under those clerks' frozen smiles. He left Diana fondling her satin and got as far as the front door, but the manager blocked his path.

An imposing figure, tall and brawny as a lumberjack inside his fancy suit, the man spoke in a southern drawl. It was closing time, he said, and my father would have to use the rear exit.

Dad didn't argue, just turned and went back through the store down the short flight of stairs indicated. But the lumberjack got there ahead of him and barred my father's way again.

This time he was openly sneering. "You yellow bastards. What's it take to make you see the light?"

He jabbed his finger into my father's chest. "Didn't you get the message when we dropped the bomb? We don't like you coming into our stores. And we sure as hell don't want you spitting all over our water fountains and laying your filthy hands on our goods and women."

Joe heard Diana's heels clicking on the steps behind him. "Joe! What the . . ."

The man had backed my father up against the wall and was ramming his large, white thumb into Dad's breastbone.

My father grabbed his fingers and pushed them backward until he winced. He still towered over Dad, but his size was his only advantage. My father didn't even have to raise his voice.

"You dropped the bomb on the Japanese, you bloody idiot," he said. "Now get the hell out of my way."

The man looked as if someone had just pulled the seat out from under him. His brow squeezed with the effort of some serious mental gymnastics. My father dropped his hand and grabbed Diana, whose face had gone absolutely white. They pushed past.

"The door—the door's locked." Diana was hardly breathing.

"Open it," my father ordered the man.

He stammered. He shuffled his feet. He turned the key and my parents passed through to the alley.

Finally the dimwit puzzled it out. "So you're a chink," he shouted after them. "One yellow slant-eyed bastard's just like another. You keep yer commie ass out of here."

Diana was sobbing by the time they reached the street. The heat and the traffic, relentless.

"We'll have to find a bigger place to live," Joe said. "A different neighborhood. For the baby's sake."

"I wasn't thinking of Chinatown at that moment," my father told me. "We could have moved to the suburbs. We could have moved to the country. But Diana would have none of that. Bad as the clerk had been, she kept insisting suburban and rural bigots were worse. That was why he upset her so—because he reminded her of the jackasses she'd moved to the city to escape. Her idea was to move to Paris or London because Europeans were more open-minded."

I remembered what my father had told me about the British and French boys attacking him at school. "But you knew the Europeans were just as bigoted as Mum's farm folks."

"I had no desire to live in another international settlement, that's true. Anyway, we had no money to travel, and since Diana seemed inclined to keep her job, we had to stay close to Manhattan. Chinatown was an afterthought."

"But how did it even come up?"

"Diana announced one day that it might be 'amusing' to live closer to my roots. Whatever the hell she meant by that."

Tai had told me about landlords "frying real estate" to make it hotter and hotter until only the rich Hong Kong and Taiwan tycoons could afford it. "Chinatown real estate's no bargain now. Was it ever, really?"

"Yes and no."

My father opened the window, letting in a flow of cold air and the dim strains of jazz from the party. If the terrace wrapped all the way around, he'd have nowhere to hide from Mum's pals; fortunately Dad's room faces the street.

He turned. "When Diana gets an idea in her head, she's like a cat stalking a bird, you know? There wasn't one Chinatown apartment advertised in the paper, but she insisted we go look for signs, ask around."

"And that's how you found our apartment?"

He scowled at me and waved his arm. "Wait. Just wait. We found nothing, she'd about given up when we passed a shop with this old inlaid chair in the window. Rosewood. It was identical to a chair that belonged to my grandmother in Hangchow. Christ, that miserable chair! Every year when we made the pilgrimage to the old bitch's estate, my sisters and I had to sit in that chair and have our picture taken. I loathed those sittings. The little man beneath his drapes, decades behind the technology of the West . . ."

"An inlaid chair." I felt as if the pieces of an invisible puzzle were about to drop into place.

"I wanted to walk on, but she kept badgering me, and eventually the shopkeeper saw us and came out. He recognized me."

"It was the same chair."

"Yes. He'd been a friend of my father's in Shanghai before the war. They both raised money for the Republic—pulled in something like ten million between them. Those were uncertain times, and they promised to look after each other's business and personal affairs if the need should arise. After this fellow threw his support behind Chiang Kai-shek they became political adversaries, but he never forgot that promise. Personally I never wanted to see him or that hideous old chair again, but the next day he telephoned about the apartment on Mott Street. His association owned the building."

I felt the words cutting into the sides of my mouth as I spoke them, clearly, slowly. "It was Li, wasn't it? He was the reason we lived there."

My father's hands trembled as he fought with a match. I grabbed a massive desk lighter that he never used, held it for him.

"Yes."

"But why? Why did you hate him so? Why wouldn't you tell me when I asked you?"

"I told you about a boy I knew. Nigel Halliday."

"Of course. The one that tried to drown you."

He stared at a blank spot directly above the door for a good minute before he continued. "Li was an operator for Halliday's father, the arms trader. He had the scruples of a gutter rat, but he covered it up with all that crap about Chinese tradition and face. He was a bloody liar, Maibelle."

According to my father, Li had not left China after the Japanese invasion, but stayed on for years brokering munitions deals between the Hallidays, the Japanese, and the gangsters who ruled Shanghai in league with Chiang Kai-shek.

"He did it all under the guise of patriotism, but when the time came, it wasn't the British or the Japanese or the Germans that made him grab his precious antiques and run, but his own countrymen. Men like my father."

Dad's cheeks pulled tight. "The reason I went back to China was to try to find my father. Instead I found Li. He lured me in. He promised to help me."

"Did he?"

"I told you. Li was a bloody liar."

But I couldn't—wouldn't—believe him.

"I loved Li, Dad. He treated me like his own daughter—friend. I felt safe with him."

The light was too bright in my father's workroom. It made my eyes do curious things. Like turn my father's face gray and white. The switch was within reach. I could turn off the light and we'd be sitting together again in the dark. Instead I picked up a small brown box filled with air.

But when I let it go he was still there, still patched with gray and white, looking older than I remembered ever seeing him before. The sight of him filled my throat and squeezed and squeezed until I couldn't bear it. I reached for the lock and tumbled it.

"He's dead, Maibelle. We don't have to worry about him anymore."

Through the crack poured an old song, familiar and slow. Late sixties? Pulsing like a dirge and strangely cold, a Doors song. "Hello, I Love You." The year after we moved out of Chinatown. Before Li died. "Hello, I Love You," on the car radio for just a few seconds before Mum switched it off. We drove, surrounded by pine and peach trees, in a Connecticut wonderland. Another place and time.

With a savage blow I knew exactly who Nigel Halliday was. Not the boy but the man. I had met him.

I drew back from the door and lowered myself onto a stool.

"It's all right. I'll stay a while longer. Make another of those boxes, Dad. Show me how they work."

The grayness lifted and he smiled a little, turned to his bench.

"So simple." As he surgically cut through the paper, I slid back fourteen years.

* * *

A Sunday in late spring. I had just turned fourteen. Anna was off at college (or so we thought; actually she was doing "independent study" at a retreat founded by her comparative-religions professor somewhere near the Canadian border). Henry was spending the day at a workshop learning to be a conscientious objector. The previous summer Mum had signed me up for riding lessons in Central Park; now my parents were extending that education by taking me to a polo match in Connecticut.

I could sense Dad's excitement as we left New York and he shoved the Rambler into high gear. He wore a pair of jodhpurs that must have been forty years old, and as he drove he talked about playing polo in Shanghai. They'd practiced in Jessfield Park, he said, by the university. "Some bloody good players in those days."

One of those players ran into us at the polo grounds. He was about my father's age but taller, massive. His jodhpurs stood out from his hips like cardboard. His helmet sat squarely atop his blond head. I thought he must be some kind of royalty. He was that handsome.

My father grabbed the man's hand and pumped it up and down. "I'll be damned," he said. "Nigel Halliday. Twenty years if it's been a day. Burma, wasn't it?"

"Right you are! Caught you photographing one of General Chennault's shipments of silk stockings or toothbrushes or some such thing, eh what?"

"Oh, Christ, don't remind me." My father laughed and shook his head. "What the hell are you doing here?"

"I live just down the road a bit." Halliday turned to my mother and me. As the introductions were made, he brushed a kiss across Mum's hand and held onto it until she began to blush. She tipped her head back, smiling, breathless.

He invited us back to his house after the game. "You live nearby, too, old boy?"

My father placed his hand lightly on my mother's shoulder as they began to walk. "We have a penthouse on Central Park West."

"Doing well for yourself, are you?"

"Can't complain."

It all sounded so glib and easy, but as I trailed after the grown-ups I caught Mum shooting Dad eager glances. I also became conscious of the sweat wrinkles on the back of my father's shirt, the way his old jodhpurs sagged in the seat, and I wondered why he was suddenly talking in this emphatic British accent.

A small perfumed crowd coiled around the spectators' area talking and smoking and sipping from lavender paper cups. Nigel led us through to the front row of chairs, where a young Chinese woman with waist-length hair sat alone reading a paperback Bible. She was dressed in a crimson silk blouse and a tight black side-slit skirt, her hair twisted into an ornate gold lacquer comb designed like a peacock's father. Halliday introduced her as his wife, Lydia.

The adults went through the usual back-and-forth about whether our visit would be an inconvenience. As if there were any question. Mum was about to expire from curiosity. Dad was like a dog on a leash. And Halliday had issued the invitation as if it were an imperial edict. Lydia quietly assured my parents that we would be no trouble at all.

It was a fast-paced game and by the fifth chukker the horses' flanks were steaming and most of the riders were swinging wild. Only Nigel was able to sustain the tight grip of horse and mallet that guaranteed control of the ball—and his team's victory.

Afterward, we followed Halliday's silver Mercedes through a fieldstone archway and on past a small lake dotted with swans, on between wildly blooming fruit trees to a country palace that belonged on the cover of *House Beautiful.* After some discussion, it was agreed that Mum and Lydia would tour the house, "the riders" head to the stable. I chose to be a rider.

On one side of the path a squadron of black-faced jockeys stood holding lanterns, on the other a cluster of cherubs peed into an enormous swimming pool. In the stable yard wing-footed huntsmen shot water into a fountain. Frozen midget slaves seemed a recurring motif.

Fortunately Halliday's stable boy was full-scale and alive, and in minutes I was astride a white filly named Lotus, my father and Nigel on stallions. As Nigel led the way down a steep bank and across a narrow stream, I concentrated, kept my back straight, thighs tight, reins loose under my thumbs as I'd learned from my lessons.

We reached a glen where the trail was wide and flat, and Nigel nudged his mount to a trot. Our horses quickly followed suit, and I fought the impulse to flop back in the saddle. Though my rhythm was uneven, I managed to get enough control to convince myself I was posting.

At the edge of a freshly mowed meadow, Nigel upped the ante again, and the three of us took off in a canter that sent me lurching forward with one hand clutching the pommel, the other Lotus's mane. I inhaled the horse's warm, musty odor, the surrounding scent of cut grass.

Dad glanced back and smiled. "Keep it up!"

Nigel heard and misunderstood—or else understood all too well. He dug in his heels and took off at a gallop. My father and I followed suit, Dad's shouts to slow down unheeded.

I had too loose a grip on the reins to pull back on the bridle, and without that cue to stop, Lotus instinctively began to race, running downhill back into the forest, then onto a wide dirt lane, closing the stallion's lead.

I let my upper body go flat and reached for a hold along the bulging muscles of the filly's neck. My feet had lifted out of the stirrups on the first leap forward and though I felt around to reseat them, the stirrups were flapping too wildly and so I was left with my feet dangling free, clenching the horse with my knees.

The foliage blurred, then spun and blended into a tunnel of green that made me feel as if I were suspended inside a mammoth wave. The movement seemed to spiral outward, leaving my body and mind quite still and replacing my initial terror with a strange ethereal joy. I gulped the wind and breathed the fluid movements, surging up and forward with each clap of hooves. It was a paradise of motion.

Like flying.

The road curled up a long hill that wore Lotus down to a slower pace, still galloping but relenting. Now I dared to lift my head and saw at the end of this tunnel of trees the shadow of a horse and rider, black against the light beyond. And my exhilaration gave way once more to terror.

It was Glabber coming out of the woods.

The demon in the basement.

I wanted to scream, to wake up, but there was no escape. And so, instead, I shut my eyes and hugged Lotus even tighter.

She must have picked up the tension in my body, because just as we reached the edge of the forest she did a nervous two-step and came to an abrupt stop. I would have hurtled straight to the ground, but my fingers were so deeply entwined in her mane that, when my hips launched into space, my hands were held in place. I was drawn into a smooth rotating slide, my body falling right around until I hung like a human kerchief under the animal's throat. Whether out of fear or relief I'm not sure, but I started giggling as I hung and soon was laughing uncontrollably.

I suppose the sight of me was pretty funny, and Halliday began laughing, too. Then my father, who'd been thrown while giving chase, came straggling up the hill on foot just ahead of his horse.

He was not amused.

I dropped to my feet and ducked out from under the horse's cheek. "I'm okay," I said.

Dad gripped my shoulders as he checked me over.

"Really, I'm fine." But I was actually shaking, and so was he. I squeezed his hand to reassure him.

"Hell of a rider, you have there." Nigel joined us on the ground. "Now, you, old man, I'm not so sure of. Made a bit of a side trip there, eh what?"

"I see you haven't lost your touch." But to my surprise Dad didn't sound angry. No, his voice was flat, stunned, the same as it had been on the night the Chinatown chicken died.

"I'm *all right!*" I insisted.

"Well, Mei Mei," my father said quietly, "enough riding. We'll walk the horses back from here."

A few steps on he whispered in my ear. "Let's not tell Mum you fell off the horse."

I smiled. "You fell off *your* horse, you mean."

"That either."

Back at the house, Nigel led us through an immaculate parlor to a solarium where the women sat chatting. Dad and I took chairs next to Mum. Nigel seated himself on an overstuffed sofa across from his wife and extended one leg in midair.

Lydia knelt before him. Her skirt pulled tight, the slit falling open along her thigh. She took her husband's heel in one hand and grasped the toe with the other. He thrust his foot toward her face, and with a quick jerk and a stifled gasp she fell back clutching the boot. Then she returned to a squat and did the other foot. The job done, Lydia fetched Nigel his slippers from a closet in the corner and placed them on his feet.

"You can bring the tea now," said Nigel, and Lydia, lowering her eyes to avoid my mother's appalled expression, scurried from the room.

By the time she returned, Halliday was telling stories about Dad. My father, he said, had stood up well to the ribbing he got as a Chinese boy in an English school.

"It was you, wasn't it, who coined the nickname Doughboy for that poor Italian slug in fourth form?"

"Manetti," said Dad.

"If you say so. I only remember Doughboy. Doughy for short. Ha!"

"Please," said Lydia. "Would you like some tea?"

"Or a Scotch?" said Halliday. "Darling, get me a real drink."

Lydia handed my mother her tea, then stepped to the bar at the back of the room.

"Joe?" said Halliday.

"Why, all right. Scotch and water, please. Light on the Scotch."

"Ah, yes. Chinese temperance. Does the booze make you go all rosy, too? If Lydia drinks a drop, she turns red as a bloody fire engine. Damned unsightly. But amusing."

My father didn't answer. Lydia gave the men their drinks, then seated herself next to her husband and passed me a plate of cookies. Her face was like a mask. A flawless white mask.

Halliday continued. "It was remarkable, really, the way you fit in, old boy. Turned the other cheek even when the boys called your mother—what was it?—oh, yes, a Chinaman's whore."

My mother, whose enchanted smile had stiffened considerably by this point, gave a cry that sounded as if she were being strangled underwater.

Halliday tut-tutted her. "Oh, don't be shocked or think me a boor, my dear. There were so few white women in those days who would even consider marrying yellow." He rolled his arm around behind Lydia, who appeared engrossed in her tea. "Communist to boot, wasn't that true? Did you ever discover what became of the old boy?"

"It wasn't the others. *You* called her that." Dad was sitting as straight as a bayonet. He set his untouched drink on the table beside him.

"Yes, well. She didn't survive the war, as I recall. The Japanese, wasn't it?"

"She died in the *Idzumo* bombing."

"Ach. Nasty business, that."

Halliday sipped his drink and played with the ornament in Lydia's hair. Lydia didn't move a muscle.

"And what of the lover?" asked Halliday, not looking at Dad.

There was a long pause. My mother stared at my father. My father glared at Halliday, who continued to fiddle with Lydia.

"Well, really, old boy," said Halliday. "It was common knowledge."

Suddenly my father was on his feet. "We've imposed on you for too long."

Halliday lifted his face and grinned. "So good of you to come, old man. We must do this again sometime."

As we passed through the foyer Lydia stopped me. She put a finger to her lips, smiled, and passed me a small wrapped candy. In the car I undid the paper and found a piece of crystallized melon, pale and round as a pearl.

A pearl as pale and round as the moon outside my father's window. The night sky was clear, the incoming breeze edged with a promise of fall. Then winter and snow. That bastard!

I breathed hard and deep, the memory of my mother's unwitting complicity angering me as much as Halliday's torment. It was her social climbing that had driven them to accept his invitation. The same grasping ambition that made her hoard Dad's pictures, tell lies, keep secrets. She could excuse anything in the name of money or Art!

The stink of Dad's smoldering ashes was making my stomach cramp. He bent over his folded paper, not seeing the night, not hearing my thoughts.

That cigarette. The tall blond man. I shut my eyes and tried to see them again. Halliday with his helmet and crop, dashing, impervious, sneering. The man smirking in Dad's photograph.

"You saw him in China! You photographed him."

My father opened his finished box with a snap. "Who?"

"Halliday. Nigel Halliday. That creep in Connecticut. He was in one of your photographs."

"What photographs?"

It was the puzzle. The sense that I had the invisible pieces in my clutches. I was close to the solution and had blurted it out without thinking. What photographs?

"I saw some of your work."

"Where?" He put down his paper construction. His glasses obscured any expression of his eyes. His voice could mean anything.

"One of my college teachers." I wasn't lying. Strictly speaking, I wasn't lying. "She had copies from old magazines. *Life.*"

He pulled his lips in until his mouth was just a thin flat line.

"It was him, wasn't it? A picture of him in China with some people pushing a body on a wheelbarrow, and him looking as if he could give a shit. That was Halliday."

"What does it matter?"

"What matters is that you knew. You knew how cruel he was. Why did we go to his house? Why let him treat you like he did?"

He saw then where my thoughts had been for the past half hour. He saw what I remembered.

"Sometimes there are things you spend your whole life wanting to make right, Maibelle. Lies you tell yourself about people to make the things they do more bearable. To make yourself feel less responsible. But eventually the people die."

It sounded as though he would go on, but he shook his head.

"What about Halliday?"

"He died. Finally." His face changed. "Where did you really see that photograph?"

Halliday abruptly fell into place, and I searched for some glimmer of the rights and wrongs on either side of a far more immediate challenge. All I could see was my mother's deceit. And my father's innocence.

"She's been collecting your work, Dad. For years. Foucault doesn't know anything about it. No one does. She's got drawers full."

"You knew." He removed his glasses and wiped the lenses on his sleeve.

My hands began to shake. If I closed my mouth, my teeth would chatter. It was like talking into a freezer, but I kept going. "I just found out the other week. She has this stupid idea about showing our work together. I got furious. She was going behind your back. She lied to us both—"

The band stopped playing outside, which meant most of the guests had left or were leaving. Mum would find us soon.

My father put the glasses aside and lit a cigarette, still not looking at me.

"I debated telling you, but she said you'd try to destroy it all if you knew. I couldn't risk that. Dad, those pictures—"

"Don't say it."

"But—"

My brother pounded on the door. "Maibelle. I know you're holed up in there. Can we go?"

My father stood up. "It's not her fault, Maibelle. Or yours."

....

16

I am running in the new dream through a maze of doors and wrong-way escalators, jumping barriers through an airport, one closed gate after another. My parents are coming, and I have to meet them. I have to bring my child home or she'll die.

Through the thick glass I watch a jet touch down, huge grasshopper landing, skidding, faces like small white eyes in the windows. I am in the wrong place, my hands and feet heavy. Up another down escalator, dragging the weighted trunk behind me. Closer, but now a mob surrounds me. Lights popping, reporters, a gala arrival. Hedda Hopper surges through, laughing, cigarette wand flying, rhinestone sunglasses. She laughs my mother's laugh and I dive past, toward the opening jetway.

Through the long green tunnel I spot them, straining forward. The hole fills with the scent: Chanel No. 9. They are bundled in tweeds, my mother taller, ahead of my father and talking at him, around and through him. I lift my arms, one longer than the other, gloves black against the metallic luster. Sunlight glares through the tall exposed windows and the new arrivals part like sheaves of grass as I fire. Once. Twice. We all fall down in a blaze of white explosive light.

"Murder?" I hear the reporters cry. "Murder, or suicide?"

My head, banging against the wall, woke me as I thrashed out the light. The television was on low. Al Greene crooned softly from the other room. I flipped off the TV, gathered up some bedding, and entered the living room, where my brother lay in his underwear, facedown, one arm dangling over the side of the couch. A lamp burned like an interrogator's spotlight above his head. I switched that off, too, leaving the room to the darkness, my brother's soft, rhythmic breathing, and the steady heartbeat of Al's sweet voice. I kissed the fingertips of a hand I once thought I'd never forgive, and waited for the night to end.

• • •

A few days after my mother's party I called my father to apologize. Henry was out, and I knew my mother would be at the gallery. I thought we might talk more easily on the phone; that what I really needed to say might come to me.

"I shouldn't have told you."

"Maibelle, I'm busy right now."

"I was so sure you ought to know, she was wrong to hide it from you, I never thought to ask if you'd want to know. I feel so stupid, Dad."

"You're not stupid."

"Have you told her? Have you two talked about it?"

"Look, there's some interest in the box patent—"

"She doesn't know I told you, then?"

"No. Maibelle, I'm late for a meeting. It's not that I don't care—I just can't think about all that now."

We hung up. I spent ten minutes turning my father's words in every conceivable direction, then called again. No answer.

I had no further word from either him or Mum for another week, during which I decided my guilt was misplaced. My mother had overdramatized that cache of pictures just as she had my artistic potential, the tragedy of my flying career, and now my refusal to let her plug me into the Network—perhaps even the mystique of my father's lost celebrity was more a function of Mum's theatrics than any reality.

He'd said it wasn't her fault. I couldn't buy that. I was the one who'd been lied to and used. She'd probably wanted me to tell Dad, because she didn't have the nerve to. The act of telling was the real treachery; the content of the story just another buried fact of my parents' life. I'd hold the guilt of betraying both my mother's confidence and my father's complicit ignorance while, between them, nothing would change.

Nothing except a quarter of a million dollars. That's what Dad's magic box is worth to a Swiss candy company with factories in New Jersey. The reclosable carton, it seems, is just what they need for a chewy mint that hardens if exposed too long to the air, and the resemblance to a cigarette hard-pack will help persuade consumers that the candy is meant for adults. They're buying three years of nonexclusive use. Dad wants to spend the first installment on Henry's software program; Mum wants to buy into a loft co-op in SoHo where Henry could live and I could work. Henry's encouraging either plan. Except for congratulating Dad briefly, I've stayed out of the whole discussion.

"It's Dad's money," I told Henry the night Mum weighed in with their spending proposals. "Why you'd want it hanging over your head is beyond me."

"Right. You'd rather be on the payroll of the Mott Street triggerman."

I burned my tongue on my tea. This was the first Henry had mentioned Tai since the party. I hadn't been back to Chinatown since then, either. With Henry moving in I decided it was best to stay on Harriet's good side as much as possible. That meant paying the rent on time. Which in turn meant halting my shoots in Chinatown and accepting the extra catalog work Noble was offering. Really I was avoiding Tai. Henry surely knew that.

"You're changing the subject."

"Am I?" Henry pulled on a blue argyle sock and slipped his foot into a loafer. He was getting ready to go out. He seemed to be going out more and staying out later since the day he'd found me lying awake on the floor next to him.

"He wasn't paying me."

"You said he was."

"Only expenses." I began putting away the lights around the set. Quality of company notwithstanding, it was a squeeze with Henry living in the middle of my studio.

"So I was right. You are seeing him."

"Not now, I'm not. What's this got to do with you taking Dad's money?"

"Why can't you think of it as investment? You're making an investment in Tommy, and as part of that investment you ignore things about him that might turn other people off."

"I wasn't doing it for him."

Henry shrugged on his jacket and surveyed himself in my bedroom mirror, turning up his cuffs, adjusting his collar. He talked to my reflection. "Well, maybe this thing with Mum and Dad works the same way. Maybe they're investing in me, maybe they're doing it for other reasons. Either way, we can ignore certain things about the arrangement that you apparently can't. Frankly I don't see why you're so determined to shove Mum out of your life when you let scum like Tommy walk right in."

The cord in my hand moved like a snake. I imagined it coiling, swaying, rising to strike.

"You held a gun on someone once."

"Not knowingly."

"You knew you were holding a lethal weapon. You knew the damage it could do, and you liked that."

"I never touched one again, Maibelle."

"He never pulled the trigger."

"You don't know that."

"Neither do you."

"Intent makes all the difference in the world."

I felt as if I'd just swallowed a chunk of dry ice. "I'm not defending him, Henry."

"Aren't you?" He slid his wallet into his pocket, kissed my cheek, and left.

When I opened my hand, I found that the cord had left deep white indentations across my palm.

Henry didn't come back that night or the next, and then he only returned to pack. I gave him a key, told him he was welcome to come and stay anytime. He said he appreciated how much I valued my privacy and independence, but he accepted the key and thanked me. A few hours later when Harriet banged on the door and demanded to inspect my apartment because she was sure she'd seen a man coming and going, there was no trace of him.

He left me out of respect, I tell myself as the spaces he briefly occupied fill up with wooden Easter eggs and personalized angel tea cozies. I tell myself it was also respect that kept him from letting the argument about Tai go any further.

But in his absence I've slowly, steadily pushed the burden of blame onto his shoulders. Henry was wrong. Tai never meant to use the gun. It probably wasn't even loaded. Of course it wasn't loaded. Remember Henry's face as he dialed the phone after shooting Johnny? People make mistakes, accidents happen. Tai's crime was nothing compared to Henry's, which is naturally why Henry took such offense.

Maybe it would be different if Henry had stayed, if there were anyone else. But there isn't. Not even Miss Madson. Her bird never returned, but my nightmares have. Ever since I stopped working in Chinatown, and full blast since Henry left. Including the old one. Falling into blind pain, the images from Dad's photographs, the impenetrable cloud of white silk.

Last week I saw Jed Moffitt sitting alone in the window of Ray's. He noticed me across the street and beckoned, and I almost went to him. He saw me hesitate, and he smiled. I ran to keep from caving in.

Then two nights ago the police came for the first time in four months. I refused to open the door. Harriet was suspiciously silent, delivered no threats or warnings. Last night I gagged myself at bedtime to make sure I wouldn't wake up screaming.

Tai's committed no crime against me.

• • •

And so on this cold metallic Monday in October, with the most recent of my catalog assignments shipped, a rent check in Harriet's mailbox, and a sense of anxiety out of proportion even to the oppressive weather, I ride the subway with Tai and David Ling to a graveyard in Queens. We are meeting David's sister and mother, visiting from Phoenix, to pay respects at his father's grave. Death is important to the people of Chinatown and so a necessary component of Tai's book. He says he's been avoiding it, but the time has come at least to get some pictures.

Tai and I are back to visual tag. He has not challenged me about my month's absence. He understands the demands of economic duress, and his book will require months of writing before there is any pressing need for completion of photography. Having seen that my pictures are going to work, he has no basis for complaint. And now that my bills are paid, I've returned, and it should be as simple as that. The same thing could well have happened—I tell myself it would have—even if Henry had kept his mouth shut and refused to answer my repeated questions. Even if he'd done me the favor of lying.

But I still can't meet Tai's eyes.

Instead, as the train dives into the long, blank tunnel below the East River, I concentrate on David's description—background preparation for our day's mission—of his father's funeral. The family had moved to America only the year before and his mother blamed their new home for the death, hence insisted on a large, traditional Chinese funeral with plenty of ritual sacrifice to endure Mr. Ling's safe passage out of American spirit hell and back to China's ancestral paradise. She borrowed heavily from the Ling fong to pay for musicians and official mourners dressed in sack cloth. White paper lanterns on bamboo poles, gongs and incense. Silver and gold joss money, paper clothes, all burned at the grave site. Fruits and cake, roast pork to sustain David's father through his journey. And an uncle, chief mourner, unwashed since the death, who wailed and keened, bent double with the pageant of grief.

David's description inflates to fill the half-empty subway car, carries us up and out of the tunnel, colors the dreary day outside. It distracts and bothers me.

"I was only seven," he remembers. "My job was to carry flowers to the casket. It was open. My father looked like a wax figure. My mother, aunts, all kept staring, waiting for me to cry. But I couldn't feel anything. He'd never talked to me except to say be quiet, get better grades, work harder. You have to love someone to cry for them. My father never let me love him."

David's voice folds back on itself, pitiless. He turns his still-dry eyes to the window. Tai studies the backs of his hands.

We are passing Shea Stadium, Flushing Meadows. The Unisphere looms, a globe full of holes above browning lawns. Remnant of the World's Fair. I struggle to remember. I know that, but I don't remember the details. The only image that comes back to me is the *Pietà,* a dead man, stone, sunken into a woman's lap, both of them drenched in a nightclub-blue light, my mother's voice arching beyond a whisper, condemning Vatican taste. That blue light. "Peace through Understanding" was the theme of the fair, the concept behind the Unisphere. I remember standing beneath it and looking up, the great, crushing ball a web of black metal against a blinding hot sky.

"I was nearly frozen by the time they put him in the ground," David says. "The kind of wind that feels like a whip. I started crying only because I was so cold. I got furious when my aunt put her arms around me, told me what a good boy I was to weep for my father. I curled up into a ball. They had to pick me up like that, carry me. I didn't straighten out until I was in the backseat of the car and we'd started driving home."

A chill runs up my back as I imagine my own father lying in an open casket, a stone man like old Mr. Ling. I begin to sweat and wonder, distractedly, if I'm getting a fever. I have the sense of pulling away, being torn. The park behind us, we enter another tunnel and the lights go out, the noise is deafening and a crushing pressure builds behind my left eye. My hand twitches with the impulse to reach up and yank the emergency cord above my head.

Suddenly the overpass is behind us, the lights are back on. Tai and David are talking above the train's noise. We occupy a booth, two seats facing each other. Tai must feel my eyes, because he looks over, half smiling. Then he stops, pulls a handkerchief from his pocket. White with a monogram. I stare at it coming toward me.

But Tai has no patience. He reaches over and presses the cloth around my thumb. I look down for the first time and see the blood seeping through. I have ripped the entire nail away. And felt nothing.

Neither of them says anything about it. I push the damage, clenched tight, into my coat pocket. By the time we reach Flushing the bleeding has stopped and with it the headache. A short bus ride and we reach the cemetery, where Mrs. Ling and David's sister Jenny are waiting for us. They are two of a kind, compactly rounded and stuffed into woolen bundles topped with complementary tam-o'-shanters, pink for Jenny and vivid green for her mother. They smile, mostly with their eyes. David said she was pleased to have us come along to photograph the family ceremony, but as Mrs. Ling bustles us through the gate I think she would rather I were not here.

The sun glows cold, pale as a mushroom against the pewter sky, and the rows of headstones seem to stretch for miles in every direction. I see them briefly as short white hairs standing up from an old giant's scalp. I resist the urge to photograph them that way, disguising the bones below, and hurry to catch up with the others.

Mrs. Ling has brought a shopping bag full of gifts, plus a picnic hamper. Her husband's grave is in a distant corner, with a view through the fence of intersecting roads and, across, a pink and yellow mini-mart. We are the only people in the cemetery, but traffic is busy outside, and the deli at the mini-mart appears to be doing brisk lunchtime business. The iron bars that separate these two worlds make me feel as if I'm in prison.

"This is a lucky plot." Tai calls me back. "Close to the road. Easy to get out if Lao Ling ever wants to."

"Then I'm sure he's long gone. They're wasting their time."

"This isn't for him. It's for them." He taps the Leica beneath my mutilated thumb. "And us."

Under their mother's strict supervision, David has swept the grave with a long whisk broom and spread a red cloth in front of the headstone. His sister is laying cups and plates and chopsticks, three of each. To either side of the cloth they slide incense sticks into the earth and use rocks to anchor piles of joss money made of tissue glued with silver and gold foil. Jenny fills the plates with chicken and bao, the cups with wine and tea from a thermos. Steam twists off the surface of the tea. The food is still warm, too, but no one here will eat it. It will stay even after the dishes are retrieved, a gift for the dead to be consumed by insects, stray cats or dogs.

This is all supposed to assuage the grief of survivors, I suppose. To build a bridge between the living and the dead, to con those left behind into believing that mortality runs in two directions. It doesn't. The man who lies beneath my feet will never touch this food.

I don't know how David's father died, don't want to know. I am working hard to restrain these thoughts and keep my attention on the surface. The spell on the subway was enough for one day.

Across the graveyard a man Tai's size and build, but older, stooped and ragged, picks his way between the stones. He curls his head toward the ground and hugs his arms tightly into his chest. There is an unearthly quality about him, so that I half expect him to vanish when I blink, but he remains, progressing by inches, neither toward us nor away. He will not raise his face.

I jump when the real Tai touches my wrist. My camera is pointed the wrong way, my body turned back toward the intersection. The traffic light blinks yellow.

"Party time." He leaves his hand just long enough to steady me, then takes his position behind Mrs. Ling. The man across the graveyard is gone.

I scramble up onto a nearby tombstone and position the lens at an angle that won't read the language of eyes but only the gestures of bodies: Jenny and her mother standing side by side in front of the grave; David lighting first the joss sticks, then the stacks of money, and slowly returning to his mother's empty side. The air fills with the lurid sandalwood incense and a brief, minimal warmth from the flames. Everyone bows three times to the dead man's spirit as the burning bits of silver and gold tumble across the dirt, then flicker and rise on a wave of air, pulled by invisible strings.

Just as the ashes are disappearing through the iron bars to the crossroads, skeletal hands clamp my arms. The ghost turns me.

Tai's mouth. Tai's jaw. Black hair bleached to the pallor of stone and white eyes from the dead.

I hold onto my camera and curl my tongue to keep from crying out that Lao Ling has not escaped. He is trapped. My film has caught his entrapment. I have dishonored him and now must be punished by demons.

I hold onto my camera and shout without sound. What face can a ghost man have?

He turns me with fingers biting into my bones. A calm like ice pours through me as the wraith's mouth opens. His face is crevassed with lines. It is not Tai's face.

"You," the ghost-demon accuses. "You survive."

I hold. I hold onto my camera and finally press down. Down, down, down on the shutter.

"Maibelle!" Tai calls from another world. By the time he arrives my arms are free. The ghost has faded away.

"You all right?" He cranes his neck to see beyond me. "Don't be frightened. That's Winston Chang. He's a homeless guy used to live in Chinatown. A little crazy, but he's never hurt anybody."

"I'm all right," I say. He lifts the camera from my grip. "I'll be all right."

* * *

We part company outside the cemetery. David goes with his family to their cousins' in Queens, Tai and I take the subway back to the city. We don't talk much, but I can feel him waiting. He holds his notebook awkwardly, upright in his lap. It bobs forward and back with the train's motion. He positions his mouth to speak, then doesn't, instead fixes on the striped stocking cap of the woman in front of us.

"What *is* it?"

He startles, looks over. "The stripes. They remind me of noodles." His eyes wander around my face. "Are you hungry? I could make us noodles with shrimp."

The notebook falls flat. His cheeks strain against a smile.

"Yes," I say. "Yes. I'm starving."

It's the first time I've been back to his apartment, and I'm not prepared for the sight of packing boxes, the absence of pictures from his walls. Only the prayer rug is still in place.

"You're moving?"

"My cousin's decided the real estate's hot enough. Time to sell."

"But where will you go?"

"I've sublet a loft. It's a little raw, but big. I can have it for three years."

"Where?"

"Fulton Street. Brooklyn."

"You said you'd be stranded anywhere else."

"I've been stranded here." He waves his arm at the squared-off walls, the plywood doors, and confetti floor. I know what he means. It's like a motel room. Not even my mother could transform it. I just assumed that didn't matter to Tai. Certainly not enough to leave Chinatown.

He moves into the kitchen and begins pulling out pans and food. Outside the sliding glass, the sky has softened to a loose amber color that brightens the spurts of rooftop smoke leading down toward the river. The water itself is black as a paved road. It pulls, drawing me toward the balcony.

Tai puts down his knife. He lifts his hand, beckons me back.

"Come. I can use your help here."

I stay where I am but turn away from the glass and the light. A clock hums in the kitchen. I try to concentrate on the sound, to use it as an anchor, but Tai's presence is stronger. The quality of his silence. The stillness of his waiting face. So different from that ghost-man in the cemetery. How could I have confused them?

Unbidden, the words unravel into each other, bend backward in circles and squares. He comes forward, leaving his tools, his task. We sit on the floor. Darkness sweeps the room. The words keep spinning out of me, but he catches and keeps them.

As I talk, the space between us shrinks, the strength of Tai's listening holding us in balance. He hears my dreams as if casting for a fish. His attention is his hook, his attention and the even softness of his gaze, which sinks, touches, pulls one buried image up after another. I'm afraid of the pictures inside my head, of the memories behind them. I'm afraid of what I am likely to see each time I close my eyes. But he's not afraid. He's not fishing, either.

By the time I reach the most recent nightmare, about killing my parents, I am breathing hard, perspiring, hot, as if I've been sprinting or fighting. But that changes after I finish to a sense of incredible lightness. Almost giddiness. I feel unsprung.

"As if you've reached inside," I tell him, "and pried open the fingers of a huge fist."

"A giant's fist?" He touches my wounded thumb. We are facing each other on his prayer rug. "You did the work."

"But you listened."

"I think dreams can tell you things you need to know."

He is wearing a pale green shirt, open collar. Cross-legged, his jeans hike up to expose a strip of smooth skin above the tops of his socks. White socks. Black sneakers. The edges of the soles are wearing through to canvas, the middles pressed into wave patterns.

"Maibelle?"

"I'm sorry."

"You don't have to confront them alone."

"I don't think—"

He leans forward and kisses me. Swiftly. Fully. His lips are soft and comforting.

I push him away.

"That won't help. I've tried."

"Not with me."

"It won't be any different."

"I think it will." But he doesn't try again. "Would you listen to me, then? My nightmares."

I nod. The sounds and smells of cooking seem to simultaneously erupt in apartments above and below. We continue to sit in darkness. It's hard for me to listen. I'm not like Tai. The thought shames me. I try harder.

He is telling about Lao Li, how he changed after I left, his love for Old China becoming an obsession.

"He organized his own gang of Boxers."

I grope for the connection. "Boxers?"

Tai explains that Li talked endlessly in his final months about the "foreign devils" who had ruined his country and left it to rot. He had trusted them, thought they were his friends, but they were evil. All of them. He talked himself into believing that it was still not too late, he could bring back the old ways and stop the barbarians even now. He would resurrect the Boxers, the antiforeign movement of the last century whose Chinese name meant "Fists of Righteous Harmony" and whose mandate was to preserve the dynasty and destroy all foreigners. Li convinced Tai to join.

"He told us to think of tourists as foreign oppressors, encouraged us when we roughed up a few Jersey kids. Still, I couldn't think of it as what it was—a street gang—until he gave us weapons . . . I pulled a gun on someone."

The reds and blues of the prayer rug vibrate in the lamplight. I follow a river into a flower into a circle.

"But you didn't pull the trigger."

"No, I couldn't. But I came so close, Maibelle. It terrified me. I told Li I had to quit. He went crazy. Yelled that I was betraying him. My family were all cowards. My father—he said terrible things. Unforgivable things. A few weeks later he died. They said it was a brain tumor. So I thought, that's why he changed so, became so cruel and obsessed. But the damage was already done."

I press the nap to calm the colors. Li. Tai's words squeeze my memories of him into a tight, unyielding ball.

"The gang start calling themselves the Dragonflies, hook up with one of the tongs. They say my father has to pay *lixi,* but he tells them no, Li protected him. My dad doesn't understand why things change, now he's an old man."

"You didn't tell him how Li had changed?"

Tai makes two fists and presses his knuckles together. "He believed Li was his friend."

"But you made him understand he had to pay!"

"They wanted too much." Tai turns away, toward the window, and speaks to the darkened glass. "Late one night I come around the corner down the block from my parents' store and see the gang out front. Six of them. They're laughing, shouting, like who cares if anybody sees them. A couple have switchblades out, goofing around like kids. The others crouch on the sidewalk, all business. Tying rags around these stones, soaking them with gasoline. I knew but I couldn't move, couldn't yell."

Tai faces me, searching. "It was like I was asleep, Maibelle—you know how sometimes you scream in a dream and no sound comes out, you run and run and don't get anywhere—that's my nightmare. All I could do was watch. I watched them light the rags. Chuck the stones through our window. I watched them laugh and run away. A second later the store blew up."

I feel sore, as if I have a blister inside my chest. I close my eyes and see the muzzle of a gun rising. I look quickly, catch his gaze. The irony and rage I find there stay the gun but burst the blister.

"They used firecrackers. Firecrackers, three to a bundle—same as for New Year's, you know? But these were packed with black powder."

I scoot forward, pull his hands into my lap. On the soft insides of his wrists I feel his pulse beating steady, persisting in spite of his words. They are only words. Only story. But he won't let it end.

"My mother was in the back room working late. We had bars on the windows and doors. The explosion was so powerful—it lifted the desk, slammed it against the window. We found her crushed between the bars."

I picture the Mrs. Wah of my childhood—a squat, energetic woman in a pastel housedress and flapping galoshes. A grin too wide for her face. She gave me butterscotch candies and called Henry her number-two son. Her forearms were as tough as baseball bats from hacking up all those chickens, but that didn't do her much good in the end.

I imagine Tai's pulse weakening, stopping, and rub his hands hard, to awaken the blood. He reclaims them and his voice pours over my head.

"I remember the roar of the birds in the basement, beating their wings against the cages. It wasn't the explosion or fire that killed them, you know? It was terror."

"I know."

Tai's face seems to graduate into shadow, not crisply halved, but gently, the way twilight blends toward night. You sense things at twilight that you can't fully see, and in just this way I know his eyes are following mine as I trace the hard, smooth angle of his jaw with my forefinger, find the flat, dime-sized tip of his chin, and turn back and up to the deep, hidden space just below his ear where the resistance of bone gives way to softness.

His kiss is even softer. He smells of the night and, dimly, reminiscently, sandalwood. I gulp that scent, yank it around and into me like water. I can no longer tell if my eyes are open or closed, whether my feet are on the floor, where his lips stop and mine begin. I draw closer, and he gives a low, earthly sob, pulls me against him, molding his body to mine until I can no longer touch the space between us.

He starts to undress me, but I pull the clothes off ahead of him.

There will be no more words, just his lips, the roughness of his shirt. And when the fabric slips away, the smoothness of his skin. We will make love. Love. Love.

I feel the darkness of his eyes on my face, the lines of his body, his hair. At his touch my skin springs into gooseflesh.

"You never told?" I whisper.

"Told?"

"About your mother. What happened to your father?"

He stops moving. "There were threats. I left instead. My father died of a stroke a year later."

"But you never told."

"Not until tonight." He cups his hand over my shoulder.

The hand tightens. I want to trust him, I have, but the light behind my eyes breaks into a deep white glare so powerful I no longer can see him. His bones squeeze against me. Not just my shoulder, my wrists and feet, dragging me down. A weight on my chest, pushing. Pulling. How can it be so black and so bright? Like a flare through a blindfold. His hands grope.

I sniff the air around him. Not sandalwood now but fish. A deep, briny silt. The odor seems to steam from his skin, from his pores. Salt, brine, raw as sex. Not love. The smell pours over me, into me, stronger than the darkness. I can't breathe through the stink of this man. This lover. I can't breathe.

The smell becomes a pressure on my throat. Voices laughing, crying. I look down but can't see, can't fly away. Hands like insects crawling inside my skin. The smell makes me sick. Down. I'm looking, falling. They've cut off your wings, Johnny tells me.

Get out!

I rear back and snatch my clothes. This man isn't right. Not blond. Not Johnny.

"Maibelle, what is it?"

He sounds breathless. I lunge for the door, one leg, then both. Shirt. Shoes without socks. Find the knob and turn.

He stands and steps forward. Arms widen. Naked.

"Don't touch me. Please don't touch me!"

If it's locked, there's the window. Flight. No, that's crazy. No wings.

The door opens and I run. Down the endless, echoing fire stairs. Out into the street and crowds of people. I run between cars. Point uptown and go. If I stop, they'll come after me, back to the white light, splitting pain.

"Get out of there," the White Witch yells as I run. "Protect yourself." She means with my weapon. My camera. But I've left the camera behind with them. With him.

In the moonless dark the orange eyes of cigarettes blink and jab. Voices climb as I pass, and behind, some shout. The stink of fear surrounds me.

There are no cabs for blocks. Some streets have no light. But Canal Street, ahead, is lit up like Vegas. There waits a Checker but when I look in the window the driver's head seems to lift off his shoulders. Murderous blue eyes, hair as shiny as a plastic bag. His cheeks are on fire.

I run on.

I see myself as a madwoman like the old Bowery pawnshop ladies. Gray skin, empty eyes, caved-in bodies. Alone. So alone they're untouchable. I slow down. Can't let that happen to me. I can't but it will. It's already started. I have to shake myself out of this. Else I'll be damned.

I am walking by the time I reach Eleventh Street. I can still feel my heart twitching, but I pay attention to my breathing. I check periodically, no one is following. No eyes in the dark. Only people, coming and going, their voices making clouds in the chill night air.

A cab waits outside my building. He gets out and hands me my camera bag. I take care to avoid his touch, his eyes.

"Why, Maibelle?"

I pull away and run inside.

....

17

That night the phone rang. And rang. I was afraid it would rouse Harriet. I assumed it was Tai and so took the receiver off the hook. Afraid to sleep, I was just filling the developing tank in preparation for a night in the darkroom when someone hammered on my door.

"Maibelle." A man's voice in a high whisper. I didn't recognize it.

Telescoped through the peephole, my brother stood waiting outside. I flung open the door to welcome him.

"Good, you're dressed," he said. "Your phone's broken."

"What's going on?"

His arms hung, jerking, at his sides.

"Dad's collapsed."

My father was in the emergency room at New York Hospital with my mother waiting for the surgeon to arrive. Henry said something about sending a telegram to Anna, but I couldn't listen. I was transfixed by an older couple dripping blood. In their late eighties, someone said. Attempted a double suicide. Dark red stains bloomed like carnations across their sheets. My father's lung had collapsed. They'd already taken the X rays. Cancer.

When I finally worked up the courage to look at him, I was astonished to see him blink. It was too hard for him to speak—I could see the pain clasp his face with each breath—but despite this he gripped my hand. His nails were still bitten to the quick. His hair was a little damp. The moonpuffs soft and full. His head seemed immense by comparison with the rest of his body, veiled by a sheet.

Whatever had happened earlier in the evening was pushed aside by the pallor of his skin. No nightmare, nothing that could happen to me, could possibly be worse than this. I had told him about the hidden pictures, and now he was dying.

My mother leaned over him, kissed his cheek, and rubbed his other hand.

The emergency room seemed unnecessarily dark and, except for the moans of the old people, too quiet. I looked around for someone to complain to. Some soothing light, music. And heat. This wasn't a morgue!

My brother put his arm around my shoulders and drew me away.

"Calm down."

"I'm calm!"

"You're shaking. You're crying."

I hadn't noticed.

"He's not dead, Maibelle. We don't have a prognosis yet. Don't make it worse than it is."

But I couldn't help it. I kept seeing him trying to claw his way up to the plates of food, to the intersection of roads where he could choose his route of escape.

My brother sat me down. I got up. The doctor arrived. I kissed my father before they wheeled him away. His cheek was icy.

"Give him some blankets!" I yelled down the forbidden hallway. "Can't you see he's freezing to death!"

• • •

He's come out of round one, minus the fallen lung. He may have weeks or months, the doctors tell us. But the cancer has spread too far for further surgery or chemo.

The first of those weeks passes in a haze of exhaustion and dread. He looks like a high school science experiment with all the tubes and bottles and computers hooked up to him. His skin has yellowed, his hair leaves grease stains on his pillow. He can't speak, but my mother does—about the coming elections, the latest teachers' strike, a Van Gogh that sold for two million. My brother hoards the TV controller and channel-surfs. I hold Dad's hand.

Only if we are alone do I talk to him. I don't bring up the pictures since I have no proof that they hastened his sickness and, whether they did or not, he is in no position to discuss them. Or much of anything else, for that matter. So I tell him stories. Li's stories, though I don't mention Li. The Fairy's Rescue. The Pearl-sewn Shirt. I tell him Chinese versions of Romeo and Juliet and Cinderella. Sometimes he falls asleep before I finish. Sometimes he stares at the ceiling with that faraway look. Sometimes I feel his eyes roaming my face as if drinking my image. He gives no sign of protest. I like to think the stories carry him to another place where he can be young and make new, different choices. The only one I hold back from him is the one he once told me himself. The Man Who Chopped Trees on the Moon.

My father's known for weeks about the cancer. He went to the doctor a few days after Mum's party. After I betrayed her secret. A connection? That eternal clucking in the back of his throat was not disapproval but disease.

He knew and told none of us that he had been condemned.

• • •

We took turns, as families will, standing watch at the hospital. From one day to the next I slept too little to dream, worried too much for my father to feel my own ineffable terror. I recognized the piercing irony, that it took my father's devastation to ward off my own, but there was no relief, either way.

* * *

I went back to my apartment just once that first week, to pack a suitcase to bring uptown. This note was in my mailbox.

> I'm sorry, Maibelle. I never meant to push you, never would have if I'd had any idea. If you'd let me know that much more.
>
> I once wrote that silence is a prison and stories a form of refuge. I knew this was true from my own experience, and yet knowing was not enough. My story held me hostage for twelve years until you gave me the courage to break the silence. I could not do it alone, could not even have imagined how it would feel. Like coming up out of a well into the light, out of water into air. Please. Finish telling me your story, so I can try to help you as you have me.
>
> I love you, Maibelle. Believe that.
>
> Tai

When I got back to the hospital, I called David Ling at the seniors' center and left a message for Tai about my father's illness. I wasn't sure what I was saying. I didn't answer Tai's note. "Indefinitely." I used that word. Several times, I used it.

Otherwise, I didn't dare think about Tai. I didn't know if or when I ever would again.

• • •

Five days after my father enters the hospital, just when it seems he is out of immediate danger and we can try to formulate some semblance of a routine, my mother is summoned to the phone at the nurse's station. She is gone for about ten minutes, and when she returns, her left eye is twitching. She bends to kiss my father's cheek.

"Maibelle and I have to go out for a little while, Joe. Henry, you stay here till we get back?" She grabs my elbow. I hardly have time to scoop up our coats, which we put on haphazardly while racing down the corridor. The elevator is packed, overheated, no place to ask questions.

"What's going on?" I yell as she sails into the grim autumn bluster outside.

She puts two fingers into her mouth and whistles for a cab. I didn't know she could do that. I never could. I thought only Henry could. Two taxis vie to claim her. She picks the first, which is not the Checker but a crummy yellow Chevy, something she would never ordinarily do. She gives the driver the gallery's address, and he grumbles; it's only a two-dollar fare.

I slide the inside window shut. "So, what is this?"

Her hair is all over the place. Her coat is buttoned out of order, and her eyes, fixed on the driver's photograph up front, look like animal traps.

"Foucault died."

My initial impulse is to laugh. I stifle it. "That's what you've been waiting for, isn't it?"

"Not like this."

We lurch, skipping through a red light. I'm not sure what she means, and the way her lower lip is trembling, I'm afraid to ask. The metallic surface, the glint of sharpened teeth, are just cover. My mother's tenacious bluff. She reaches for my hand and squeezes hard. Something about it reminds me of when I was very small, when sometimes she'd wear white gloves and take me shopping, the feel of her hand through the kidskin gripping mine as we crossed the street. Only this time it feels as if she's the one who needs to be shepherded across.

The gallery looks dead now, too. She left it closed, pictures hastily removed from the walls when Dad got sick. The only sign of occupation is the security light in the back. She stares for a moment while I pay for the cab, and sighs as if she's relieved, as if she expected maybe to see the whole thing blown away. Then it's all business and she hurries up the steps. Her key is in her hand.

I picture Foucault's beaked face emblazoned on the building's white granite front, like one of those great proletarian banners of Lenin or Mao in holograph nodding, blinking, warning us away. "Mine!" he mouths.

I've been without sleep for too long. This is all right. Mum's finally got what she wants. Her hidden cache at the very least. After everything she's been through she's entitled. When Dad dies, what will it matter?

She is at the lock, worrying the key.

"Come here," she calls over her shoulder. "Help me with this."

But it won't turn. The brass of the tumbler is brighter than the plate, unscratched. And then we hear steps inside. A light comes on in the foyer. My mother's nails bite my skin.

A man's voice from inside calls, "Pull out the key." A British accent. Young.

I withdraw the key, her hand still clutching my wrist, pushing against me.

We step backward, almost over the step. I catch the belt of her coat to keep her from falling and note again the missed buttonhole. But there's no time to change it.

"How d'ye do? You must be Madam Chung. Coralie said you'd be popping 'round."

He looks like a club bouncer. Large square head with hair too far back, massive shoulders busting out of that houndstooth suit. A single furrow, an exclamation mark, down between his eyebrows. He's smiling, extending an open fist. I think of my grandfather's flyswatter.

"Who the hell are you!" My mother's voice booms as she pushes forward. He catches her across the shoulders and shakes his head, smiling, but not apologizing. The way a parent would stop a child. He's easily half her age.

"Executors say I'm not to let you in, I'm afraid. 'At's why we changed the locks, you notice. You're a sort of persona non grata, according to the old man's will."

She stomps on his foot, twists her body around, reaches for me to move forward. Two against one. I glance at the stairs. I could slip by and make it up there, but then what? I don't care about the rest of her trove, and my father's work is in the safe.

She wrestles out of his grip and stands glaring up at this hulking obstacle who no doubt is much quicker than he looks. "You're out of your mind! I own this gallery!"

"Not the way I read it, mum."

"Don't you dare call me that!" Her eyes now belong to the cornered beast caught in her own trap.

"Miss Coralie—"

"How do I know you're not a burglar? I'll call the police and have you arrested!"

Never in my life have I seen my mother like this. I pity her, yet she mesmerizes me. I wonder if this is an act. If not, she's got even more guts than I realized. This man could kill us both with a single blow, and she's treating him like a schoolyard bully.

I lay my hand on her arm. Her whole body is quivering. "You must have some authorization."

He raises an eyebrow, as if suddenly I'm his coconspirator, and slides a hand inside his jacket. A pellet, dry and frozen, rattles briefly in my chest, but he pulls out only papers. Papers sealed by a London court and signed, in a shaky scrawl, by Gerard Foucault. A second order for the guard service is signed by the executors of the estate and undersigned by Coralie Moutiers, the new president and owner of Galleries Foucault International.

"They seem to be in order, Mum."

"Let me see those." Her voice is clammy. She takes the documents and steadily rips them to shreds.

"It's all right, miss," the guard says to me as I scramble, hissing, to retrieve the pieces.

My mother kicks me in the ribs. I push her foot back firmly on the floor, and she doesn't strike again.

"These are only copies. I've another set in the back. The originals are in a vault in London. But I think you'd better take her away, 'fore she does any more damage to herself."

"At least let me get my personal belongings."

I half expect her to wink at me, she must have a plan. Doesn't she always? But she's sagging. She won't look at either of us.

"I can let you into the office, but I have to escort you and make a note of everything you take."

So we march, ahead of him. I wonder if this is how prisoners felt on the way to the guillotine. There's nothing she wants or needs in the office.

She sits in Foucault's chair at Foucault's desk and pulls the top drawer.

"My cosmetic bag, with my initials on it." She holds it for him to see. "My address book, also with my initials."

"I don't know about that, mum."

"This is mine. Here's the Rolodex. I wouldn't dream of taking that. But these are my personal friends." She rolls her eyes up at him, the expression of a silent-movie queen in distress. "My husband is in the hospital dying of cancer. I would like to be able to notify my friends when he passes on."

"That's true," I say. He shrugs and flutters his giant paw.

Some bills, still in their envelopes, addressed to Mum at home.

"Maybe you'd like to take care of these for me?"

"Go on with you. Finish up."

From the next drawer a box of diet bars, Kleenex, a silver pen also engraved with her initials that my father bought for her on sale at Tiffany's, and from the bottom drawer a framed photograph of Henry and Anna and me, must have been that last year at the farm. I recognize us, smiling together, but I have no recollection of the picture being taken. Mum's kept it here for fifteen years.

The guard looms over the desk, making notes. "Nice-lookin' family."

"Yeah. Well, I guess they're all I've got left, aren't they?"

I pick up as many of the belongings as I can hold. We don't have a bag. We would never have gotten out with what we really came for.

I draw a bead on the back of my mother's blue velvet collar, still marginally askew but straightening rapidly, and follow her out and away from the gallery. For the final time.

* * *

Later, standing in the kitchen with a tumbler of Scotch, she tells me the salient details. He drowned in the South of France while swimming in a mineral pool reputed to prolong life. Coralie was with him.

We stare at each other while the words sink in. I start to laugh. Mum watches, wide-eyed with surprise or anger, I can't tell which, but it doesn't stop me and soon she, too, is bubbling over, helpless chortles branching into raucous guffaws. We wipe our noses on paper towels. The laughter fills the cold white room like helium in a dental office. We refill our glasses with the Dewar's we've been drinking for over an hour. It almost feels as if we're having fun. We keep it up until our faces are slick with tears, and stop abruptly.

The Bauhaus clock reads six. Outside, the sky is ashen, city lights reflecting intermittently off of low clouds.

She has her arms twisted around each other tight against her chest. Suddenly she whirls to the sink, grabs a scrub brush, and attacks the tile grout.

"You could fight in probate," I say. "You could get your customers and artists to testify that Foucault only succeeded in New York because of you. There must be some precedent for this, like commercial palimony? Mum, that gallery was your life, you can't just let it go without fighting."

Her body slowly stops working. She lets go of the brush. When she turns back to me, she is biting her lip. The rims of her eyes are red and glossy, and I expect her to say something about the hidden pictures, the part of the gallery that is most hers, which she can never claim.

Instead she says, "That's really what you think?"

I stare at her shoes. Black round-toed Ferragamos with small pleated bows. She's had them for years, but they look brand-new. "Well, Art was, anyway."

She tears a Kleenex from the heap of retrieved goods piled on the counter and blows her nose. Hard. "Your father was my life, Maibelle. Everything I've ever done has been for him. That's the only thing I regret about the gallery. The only thing."

She gasps. Her eyes roll wide, thick with tears that have no part of laughter. She gulps air. "I don't know what I'm going to do. What am I going to do now?"

I come toward her. She stands sobbing, pulling tissues. She won't look at me. Her hair falls loose, dull and wispy as an old feather. I want to hold her, to hug her, be small in her arms again. To feel warmth and the certain squeeze of her love. But her body is closed and smaller than mine now.

"It was my fault, don't you see? Coming back. Settling in. Babies. None of it—"

I picture her clawing at a locked door. A pink satin pillow. Sobbing. My father leading her to safety.

"He never would have quit if it hadn't been for me."

"That's not true, Mum."

"It is." She takes my head between her hands and squeezes until I can feel the contours of my own skull. Her eyes dig into mine. "You don't know. None of you. The way he just disintegrated."

Suddenly she straightens as if someone's put a prod up her back. She releases me and shakes her head, smooths a final tissue below her eyes.

"Look at me. Who has time for this! It's all right, Maibelle. As soon as the word is out, as soon as Joe's better and I can put my mind to this again, people will call."

"Delong. And Scott?"

"Absolutely."

• • •

After that one brief lapse, Foucault's death seemed to engineer my mother's grief over Dad, gave it the sharp, crisp edges of an executive career. The day we brought him home from the hospital she filled the apartment with balloons and loaded his bedside with the best of his gadgets for invalids. Rotating cup holders, folding trays, side bags containing magazines, newspapers, cards, and notepaper within easy reach. Considering the disdain with which she's treated most of his inventions, this was a sweet and meaningful gesture.

Sweet and meaningful does not describe her dealings with me and Henry. The contrast, after the first days at the hospital when every word between us throbbed like a stab wound, was both a relief and a serious annoyance.

After the shock of Foucault's betrayal subsided, she didn't mention the gallery or her future plans again. Instead, Dad became her consuming passion—and a macabre Pollyanna passion it was. In complete and unilateral command, she reported every development as if Henry and I had just dropped in from Outer Mongolia. Told us over and over how marvelously sensitive the radiologist was, how humane the treatment (which, because of the extent of the cancer, consists of little more than painkillers), and how open-minded the oncologist (because he gave Mum the number of an "alternative" medicine man whose coffee enemas and herbal infusions Dad won't touch). She studied homeopathic textbooks, restorative cookbooks, became an overnight expert on resuscitation techniques. The kitchen became a laboratory for Dad's new whole-grain, raw-vegetable immuno-boost diet. Once again, her entire existence served a master plan.

When I suggested that the best treatment might be simply to cherish the short time Dad had left, Mum repeated a phrase I'd heard so often. "You don't really believe that," she said, then more softly, "We can't quit."

While I told myself she was more than entitled to whatever defenses she could muster, at that moment I began to fantasize about scrawling "Death Kills!" in blood red across her living room chevrons.

Henry finally bailed out. He'd visit Dad every day like a dutiful son, but he just couldn't handle round-the-clock exposure to Mum's Florence Nightingale routine. So we've traded places, in effect, with me helping Mum uptown, he braving Harriet and the other white witches of Eleventh Street.

And then the weekend after Dad came home, Anna arrived.

• • •

From the living room I could see the foyer as my mother went to unlock the elevator door. I watched it roll back, saw the duffel bag and backpack and, beyond, a thin figure with cropped brown hair. She was wearing blue jeans, a turquoise-green pullover, dark glasses. She gave us all hugs, no cheek pecks. She smelled like a Big Mac and handed Mum a bottle of Oregon wine for a homecoming present.

As Anna hurried down the hall to see Dad, Henry voiced what we were all thinking. "Ding dong, the guru's dead!"

Later in my father's room, Anna (she was, again, Anna even unto herself) told us the story. The Dhawon, it seems, had objected to her leaving the ashram. He told her she had taken a vow to serve him as daughter and wife, that her spiritual family consisted solely of other devotees. The outside realm was of no consequence. Not even if her "biological" father was terminally ill. By leaving without permission she would forfeit her place of favor in the Inner Circle.

"In other words, I'd go from being his mistress to his janitor. Somehow, I felt I had a right to my own father. Besides, I always hated the way I look in red, and I had a terrible craving for beef."

Dad smiled. "Me, too," he whispered.

Anna kissed his forehead. "Which part? The red or the beef?"

"Whopper."

My mother started to shake her head. The nutritionally correct diet she'd been feeding my father made the Dhawon's menus seem positively sybaritic. But the rest of us were united on this one.

"If he can't smoke, he can at least have a good greasy hunk of meat."

Without any further discussion Henry and Anna were gone, my mother pounding after them.

"Lock the door." My father propped himself up, wheezing with the effort of speech.

I did as instructed and tried to plump up his pillows, move away some of the books that cluttered his bed, but he waved a sheaf of handwritten papers in my face to make me quit.

"Sit. Read this."

"Maibelle? Are you in there?" She called but didn't try the door.

"Yes. We're fine. Take a rest, Mum."

"You'll let me know if he needs anything?"

"He doesn't need anything, Mother. Relax."

But I could hear her pacing the hall a few times before her footsteps finally retreated to the kitchen, where they were soon replaced by the roar of the Cuisinart. There was going to be a showdown when the Fast Food Kids returned.

My father was watching, taking one labored breath after another as he waited for me to attend to my reading. There were pages of his cramped chicken scratch. I dropped into a chair beside the television, which was tuned to a rerun of *The Avengers* with the sound off.

"This will take a while. Want me to turn up the volume?"

He signaled for me to just read.

"Dear Maibelle—Mei-bi," I read. "Mei Mei."

He had his mouth pursed around an imaginary cigarette and his eyes were aimed toward the television but moved in quick, side-to-side jerks as if he were dreaming awake.

> You were always fond of stories. I'm not sure if you yet realize, the best photographs tell stories better than words. So that they rise beyond the tale, reveal history. I made a few pictures that qualified in my day. Maybe Mum has some of them in that secret cache you told me about. Maybe you've seen them. I hope so. But most of my work fell short because I refused to put *myself* in the story. (I don't mean physically being in the photograph, you understand. I'm talking about more of a spiritual presence, as Anna would say.) I always knew that one day you would insist on the truth. Henry and Anna would go their own ways, but you . . . from the very beginning you wanted to know what I was incapable of telling you. It seems that by telling me about Diana's secret—by offering to show me what you've done with the Leica—you are again asking the unanswerable.
>
> I came across one of Diana's old gardening manuals the

other day, and it struck me that history is nothing more than a universal plant. It propagates. It proliferates. And over time you have a tangle of roots, branches, leaves, and buds all carrying exactly the same cyclical pattern. History doesn't merely repeat itself. It expands and multiplies, over and over until there are so many regenerations that the pattern is impossible to kill. Or to escape.

I tried to make a break with my history. Destroying my photographs—banning them—was part of that. So was my silence. I never told anyone why I had to make this break. If I had been able to tell Diana, maybe she wouldn't have tried—and succeeded—to thwart me. Maybe she wouldn't have been so determined for you to fill the space I'd abandoned. Maybe she'd have persuaded me I was wrong, that quitting was no escape. But you can't quit your own cowardice.

It's about my father, Maibelle. About 1948, when I went back to Peiping to find him.

I hadn't seen him since early 1935, when I left Shanghai for New York. He had sent me just one letter, warning that any further correspondence would endanger him. Not long after that letter was postmarked, Chung Wu-tsai put my mother and sisters on a ship bound from Shanghai for San Francisco. That night Shanghai was bombed.

I've read accounts of that day. One family was driving to a wedding reception. There were couples dancing in the Palace Hotel. A refugee center had been set up on Nanking Road just the day before. Children begging on the Bund. All gone. Others were killed at the top of the roller coaster at the Great World entertainment complex in the heart of the International Settlement. Bodies dangling from twisted steel pilings. Streets knee-deep in shattered glass and flesh. Heads lopped off, still with their flowered hats on . . . I used to wonder what my mother was thinking, what they did with her body. My sisters. But there were no eyewitnesses in their compartment. And there was no compartment afterward. Only a bloody hole. I spent years searching for pictures that matched my imagined snapshots of that day.

The Japanese did not drop those bombs. They were Chinese pilots trying to hit the Japanese ship *Idzumo,* anchored just offshore. Instead they killed nearly a thousand civilians and wounded twice as many. Afterward, the foreign powers finally began to take the war in China seriously. Some people said those pilots never intended to hit the Japanese warship.

It was a Chinese who killed my family. One of my own people. So I thought at the time.

I never heard from Father after my mother died. It was as if he, too, had died, or I had for him. Even after I was assigned to China, it took me nearly a year to find out he was teaching history at Peita University.

We had a meal together. He said he'd remarried. His new wife was Chinese, and much younger. They had a baby daughter. My half sister. Father promised to take me to meet them. Maybe the next day, he said.

It was not an easy conversation. Though I had been trained to admire and respect my father, I didn't know the man. The news of this substitute family came as a complete surprise, but my only response was a mild curiosity. It was too late for jealousy, too soon to feel any hope of reentering Father's life. Anyway, I rather suspected that he felt more keenly about his students than any member of his own family, past or present. The students surely knew him better and had more in common with him. When he suggested I come to a demonstration scheduled for that evening, I accepted without hesitation. I wanted to see his chosen sons.

The rally was held on "Democratic Ground," a vast square located just outside the university. Students from all the colleges represented in the North China Student Union assembled to protest Chiang's regime and, specifically, the shooting and arrest of students in Shanghai and Peiping in previous days. Several thousand young Chinese packed together in front of a makeshift stage. Many waved painted banners or placards with slogans denouncing Chiang's "antidemocratic government" and that "ally of reaction," the United States. Similar phrases lined the handwritten newspapers plastered on nearby walls. They also cropped up in the speeches of student leaders and sympathetic professors, including my father. The audience listened intently, occasionally breaking into cheers and applause, joining in with enthusiasm when the revolutionary songs began.

Through the show I made frame after frame of rapt faces, raised fists, and, toward the end, the long procession snaking around the square. I hoped to try the pictures at *Life.*

My father and I were to meet again the next afternoon outside the Forbidden City. That night I returned to my room and developed the film. In the morning I went out for breakfast. I'd intended to return and make a few prints to send back in the pouch that evening, but I ran into a fellow I'd worked with briefly in Singapore who convinced me to go with him to Pachiatsun, on the outskirts of the city.

The scene at the front was eerily calm. We could see the hazy purple of the Western Hills, the rooftops of the Empress Dowager Tzu Hsi's Summer Palace, endless raw, brown fields, and the smokestack of a former textile factory Chiang's people were using to manufacture arms. A half mile beyond the factory, across an invisible line, lay communist territory. Hard as you looked, it was impossible to distinguish one side from the other.

I arrived back in the city late for my meeting with Father. A crowd had gathered in front of the Gate of Heavenly Peace. I heard the familiar slogans. Some students were organizing an impromptu rally. I remember their breath in the cold air formed clouds shaped like dragons.

I assumed my father would be somewhere in this group, but the traffic was thick and moving against me. I raised my camera. People hid their faces and stepped aside. I had just found him in the lens, just focused when his face flew apart.

I was no novice. I had been on battlefields, photographed the shredded bodies of men I'd shaken hands with moments before. It was not merely the sight of blood, raw flesh, or the danger of my own death that stopped me cold this time.

The crush of people forced me down, despite my attempt to flee. Machine-gun fire roared overhead, ricocheting off the Imperial Palace. People dove under each other for cover. I could no longer see my father but was kneeling in his blood.

Then, as suddenly as it had begun, it was over. The open-bed truck of the "Discipline Supervisory Corps" sped off. The mob pulled back. My father and two of the three young men who had been leading the group lay dead on the pavement.

I watched my father's students load his body onto a cart. I forced myself to run with them to the hospital. I listened to doctors verify his death as the students wept for my father. Strong, young, idealistic Chinese, they claimed both his body and his memory. They appointed a group to inform his wife. I followed at a distance.

The students led me through the maze of Tungan Market, finally turning through a high archway and down a deeply shadowed *hutung* to a tall, red-lacquered gate. The gate closed behind the students.

For the rest of the day I wandered the city, losing myself

among the beggars, vendors, and rickshaw drivers. I watched soldiers stop and search young boys. They crushed an old man's skull with the butt of a gun. I kept walking past the midnight curfew, until an armed patrol stopped and threatened to arrest me. I put up a fight, insulting them, daring them to shoot, but I was not Chinese. They demanded my identification, then tied my hands and drove me home.

The next day I returned to Tungan Market and went through that lacquer doorway. My father's house was old, elegant, with a quiet courtyard and lovely moongate. His wife answered my knock herself. She was not as young as I'd expected, forty or even older. Already she had dressed in the ceremonial sack cloth of mourning. Behind her stood a beautiful young woman, also white-robed, whom I took for a servant.

My presence seemed to bewilder them both. I said I was a business acquaintance of Chung Wu-tsai, and had heard of his untimely death. This satisfied the wife, who introduced herself as Ming-yiu. The young woman was Wu-tsai's daughter. Her name was Chung Ling-ling.

They offered me tea, which I could not drink, and cakes, which I could not eat. I do not remember the subtleties of my half sister's face, only that she wore her hair in a long coarse braid and had a jade moon in each earlobe. Only that she could not have been more than a few years younger than me. I knew I would never see her again.

I do not remember what was said, except that it was all lies. They deserved better. They deserved the bloody truth. But I couldn't blame them, and I had no desire to hurt them any more. Their lives would be difficult enough if Chiang remained in power. In any event, it would do them no good to know of my father's double life. Of my mother and sisters and me, and the family my father had sired in Shanghai's International Settlement.

My mother's pride had blinded us all. If she knew, she never showed it. Always the wife, never the concubine. But Wu-tsai had different ideas. He had proved he could tame the White Witch. Now he would keep his conquest and take a real Chinese wife.

How convenient for Father that I had gone to America and the others had died in the bombing. His white wife and children might never have existed. Perhaps, for him, we never really did.

Somehow I conveyed my regrets and got away. If I had even for a moment imagined some kind of bond with these half relatives, my past was closed against me now. I would process the last of my film, ship it off with a request for immediate reassignment.

I forced myself to develop the frames of my father's dying moments, the faces of his friends and supporters, the sights of Peiping, his home, on his final day on earth. But it was not until I lifted the first strip from the bath that I remembered the other shots. Those negatives from the university protest—I'd left them on the line to dry and now they were gone. I ransacked the drawers, searched every crack of that dank basement cubicle. But I knew.

Two weeks earlier, days after I'd accompanied a French journalist to a village north of Chungking, twelve of the peasants we met were publicly tortured and disemboweled by KMT soldiers. The anonymous interviewee, a Red collaborator, had refused to let me photograph him. He was never even detained. The twelve who were killed had asked to pose to show off their children and pigs. But I'd refused to admit the connection. I refused to accept the blame.

Chung Wu-tsai was a man I barely knew, a man who turned away from me just as China was turning me away. He was a stranger and the source of my greatest confusion. But he was my father. And I had killed him. Without intent or premeditation. What the hell! Without honest grief or even remorse.

In death he continued to shame me. And I, in my ignorance, had once again proven myself the fool.

Instead of requesting reassignment, I resigned. I burned all negatives in my possession and by week's end left China.

I have never experienced such loathing as I felt for myself on returning to America. I could not bear to lie anymore. I couldn't bear to tell the truth. So I held back, hoping that in time this would all just fade away. Become ancient. History, as it were, immaterial.

But as I've said, history seems to proliferate. Mine has been concealed for so long it now seems to burst at the seams. Hiding does not, as I wished, make things go away. It's only hurt us all.

So I am writing this. The next step is to talk the story, but that takes more strength than I can manage now. Not just because of the cancer, you know. The shame still runs too deep.

And yet, I heard a young, American-born Chinese artist on the radio the other day say, "Only when the question of identity is settled can we do justice to other concerns." I think that's about right, don't you? Perhaps this will help.

I love you, Mei-bi.

Clipped to the back of the note were the sad-eyed picture of my grandmother Alyssa as a child and the notice of her death. I hadn't even noticed they were missing from the China box all these years.

This time when I looked up, Dad was watching me as closely as if he'd been reading over my shoulder. His face was the color of ivory, sunken with pain and concern. In his eyes I saw the flash of gunfire. Blown-away flesh. Pain and noise and consequences. And guilt? Could he really have borne the blame for so long?

"None of that was your fault, Dad. You were set up. By all of them. You loved your father. You showed the truth."

"What truth?" He pulled the glasses off his chest and rested them over his nose. A large nose. From his mother's side. His mother whom he'd suggested his father had wanted to kill.

"It's too cruel, too bizarre. People don't treat people they've loved like that!"

"You don't know."

"Well, if your father was really so awful, you're lucky you got away. You escaped. But if you'd told us—"

"What?" Each gasping syllable was torture. "If you knew—?"

"You and Mum. Everything would have been different. And I wouldn't have kept hounding you."

He patted the bed for me to come sit beside him. I took his cold, mottled hand in mine, felt the tension through his skin as he spoke.

"Diana wanted—a prince. If I told—" I held his inhaler for him. "She'd leave me."

"No, she wouldn't!"

"If I told her." He cleared his throat. "I couldn't face her."

My father's fingernails were chewed to the quick, the tips of his fingers flattened, some blue as bruises. I showed him mine. "We both mangle our fingernails."

He smiled, but the moment passed quickly into the suppression of a cough. I was feeding him his medicine when I heard the stomping of the family hunters, my mother's adamant protests. I unbolted the door and looked back at him.

"I love you, Dad."

They came through en masse. While Mum stood by with her prescription gruel, my father bit into his Whopper as if it were take-out from Lutèce.

• • •

Before he left that night my brother gave me a letter. He said it was the only mail I'd received that looked personal, and therefore interesting. It was written in Tai's even handwriting, though there was no return address. I took it into the bedroom after Henry was gone, while my mother and Anna were in with Dad.

I was still reeling from my father's story, trying to decide whether he'd told me in the hope that I would tell the rest of the family or to stop me from telling what little I already knew. I didn't feel as if there was enough space in my head to think about Tai along with all the other spinning fragments of my life. But the letter seemed to be waiting, almost breathing.

It was not, after all, Tai's fault that I'd bolted the way I did. Not his fault everything had turned inside out, or that I was afraid to see him. I wondered if Dad had had some of the same feelings about going back to China to find his father—the need for his love fighting against the dread that meeting him again would unleash some horrible truth. And even more horrible consequences.

But that was Dad's story, not mine. My fear of Tai was as irrational as my terror of Chinatown had proven to be. As my pursuit of young blond men had been. Something I demanded and then rejected or fled from.

The envelope smelled faintly of garlic. Tai's cooking. Like the smells at the back of Li's shop. No fish. That, too, was in my head.

> Dear Maibelle,
>
> David told me about your father. Thank you. It makes me worry less—and more—for you. I remember when my mother died, and then when my father had his stroke, I tried to think of something people could say that might cheer me. There was nothing. I remember feeling so powerless. And guilty. When people said they were sorry, I wanted to say, yeah, me too. In the end it's only words. And the words are only as meaningful as the feelings underneath them. Nothing words can mean the world sometimes. Eloquent statements can ring hollow as bamboo. I'm sorry.
>
> I keep seeing you, Maibelle. And maybe this isn't the

> time for me to say it, but I need you to know. You said you were surprised I remembered about your childhood sweetheart in Wisconsin, but of course I do. That day I saw you in the street after he died, you ran away from me but I saw what was in your eyes. I remember thinking as I handed you my handkerchief. I remember thinking how beautiful you looked. I remember thinking maybe Lao Li's matchmaking scheme wasn't so crazy after all.

It went on a little. He was confused. Hurt and afraid he'd hurt me. He didn't understand. I folded the paper carefully into thirds, following his own creases. White onionskin. His ink was blue. The writing slanted on the lineless page and seeped through to the back in spots. I imagined him sitting in that bare white cube of his, leaning into these words. Meaning them.

I imagined the cool, smooth sweep of his skin against my face, the rounded motion of his arms. And then it was as if an iron gate crashed down, and I couldn't think anything at all.

Part VI

Dragonflies

....

18

My sister and I are sharing a room for the first time in thirteen years. She lies kitty-corner to me, with her feet near my head, and tells me the real reason she joined all those cults was that she loved the colors. Any colors. But bright. Rose, orange, mustard, even white. Anything but black and gray, or, God forbid, neutrals. She stares at the ceiling. Beige. The whole room is done in what my mother calls earth tones. I see I'm not the only one with fantasies of bloodred paint.

"How does it feel to be back, Anna? I mean, if you can separate Dad's being sick."

"Like a large question mark."

"Didn't it always?"

"No. For me it felt like a blank wall at the end of a tunnel."

She sits and pulls her knees to her chin, wraps her arms around them. "After I left I got into some places where the wall wasn't just blank, it was made out of concrete, and the only way out was to go back through the dark and start over. I did that. Over and over. But coming home this time, I realized the wall here is just cardboard."

"And the question mark?"

"What's on the other side if and when I work up the nerve to push through."

Propped up on one elbow, snug in an old flannel nightgown of my mother's, Anna resembles none of her past incarnations. Her hair is shorter than I've ever seen it, her neck longer and skinnier. Her normally dark eyes have acquired a golden tinge, like a cat's. It never, ever occurred to me that nerve was my sister's problem.

"You still believe memories don't matter?"

"Hmm. Maybe not that they don't, but I do believe they shouldn't. You have trouble with that, don't you?"

"Saying they shouldn't is like insisting we repress them."

"Is that so bad? You get on with your life. Every day's a clean start."

"Or a new tunnel." I lean against the wall and listen to the apartment's quiet. Mum and Dad have been asleep for hours. "I know why Dad quit photography."

She twists a sliver of hair between her fingers and trains her cat's eyes on me.

"He thinks his father was targeted for assassination because of some photographs he took. He's carried that guilt around all these years and never told anyone. Not even Mum."

Anna frowns. Then shrugs. "Maybe especially not Mum. So how come he told you?"

"He didn't exactly come right out—I've sort of been badgering him since I came back from California. For information."

"Probing his memories."

"Didn't you always want to know?"

"You said it yourself, all the remembering has done is prolong his guilt."

"But you can't *forget* something like that!"

"I guess he never did."

"You sound bitter."

"Well, he wasn't exactly around for us, was he?" Anna gets out of bed and stands with her back to the wall, slides down to a sitting position. Her nightgown hangs over her knees to the floor, so you can't see there's no chair beneath her. "This is good for the hamstrings."

"You don't even want to know the details, do you? But you blame him."

"No, I don't. Want the details or blame him. I'm just sorry he's wasted so much of our lives blaming himself." She grunts and staggers up out of her seat. "Stings." She squats, rummages through her duffel bag. "Dad's an innocent. Like you. Here."

A small round object flies across the room and lands between my knees.

"I've kept it for years, but never really felt it belonged to me. I realized watching you with Dad. I was keeping it for you."

The size of a half-dollar but heavier and octagonal, bronze maybe, with a hatchwork of symbols, characters.

"This is the coin you found in Columbus Park!"

"Take it back to Chinatown. Find somebody who can tell you what it is. It might be worth something."

"You don't want to sell this!"

"That's my point. If you hang on to things too long, you can't move on. Everybody loses. Look at Dad."

I slide the coin under my pillow as I wait for an answer to form. Somewhere she's acquired the habit of staring straight into the person she's talking or listening to. It is almost impossible to catch her blinking, but I am painfully aware when I close my eyes, or look away. I sit up and wrap the blanket around me. A draft is coming beneath the window.

"You're having nightmares again, aren't you, Maibelle?"

I flinch. "Again?"

"You had them as a little girl. I think it was the way you dealt with things that bothered you. You never said anything, but you dreamed it. Used to get into bed with Mum and Dad, remember?"

"Yes."

Anna turns to plump up her pillow.

"But that's not what you mean, is it?"

She eases back, covering herself. She presses down on the blanket to force all the air out and answers slowly. "No. The worst were after that time you got pregnant. You would call me at school, sometimes in the middle of the night. You'd be crying. I remember I could actually hear your teeth chattering over the phone. You said I was the only person you could tell, but all you ever told me were your dreams."

"What are you talking about? I never called you—and you weren't in school then, anyway. You'd been out for years."

"I was a sophomore. I remember I had to rush back for an exam on Flaubert."

"I never told you about being pregnant."

I'm starting to spin. Or the room is. Shadows dance around hidden corners and holes. Her letter. In the chaos of the past weeks I've forgotten all about it.

Anna gets up and comes over to my bed. She doesn't touch me, but she sits close enough that I can see the whitened tips of her eyelashes. Close enough that I can feel the warmth of her body brushing the solid cold of mine.

"Of course you did," she says.

"Henry must have told you."

"You never told this to Henry."

"He's the only one I told."

"Maibelle." She reaches for my shoulder. I shrug away, suddenly shivering so hard my bones are rattling.

"Maibelle, what happened to it?"

"I had a miscarriage."

"How old were you?"

Why is she interrogating me like this? Our father is dying. I was just trying to tell her about Dad, and she's turned it around on me.

"Twenty-two," I say. "I was twenty-two."

"No. Well, maybe, but what about the first time?"

My heart sounds like a vacuum cleaner. The room is darkening, red around the edges. I can't breathe.

"You were fourteen, Maibelle. You called me, made me drive down from school to help you, not let anybody know. You never told Henry about this, or Mum or Dad. You couldn't have."

"Who?" is all I can manage.

"You wouldn't say. I figured it was some jerk at your school. Fortunately some of my friends had gotten knocked up, I had the name of a doctor in Pennsylvania. You really don't remember?"

I want to scream that she's making it up. I try to, but no sound comes out. My bare feet are frozen to the floor, and still that's not good enough. She moves to a chair directly in front of me so she can pin me with those eyes of hers.

"You fell asleep in the car on the way back. You were having one of your nightmares then. But it was an old one, about Johnny Madison. You kept crying out that he was flying. You shouted at him not to fly."

I press my eyes shut against her stare. "I don't remember."

"I dropped you off back here. It was late. Mum and Dad didn't know I was down, it was all so hush-hush. I went back to school. I tried to talk to you about it a few times, but you never said anything except about your dreams. Then they stopped—or you stopped calling me, anyway. I figured it was history. You'd as soon forget. I know I would, in your place. Then I was off on my own thing. Tell you the truth, I forgot all about it until I sent you that letter. *That* was the weirdest thing. What are you getting dressed for?"

"I need air."

"Are you crazy? It's nearly midnight."

"Anna, please. I can't stay here. I—I need some time."

"You remember, then?"

• • •

I remember fragments at first. A sky like spilled ink. The Pentax my mother had given me for my fourteenth birthday. Fish scales glittering like sequins along the sidewalk. Li was dead, but I didn't know it. I hadn't been back in so long, was feeling guilty about not seeing him. Too guilty to go specifically to visit him, but the camera gave me my excuse. Like my house key, I thought, like my balcony. My justification.

I wanted to shoot the storefronts. The ginseng and strangled ducks. The dancing chicken. Then I'd drop in on Lao Li.

Chinatown wrapped around me as if I'd never left. It was a few days before New Year's. Twinges of orange peel and incense in the air, the calliope of Chinese voices. Storefronts filled with merchandise found nowhere else, that was more a part of me than any of the designer *objets* with which my mother filled our uptown home. Even my own reflection—taller, paler, and more out of place than ever—seemed part of the package luring me back, no longer cause to run away.

The cage of the dancing chicken was empty, but I managed to fill most of a roll with faces of children and old folks, dead birds and fish. The temperature had dropped suddenly, a sure sign of snow, and it was darker than it should be for the hour. I was heading for Li's shop when I saw a boy I recognized squatting, playing craps with a group on the corner of Henry Street. Long arms, a short neck. He wore a bright green scarf and was tugging at his hair. It was the intensity of his eyes as they followed the cards, an intensity I knew I'd seen before. He won the round, was gathering up his winnings when he felt me—or rather my camera—staring and waiting for him to look up. He obliged, shooting back the same triumphant grin he'd fired past me after losing his cricket fight nine years earlier.

"Hey." Only this time it was intended for me.

Fourteen years old with a Pentax for protection. Old enough. Young enough. Straddling the invisible line that separated one warring territory from another.

I was disobeying my mother.

"You're not to go traipsing to the far ends of the city on your own."

"I'm fourteen years old!"

"Precisely."

I smiled back at him with a flood of relief and gratitude that I'd been holding in wait all those years. I felt foolish, a near grown-up suffering the emotions of a baby, but I could not stop grinning. I finished the roll while the boy preened and swaggered for the camera. It was the camera that attracted him, as it had been the pigeon before. Underneath my pleasure, I knew that. But I could use the camera to gain his favor. It wouldn't fly out of my hands. I could hold onto it and hold I did, pushing the shutter long after I knew the film was gone.

Finally he'd had enough. The game was over. His companions, fed up with his antics, had left. He came over and threw an arm around my shoulder, asked my name. He said he remembered me, but not my name. I believed him.

"Maibelle," I told him. "Maibelle Chung."

He guffawed. "Right. Married to a Chinese, huh?"

I smiled and swallowed his ridicule, didn't answer. He didn't really remember me, but maybe that was better. We walked. He kept his arm around my shoulder.

We passed a store window with a clock. It was nearly four. I'd told my mother I was going to the Y to use their darkroom. I often lost track of time in the darkroom, so she wouldn't expect me till late.

He was skinny, tight jeans, a black bomber jacket with red zigzag stitching. He had acne scars across his forehead, like Anna's. I think those scars, plus the memory of him under Old Wen's arm, made me trust him. He didn't swagger when we walked together.

"Maybe you knew my brother, Henry. In school."

"Here?"

I nodded. The motion yanked my hair under his arm.

"I did school in Hong Kong. Just moved back last year."

That was why I only remembered seeing him that one time. I worked hard to steady my voice. "What's your name?"

"Mike. Hey. Mike and Maibelle. Sounds good, huh?"

I bit down hard to keep from blushing.

"Want to see inside an association?"

He could have asked me if I wanted to see inside the boiler room of the *Titanic,* I would have said yes. As it happened, I would very much have liked to see inside an association. But that's not exactly what he meant.

He took me to a building on Doyers Street with a fishmonger below, five stories of tenements overhead. He opened the door to the stairway and, when he saw me holding back, said, "Just got to pick up a friend. Come on."

He couldn't have been older than sixteen. Just enough older than me to look up to, not enough to fear. The stairwell was dark and smelled salty and damp. I stayed close to him. At the top a door stood open to the roof. Cold air and gray light poured through. We climbed three flights, and he led me into an unlocked apartment. The shades were drawn, no lights on. I could see my companion's outline, the shape of a couch, chairs, a table, nothing in detail. The room was thick with the stink of fish and diesel fumes from outside. He made no move to switch on a light. He locked the door.

"Safety." He pocketed the key. "You never know."

My foot struck a can that was lying on the floor and liquid trickled across my toe. Beer. The stench came on suddenly, mixing with the other smells. I felt queasy.

"Please." I pulled at his sleeve. "Let's go."

But suddenly there were five of him. They must have come out of another room.

They jabbered in Chinese. The only words I recognized were *gui lou fan.* Barbarian.

My teeth began to chatter when they turned on a light and I saw the room, my captors. Cans, cigarette butts. The walls and furniture were scarred with graffiti and knife cuts. Take-out cartons filled a fireplace and were strewn across the floor. The sofa had been slashed so the stuffing popped out in fat, dingy wads. So much black. Hair, eyes, clothing, sunglasses in the dark.

They fanned across the room, some staring, others casually avoiding my gaze. Mike picked up a can of Schlitz from the windowsill and emptied it down his throat. My teeth were going like castanets and the chill up my spine made it impossible to keep the room in focus. I felt rather than saw them closing in.

Then I must have passed out.

* * *

The next thing I remember is the cold. Like steel wool against my skin. Stripped from the waist down. My shirt up around my shoulders. I felt the nakedness, couldn't see it. What I saw was the gleam off cars, lights below turned to bulbous stars through softly falling snow. Head down, arms up and behind. Someone holding me by the wrists. Tight. I started screaming, but they'd gagged me. My tears froze in my eyes, turned the lights to crystals. My skin burned. My insides burned. They were taking turns breaking into me, cutting deeper and deeper, so much farther below the surface than I'd ever imagined I could be hurt.

The pain's like fire, but it doesn't seem real, like it's somebody else's fire, don't you see. It's mine. Let me take it from you, Maibee.

Something was splitting inside me, looking away and up at the same time, seeing sky, though I could not turn my head, white and black, no gray. Then suddenly I pulled forward and down, down five stories. Stories. Women hacking at carcasses, stacking oranges, wrapping money in red and gold papers would look up, see a bare-assed bleeding girl fly by. Split like a chicken. Dropping, spreading, lifting and soaring out of the picture, the story. Escape.

Johnny told me the blood wasn't mine, had nothing to do with me. It was a sign.

Still the smell of fish, stronger, stronger. The part of me that was no longer part of me began to retch.

The convulsions warned them, they hauled me back over.

Their voices were hushed now. Dark shadows in the moonless night. The vomit, flowing through my gag, overpowered the fish, the brine, the smell of sex. Until a pail of water hit me in the face and backside, followed by fabric. My clothes. They released my hands but flashed the blade of a knife before my eyes. It was snowing.

"Get dressed." Mike's voice, hard as a chisel.

I scrambled, choking and swallowing, gagging once more. I began to faint again, but stopped myself, lest the nightmare start over. Let it play out. Let it end.

Fingers pinched me as I worked, grabbed at my waist and breasts. Giggling and jabbing. Pulling my hair. All in Chinese.

"Bai xiangku." White witch.

That's when I felt Johnny reaching down, offering his hand. To lift me? Or push me?

Up and over the wall, Maibelle. You can fly. You've done it before. Just look at me. I flew and I escaped!

They didn't expect me to go that way, and I almost made it, had one leg over. Fabric ripping. No fire escape. Five flights. Then a car below sounded its horn, and I looked. The street swam at me like a drop of pond life I was examining under a microscope. Infinitesimally close and utterly removed. I would never get there.

That instant of doubt gave them all the time they needed to yank me back.

"Don't be stupid." Mike's voice in the darkness. Mike, my friend. "We're just having fun, you know?" Two of them held me. I felt the blade's point on the nipple of my right breast. "Got it?"

I must have nodded. They pulled me away from the edge, and back downstairs, wrapped plastic bags around my hands and feet, around my mouth to replace the soaked rag. One of them kept flicking matches in my eyes, singed my hair with cigarettes. The smell, familiar and awful, and then from outside came the roar and clatter of firecrackers in the street. And I remembered being trapped and terrified. My father's death-mask face. But my mother had rescued me. My family had rescued me.

They were playing a game. Throwing fingers and fists. I watched them to avoid the flame. Boys. The kind of boys my brother had looked up to. The light moved and color broke from the wall behind them. Again, it flashed. Small flecks of color and shine, I now saw, covered a board leaning against the mantel. Iridescent wings. Not butterflies. They were transparent, visible only when the light hit them. Dragonflies. With their wings pinned. Dead.

Paper. Rock. Scissors. They were playing for a reward. The knife in the center of the circle.

I could feel the worms already crawling from my skin. I could see forward and backward in time, could move in and out of my body and its pain. My senses were warped by madness, which perhaps explains why one arm of my mind stretched beyond it all, untouchable. This dreaming arm reversed everything. Glabber, the basement demon, the pieces of nightmare bodies in the street, they were here in this room, no less real than the singed hair or cigarette. I was the one no longer real. I was dead or haunted or insane. If they were going to kill me, they would kill a crazy person.

I stared into the flame the fat one kept waving at me. I didn't blink. Again and again, until the muscles around my eyes burned with the effort of keeping them wide. My body rigid. The effort kept me from thinking or feeling anything else. And I counted. Slowly. From zero to forty, to seventy-six. Watching the numbers swallow time.

Even when the door opened and an overhead light momentarily blinded us all, I kept count. A new voice barked at the others. A familiar voice, low and smooth. Tommy Wah! Lost in the crystalline madness, I actually believed he had come to rescue me. Still, I didn't look or move. I reached two hundred.

He entered my field of vision, tall as Tommy, dark, but older, better dressed. He looked familiar. Felt familiar.

I had never seen him before.

I retreated back into my crazy eyes, let the numbers fill my face, mend my body, stop its shaking. They seemed my only defense. Aside from dying.

He walked over and peered at me. He still looked like Tommy. He did, and the comparison threatened to make me lose count. But he wasn't paying attention, anyway. He stood away from me as if the fluids that soaked my clothing, skin, and hair might contaminate his gabardine trousers. He wrinkled his nose at my smell and shook his head, fired an angry tirade at the boys.

Three hundred ten.

The man kicked out everybody but Mike and the match man. Then he squatted next to me. He wore penny loafers. Shiny. With Chinese coins in the penny holders. Chinese coins. Anna had a Chinese coin like that. And suddenly I couldn't remember what number I'd reached.

I stared at his shoes so I wouldn't have to look at his face, so like Tommy's, hear his voice. If I stared hard enough, I could transform them; when I followed the legs up to his waist, his chest, his face, it would be Tommy, years later. He would take my hand, swing arms, and walk me safely uptown.

But I couldn't stare down the words.

"I know who you are. You don't move. Don't scream. Understand?"

The crazy act wasn't fooling anybody. I nodded. They made me squat, shoved me into a garbage bag that was slimy and stank of the fishmonger's trash they must have emptied out of it.

Would they bother to threaten me if they were going to kill me? The rest of it—the pain and filth, my revulsion and panic—all paled beside this single shaft of hope.

They weren't going to use that blade on me. Not yet.

But I'd already been cut too deeply.

• • •

Tear the scab away and a hole remains, deeper than you could ever imagine. Like a swimming hole without a bottom. Like a well without a top.

I ride the elevator up twelve stories and bang on a door smeared with greens and blues. Water, I think, still pounding until the sleeping blond man awakes.

The door opens and I throw myself on Jed Moffitt with kisses for his blue eyes, hugs for his thin ribs, fingers swimming through his long pale hair.

"Maibelle!"

"No. Don't say anything."

I push him backward into his darkened hallway. With the door closed, the surging, gurgling colors rise and fall like supernatural pets. The place is a wonderland of liquid color and light.

I knead him, smooth him. He doesn't resist. He is tall, golden. I play blind, moving my palms over the lines of his face, closing my eyes and making my own dream picture. He wears only a T-shirt and shorts. His skin's cold as marble, but his hands move quickly, responding with grabs and tugs. He strips me, then himself, falls on me stroking.

I want him to numb me, let me believe. I want him to turn into Johnny and take me away, back before. To not have to remember or forget. This stranger to become a friend, a lover, to render me capable of love and forgiveness. To force me to trust him.

But his nails scrape my skin like the tips of forceps shocking with each touch. And instead of numbing the surfaces, welding them, the jabs just keep sharpening. Now his arms and legs become whips, flicking lightly, then harder, piercing.

Not Johnny.

Jed moans, exhausted and thrilled. I roll away in disgust, feel the sneer before I hear it.

Chinaman's whore.

At the end of the darkened hallway outside Jed's apartment a window stands low to the floor. It is crusted with soot. The frame is blistered and cracked, the lock broken, catch missing. I don't look past the filthy glass, but I feel the cold air splashing through a bullet-sized hole with cracks fingering out in a web. Where this air comes from you can either float or sink.

The sill hits my knees. The panes climb nearly to the ceiling, each sash the size of a steamer trunk. The grinding vibrates down the hall, and I worry someone might wake. Another shove, though, and it's open.

No moon tonight. Just blackened rooftops and the pinked blur of streetlights below. Spidery limbs of leafless trees in Sheridan Square. Twelve stories down. No spinning. No blur. No dizzying outward mental plunge. Just the perfect, unbearable clarity of this empty patch of air. My heels kick against the granite fall. My hands clasp the sill. Straight down. No fire escape. No moon tonight. No witness.

I tip forward, back. A human seesaw. Unclasp my hands and reach into space, grabbing the steam that spurts from my mouth, steam that hangs weightless from invisible threads. No thought.

I touch the child's golden heart that still, belatedly, hangs at my throat. The only reply is the tug of air. No comforting voices. No Marge or Johnny. No White Witch or Tai. I'm on my own here. They want no part of this.

The low moan of a pump nearly unseats me. A road crew. Pale helmets like snails crawling up out of manholes. I can't see bodies or faces, just the glow of lanterns, black holes in the ground.

An inch forward, and the balance tips. Gravity will handle the rest. They don't notice me, those men. I am no one to them. Nothing but soiled shards of bone and bent pieces. A shattered lens on the earth's smooth, unyielding face.

Just another fallen object.

....

19

It was nearly dawn when I returned to Eleventh Street. I needed a shower. To rinse and sponge and soap away the filth, the stench of fish and beer that still clung to me. To scrape my skin free of the memory I'd finally retrieved and now longed desperately to abandon. In the end I had neither jumped nor fallen nor flown from the window outside Jed Moffitt's, but even with my feet flat on the ground the distance below seemed endless.

There was music softly playing inside my darkened apartment and perfume in the air. Wine. Gardenias. Otis Redding.

I leaned into the door, all the breath gone out of me. I wailed something unintelligible and dented the refrigerator with my fist.

My brother appeared through the darkness, ghosted in a sheet. "That you, Maibelle?"

"Henry . . ." It was all I could manage. The night had been too long and too wide, and now, suddenly, I was drowning.

"Hey, Maibee." He stepped forward and held me. "We all knew it was coming. God, I feel terrible not being there. That's okay, go ahead and cry."

"Knew what?"

He became very still.

"About Dad?"

I was talking into his shoulder, but couldn't bear to pull back.

"What about Dad?"

"Isn't that why you're upset? It's all over?"

I began to breathe. And choked. It was the closest thing to a laugh I could produce. Not that laughter would have been any more appropriate.

"No, that's not it. Henry, no. Don't let go. I can't tell you what's happened. But I'm so tired. Please, just let me lie down next to you for a while. Maybe then I could sleep."

"Hey, Maibee." He kissed my forehead, but his mouth was hard and nervous. "Maybe you should tell me what's going on."

He pulled back, and I was suddenly aware of the darkness turning. A bird trilled outside. Through the pale tissue of light I saw the muted squares that I knew were Marge's photographs against the far wall, the slumbering form of her couch, the blackened entrance to her darkroom. I felt the White Witch and her children warning me not to stay.

"Henri?"

Only then did I realize we weren't alone. Coralie huddled in the bedroom doorway, in my brother's shirt.

"It's all right. My sister."

I grabbed his hand as he made a start back to her. "Both of you, then. Please, Henry. Let me sleep with you—or get out!"

"Yes, all right." She took my other hand and led me forward. There were no more questions, no need for answers. They opened a safety zone and I crawled in just as I had when I was young enough to find comfort in my parents' bed.

But unlike those childhood nights, I did not dream of gliding through air or dodging bullets in lower Manhattan. I did not go into free fall, either.

I awoke with a queer sense of peace, like the solitude you feel staring out over hundreds of miles of uninhabited land. A kind of peace that, in a blink, can switch to terror.

Henry and Coralie lay still sleeping, their backs to me, their faces away from each other. More secrets they possessed. When I left the bed, they rolled naturally, fluidly together. Children yelled in the playground, and a soft, rhythmic thump of tambourines fell from the floor above. The narrow bedroom was tinted orange by sunlight working through the window sheet. Coralie's hair fanned across the pillow, drawing Henry closer. I felt an intense spasm of love for them both for receiving me, and for letting me go unnoticed.

Everything in the living room was as I remembered it. The White Witch and her children. Marge Gramercy's children. My equipment. Yet it all looked foreign, the edges too sharp, shadows too dark. It was like a word I'd written thousands, millions of times turned suddenly unrecognizable.

A ceramic mug sat amid a shelf full of gadgets. Blue-green mold covered the surface of its contents. Mold takes weeks to grow like that. Months. It must once have been coffee, but I couldn't remember holding it, putting it down, abandoning it. It seemed important that I remember when I last noticed it, but I couldn't. One of millions of instants that make no difference, except that without them the thread falls apart.

I took the cup and rinsed it, watched the mold separate, the tap water push it through the holes of the drain until all trace of spoilage was gone. I paid attention as I scrubbed the bright red glaze and set the mug down on the lip of the sink. If I paid attention, I would remember. I would know that something happened to me. I would be able to explain.

When I turned around, I noticed the Leica where I dropped it that night weeks ago, before learning my father was dying. Before I understood what I'd been chasing all these years. It sat on the windowsill facing out. If I tipped it straight down, it would frame the old lady's garden. But what would be the point of that now?

I put the camera to my eye and rotated slowly, reducing the room to a continuous stream of rectangular frames. My mother used to encourage me to do this as an exercise when I was new to photography. "Find odd corners," she'd say, "shapes you haven't noticed before."

There was so much I never noticed. The chip in the mantelpiece.

The hairline crack running the length of the wall. Dustballs behind the backdrop paper. A web clouding the top of the curtain rod. The camera framed dirt and breakage; if I planned to stay, I would lay down my eyepiece and get to work scrubbing, dusting, sweeping. I would revel in the motions of my arms, the fresh smell of soap, and the sparkle of water on wood. I did not plan to stay, though. I wanted to be gone before Henry and Coralie woke up.

The viewfinder caught on a pile of mail that I could not have noticed before because it had arrived during my absence. I set aside the camera and pulled from the top of the stack a large manila envelope bearing Tai's careful block lettering, postmarked a week ago. It was overstuffed, as if booby-trapped.

He was not there, I told myself. Whatever happened between him and Henry, he had no part in my attack. He was no more guilty than I was.

Nevertheless, he was linked in my mind. An unwitting accomplice and now a reminder. I dreaded this package almost as much as I dreaded seeing him again.

Fortunately the rest of the pile was tamer. An overdue check from Noble for the work I finished before Dad got sick. Some junk mail. And a message from Stein & Stein, the rental agency for my building. Harriet had finally delivered. Violation of the lease's single-occupancy clause. One month's notice of termination. I placed the letter in the refrigerator where Henry would see it when he poured his wake-up orange juice. The heavy white metal door shut without a sound.

I turned back to pocket the check and for the first time sighted my portfolio. Could I really have left it out all this time? I remembered neither putting it away nor seeing it since that night Tai was here. The size of it, the blackness of its leather, seemed equally unfamiliar. I stepped closer, but the object remained alien, challenging. The binder was unnaturally heavy. The zipper stuck. In the other room bodies turned and sighed. I froze, but there was no further movement.

Slowly, slowly, I pulled the metal tab around the corners and peeled back the covers. Not ringed pages but loose glassine envelopes. Not my photographs. Not my portfolio.

I was stupid from the night of fear and remembering. Like a demented child faced with the simplest of puzzles, my mind snagged on the surfaces, unable to fit the underlying forms together. I knew some of these surfaces. My father's pictures.

They were all there, many more than the seven my mother had showed me. Shattered bodies, lost children, faces out of place and time. I came to the body sprawled on the platform of a crude wheelbarrow. A body without a head. And Halliday.

Only the invisible presence of my father on the other side of the camera's eye stopped me from tearing the print in half, from beheading the monster just as Anna did Johnny. He was dead, Dad had said, so what good would it do? Only destroy the evidence.

Instead I turned to the next photograph and faced him again. A party. A banquet. Dad told me about these. Fifteen-course banquets and goddamn lawn parties. Kuomintang affairs. Men in Western suits. Oriental women in shiny skintight dresses and faces like pretty masks, as decorous and artificial as the dishes of elaborate, exotic food. Halliday is the only white. He holds a drink and swivels his body toward another man. Older. A thin Chinese face with knives of shadow beneath his cheekbones. Small, deeply set eyes. Black hair pomaded to one side. The two men lean toward each other as if plotting something.

The man with Halliday is Li.

My father had told me Li worked for Halliday, now here was the proof. Dad had seen them both together in China when he went back. What was it he said when I asked about that day in Connecticut?

There are things you spend your whole life wanting to make right.

I glanced up at the White Witch to get away. Away from my father's failed memories.

Look closer, she insisted. There's more.

Only then did I see him. Behind Li, hand on his arm. A younger Li. A ladies' man. An older Tommy. Tai.

No, impossible. This was—must have been when? Again, my brain stalled. Thirties? Forties? Before Tai was born, and yet there he was. In his teens. That same rounded forehead, flying brows. I'd seen that face before.

The ghost-man from the cemetery. And the man with the coins in his shoes. They were all the same.

I couldn't look anymore. I was losing my mind. Coralie was not in the next room. These were not my father's photographs. Just another nightmare. All of this. Another nightmare that made no sense.

"Maibelle?" Henry's voice stretched across my dream like a wide, slow rubber band.

At the last possible moment I grabbed Tai's envelope and got out before they rose.

• • •

There is a coffee shop on Sixth Avenue where the waitresses wear aquamarine polyester dresses and running shoes and have names like Shirley and Suzette. That coffee shop was as far as I could go without thinking about where I was heading. I sat in a booth with my back to the wall and ordered coffee. The bitter black liquid burned the roof of my mouth, reassuring me I was finally awake.

My father was dying. That's what mattered. What happened to me happened fourteen years ago. Ancient history. Dismiss it. Forget it. My father failed to forget and his history buried us all. Anna was right: if he'd only been able to leave it behind, everything would have been different. Mum wouldn't have felt she had to save him, or maybe she would have left him. Maybe he was never meant to marry her in the first place. We could have stayed in Chinatown, and he'd have found someone there. Then we would have been accepted, known. I would never have become an outsider, would never have been raped.

Instead, Mum kept thinking she was to blame and defied him to salve her own guilt. Dredging up the evidence without even realizing what she was doing. And now Coralie probably thought she was doing us a favor. Twenty-five years ago maybe she'd be right. Twenty-five years ago I wouldn't have known Li yet, wouldn't question what he was doing with Halliday or why he was in the picture at all. Twenty-five years ago that boy in my father's photograph would have meant nothing to me.

"You all right, hon?" Cocoa: the embroidered letters shone on the waitress's stalwart bosom.

I didn't know I was crying. Not sobbing. My body was locked in place. But my face was wet.

"Boyfriend problems, huh?" She handed me a handkerchief.

"No. Sorry, thanks." I blew my nose on my napkin and pulled deeper into the booth.

She refilled my cup. "I'll bring you a muffin. You should eat something."

Her attentions warned me to pull myself together. I remembered the package in my lap. Tai did not rape me, and he was not the boy in that photograph.

I set the envelope on the table, used a knife to slit it open. There was a folder inside, and a letter, but what fell out first was a drawing. Watercolor, actually. On rice paper. The colors were soft but certain, a fluid green and sky blue. A penciled grid ran through them, creating panes of a window, divisions of a screen. Within each pane floated infinitesimal shapes of bright, vivid color, like birds or insects dwarfed by the vastness of the space around them. The drawing had a quiet, elegant beauty that clamped itself around my heart and squeezed until it hurt.

> Maibelle,
>
> I called your apartment and talked to Henry. I asked him not to tell you I called, I just wanted to know how your father is. I'm glad he's home and you're with him. I'm glad you have this time together. If you'd like to talk about it . . . well, you know.
>
> I've moved into the loft I told you about on Fulton Street. It's very quiet here. Not much of a view. My neighbors are mostly women. Artists. They're rubbing off on me, I guess. My work on the book hasn't been going very well. But I've started to paint. Little watercolors. Meditations, I

call them. Like this one. I don't know what it means or where it comes from. But I know it's for you.

There's something I need to tell you, Maibelle. I should have before. I meant to. I thought there would be time. I'd still rather tell you in person, but I'm afraid your father will lose his strength, and I think you may want to talk to him about this. It's about Li, something he said to me after you were gone. It could have had to do with his craziness that last year, I don't know, but I think it was the truth.

I told you, I always knew Li loved you. After you moved away, one day I came to his shop and found him holding that picture, the one he gave me for you. That one you call the White Witch. He told me her name was Eliza. He was crying and asked me never to tell you. I realized then the reason he kept her there all those years. He loved her. He told me she was your grandmother. He said that child in the baby picture was your father. No, he didn't say that exactly. He said that baby was his son.

I opened the folder to a portrait of a miniature woman with bound white feet and haunted eyes. This well-used page, like the others below it, had been surgically removed from a magazine, so long ago the edges were browned.

• • •

The trunk of a car is like the cargo hold of a plane. Freezing cold, an echo chamber for the noise and vibration of the journey, each bump a separate punishment.

After we start moving I track the changes as best I can, losing the thump of potholes and the blast of city traffic to the dull roar of the highway, the whine of grating as we cross a bridge. Brooklyn? New Jersey? I worm one hand free and push through the bag, find no tire iron. No wrench. Not even a screwdriver. The frozen air helps hold down the thickening smell, and pinhole cracks let in weak, pulsing veins of light, but I might as well be in a straitjacket.

I resume counting. On trips to Wisconsin I used to count lightposts when I was bored. I once got up to ten thousand fifty. Now I understand that I will never be bored again. I have only reached two thousand eighty-nine when the ground beneath us changes to gravel. I duck back into the bag just before the trunk flips open.

Footsteps on grass. A quiet tapping on the surface of the plastic—I remember it is snowing. Fingers grab, clutch my arms through the plastic. Up and over a shoulder. He staggers under my weight. Cars, the drone of highway like a swarm of bugs. Mosquitoes or gnats. Not dragonflies. Dragonflies make no sound. A plane surges overhead. If the pilot looked down . . . But no, though we are outside, they must not be afraid of being seen. Three men and a sack of garbage. I am up above again, watching with Johnny, trying to laugh.

I count three thousand three hundred ten, and they let me go. My head strikes a slab of stone or concrete. I don't move.

"Li Tsung Po."

Once, twice. I distinctly hear Li's name. Like the snap of a twig. If I hadn't gone back to see Li, none of this would have happened. But I never mentioned him to Mike. Why, then, are they talking about him?

They argue. Then the man with Tommy's voice speaks in English. "Li's girl!" I can't tell if it is a question or a statement.

No one speaks right away. Then Mike's voice. "What's it matter. He's dead now."

The other man snarls, and I hear the whack of skin. I feel it like a punch, though I am not the one being hit.

"Look you." It's Tommy's double again, too close, as if his face were inches away. I can't see through the plastic, but I feel his hand at the back of my head, my neck. I pull out of my body, try to picture him on the other side, but there is no light.

"You never see these boys," says the soft, even voice. "You forget this night, everything be okay for you. If not, I know where you live. I know your mama, papa. Lao Li tell me. You know."

His hand remains as if testing to see I am alive. He wants to make sure I have heard. "You wait, we go away. You go home. Forget tonight."

Then he gently lets go, and a moment later someone slits open the bag and releases both my hands.

My head throbs so loudly, I begin to count my own pulse as I hear the earth lead them away. I will never see them again. The man will get rid of them. Move them somewhere else. I will forget this night.

After counting another hundred, I tear away the bag and tug the cords from my ankles. I am in a huge open space, flat lawns in every direction crisscrossed by lamplit paths and not a human being in sight. It's eerie, foreign, recognizable territory, but I don't know where I am.

Beyond the lawns fly the headlights of expressway traffic. Too much traffic for the middle of the night. It's still evening, I realize with a shock. Hours have passed, not an eternity. Snow as fine and soft as a film drifts down around me.

Film. I remember they've given me back my jacket. In one pocket I find a subway token I don't remember having. In the other my hand folds around a metal box. Before I can question what I am doing I open the compartment.

I needn't have bothered. They let me keep the Pentax, but destroyed the film. I put the viewfinder to my eye, start looking for clues. A low growl pulls me to the left. Track and train. A subway station how far off? A mile? Two? Half?

I consider the token again. That man. Go home, he said. He wanted to make sure I got there.

Now that I am alone, the quiet and snow—and something else about this place—make me feel protected. There's no hurry. No need to test my legs before I am sure they will hold me.

Johnny is calling. I can hear the smile in his voice as I did the day he asked me to marry him. Smiling and eager and unsure. I look up and through a world. A globe. A globe full of holes to the other side, where he waits for me to join him. But not yet. I'm not ready yet.

If I just keep quiet, I'll be safe. Mum and Dad will be safe. Forever.

....

20

I had called Tai after leaving the coffee shop, arranged to meet him at Grand Central at noon, but I arrived at eleven-thirty and bought a ticket for the 11:55 to Providence.

Providence. I'd never been there. The name made me think of white buildings, sun-drenched and spotless as fair-weather clouds. No one would imagine me in such a place. I would take pictures of people I didn't know, faces that had no bearing on me, and when I discovered Providence had not, could not, make me as clean and anonymous as I'd imagined, I would move on. Searching for someplace where day and night fused and time slid forward without notice, and I could be lost all over again.

I liked the idea of going as I had liked the idea of flying. Only now I understood why. Because I knew it wasn't a dream. I wasn't safe here, and no one was safe with me. I was like a time bomb with a fuse that burned faster some places than others. The farther from Chinatown the slower the burn. The farther from my parents the less the temptation to hurry the spark.

The danger was not just in my mind. The danger spoke with blades and bullets and flames. The man tailing me in the graveyard. In the photograph. Shadows in the park. Thugs in front of Li's store.

Li. My friend and, according to Tai, my grandfather. I loved him and was raped by his followers. The same Dragonflies that killed Tai's mother. I felt sure of this, just as I was sure that somehow the man who had spared me in exchange for my silence was the same man in my father's picture with Halliday and Li. He'd meant it when he said he knew who I was, and now, today, he was still following me. He might wear the disguise of a ghost, but he was no ordinary crazy man.

Eleven-forty. The big clock glowed white as a full moon below the ceiling of stars. I carried a small duffel bag with some clothes, film, the Leica. Other women carried efficient-looking briefcases, canvas totes, babies in Snuglis. A congregation of homeless women clutched torn paper bags. What ladies carry tells who they are, sometimes more accurately than where they are going or even what they are wearing. My sister with her backpack. My mother with her old Italian tote and *Interiors* magazines. Marge Gramercy with her handwoven baskets full of camera equipment and Polaroids of the children she loved.

I hoisted my airline-issue bag over my shoulder and walked. I had not looked for Tai, and did not now, but paused at the gate to check the listing of towns where my train would stop. A whistle blew from the platform. It was dark as a coal mine inside, the tunnel's heated breath ballooning out into the terminal. The ramp down to the trains stretched like a tongue, and I imagined the cars traveling down, down the back of that tongue until they rolled through the fiery belly of the globe and came up in Wisconsin. In the shadow of Mount Assumption. Where no one was home anymore.

Johnny's flight did not bring him closer to heaven but thrust his face in the earth. I had finally to understand that even if he'd survived he would have become just another man. No better at rescuing me than I had been at saving him.

The conductor gave his last call and I boarded the end car. A No Smoking sign hung above my head. Plush, upholstered seats marched up the aisle. I counted twenty-seven heads, mostly women at this hour, and only when the train jerked forward did I permit myself to look out the window.

The platform was empty except for a kid selling commuter sodas and a man waving his arms for the train to wait. It didn't.

Time passed. I tried not to think as the train slid deeper into the tunnel. I tried to block the image of my sister's concrete wall clattering closer and closer but, still, when the tunnel finally slid open and we rolled up into daylight, I breathed a little easier. There was Harlem, the river. Bleak warehouse and factory districts. The train rocked with the rhythm of its wheels. The sky pressed down like an iron glove. When I closed my eyes, I might as well have been back inside the tunnel.

The woman seated across from me had incredible nails. Must have been three inches long, curling at the ends. In Old China only scholars and the rich were allowed to have nails like that. I wondered if the man I'd always thought was my grandfather had such nails. This lady didn't look like a scholar. She'd painted her claws alternating colors, half purple, half tangerine orange. Each nail was embossed with a golden charm. One a tiny key, another a cupid's bow. You could do a real number on somebody's eyes with nails like those. I wanted to lean over and ask if she'd ever been attacked. If she'd used her nails for self-defense.

But I was distracted by the train slowing. We'd stopped before, I hadn't paid attention. Now the door slid open and two women carrying attaché cases walked off. Beyond the platform I could see a tree-lined street that looked straight out of Mayberry. There was a brick café that boasted an ice cream fountain. A white clapboard stationery store with one of those coin-operated horses out front. Cars and people alike seemed to move in slow motion and the colors of things had a polished edge to them. Even the air blowing in through the open door felt as if it had been freshly washed and iced. It smelled of high tide.

I suddenly recognized where I was, grabbed my belongings, and made it through just as the train jerked forward. I checked my bags with the stationmaster and set off walking.

* * *

Time had stood still here. The distance was longer than I remembered, but the houses along the way, the verandas and widow's watches, the fieldstone walls hadn't budged. I found the beach where my father had cast his rock. It had been low tide. Now the sand where he'd actually stood was concealed by water as green and luminescent as moonstone.

I stood with my toes on the tide line and permitted myself to speak the words aloud.

"I am running away."

Everything had happened so fast in one sense, and so slowly. It was hours since the moment in the coffee shop when I'd decided I wouldn't let myself think about it, just run. Back to the apartment where Henry and Coralie lay sleeping and oblivious as I packed the few things I was taking. Uptown without calling Mum or Anna. Without saying goodbye to Dad. Just leave them all be, I told myself. That would keep them safe.

The breeze stung my face with a cold spray of salt. I put my tongue out to catch it. It tasted like tears.

I was wrong.

My leaving would not protect my father; it would only prevent my being with him when he died. And he would die. Nothing I could do would change that. I could only make it worse.

As I already had by exposing the raw film of Dad's life to daylight. The lover, as Halliday so indelicately put it. Dad must have known yet kept the secret of his mother and Li through all the years we lived there. And all the time I spent with Li. He'd photographed him when he went back to China. He'd photographed the whole lot of them. But had he known Li was his real father?

I picked up a rock covered with barnacles and slippery green threads of seaweed. The hatches of the barnacles were closed up tight, the animals inside hiding or resting or dead. I pulled at the green hairs until I'd stripped most of them away and could see the shape of the underlying stone. What had been concealed was riddled with holes.

The doctors said Dad's body was riddled with cancer. They said it had gone too far, and now we could only hope for a year at most. This stone would go on a lot longer than that, supporting all this life in spite of the holes.

If it were my mother, she'd be like the stone. Let the disease grow, consume her, and yet, perversely, turn it into the very fuel that kept her moving, shoving everything and everyone out of her way. Because she'd been damaged she would feel entitled, but because she was entitled, she would never have enough. She would demand the impossible. To be whole, unspoiled, constantly renewed. To refill those holes and disguise them. And remake history.

My mother didn't have cancer, but she bore her share of shame, which she treated in just this way. A very Western approach. American. If you don't like what's happening to you, dismiss it. Don't run from it but over, around, or straight through it. That's what Gramma Lou meant when she said Mum paid more attention to the obstacles in her way than what she was aiming for, when she said Mum was just like her father. My mother must have had secrets that dated back long before Dad. But she kept going.

My father's response to shame, just like his response to his cancer, was typically Chinese. Swallow it, tamp it down, sink with the weight of it. What had been done to him he kept on doing to himself until it became a reason to quit. To hide. But never point a finger. Never blame or complain or admit to pain. Better to disappear than lose face.

The cancer would succeed in killing my father but it would not claim the victory of his death.

I crouched down and held the stone just under the water's surface until the barnacles began to open. Tiny feelers waving, grabbing, feeding on nutrients too small for the eye to see.

In the end the stone's ongoing life, its survival beyond either of my parents, depended on everything but the riddle of holes. On the contrary, each empty space represented a cancer that had been cut out and discarded. The tracing was a scar, a memory. That's all. Neither Western nor Chinese but a combination and something else entirely. A third possibility.

Once the cancer is surgically removed, the memory and the possibility of recurrence will remain forever, cannot help but remain as essential ingredients of character, but when the imminent danger is gone it is possible to carry on. Not to keep reconstructing what is dead and rotten. And not to reject the sorrows of the past or the lingering fear, but to use them to move forward.

I opened my fingers and let the stone fall, slowly, luxuriously, through the green water. In an hour's time the tide would drop, exposing those surfaces to the pounding waves that would gradually dig out new trenches, add to the scars, and reshape the form. Yet if I came back next month, next year, and found this stone, I would still recognize it by its older, deeper markings. I would know it.

I walked out on a natural jetty of boulders past the point of beach. The water came at the shore in wide smooth bands. A barge, moving as slowly as a minute hand, was the only traffic on the Sound. I was completely alone, but if I squinted deeply into the silvered light, if I faced south and made the effort, I could still see the shadowed spires of Manhattan reaching for the clouds.

I pulled my father's Leica from my pocket, focused, and opened the shutter once. Just once.

I would not be able to live in Chinatown again. I understood that now. But I could not escape it, either. No one in my family could. It didn't matter how far I ran.

As I was buying my return ticket a train pulled in on the northbound track. When I looked up and noticed him, Tai had already spotted me through the window. His face seemed to float behind the glass, his dark, angled features and hesitant expression out of place in these New England surroundings. But he stood ready and waiting for the train door to open, as if he had known he would get off at this stop.

I smiled as he stepped down. "You win."

He came empty-handed, dressed in a navy peacoat, jeans, and cowboy boots. He looked good.

He glanced around. "You described it well."

"The real test would have been if you hadn't seen me."

He stuck his hands into his armpits. "I'd have found you."

"Buy you coffee," I said.

We sat at the back of the café where my father had brought me and Henry. It was busier than I recalled, brighter. Mothers encouraged their children to eat grilled cheese sandwiches and hot dogs. Teenagers held hands. The flecks in the Formica table reminded me of the floor where Tai no longer lived.

He clasped his mug of coffee as if he was still cold. I took off my coat and the sweater underneath. I should have felt awkward and embarrassed, but I didn't. I felt as if Tai and I were right on time for a long-standing appointment, as if the past year had never happened and I was responding to his letter for the first time.

"How's the book going?"

"I've figured out why you're leaving," he said. "Why you run."

"I'm not leaving."

He tilted his head until the hair at the back of his neck caught his collar. We were sitting across from each other in a booth surrounded by Muzak, the clink of utensils, and limber suburban drawls. There were lots of blondes in here, several redheads, and a few brunettes. No one else as dark as Tai. No other Oriental eyes.

"I've lived in places like this," I said. "I never felt I belonged."

"I know." He was pressing so tightly his nails turned white, so tight it didn't take much imagination to see the cup cracking, scalding coffee streaming down his arms.

"Go on."

"There are always stories in Chinatown, Maibelle. Gang stories. But even when there are witnesses, no one knows how much is true, how much made up to keep the pressure on."

His skin would turn pink then red, would burn. He would cry out in pain. "Were there witnessess?"

"No one knows."

"No identifying marks or details." I pulled my hair back off my shoulders, twisted it into a knot. I could feel beads of perspiration popping across the top of my forehead. Tai's Adam's apple made a shadow that slid up and down as he talked.

"Only that the girl had red hair, was a teenager. Rumor was, she came from outside."

I spooned an ice cube into my coffee. It melted surprisingly slowly.

"Maibelle, after that night you ran from my apartment I had to know what had happened to you. I couldn't stop thinking about you."

"So? How'd you find out?"

"I remembered the look on your face. The same look when you ran from me as you had when you saw Winston Chang."

"Who?"

"Li's gang's *dai lou*." His right eye flickered. "The man in the cemetery."

I placed my hand over the top of my coffee, let the still-hot mist coat my palm and finally turn cold. My heart felt flat and slow and heavy as that barge on the Sound.

"I started asking the old guys at the seniors' center about him—" Tai leaned forward, pressing down on his elbows. "Believe me, I didn't know that day, or I would have warned—"

"Would you?" I poured cream in my coffee until it was as beige as my mother's decor. I swallowed some but couldn't taste. "I saw a picture of him with Li. Back in China."

"Winston was Li's nephew. A big deal with the KMT in Taiwan. Li brought him over after your dad moved away. Put him in charge of his Boxers."

He looked as though he thought this would shock me. I squinted at him, and the subleties of his face blurred into broader, more general planes.

"He looked like you."

He stared into his cup. When he raised his eyes, I realized how deeply my remark had cut him. He didn't answer.

"What happened to the rest of them?"

"No one knows. The tong got them out of town right after. They never came back. Only Winston stayed, but he had a kind of breakdown, wouldn't have anything to do with the tong. Next thing, he was wandering around Queens like you saw him." He hesitated, his lips stretching in an apologetic smile. "They say there was a curse on them all."

"Right. The White Witch."

"That's what the old-timers say." He gulped his coffee and grimaced.

"You believe Li was my grandfather?"

"Yes."

"Why?"

"Because of the way he loved you." Tai reached but didn't touch me. "It never would have happened if he were alive, Maibelle . . . Or if I'd been there."

"You're the one who sits with his back to the wall."

"If I could have eyes in the back of my head, I would. Fear gets to be instinctive. You can use it—or let it destroy you."

He picked up his napkin, folded it in half, and half again, then laid it flat.

Two policemen walked in and took seats at the counter. They were big and doughy, red in the cheeks. They settled onto their stools with a jangle of keys and clubs. They didn't threaten me, but they didn't make me feel protected. I'd grown up around police, watched them prowling the corners of Chinatown, circling Little Italy, patrolling the street in front of my parents' building uptown. It was as if they belonged to another species. The uniform. The uniform did that, the special knowledge, the equipment, the borrowed authority. Passengers had watched me with the same removed curiosity when I worked a flight or waited in airports for the motel shuttle. If a plane had gone down, they would look to me to save them, and only I knew how slight was the chance I'd fulfill that expectation. So much had to do with circumstance, so little with equipment or training.

When I looked back at Tai, his eyes had widened, seemed impossibly round. "I need you to forgive me, Maibelle."

"Don't." I picked up my spoon. In its curved fun-house surface the room flipped over. My face was distorted and ugly. "What for?"

"For what I had no part of."

We both looked at his hands spread flat on the table. A writer's hands, now a painter's hands. More cautious, by necessity slower than a photographer's hands. With pale square nails and full moons the color of pearls. Beautiful hands.

I slipped my bitten fingertips beneath his palms. It was the first we had touched. He didn't move except for his eyes.

Then he lifted my fingers in his beautiful hands and kissed them softly, gently. Shockingly. A kiss of absolute gravity and release.

• • •

The elevator door slid open to Edith Piaf's rich and mannish moans. Over the music I could hear my mother in the kitchen exclaiming, pronouncing some critical imperative. Then a lighter, genial woman's voice. Coralie. Light but firm.

Business talk. A deal was being struck. Or maybe an outright gift. I heard it in her voice. Coralie was in love with my brother. She was prepared to pay the price of admission.

The music rose. The ladies concurred. There was no sign of Henry or Anna, and I'd lost all sensation of time.

When I entered the bedroom, my father was seated by the dimming window, struggling to look and breathe. He smiled when he saw me. His smile had withered to a clench of muscles around his jaw. Each day now took the toll of a year.

He was holding one of his new boxes, a prototype printed with a colored drawing of mountains and flowers and the name of the candy—Pearls. He worked the lid with his thumbs, popping it open, shut, open, shut, the click of cardboard a steady, soothing percussion.

"Been gone." The words made me think of rough water on stone.

"I needed something downtown. It took longer than I expected."

He let the box drop and reached a hand. I pulled up a stool and sat beside him. His skin was cold, full of bones. Like Li's.

I remembered the two of them facing each other the day after Johnny died. The way the air between them seemed to tremble. The silence as thick and hard as glass, holding them at once together and apart with me in the middle.

I waited for my father to regain his breathing, then handed him the bag I'd brought. He took out the photographs one by one. Cold currents of air eddied around the bottom of my stool, made me pull my knees to my chest. I could see by his face, he'd known I had them and probably thought I had them all along.

"It's your mother, isn't it? Alyssa. Li called her Eliza."

He took a corner of the blanket and wiped the glass above her face. Sad eyes, frozen. Trapped. In the photograph his mother was a young woman, hardly older than me.

"That letter you wrote me about your father."

"Yes." His voice surprised me with its strength. He stared at the pictures. An infant. A toddler holding his amah's hand. A boy with two sisters.

I thought back to the photograph in that old basement box. Chung Wu-tsai was thick, with a head like an egg, already balding in his youth, and flat-faced below slitlike eyes. He looked nothing like my father. Lao Li at least had moonpuffs, and now in my father's ravaged face I could see other similarities peering through, like the ghost of someone within. The same shadows dug into my father's cheeks, the same distant glimmer in his eyes. Dad's hair was thinning and whitening, not receding like Wu-tsai's.

"Your mother loved Li."

He closed his eyes.

"And the man you call your father lied, deceived you all. Why do you—why tell us you were Wu-tsai's son?"

His lids flew open.

I pointed to the baby picture. "I know your mother had a son by Li."

He gave me back the stack of frames and reached to the floor beside him. For a second I thought he'd collapsed, but he came back up slowly, lifting something in his arms.

"Let me help you."

He waved impatiently. He had Coralie's portfolio, unzipped as if he'd been going through it. It fell open in his lap and he threaded through the familiar pictures until he came to the one of Halliday and Li and Winston Chang.

I heard my own voice from a distance. "Li's nephew."

And my father's too close. "Li's nephew—" He jabbed the young man's face with his finger. "Li's son!"

"Li's nephew," I repeated quietly, carefully. "Li's son. Which is it?"

My father watched the picture as if it were about to spring to life. Or as if it had never stopped. "Son."

The music died at the far end of the apartment, but the photograph was full of its own noise. The heavy wooden scrape of chairs, dishes clinking, music and voices. The smell of salted meats, men's perfume, expensive wine and wartime. Li's and my grandmother's bastard son.

The game of blindman's buff was over, and I was cold. Stone cold.

"Li's sister—" My father started wheezing and reached for his inhaler. "Married name Chang—they took him—raised him."

"Winston Chang." I proceeded slowly. "I met him once. After we moved out of Chinatown. After Li died."

My father's body quieted. He didn't ask for clarification. He didn't demand the truth. He stared through the window at the blackened sky as if looking for something far, far away. I lifted the photograph out of his lap.

He was in the same room, smelled the food and perfume, was distracted by the same noise. He was there, behind the lens. There with his half brother. And, in effect, his stepfather. And his childhood classmate. But there is no recognition in these faces. They talk and smile, exchange pleasantries and secrets as if they don't know there's a witness. Meanwhile the photographer hides behind his camera, as anonymous in his line of duty as if he'd pulled out of his physical body, become invisible and untouchable. As if he were a ghost. But Dad wasn't that. Not then.

Anna had it right when she said our father was a spy. That was his true nature, anyway, and it must have run in the family. Now when I looked at the young man's face I no longer saw Tai. He was no more like Tai than my father was like Li. The resemblance was between the two brothers, as it had been all along. My father's younger brother. My uncle. He had known where we lived. He hadn't lied. He had threatened me with the truth. And saved my life.

"You knew Winston was here, didn't you?"

Dad grabbed the edge of the blanket and pulled it higher. I laid a sweater over his shoulders. He turned aside to cough, and his face blanched with the effort.

"I found out," he said in a toneless voice. "Too late." He pointed to one of his bedside pouches.

Inside I found a folder labeled "Winston." All it contained was a one-paragraph newspaper clipping. "Man Drowns Self in Queens." A blue-ink star drew my attention to Winston's name.

> The body of an Amerasian male washed ashore in Flushing Bay, October 28. Investigators identified the victim as Winston Chang, 59, a homeless vagrant. He drowned in an apparent suicide. Chang left no survivors.

I had seen him in the cemetery in Queens just three weeks earlier. He'd recognized me, and the White Witch had cast her curse.

"He was crazy," I told us both. But even as the breath left my mouth I could feel water closing over my head. Winston Chang. The name inflated, buoyed up to the surface, dragging me with it. My lungs burned. Tai and the old-timers all believed Winston was Li's nephew.

"Did he know, Dad? Did Winston even know he was Li's son?"

He started to shrug, then shook his head no.

"But why would Li never tell him?"

"Face," said my father in one gnawing breath. "Too much lost face."

I wiped his forehead gently, carefully, as he pulled a very different picture from the portfolio still in his lap. A young boy stood in the midst of a bustling Chinese market with his head tipped back, eyes half closed, as if he expected the sky to reach down and kiss him.

Dad gazed at the photograph. "I remember."

He strained for each new breath, each word. "Clouds in the river— Heat— Smells. The light."

"China."

He moved and grimaced with the pain shooting deep inside his body. I reached for his medicine, but he shook his head.

"Just to know— It was no dream."

I took in the boy, his waiting upturned face. My father's memory. "Like looking at a photograph."

"Yes." My father turned to the window and, beyond, the blinking light of a night plane flying west. "Like that."

• • •

Early in the morning, I raise my lens and click off half a roll. An overnight freeze has left the shop windows and awnings glazed, released geysers of steam from manhole covers. Fire escapes shine silver and old brick walls gold. A merchant pushes back an iron gate while stray cats dart among the shadows and breakfast noises spank the airspace overhead.

Tai stamps his feet against the cold. I photograph him, tall and uncertain, against the storefront that was Imperial Poultry. Chrysanthemums still dot the guardrail of the balcony overhead, but their frozen heads droop brown and the surrounding windows recede, faceless and dark.

Farther down Mott Street, doors are opening. Inside fingers arrange baked goods in the windows of basement coffee shops. Women in thick coats and scarves bustle past us. We move on.

"You're nervous. Give me your hand," he says.

We have no more than a block to go. He touches my hair and kisses my forehead. His lips are warm and gentle.

"We don't have to do this now—or ever."

I stretch as tall as my height permits. "If I'm not scared, it won't mean anything. If I don't do it now, I'm afraid I'll be scared forever."

We walk on, more slowly, blowing steam from our nostrils like dragons.

Doyers is an easy street to miss, a blind horseshoe hardly wider than an alley and just one block long with a half dozen shops. It should be odd that Tai and I have missed this center-of-Chinatown passage on our wanderings, but we've had no reason to come here. There are no sweatshops, no day-care or senior citizen centers.

I am trying to remember the way it was. White tiles and cracking red paint. Dirt-streaked glass. Fish eyes staring, glassy as marbles. But the fish store is gone, the tiles cracked and grimy. The paint has aged to brown. Now stacks of hand-embroidered polyester clothing lie where once I passed eels and squid. Around the open doorway fibrous dust catches the early sun, the smell of brine long since absorbed by boxes of shiny cheongsams and jackets and synthetic shoes "Made in China."

I let go of Tai and reach for my throat, the small golden heart that hangs there. It was Tai's idea. "Bring something that will remind you, you don't have to stay or be afraid. You're safe, you know? And you can escape any time you need to."

He wouldn't say if he was thinking of something in particular, but I knew what he meant.

Tai stands waiting to one side of the door I've refused to notice until now. Two steps up, one forward, and we'll be inside. The green-painted wood and frosted glass will close off the street. The stairs will stretch straight up, light or dark at the top. And I'll be back.

The door opens with a kick. Tai's been here before, knows some of the tenants. Families live here now, he said. He knew it would be unlocked.

"You okay?"

I grip my father's Leica with both hands. "I'll go first."

The stairwell reminds me of drawings I've seen of near-death experiences. A flare of light, blinding as a star at the end of a long, black, upcast tunnel. A sense of being lifted, drawn weightless toward the light. Sounds filter through the walls, but distant and blurred. The motion of water through pipes. A laugh track. A murmur of indistinguishable voices. The cold, dank smell of damp plaster and rotting wood, reminiscent of the old basement, fills the hallway, and the first step groans.

"The bogeyman on Mott Street," I say.

Tai holds the door open behind me.

"That was Li, wasn't it? One last story come to life."

The door eases shut.

"I wouldn't put it past him."

I take a deep breath. A story come to life. If only my assailants had been playacting.

It was quiet that night, and dark, the stink of fish overpowering everything else. That boy Mike. He stood blocking me, pushing me forward. Now Tai leaves a space between us. A way out.

His footsteps echo with the hollow planking of the stairs. I can hear the thick, measured cadence of his breathing, and the light makes me squint to look forward, but I don't turn my head. I keep climbing, let the light surround me. It's warm in the sunny enclosure at the top before I step into the wind.

The door has been pulled from its hinges, and the rooftop is crisscrossed with laundry lines. Patches of yellow, pink, green, and white whip back and forth, some brush the tarred surface of the roof. The sky has brightened to a crisp, robin's-egg blue with skeins of cloud like an old man's beard over flat-topped buildings that stretch for miles, each weighted down by a short, squat water tower wearing a conical hat. It's too far to see the river, but I can smell it over the fumes of traffic. I can feel the snap of water and wind, the salted ocean it brings to the city. It all seems so much bigger than the cramped, collapsing night that slits my memories.

I stand rooted by the unhinged door. A low wall surrounds the roof with asphalt rolling up its side, darker because of the sun. Bright light makes shadows deeper, colors tougher, contrasts more intense. As a photographer I know this as well as I know that the space behind me is shrinking.

I make the necessary adjustments and begin to shoot the place where I was raped.

The camera offers a removed chamber where I can rest and wait for the glare to subside. The frame controls what I see, lens and shutter give me something to do with my hands.

The wind pushes my hair in front of the lens. I step closer to the wall and begin to see their faces through the flying strands. Rooster hair, they called it. One had a sliver of a mustache and a scar that cut his left eyebrow in half. Another had a mole between his eyes with a whisker that grew from its center. A third twitched and had a voice like a hiccup. They'd brought me up here and stood in a circle around me staring and pointing and yanking my curls. They'd struck matches to prove the green of my eyes. The one with the mustache lunged, pulled my head back, and shoved up my shirt to show the others my breasts. Mike held the knife. Mike, the one I trusted. He came forward with that blade, made me gasp. I fell backward and the fat one caught me, turned me around, threw me forward . . .

I whirl and catch Tai in my frame.

"They're not dead. There are others."

He doesn't move. "There will always be others, but the ones who hurt you are gone."

"They're here." I train my lens on him like the crosshairs of a gun.

"I'm here, Maibelle. I love you. You're safe now."

"You don't know."

"I don't know what you're thinking or feeling. But I know you have the power to make them go away."

A motion to the right, and he's gone. Into black. The camera allows no peripheral vision. In or out. Like magic.

I step closer to the edge, and the wall rises, higher than it seemed, or than I remember. Waist-high. Above it, the other side of the street pulls closer. Five stories to the ground. A window shade snaps up. A child leans her head against the glass, blows a cloud of mist and draws a line through it.

No peripheral vision. It pulls me over and down, lifts the pavement to meet me. I no longer feel my feet.

"I'm going to keep you from falling," Tai warns. His hands press, strong and quiet on my shoulders. To my left, not ten feet away, is a fire escape. Like a stile, it crosses over the wall, zigzags down, down to safety. It is scaled with rust the color of dried blood and mounds of white bird droppings.

"How long do you think that's been there, Tai?"

"As long as this building's been here."

"Fourteen years ago?"

"Yes."

"I didn't see it."

"But it was here."

"I wouldn't have had the courage to use it."

"You might if you'd seen it."

He lifts his hands from my shoulders, and my feet connect with the rough, black surface of the roof. The street drops into place. I keep my finger on the shutter and follow the slow, cautious progress of a car that has entered the alley at Division Street, creeps forward, lost, rounds the corner, and disappears into Chatham Square.

When I turn around, Tai is smiling. I lower the camera, let the sky widen behind him. A candy wrapper, green and gold with scarlet characters, dances for a moment at his feet as if led by an invisible partner, then rises on the wind and sails toward the river.

"It's cold. I'm ready to go downstairs."

A child's voice answers my knock, and the girl opens to Tai's greeting. She is about five, with curly black hair and skin the color of cocoa dusted with fine, darker freckles. Her grandmother, a small, tightly shrunken old woman with gray hair knotted close to her scalp, sits in a folding metal chair by the empty fireplace. They both talk to Tai in Chinese while I study the small, well-lit room for traces of the gang den it used to be.

It's as much smaller than my memory as the rooftop was large. A dilapidated vinyl couch and card table fill it. As decoration, New Year's calendars and the labels from food packages paper the walls with red and gold. Pipes and antique sprinklers crisscross the punched tin ceiling. The couch is thick with moth-eaten blankets and a cheap stuffed dog like the ones you win at carnival games.

There are voices in the other room. Men talking hushed and incessantly, as if they have something to hide. Tai doesn't seem to notice.

The light that fills the apartment is diffuse and absorbent. Unlike the stark sunshine upstairs, it illuminates even the darkened spaces, leaves no impression of shadow. I lift the camera to my eye and move forward, stepping as quietly as if I were stalking a bird, and swing around the door frame to a space the size of a closet. Hardly big enough for the twin bed inside. The window opens on an air shaft. A worn gray blanket is pulled neatly to the pillow. Two pairs of black tie shoes sit below the bed. But there are no men.

The voices come from a plastic transistor radio that lies facedown at the foot of the blanket. I reach to switch it off. The room fills with the sound of Tai's voice and the child's. She is challenging him. He speaks louder, angry.

I look back into the other room and see his arm rise high, his palm spread. She is turned toward him, hands wide to push him away. He starts to pull down, hard and fast.

"No!"

I let the camera fall and rush forward, grab his wrist and push it away.

"Maibelle, it's a game."

Two of his fingers are spread in the peace sign. He brings them together, widens them back to a V. V for victory. I clutch his wrist and struggle to think.

The child wraps one fist in her other palm.

"Paper." She gives me a gap-toothed smile. I let Tai go.

"Paper, scissors, rock," he says cautiously. "You know that game?"

I retrieve my camera. "I know it."

But as I straighten up, the child is at my throat. Her grandmother barks at her in a dialect I've never heard before, starts to rise.

"It's all right."

The little girl's fingers feel like the wings of a hummingbird. She lifts without pulling, entranced by the shine and reflection. She's a strange child, elfin and dark.

"Where's she from, Tai?"

"Vietnam. Chinese on her mother's side. Father's gone. He was American. They're here to look for him."

"Where's her mother?"

"With her aunt, out trying to find work. They just arrived a couple weeks ago."

The child's eyes are elongated, beautifully carved with the same perfectly smooth, flat lids that I used to admire in the Yellow Butterflies. But that's where the resemblance ends. As I lean close I see, this child's eyes are not black or even dark brown. They are flecked with color radiating like a wheel—slivers of gray, amber, green—but deep in the center, as unearthly and hypnotic as a summer pool, they are pure blue.

I reach behind my neck. The grandmother waves her arms to protest, and the child flashes astonishment, joy, and dismay in such quick succession that I hardly have time to insist.

"I want to take her picture. Tell them, Tai."

"You're sure about this?"

The little girl circles her fingertip over the smooth surface. I remember the way Johnny rubbed and rubbed, until life returned where none had seemed possible. Like a phoenix, he said.

I find Tai's eyes and rest in their darkness. "I'm sure."

I move back to get her whole upper body with the Chip 'n Dale T-shirt, her bright pink hair ribbons, the red plastic jewels in her tiny ears. She waits for me to adjust the Leica's settings, then sits up straight, looks me sharp in the lens, and smiles shyly, happily. Around her throat hangs a golden heart.

I wait until my tears are flowing, and begin to record what I see.